PROVIDENCE

DAVID GROSZ

Black Rose Writing | Texas

The author grants the final approval for this literary material.

First printing

ISBN: 978-1-68513-336-8
PUBLISHED BY BLACK ROSE WRITING
www.blackrosewriting.com

Printed in the United States of America
Suggested Retail Price (SRP) $21.95

Providence is printed in Minion Pro

*As a planet-friendly publisher, Black Rose Writing does its best to eliminate unnecessary waste to reduce paper usage and energy costs, while never compromising the reading experience. As a result, the final word count vs. page count may not meet common expectations.

PROVIDENCE

A story obsessed me from my late childhood into early adulthood. "I was 11, it was late August 1990," I would begin, "and my mother, father, sister, and I drove to the Catskills to visit a summer home rented by the Morrows, who at the time were our best friends." I must have run through it thousands of times, at first in my head; later out loud, to others. I saved it only for intimates—close friends, girlfriends, and more than one shrink. It was the bridge to my inner chamber, I implied between whispers, the only way to know the real me.

Over time, I recognized a second motivation for these retellings. Although I had recounted the story again and again, something at its core mystified me. Each telling was a confession, but also a plea. I was asking the person across from me for help—to comprehend what had happened, to locate the source of my obsession, to explain why I remained haunted by an incident from childhood, an incident in which I mostly watched and listened, in which I barely played a role at all.

BOOK 1

1

At the sound of my name, I spun and saw an older woman in a navy jacket with shimmering bronze buttons, glasses balanced on the tip of her nose. I looked past her, sure that someone else must have called out to me. But the sidewalk was empty, and though hazards blinked on a double-parked car, I could make out no faces through the windshield.

The woman continued toward me, her step deliberate. "Why it is you, Gabriel," she said. "Don't you remember? It's…"

Catherine Morrow. In twenty years, she had barely changed at all. The same long, straight hair (though gray, where it had once been black). The same pale blue eyes. Even her colorful outfit, an orange-and-azure-striped dress, seemed like it might have come from an old picture album. In an instant, she shot from unknown to vividly recalled, so that the one detail that clashed with memory—her worn white sneakers (her younger self wouldn't have gone out in anything so tattered)—stood out all the more.

"What a wonderful coincidence!" she said, lightly touching my elbow. "I'm on a wander through the park. Come with?"

I could think of little more tiresome than recapping decades of my life to my mother's one-time friend. Still, I fell in next to her, and we passed through the entry gate to Carl Schurz Park, walked down a bench-and-hedge-fronted path, and emerged onto a wide promenade overlooking the East River. We stopped before a gated dog run.

"These are the little ones, the big guys are over there." Catherine pointed to a larger field with a fence twice as high. "Would you believe, Gabriel, I live only five or six blocks away—in a home—*for old people*? I have my own apartment, my own kitchen and bathroom. It's probably nothing like what you imagine. And you? Are you in your parents' place?"

I had heard this question often since returning to New York after several years away. The truth—that, yes, at 33 I lived alone in a spacious co-op only blocks from this park, the very apartment where I had been born and raised—evoked from my peers a mix of envy and condescension. But Catherine's response was different. "I think that's wonderful. My boys moved as far away as possible. JT's in San Diego, Kyle's in Oregon."

She had neglected to mention Alan, her husband, and I felt obligated to ask.

"Oh, Gabriel, he's gone," she said and quickly expressed sadness at my parents' deaths, which she claimed to have heard about from mutual friends. In the ensuing silence, I thought to complete the circle with some mention of Becca. "She's an artist," I said, "lives in LA," the same shorthand I used with friends, which was so much easier than explaining that my sister was a nomad. "I don't see her all that often, but we're in frequent touch."

Catherine nodded, seemingly no more eager than I to dwell on the past. She turned to the big dog run and marveled at a dalmatian who caught a bouncing ball and a bulldog drooling over a twig like it was the first ice cream of the spring. On the grassy field behind, a few people my age, or perhaps younger, stretched out on blankets, as if willing the start of sunbathing season. "I don't care if the calendar says April," Catherine said. "It's still winter. What are they thinking?"

Below the promenade, kids on roller blades skated between hockey nets, and two solitary teens shot layups on opposite ends of a basketball court. Catherine asked if I still played basketball, and it was then that I realized I had seen her more recently than two decades prior. At one of the parents' funerals (I couldn't recall which), I had glimpsed her, in a black shawl, just an instant before some well-wisher, attempting comforting words, blocked the view.

"I'm not so sporty these days," I said. "I run when I get antsy."

"Well, my exercise is walking," she said. "But I still need to rest." And she steered me across the promenade to a bench overlooking the East River, with Roosevelt Island and Queens beyond. A red tugboat was passing, hauling a city block's length of trash. As a kid, I used to love seeing boats from the living room window. If one came by, I'd rush to the glass, smacking into my reflection, leaving impressions of my hands and face. I loved tugboats most of all, and red ones at that. Maybe they were the easiest to recognize, or to pronounce. How funny to realize that the mesmerizing vessel of my youth was just a sluggish motorboat dragging future landfill.

"In most parks," Catherine said, "the benches face inward and practically beg you to people watch. But here you have to choose—bench or people. How fortunate I ran into you."

In profile, she looked more her age, webs of wrinkles spreading from the corners of her eyes and mouth. A certain fleshiness, once high on her cheek, had sunk to her jawline. I sensed motion behind us, joggers, parents pushing strollers, dogs on leashes, kids bouncing balls, seniors dragging canes, nannies trying to keep siblings in line—a parade of pedestrians, just one block removed from the city grid. I felt restless and thought of friends I might call, Sebastian, maybe, or Peter.

But it was Catherine who stood first, asking suddenly, "Can I ask you something, Gabriel?"

My shoulders tensed with apprehension. I felt sure she was about to launch into the inevitable questions—about our shared past, about Becca—and I lamented that I had consented even to this brief conversation.

"Do you play backgammon?" she said.

"Backgammon?" I repeated in surprise. "I'm not sure I remember..."

She waved away my objections, and before I knew it, had asked for "my digits to fix a next date"—yes, those were her precise words. With a grin and wave, she walked back in the direction we had come, her ponytail bouncing with each step, an elderly woman who seemed anything but.

2

I was 11, it was late August 1990, and my mother, father, sister, and I drove to the Catskills to visit a summer home rented by the Morrows, who at the time were our best friends.

As we pulled into the gravel driveway, I saw a worn house, its walls at a slight lean, second-floor clapboards flaking white paint. Catherine appeared in a corner window, wearing a red apron above a yellow floral dress. "Welcome, Staubs," she cried. A moment later, the front door opened, framing Alan, in neat khakis and a blue Izod, and JT, brown hair flopping over his eyes.

I would tell the story of this visit dozens of times in years to come, often starting my tale earlier to include some detail from the trip from the city: Dad blasting us for being late, but then, when we were at the front door, rushing back to his room for a dusty college yearbook; our scuffed, gassy Datsun, the exception that proved the rule about my otherwise neatly tucked and coiffed, upper middle-class family; Becca's yellow Walkman, blasting syncopated beats from the middle backseat; Mom doing all the driving and Dad most of talking, and how she cast glances of solidarity at me, the other quiet one in the family; or the burst of light that entered through Becca's window at the very moment we left the highway for a dirt road, and how it landed on her rumpled Cornell sweatshirt and cast a shadow onto the seat between us—a shadow with curves, reminding me that, even if at 11 I was already half an inch taller than she was at 14, a chasm of maturity lay between us.

But whenever I started my tale, after several wrong turns and an hour late, the sun having already fallen below the horizon, we pulled into the gravel driveway of the Morrows' summer rental, and Catherine welcomed us with a shout, and Alan and JT appeared at the front door.

Mom, Dad, and Becca had visited earlier that summer—July 4th, while I had been at camp—and for this reason, plus the late hour, plus JT's taciturn, mopey style, his tour of the house was rushed and cursory. Becca and I had barely tossed our backpacks into our second-floor room when we got the call to come down for dinner.

Alan nonchalantly gripped the chair at the head of the table. Kyle greeted us with high fives and introduced his enormous friend, Connor, and his equally enormous parents, the Darnolds, who were already talking with Mom and Dad. JT slumped onto a chair in the middle of the table, and Alan directed the rest of us to our seats, trying to make his decisions seem spur of the moment when we knew full well that he had mapped out a seating plan in advance.

The kitchen door swung open, and Catherine appeared with a large ceramic tureen filled with "summer squash soup, topped with a dollop of cream and cilantro." She assumed her spot at the other head of the table, opposite her husband, and began to fill and pass bowls. From the moment of her arrival, she gave instant order to things. The fact that we had come to this dining room from various doorways and staircases, whose relation to one another still confused me, that some of us came from the city and others the country, or that some were dear friends and others complete strangers, no longer mattered—somehow, Catherine, smiling, serving, in command but making it seem that her husband was, made sense of it all.

After the soup came lamb chops: a single rosemary-sprigged bone per plate.

Then a carrot, beet, and goat cheese salad.

Amid this quick succession of plates flowed light, friendly conversation. Beyond their extraordinary size and oddly perky ears, the

Darnolds were largely forgettable. Mr. Darnold caused a minor stir when he complained about the "yuppies who overrun the area in the summer," leading Dad and Mom to exchange glances, but the Darnolds were mostly soft-spoken and affable, or in the case of the hulking Connor, curiously deferential to his friend, as when he claimed to be "the Maris to Kyle's Mantle" on their summer baseball team. Perhaps the most exciting moment of the meal's first half came when Becca raised the topic of German reunification seemingly out of nowhere ("It's a touchy subject for my Mom and Dad," she said, "but please bear with me") and then used phrases like "historical inevitability" and "self-determination" and "not blaming children for the sins of their parents"—eliciting blinks of surprise from the Darnolds, who clearly were not expecting any such discourse from this tiny girl, three years younger than their mass of a son.

But if the Darnolds were unassuming, their mere presence assured what had become traditional at these events—the telling of the story of the Morrows and the Staubs—an old and practiced routine that Dad generally initiated (hence, Becca and I shorthanded it as "Dad's story"), but which the other adults soon joined, each playing a part. Like an old couple, the families had a story of how they met, and they loved to tell it, especially in the presence of some third family. The story recounted the awkward meeting of Dad and Alan at Cornell, their close friendship and eventual drift, and then the unlikely coincidence by which Mom and Catherine encountered each other years later and reunited the lost friends; and already at 11, I sensed what I would later understand as its lessons—that through the chaos of life, it was those rare, close relationships that gave order to things, binding seemingly random, disparate moments into a tale that almost feels providential.

But we kids had heard the story so often that we had turned against it—at least, the other kids had. The moment Dad got started, JT or Kyle or Becca would fake gag or vomit, claim to suddenly have lost their appetite, or to have discovered a need for a lengthy bathroom break, anything to escape another rendition of what Becca called, "that absurd, interminable yarn."

After the salad, Catherine cleared the plates and said that she would be right back with "the main."

"You mean there's more?" Mrs. Darnold gasped.

"Of course, those were only apps."

Catherine disappeared into the kitchen and returned a minute later with a giant tray of grilled salmon topped with capers and lemon, plus bowls of braised broccoli and couscous. She placed a piece of salmon on each plate along with a spoonful of couscous, then sent the broccoli around so each person could serve themselves. As the plates circled the table, it occurred to me that every detail of the meal so far—the run of small plates, the delayed main course—were part of Catherine's careful choreography. She was determining not only what we ate, but at what rhythm, as well as when Dad began his story, when the kids made their getaway, and who knows what else to follow.

Of course, she also controlled us with her skill in the kitchen. The food was so good, it was impossible to pull oneself away from it, and the next several minutes were silent, but for the scraping of silverware on plates and the audible chewing of Connor Darnold.

But soon enough, Dad, a furious eater despite years of Mom begging him to "slow down," had polished off his plate and was lowering the napkin from his lips.

Turning first to Mr. then to Mrs. Darnold, he said, "Clint... Beth... how do you know the Morrows?"

Even before they began to talk about their encounter at the local golf club, Kyle had emitted a long groan, earning a death stare from his father.

Then, Mr. Darnold asked Dad the inevitable follow up, "What about you, Jonah? I understand you and Alan go way back?"

And so Dad began...

Within moments, JT mumbled, "I'm full, can I go?" and left through a gray door, which evidently led to the basement. Soon after, Kyle, with a prompt to Connor that he should follow, passed through the same door. Next, Becca, with a glance back at me, requesting my company. But I didn't budge. The truth is, I secretly liked Dad's story.

What the other kids found so embarrassing about it—the reliability of its telling and its overly sentimental moral—was exactly why I found it comforting. So, I stayed and listened, all the way through the conclusion, and the inevitable response, offered on this day by Mrs. Darnold, "That's quite the story."

"Isn't it?" said Dad, leaning back proudly in his chair. "You might even call it fate."

Alan, with a smug grin, uncorked a new bottle of wine and rounded the table, filling all empty glasses.

Stopping before me, he paused, "What'll it be? Another Coke?"

I nodded, but only seconds later, as Alan went to the kitchen for my soda, Catherine said, "Gabriel, wouldn't you like to go and join the others? I'm sure they would be happy to see you."

Her words were at once warm and authoritative, part supportive advice, part polite command that I was meant to leave, as the table was about to become an adult-only zone. But, as I intuited then (and would recognize more consciously years later), it was Catherine's particular genius that even as she implored me to leave, even as she made clear that my departure was necessary for the next stage of the evening, I couldn't help but feel that she was squarely on my side, that she alone recognized my dilemma as the youngest, torn between staying with the adults and joining the older kids, and therefore that she could only be encouraging me to take a step that she knew would be good for me. It felt as if she were loaning me courage, emboldening me with the belief that, even if JT were already in college, even if Kyle and Connor were rising high-school seniors and star athletes, even if Becca were about to enter high school and a star at everything she put her mind to—while I was merely a sixth grade twerp—I could go down those stairs and hold my own in that basement.

I met her pale eyes, which seemed to be waiting for mine, and asked to be excused.

"Of course," she said. "Have fun."

As I headed to the basement door, I didn't know what to expect. A New York kid, I generally found large houses to be strange and intimidating. The house I knew best was the Morrows' two-story colonial on Route 100 in Katonah, and as I went down the stairs, I expected to find a basement similar to that home's finished lower level, a cozy kids' hangout, in other words, with a giant TV, Nintendo, stereo, and plenty of fluffy couches and chairs. At first glance, the Catskills basement met my expectations. On a rattan rug sat a couch and a few armchairs arranged around a coffee table. A TV leaned against a back wall, an adjacent basket overflowed with movies and video game cartridges. But all of this was within an oasis of light, with stretches of dark all around, the borders unseen. The space was damp, even chilly, and I was reminded that basements, even a fluffy-carpeted, well-lit one like in Katonah, contained a bit of country spook, which was amplified at night, when you might hear not just a crank in a floorboard or creak of a pipe, but also the rustle of a branch or the scurrying of some nocturnal creature.

Kyle and Connor faced Becca, who was holding forth in her typical way. (Across the space, JT was splayed out on an armchair and turned to the far wall.) Upstairs, a lecture on the inevitability of German reunification; downstairs, her topic was "clubbing," a term I didn't know but which seemed to consist of a network of dark indoor spaces, room after room after room, each with its own music, its own decor, its own "vibe." *Dance clubs*, I soon realized; she was talking about *dance clubs*. And immediately a question came to mind. Was this real or BS? With Becca, either was possible. Regardless, I knew the game she was playing. She was the cool New York kid, entertaining others with her improbable precocity and exotic experience. I had done the same that summer at camp, spinning a tame mugging—after a game of pickup football in the park, I'd been confronted by someone on the losing side, who flashed a knife and walked away with my Dan Marino football as consolation prize—into a story of suspense and peril.

"I never have a problem," said Becca. "'Course it helps to be a girl, and to know the right people."

"And how do you know the right people?" asked Kyle.

"I have friends who organize these things. They make flyers, recruit kids to come. It's a network. When you're in, you're in."

Did Becca really go dancing at night? When our parents went out for the evening, to Lincoln Center or some fancy restaurant, Becca would sometimes set me up with pizza and a Bond flick and announce, "I'm off to Emily's" or "Caitlin's." Until now, I had never doubted that this was in fact her destination.

"So, we could come?" Connor asked.

"Sure. As long as you take me cow tipping or whatever else you do around here."

"Har-de har har."

As I sank into the soft couch beside her, I noticed wide eyes upon Becca—I don't think I'd ever seen Kyle look at her like that—also beer cans on the table, a pack of cigarettes, an ashtray with butts. The pack was passed around, and I was offered one, a first for me. I shook my head but grew self-conscious, realizing I had not said a single word since entering the basement. And I hardly wanted, "No," to be the first. Thankfully, Connor announced that Kyle had been working on a curveball—"he's not even a pitcher, but his breaks more than our number one starter's." They would play the next day, so we could see his curve's nasty break.

"I'm in," I said with relief. "Can't wait."

On the other side of the room, JT was so quiet that I had practically forgotten about him, but then Kyle started picking on him, teasing JT for playing D+D, calling him "a loser," who was surely "dorkimus prime" at URochester.

"It's weird, don't you think?" Connor said. "The way the younger one goes after the older. I've never seen anything like it."

I'd seen it a million times before, but Connor's observation still made an impression on me. I turned to Becca, who shot me a stern look. Of course, she and I weren't anything like Kyle and JT. Mainly because I knew better than to start with her. But now and then, I called her Thumbelina or Tiny Tim or Tinkerbell, and watched her grimace, signifying that I'd landed a blow. Still, Kyle going at JT was a whole different level of attack, sustained and relentless. I'd seen JT respond by calling Kyle a "balloon brain" or a "tard," but this night in the basement, he shook his head silently, only once bothering a tepid, "beg off," which Kyle finally did a few minutes later.

The conversation returned to New York clubs and boring Catskills summer evenings and JT got up—I figured to leave—but instead he rummaged around the shadowy far wall and pulled out a CD case. He slipped a disc in the stereo, and music came on, weird, wordless rock. Then he tossed a dark bag to Kyle.

"Dungeon master," said Kyle in a gentler tone than earlier. "Nice one."

The bag held a metal pipe and Ziploc of pot. Kyle packed a bowl and passed it around. Again, I was offered a smoke; again, I refused. Soon the conversation sped up, much of it flying over my head. I just sat there, watching, barely a part of things. At some point, JT invited me to go with him to get more drinks. Happy to have a task, I followed as he passed through one of the room's dark borders, rounded a corner, and stood before a giant fridge. He grabbed four beers and pointed me toward the sodas. They had everything, Coke, Crush, Root Beer, Ginger Ale. I grabbed a Cherry Coke and followed him back. JT tossed a beer can to each of them. Even Becca caught hers cleanly.

"Wanna DJ, Becca?" JT asked, inviting her to peruse his CD collection. "I'm curious to hear the music from the clubs." She spread out on the floor, flipping through several CD binders before saying she had found nothing that they played. Kyle and Connor shared a cruel laugh, but Becca found nothing in Kyle's CDs either and returned to JT's. "This is as close as we'll get," she finally said, a disc spinning around her finger, "to where our tastes merge."

I didn't recognize the music, but I've learned since it was New Order, early stuff, from the 80s, not their most recent album. The boys bobbed their heads and said, "Sweet" and "Awesome choice," and again Kyle and Connor looked at her with those wide eyes. The conversation resumed, but at some point, Becca stood, kicked off her shoes, revealing her favorite pair of socks (thick wool with a yellow base and green dia-monds), stepped toward an open spot on the rug, and began to dance.

She was good. Really good. She had all sorts of moves, twists, pumps, and kicks, each in step with the rhythm; it was like she knew the song so well she could anticipate its next move. She continued for a second song, and a third, as the others called out, "Wow, Becca," or "Becca Staub, who knew?" At the start of the fourth song, Kyle joined her. Half a minute later, Connor did, too. JT remained splayed in his armchair, though now he turned from the wall and faced the others.

The difference between Becca, and Kyle and Connor, was startling. She commanded the music; they could barely hear its commands. As her movements became more confident and forceful, Connor could do little more than flail his arms enthusiastically and hop around in some semblance of "good dancing," while Kyle couldn't even manage that. He was robotic, heavy limbed, off beat; his forehead sweaty. Had the evening ended there, I might have remembered it as the night I had seen Kyle Morrow—cool charismatic Kyle Morrow—look like a dork.

The conversation had long since stopped. There was just the danc-ing, the trying to dance, and the watching of dancing. The three of them—Becca, Kyle, Connor—continued song after song until there was a click and the music stopped. Kyle, picking up a vague suggestion from earlier, said, "Let's go outside," and before I knew it, the garage door slid open, Kyle and Connor collected supplies, and everyone was run-ning up a slight incline, onto the lawn.

Kyle was back in his element, his gait graceful and athletic. This was followed by Connor's thunderous plodding, JT's gawky stretches, and Becca's effortful, elbow-pumping. As I ran after them, I felt the wet of the grass, already dewy, sneaking through pores in my sneakers, damp-ening my toes. We ascended and descended a ridge, landed in a shallow valley, rose again, achieved another plane. The house was out of sight, though a halo of light above the horizon marked its general location. A sliver of moon hung above us; the sky's few clouds glimmered brackish gray. In the dim glow, I was able to make out the objects the others carried: flashlights, a lighter, mosquito candles.

And lawn chairs. But only four, so I sat on the grass, nearly jumping up at the first touch of moisture on my butt, then pushing past the momentary discomfort. The mosquito candle was lit, a handle of vodka, which had until then escaped my notice, was passed back and forth. The lighter and a pack of cigarettes made the rounds, too, then the metal pipe. Kyle smoked less than the others but drank more. There was more talk about clubbing, with Connor insisting that he had to visit and see it all for himself.

"Anytime," said Becca.

Things got quiet. We watched the stars. There was some discussion about whether New York was dangerous, which was odd because I couldn't understand how the city, always lit at night, could be scarier than this near pitch darkness.

At some point, JT stood. "I'm heading back."

He spoke so softly that I might not have noticed his departure at all, if not for the speck of light from his flashlight that dotted the black sky. As the light faded, I realized that his departure had been my chance to leave, too. Then I realized that one of the four chairs was free. But before I moved in either direction, I felt a touch on my arm. It was Becca, seated beside me, no, actually lying down on the grass. How long she had been there, I couldn't say. She pointed to the sky, the moon, the stars. "That's something we don't have in the city," she said. "There are too many lights."

"She lives in this fancy apartment building, way up high," Kyle said. "What is it, 12th floor?"

"Fifteenth, but we don't have views like this." Becca got quiet, looking up some more before turning back to them and speaking in her usual rapid-fire pace. "That's why we don't know any constellations other than the Dippers. Know what else? We don't know the names of trees, flowers, or cars. We can't tell a Colonial from a Cape Cod, but we do know the difference between a condo and co-op."

"She's wicked smart," Kyle said to Connor. "She goes to this fancy school where they teach Latin and wear plaid skirts. But the most amazing thing is how she draws."

"Oh yeah," said Connor. "What do you make?"

"Anything. Things I imagine. Things I see. People I know."

"Has she ever drawn you, Gabe?"

"Gabriel's too small," Becca said before I could answer. "He's just a wisp, a fragment. He's not fully formed."

"She does all kinds of things," Kyle said. "Faces and flowers, everything. Becca, I bet you already know where you're going to college, don't you?"

"I'm just a freshman," she answered.

"You'll probably go to Harvard, we all know it. At least I've got baseball," Kyle said, suddenly sounding mopey.

"You'll definitely get a scholarship," Connor said. "You should see him at batting practice."

"Hope so. Otherwise, it's tier 3 for me, like the Dungeon Master," Kyle said.

The handle of vodka made another round, Kyle taking two monster gulps, then wiping his wrist across his lips. I lay back, my head close to Becca's. She was looking up again. The stars were indeed spectacular.

"Too bad about the moon," she whispered.

Too bad why? I thought, and she answered, as if reading my mind, "It blocks so many stars."

"Let's do something," Kyle said. "Play a game, explore, anything. How about the woods?"

"In the dark?" Becca asked.

"We have flashlights," Connor said. He and Kyle were already on their feet. "Coming?"

Becca touched my hand, pressing my palm, the inside of my thumb, inviting. "Sure," she said. "We'll come."

We moved further away from the house. There was another rise and dip, and the grass grew higher, the dew now dotting our shins and knees. It was mostly dark, but I soon saw the outline of trees in the distance. At the point where the field gave way to the woods, I paused, wondering again if I should head back. Becca touched my elbow and ran her hand softly down my arm until she found my hand. "Come with?" she whispered. "Please."

We crossed into the trees, and the flashlights came on. Three of them. Like with the lawn chairs, they each had one, but not me. I kept close to Becca. More than once I stepped on the heel of her shoe, but to my surprise she didn't bark at me. We walked in single file; I was in the rear. The trees thickened, but there was a path, or at least a way through the dark that avoided jutting branches and thorns, that ended at a kind of clearing.

"Turn off the lights," Kyle said. "Take a look."

With the moon obscured by trees, we had a clear sight of black sky punctured by a thousand radiant sparks. I thought we would lie down and take in the brilliance, but the pause was brief. Kyle said, "Let's go," and trudged ahead. Connor fell in behind him, then Becca, then me. As we passed into new tree cover, our flashlights illuminated little more than a step or two ahead of us and we stumbled over tree roots and were scraped by the occasional branch.

Becca took my hand, whispering, "It's ok."

It's ok? I had no idea what she meant, for I hadn't said anything, expressed neither concern nor doubt, and I kept turning her words over in my mind—Ok as in, *you are safe?* Ok as in, *it's normal to be scared?* Ok as in, *you can leave, I'll be fine?* By the time it occurred to me to ask her, I saw that too much time had passed. If I responded, she'd be as baffled by my words as I'd been by hers.

3

"Come," said Catherine, leaning into an awkward hug. "Let me show you around."

My first impression of the East River Home for the Aged was of a chipped welcome desk, a standoffish receptionist, drab gray carpeting, blinding fluorescents, and a water-stained, Styrofoam-paneled ceiling. The few residents I saw were stooped, scarred with wrinkles, fingering wires of hearing aids. But Catherine quickly led me into an open space with tables and chairs before a giant glass wall that looked onto a verdant garden. "The Home's hidden jewel," I had read on the website. "It's the first place you'll want to visit." Sure enough, we continued toward the wall and through a glass door.

The garden was something less than the miniature Eden advertised on the web. Nestled within a narrow patch of city street, it was an ovular area around whose edge curved inner and outer paths, separated from one another by a row of manicured hedges, about head high. Catherine led me on the inner path, which brought us to a small fountain (with a pudgy Cupid, water gurgling from the tip of his arrow). There were benches on three sides and, on the fourth, a flower garden boasting purple and yellow buds. Catherine slowed to let me look but soon brought us to the outer path, which hugged the ivy-covered wall, where every twenty yards or so appeared a little alcove between the bushes with a small bench, perfect for private conversation. At the path's furthest point—the apex of the horseshoe curve—was a small crop of oaks, already densely leafed.

A man and woman, both notably older than Catherine, popped in and out of sight in gaps between the bushes. Another man, with a silver-topped cane, sat alongside a woman, the first I had seen with black or brown skin, in a nurse's uniform on a bench by the fountain. Even when the others faded from view, it was impossible to feel in complete isolation, with the city looming around us. The dead-end streets to either side were quiet enough, but at the garden's far end, just beyond the oaks, lay the FDR Drive, with cars stalled in morning traffic and a chorus of honks and grinding gears.

Catherine hardly noticed. She was caught up in her role as tour guide, naming the flowers—names that I, a city kid, had never learned—telling the supposed myth behind the water fountain (Cupid had shot an arrow into the heart of Hades, making him fall for the virginal Persephone, at the request of Venus, who had wanted to extend her dominion into the underworld), listing the good coffee houses and the best Greek and Japanese restaurants she had discovered in the neighborhood. Even when the conversation wandered into the past, it never went back too far. I learned that JT worked as a studio engineer, lived in San Diego, and was divorced with a child, Sophie, "who's very creative, oh, I adore her so." Less was said of Kyle, but I heard that he lived in Oregon and "worked in sales."

"And what about you, young man?"

Such a simple question, but one that still caused my entire body to tense. The truth was that, though I was home after some dozen years away, I had never felt so lost. Between my inheritance and money from leasing my parents' apartment, plus the trickle of income from occasional writing and editing gigs, I had managed to support myself over the years, but my piecemeal, odd-job existence was a far cry from the careers my striving peers were building. Nor had I returned home with a lasting relationship, let alone a family. At first, the friends I reconnected with were welcoming enough. But our lives were misaligned, and I quickly saw that they viewed me as a foreign curiosity, oddly lacking in attachments, who had passed a decade "gallivanting" (their word, not mine) around Europe, while they had followed all the rules, intent on surging into the upper-middle class, building the sort of life that my parents had led and into which I'd been born. When conversation arrived at the inevitable questions (*why had I come home? what would I do now?*), I could find no response that was both true and satisfying, but to keep everyone sane, I had shaped a rote reply—that I was a journalist and had returned to New York after more than 10 years away simply because it was time—and this is how I answered Catherine.

"I'm glad to hear you're well," she said, with a bright smile that communicated, to my significant relief, that she needed nothing more from me on this topic.

We walked some forty-five minutes, lap after slow, counterclockwise lap, and never once did I feel pressed to share anything I did not wish to, nor even to find words to fill the silence, when talk momentarily lapsed. "There is so much to explore in a new place," Catherine said after one such gap. "I'm still working my way through this neighborhood. And to think that this borough is full of neighborhoods, and the city full of boroughs. It's like I've arrived at a new home with a grand library—so much more to discover than I will possibly have time for."

We might have kept going had not the clouds darkened and thick pellets of rain begun to hammer the ground. We reentered the Home and sat at a table near the glass, listening to the steady drumming and looking at the green space before us, which seemed lush and expansive, as if this sightline, from inside the Home looking out, were its primary purpose. I thought to share this observation with Catherine, but she smiled so innocently, flashing a row of mostly white, if whittled, teeth, that it felt wrong to darken the mood.

A man in a uniform of a white shirt and blue pants approached. "Can I get you anything, Ms. To-Morrow?"

"The usual, Sir Harvey. And may I introduce you to Gabriel, an old friend."

"He doesn't look old, Ms. Cathy. And neither do you. I'll be right back with the usual. Pleased to meet you, Mr. Gabriel."

Their banter had a practiced quality, and I wondered if I might not be the first young man, described as an old friend, she had brought here.

"I hope you like coffee and brownies," she said, sweeping her wet hair back from her face. "He's always teasing my name. Cath. Katy. Ms. Tomorrow."

The coffee arrived quickly. "You'll probably think it's watery," Catherine said as I sipped. "It's how we used to make it, not like at those fancy places nowadays. But the brownies won't disappoint."

We picked at the brownies and watched the rain pelt the glass, a fog of tiny ripples and long streak marks, and soon we hit a new patch of silence, the first hint of awkwardness since my arrival, with neither the walk nor garden to use as a distraction. I sensed that Catherine had been tending to every moment since my arrival but now had finally reached the end of her preplanned script.

"Ready for a game?" she asked.

I had dismissed the stated purpose of the visit as a pretense, then forgotten it entirely, so I was not only surprised when she returned to the table with a backgammon board, but also by how practiced she seemed—how quickly she arranged the pieces, the ritualistic tapping of each side of her dice shaker that preceded each roll, her intense study of the board when it was my turn, the decisive movement of checkers when it was hers.

She crushed me the first game, as I struggled to recall the rules. But I fared no better during the second and third, even as I had a run of lucky dice rolls.

"Wow, you're good," I said.

We played several more games as the rain tumbled outside, pressing down the leafy bushes and pinging the glass window. Catherine was the picture of concentration as I tried to keep up, but I could never abandon myself to the game, periodically worrying how and when she would broach the subject of the past. My brain told me it was surely coming, though as the visit stretched on, I wondered if I had been wrong.

"I used to think it was just a dice game," she said. "A friend taught me otherwise. We met in White Plains in a park across the street from the facility where I took Alan a few times a week—for Alzheimer's patients."

"I'm sorry," I said. "I didn't know."

"It began years ago. Just one of those things," she said with a shrug. "One afternoon I was on a favorite bench, and a man approached. He had bushy white hair and a round, wrinkled face. It was a warm spring day, but he wore gray slacks and a black sports coat. He had a cane and walked with some difficulty. 'I come every day,' he said. 'Rain or shine, cold or warm.'"

"'I'm also a regular but only two or three times a week,' I replied.

"'I know,' he said. 'And when you come, you sit right here, in my favorite seat.'

"I apologized and slid over. He sat, we chatted. He had an accent I couldn't place. Somewhere in Eastern Europe or the Middle East.

"'I am Turkish,' he said, anticipating my thoughts. 'From Ankara. But I have lived here nearly forty years. My children are American, which is why they think I will like a place like this. In Turkey, you would invite your widower father to live in your home. You would take care of him, as he once took care of you. It would be an honor and a blessing. In America, they send the elderly away like trash to a landfill. My son said, 'It will be green and breezy, Baba, not hot and loud like Brooklyn.' My daughter spoke of the 'pure country air.' But they sent me here so that they won't have to listen to me tell them that they're ruining the restaurant. *Which I built.*"

"'I'm sorry to hear that,' I said.

"'But I am happy, Catherine. I am happy because it is my nature. It doesn't matter how often I tell my children that it is wrong to treat your elders so, because they think like Americans. They think what matters is whether you smile. Smiling, for better or worse, I cannot help. It is my way. I have, as they say, a golden smile.' As if to prove his point, he grinned widely, showing off a mouth filled with gold.

"When I returned to the park two days later, Ahmet—that's his name—was there again, and we spoke for hours. After that, every few days, I dropped off Alan and met Ahmet on his bench. We mostly talked; sometimes we walked small distances. I learned that his 'home' was in the very same building where I brought Alan, a few floors up from the Alzheimer's center. Ahmet was in the park, even during nasty weather. I would find him beneath a wide umbrella during a downpour or on the lone spot that wasn't white with snow. Sometimes, I tried to coax him inside. When I finally succeeded, he said, 'Then we must play backgammon.'

"That's how I started. Ahmet taught me the rules, the basic strategy, then deeper theories. And he loved to philosophize about the game. 'For many people,' he said, 'the dice are an imperfection; they say back-gammon is not a game of pure skill, like chess. To me, it is the contrary. For the element of chance introduces human psychology. Chance means uncertainty, and in uncertain situations people express who they are. You can play a computer at chess, but the joy of backgammon is its human face.'

"As Ahmet taught me backgammon, he showed me who he was. He loved the Italian singer Mina. He sewed holes in his socks. He claimed the T-bone steak was the best thing about America. He ate more yogurt in a given week than I had eaten in my life. He seemed so young and energetic when he sat, but he walked slowly, bent over, his forehead sweaty. I sometimes thought, 'If only you could combine his mind and Alan's body.'"

Catherine's eyes sparkled, and I wondered where this story was leading. Was she describing friendship or something more?

"'One morning,' she said, 'a beautiful spring day, Ahmet was not at the bench. Nor was he there in the days that followed. After a few weeks, I went to his floor of the old aged home and learned that he had fallen and bruised his hip. I was told he had refused all visitors.

"Perhaps a month later, he was back on the bench, a walker beside him. When he stood, he was so bent that he had to put his sunglasses in his jacket pocket, so they didn't fall from his face. Our walks had ended; and even chats on the bench or backgammon games inside were quickly interrupted by exhaustion.

"One day, I found him in the park beside a young man with the same thick eyebrows, though entirely black. 'Catherine? I'm Orhan,' he said, 'Mr. Yildiz's son.' He knew how to shake a hand and greet a stranger, but he lacked his father's charm. Orhan told me that Ahmet would be moving to a home in New Jersey, adding in a whisper, 'one more appropriate for his condition.'

"It's sad, Gabriel," Catherine turned to me. "There are many homes. You move from one to the next as you fall downward. But the key, as in backgammon, is timing. Not where to move, but when. You must anticipate; it is better to move too early than to move too late. That's part of the reason I came here now.

"'Let's stay in touch,' I said to Ahmet, but it was Orhan who answered, 'Of course. I understand you've been a good friend.'

"After that, Ahmet and I spoke on the phone. We wrote a few letters. One day I ran an errand in New Jersey and visited his new home. The reception room was dark, the small courtyard smelled of gas from a nearby pump station. The other residents were in wheelchairs and slow of speech. Ahmet's face had thinned, he ignored his lunch. When I took out a backgammon board, he shook his head.

"Later, the calls stopped, the letters too. For a while, I told myself that it was Ahmet who stopped trying, but in truth, it was just one of those things. A slow, gradual parting.

"Then one day, maybe a year later, the mailman stands in my doorway jokingly asking if I had a rock collection, before carrying a massive box into my living room. Can you guess what was inside? Stacks of books—English, French, German, Turkish—all about backgammon. Also, an envelope with a letter, typed and signed by Orhan:

...he grew sick and weak and refused visitors. Even me and my sister, Leyla. But his death was mercifully quick and painless, nothing like the passing of his wife, our beloved mother, from which he never fully recovered.

Catherine, my father spoke often about you. You were a dear, dear friend to him. And in the final months of his life, he revised his will to make one small change: to bequeath his backgammon library to you.

"Do you know, Gabriel, I've tried to find other backgammon partners. Old friends, strangers I meet in the grocery store, a few of the nurses here, but I beat them all as badly as Ahmet beat me those first days, and they give up, even if I occasionally lose on purpose. Isn't it wild? You get good at something and soon there's no one to play with. Who knows, maybe you'll be my new partner."

We had played seven or eight games by that point, and I had lost every time. I'd been competitive twice, and only because of good luck with the dice.

"You have a feel for the game," she said. "I could make you a strong player. What do you say… another one?"

She set the pieces and handed me a shaker and dice. I kept things close for a while and wondered if she was letting it remain that way, but again she won. Outside the rain slowed to a drizzle. Harvey returned to the table. "Anything more, Ms. Cathy?" She shook her head, and he placed a bill beside her.

I glanced around, finding more zombie eyes, plus the far more intimidating stare of the receptionist at the chipped desk. "I'm so glad we had a chance to catch up," I said and stood to leave.

"Do you know, Gabriel, who Orhan with all his skill and smarts, reminded me of? Why, your sister. Before you go, please tell me something about Becca."

"I think I told you before," I answered quickly, wanting to disengage from this line of questions. "She's a painter, a sculptor, a video-artist. She lives in LA, also Berlin. Travels a ton. I mean, it's weird to call either of those places her home. She's becoming a really big deal in the art world."

"I've read about her."

This was unexpected. "You read art magazines?"

"I set up a Google Alert. Actually, my granddaughter did. When I started seeing Becca's name in the papers, I was surprised. Well, not that *surprised*. Donna used to say that Becca was unusual. Of course, I saw it right away. The first time I met her was at a street fair. We arrived as Becca was trying to win a prize. 'Welcome, Catherine and Alan,' she said, then turned to the boys and tossed a beanbag, which Kyle grabbed out of the air. 'Nice catch,' she said. 'Come, I'll show you how we play.' She was four years old, half the boys' height, but she already had their attention. She had all of our attention, immediately."

Catherine stood, and our eyes were even again. I had forgotten how much taller she was than my mother—*Donna*, the oddness of hearing that name still rang in my ear.

"Does she still not show new work?" Catherine asked.

"Huh?"

"I just mean, I hope that we can see a show if she has one in New York."

As we walked to the entrance, I couldn't help but wonder what Catherine was getting at, if there was an endgame to these questions that went beyond interrogation, apology, and an airing of feeling and regret. Did Catherine want to see Becca's art or Becca? Did she want to play backgammon with her, too? If she thought Becca would consent to an afternoon of board games and breezy conversation, she had obviously forgotten who my sister was.

We had come to the door. Outside the sky was bright again, and the sidewalk glimmered.

"I've had such a fun time," Catherine said. "Promise me we'll play again soon."

"Of course," I answered, though I didn't turn back as I stepped into the drumming light.

4

"How about hide and seek?"

"In the dark?" Becca asked.

"The woods aren't thick here," said Kyle. "And we'll only count to ten, fifteen. You can't go far."

"I'm IT," said Connor. "One, two…"

I heard movements on both sides, Kyle running one way, Becca the other. I followed her—or rather, I followed the beam of her flashlight—past trees and bushes, over roots and fallen pine needles, never letting her get more than a few feet ahead. When she settled in behind a tree, crouching like a catcher, I kneeled right beside her.

"Find your own spot," she said.

"But Bec—"

"Find your own spot, Gabriel."

"Fourteen… Fifteen," Connor called out in the distance. "Ready or not, here I come."

I felt my way through the dark—one tree, two trees, three trees—to a trunk so wide I couldn't hug half its circumference. One hand always touching bark, I sank to the roots on its far side. Three and a half trees away, Becca's flashlight was off. There were noises, and I saw an approaching light. As seeker, Connor didn't need to mask his location, but when he drew near Becca's spot, he didn't scream, "Got you!" Oddly the light went off.

I heard rustling. "Hey," Becca said loudly. "Hey, what are…"

She stopped mid-sentence. I heard more rustling, louder, quicker, and felt a chill, partly cool night air, partly country spook. I moved toward Becca, my hand grazing the trees I passed. "Becca?" I called as I got close. "You there?"

A smacking sound, a muffled grunt, another rustle, a pulling back. "Gabriel, what are you doing?" She was low to the ground. She stood suddenly and brushed off her chest. "You've given away your spot."

A bright light shone in my eyes. "Got you, Gabe," said Connor, rising from the ground and tucking in his shirt. "That's two. Let's get Kyle."

Becca's light came on, and we were moving in a line—she allowed me to go first, so it was Connor, me, Becca—heading back the direction we had come. Kyle was easy to spot. He was sitting on a boulder, like an enthusiastic hiker who had gone ahead then grown nervous about being alone.

"You call that a hiding spot?" said Connor.

"It's pitch dark. Everything is hidden," Kyle answered.

"Maybe we should head back," Becca said, still behind me.

"You don't have to be IT. I'll go next," said Kyle. "One… two…"

I suddenly felt my heart racing. Two, three thumps, for every number Kyle called. Connor took off to the left, the direction Kyle had gone last time. Becca grabbed my hand and pulled the opposite way. I held tight, and to my surprise, she clung to me just as fiercely. We moved at a hurried clip. Coming to a crevice behind a fallen tree, I whispered, "Here?" but Becca didn't stop, nor did she let me. Keeping me close, she pulled me deeper into the woods until finally, between hard breaths, she yanked me to the ground beside her. We were on the far side of a wide tree, nestled in the groves between roots, still holding hands, our palms sweaty.

"Nineteen… twenty…," I heard in the distance. "Ready or not, here I come."

Kyle's cry seemed distant, and his first movements seemed to carry him even further away. But when I peered around the tree to see the path of his flashlight, Becca gripped my shoulder. "We're hiding," she said.

The sound of Kyle's footsteps faded, and I heard only her breathing, mixed with sniffles.

"Are you ok?" I asked.

"Shh."

"You're sniffling."

"I'm cold."

I heard what sounded like far-off laughter, though perhaps it was wind ruffling leaves. "I think Kyle found Connor," I said.

"Shh," Becca said and again squeezed my shoulder, but this time I broke free of her grip and swung to the tree's opposite side. In the distance, I saw a flashlight beam cut an angle through the dark.

"I can't tell which way they're going," I said.

"Shh."

The light shifted further away. With each step, they were cold, cold, colder. "They aren't coming toward us," I said. "Maybe we should we turn on our light."

"Gabriel, can't you be still?"

The sounds had grown faint—as had the glimmer of the light. I could no longer tell if I saw a flashlight or only hazy moonglow.

No, it *was* a flashlight. Far away, but I could see it. Until I couldn't. I didn't note the exact instant it vanished, but at a certain point it was clear that the light was gone, and in the distance, I saw only black forest.

Becca's heavy breathing had faded, too. I slid to the tree's other side, seeking her with my outstretched hand, thankfully finding her shoulder. "Shouldn't we give them a hint?" I asked. "Turn on the flashlight. Talk loudly."

"We're hiding."

We went on like this. I wanted to call out, shine the flashlight, rattle branches, make ourselves found; Becca urged silence, patience, that we remain hidden, or something like that. Mostly she just said, "Shh."

But eventually she rose and stood so close to me that our shoulders pressed against one another's. "It's ok," she said, squeezing my hand. The same words as when we had entered the woods, but this time I spoke up.

"What does that mean?"

A click. Finally, a new beam of light. She pointed her flashlight, which had been off this whole time, toward a tree directly before us, then circled, as if exploring our environs. Trees, trees, and more trees. Some with hulking trunks, others just skinny twigs. A floor of pine needles, patches of grass, pebbles, networks of roots, the odd jagged stone, a thick patch of moss. The pace of her movements was lackadaisical, even playful, which unnerved me further.

"Becca, we have to call out," I said. The light went off, and it was dark again—darker, for my eyes were no longer adjusted.

"I'm listening," she said. "Shh." She clicked the flashlight on anew, a dancing beam, figure eights, spirals, zigzags. Faster and faster until it became a riot of fireflies, momentarily hypnotic. The chilly touch of a hard gust stirred me from my reverie.

"Kyle," I screamed. "Connor."

No response.

The flashlight slowed to a more measured pace. Like a wand, or a paintbrush. Then, it zipped across the forest floor, jumped between crinkly leaves, fallen pinecones.

"Don't be an idiot," I said. "Point it upward."

I grabbed for it, but Becca yanked her hand away. "There's no point."

The light went off, and I felt her hand holding mine. We began to walk, at times squeezing tight, at times linked only by the curl of our fingertips. My eyes readjusted to the dark, and the risk of stumbling dissipated as I began to decipher what was object and what was shadow, what was solid and what was empty space.

Eventually she turned the light on again, beaming straight ahead. Trees, overhanging branches, trunks, thick and thin, grooves running down their length, holes, where a bird might nest, or a rodent, vines twisted on thin branches, pinecones, dried leaves, tangled bushes. Forest. Nothing but forest. Becca pointed the beam upward, and the light vanished into the sky.

"Kyle," I shouted. "Connor."

"What's the point? If they wanted to find us, they would have called out."

"You mean, they left us on purpose?"

"Duh."

"But why would they?"

"Beats me. They're jerks?"

"No, Becca. *You* left them." I don't know where that thought came from, but it felt right. "You took us so far away. The wrong direction, on purpose. You wanted to get lost."

"You can't be serious," she said. "We were playing hide and seek."

We marched on, in single file. The beam of light; Becca; me. The flashlight glanced left and right, but nothing changed. Woods. More woods. That's when I thought of Hansel and Gretel. Abandoned in the forest, they had marked their trail with pebbles. I felt along the ground and picked up anything solid—stones, twigs, chips of bark.

"What are you doing?" Becca asked.

When I told her, she kicked an acorn from the path. "That's silly, Gabriel."

"So, you know the way back?

"I think so."

"Prove it."

More silence. Where our hands still touched, there was no longer warmth. I kept marking the trail, but less frequently, and with softer, quieter items, seeds and twigs, pinecone fragments, less likely to draw attention.

After a while, the ground was damp, and the sky opened above. A clearing. Stars. Moonglow.

"Look, Gabriel."

The flashlight circled the clearing's edges.

When we had first entered the woods, even before the game of hide and seek, there had been a clearing. Was this the same one? "Do you know where we are?" I asked.

"I think so."

"And you know the way out?"

She led us to the clearing's edge, and then past it, back under the trees. At any moment, I expected a burst of open sky, soft grass beneath our feet, a sliver of the Morrows' roof in the distance. But there was only darkening canopy.

"I thought you knew the way. Shouldn't we go back to the clearing?"

"It was dewy. I was getting wet sock."

"Are you kidding me?"

"Shh, Gabriel. I just need to sit for a second."

She slumped against a hefty tree, turned back on the flashlight, and waved it around again. Not that frantic rush of earlier, but the magical wand thing, the painting thing.

"Cut it out," I said.

"It helps me think." More sweeps of light. A slow looping cursive. A careless doodle.

"What about the batteries?" I said.

That made her freeze. One heartbeat, two, three. Then the flashlight moved a few inches, shining on an opening in a tree trunk some ten feet away, perhaps an owl or squirrel hole, maybe just a purposeless void. I could feel Becca considering my words, testing their logic. But after some thirty seconds, the flashlight began a new round of twists and twirls, faster now, driven by a new nervous energy.

"Becca, quit it."

The dance lightened but did not slow. A ballerina on tiptoes. A butterfly's flight.

"Becca, stop—"

I grabbed for it. She yanked her arm violently. I lunged further, leaned directly over her body.

"Oww," she screamed, rolling and shoving me away. "Get off."

I had touched the cool metal for a moment but never gripped it firmly. There had been a clang, followed by muffled sounds.

Becca was crawling, patting the ground. "Nice one, Sherlock," she said. "It's gone."

I joined her on all fours, searching frantically, finding only soft dry dirt and pine needles, which felt nice, surprisingly comforting.

"Got it," she cried, but when I heard a click, and then another, I saw nothing.

"What happened?" I asked.

"You broke it, doofus."

"I didn't break anything. It's the battery. You were wasting—"

"No, Gabriel. You broke it. And you hit me. It hurts. It—"

"Was that the same clearing as before?"

"Did you hear me? I said you hurt—"

"But you know the way back, right? Why do we even need the flashlight?"

Becca dragged me beside her against the tree. "Let's wait here," she said. "Until morning. It won't be long."

"You said you knew the way."

"Shh, Gabriel. I'm sure you're tired. It's best this way."

I protested a while longer, but I saw that even if I insisted on continuing, she would refuse and I would be on my own, without any light. A country basement was scary enough. But to be alone in the dark woods—it was the last thing I wanted, the very last. So, I did as she suggested. I leaned into the tree as if were a big lumpy armchair. Though my heart was pounding, though I jumped at each owl hoot and even a flash of some foul odor, I managed to nestle into the trunk, which, to my surprise, could be almost as comfortable as a real armchair, even a bed—almost—if you let it be.

5

"Pick me up at 73rd and York," Catherine said. "I'll be waiting."

She had called a few days after our meeting at the East River Home and suggested a stroll along Madison. Not a word about Becca or any other fraught topic; it was light and surprisingly fun, easing my misgivings about another visit. Now two weeks later, Catherine and I had seen each other several more times. We'd been to Dalmos, her favorite Greek restaurant. We'd passed an entire morning at Starbucks, sharing the Sunday *Times*. On consecutive rainy days, we'd sat before the glass wall of the East River Home playing backgammon, and the next day, when the weather broke, we went to the Central Park boathouse to watch toy sailboats race across the shimmering pond.

Catherine had appeared in my life at the perfect time. After a few months back in New York, the city's newness had worn off and I was left to confront my state of utter confusion. It was about everything really—what to do each day, what to do with my life—but nowhere was it more apparent than as I attempted to muddle through social life. One day, I mumbled incoherently to girls at a party. The next, I leaped into an awkward exchange with a bartender that required a friend's rescue. And there were many lesser sins, which friends hinted at with a mixture of smirks and befuddlement: that I hummed horrid Euro Pop, that I wore pants that were too tight, that I pointed out misspellings on menus, that, when I was drunk, my accent shifted to somewhere in the mid-Atlantic. I had become a bumbling fool, a study in guilelessness, a walking social disaster.

But Catherine made me feel like none of these foibles mattered. Each time I recounted a new mishap, my latest awkward attempt to re-connect—with Sebastian, Carlos and Laura, Michael, Peter, Vic and Helene, Casper, any number of friends from the past—the event seemed to transform as we discussed it, from ghastly faux pas into the softer stuff of comedy.

I spotted Catherine across York Avenue. She was overdressed, given the day's heat, in a pale blue dress and green knit sweater. She wore a fanny pack and her beat-up sneakers, which I had learned were Keds. Her hair was cinched in a tight bun, revealing the papery surface of her forehead.

She greeted me with her usual quick hug, and off we went.

"You were going to tell me about a girl you met in Paris," she said when we had walked a few blocks.

"Right," I said. "This was probably 2006—so I'd already been in Paris several years—and one afternoon I went to what had become my favorite café. The place was busy, I had to ask to share a table. 'Je vous en prie,' said the woman sitting there. She returned to her magazine, but I felt unusually bold and started talking.

"Cassia was her name. A foreigner like me, from outside of Naples, she worked at L'Oréal, the perfume division. Our conversation was easy, led seamlessly into dinner, then a walk. Soon, she was leading me to a spot on the Ile de la Cité, where I had never been, though I'd often watched enviously from above, as kids congregated with guitars and cheap wine and notebooks and backpacks, an outdoor frolic on sum-mer eves. On this evening it was cool and drizzly, and we were alone. She took me to a private corner beneath a rocky overhang and ... well, it's hard to describe, Catherine. I mean, I'd had other flings in Paris but this happened so naturally..."

"I'm not surprised."

"What do you mean?"

"Well, you are easy on the eyes."

I paused, catching the awkwardness of the moment, of sharing such detail with an older woman I barely knew, of hearing such words from her in response, but Catherine continued. "Don't be alarmed. I understand how these things work. I'm the mother of two sons, you know, and a woman myself. Don't let the gray hair fool you."

Her eyes were gentle, and I was struck, not for the first time, by how effortless our friendship seemed, how she offered a judgment-free space, in which I didn't need to defend my actions, or lack thereof. Only with Catherine did my life as presently constituted compute as acceptable. Being with her was the perfect antidote to whatever mysterious pall of alienation darkened my encounters with peers.

"Those other flings didn't last," I said, "but I knew right away that Cassia would be different. She was delightful and sexy, easygoing but also exciting, and she quickly became the center of my existence. But one evening only months after we met, on another walk by the Seine, she led me to a bench overlooking that same corner of Ile de la Cité and told me, between kisses, that she would be moving to Milan—*at the end of the month.*

"The news hit like a bomb until I realized that this was an invitation, which felt like a different sort of bomb. Ten weeks hardly marked a serious relationship, and this was not *amour fou*. On the flip side, little tied me to Paris beyond inertia. A phone call with Becca helped clinch my decision. 'I don't get this front of resistance, Gabriel,' she said. 'If it doesn't work out, you're right back where you started.'

"But something stopped clicking in Milan. From the first, our balance was off. In Paris, Cassia and I were both on foreign ground, equals, but she had moved closer to home, while I'd gone further from mine. Disagreements that had been easy to overlook suddenly took on grave importance. She was moody, but I tended to ignore her snide quips and performative sourness, rather than draw her out into a happier place, which I later realized is what she wanted. Silence and then apathy seeped into the relationship, and it seemed like we needed to rouse ourselves into arguments to motivate for anything, a dinner out, a conversation about politics, sex.

"And there were real fights, too—about how late she worked, socks lying on the bedroom floor, toothpaste on the rim of the sink, big weekly cleanings versus small daily ones, how much to scrub before loading the dishwasher, who was obligated to make the second pot of coffee. Living together revealed basic incompatibilities, and for a while it seemed like we had nothing in common but a refusal to compromise. Still, when she announced, maybe two months after our move, that she would return home to Campania for the weekend, claiming that 'time apart might be good,' I protested vehemently. Recalling an earlier fling, which had ended after the girl had gone home to Toulouse for a few days, I insisted on accompanying her, despite a warning that her mother 'would size you up in an instant. Mi raccomando.'

"It was a pleasant enough weekend in a hilltop town with giant lunches and even larger dinners eaten on a sunny rooftop, and to me her mother (and aunt and cousins) seemed friendly, but the moment we returned to Milan, Cassia said, 'It was exactly as I feared,' after which she detailed her mother's critique of me—I was not affectionate enough, yet too deferential; that I had failed to notice her contempt was proof of my naivete—which happened to align with the very complaints Cassia made whenever tensions arose.

"Maybe a week later, after morning sex (Cassia instigated, a pleasant surprise), we dressed and went for a walk. It was a spectacular day, cloudless, the sun perched on rooftops. We wandered—directionless—or so I thought until I realized we were only blocks from the train station. 'Shall we sit?' she asked and settled on the front steps of an office building. She pulled out her Marlboros and offered me one—she always asked, though I always refused. Between puffs of her cigarette, she said, nonchalantly, that it was over, 'it just didn't feel right.' She'd bought a ticket for Naples, she'd go for a week, then return to Milan and get her stuff. I thought she was joking, then that there had to be more to it. I called all week, begging for an explanation, getting none. Finally, she requested that I not call again. 'Gabriel, je vous en prie,' she said, closing the circle. A week later, a friend picked up her stuff, and that was that. Except that I was alone in an apartment I didn't like, in a city I hardly knew, with oodles of free time and no idea what to do with it.

"Young love," said Catherine, smiling with sympathy. "So mysterious." I kept waiting for her to ask if I stayed in Milan, to ask what happened next, but she seemed content to pat my shoulder and hurry us across a busy intersection, the light blinking yellow.

But we mostly proceeded slowly. We were passed by kids, by seniors. Before the backgammon board, Catherine was master and I the disciple, but here on the street, though plenty eager, she had little stamina and struggled to match my considerably reduced speed.

At a red light on 44th and Lexington, she reached for her knees, breathing heavily.

"Should we stop for lunch?" I asked.

Between gulps of air, she pointed to a Starbucks across the street. "Or a coffee?"

We sat by the window looking onto Grand Central and made fun of the harried pedestrians straining their legs to move as quickly as possible without breaking into a run, and also the bewildered tourists stepping tentatively from the station, looking left and right, trying to find their bearings—the only two types we saw, New York as ever a city of extremes.

"Aren't you becoming the jaded New Yorker?" I said.

"Maybe a little. Feeling superior is quite the rush." Her breathing had steadied and her face, momentarily flushed, had returned to its lighter shade.

"I'm heading to the station," she said.

"We can ride the subway together. Or a cab. My treat."

"Actually, I'm taking a train to White Plains."

I was puzzled, but she soon corrected a misunderstanding that had persisted over our several meetings. Catherine had said that Alan "was gone," which I had taken to mean deceased, but, no, he was instead lost to an Alzheimer's fog and living in an institution. She was going to White Plains to visit him.

I left her at the ticket line in Grand Central and continued to Union Square, where I sat on a bench, flipping through an abandoned newspaper and peeking at a crew of skateboarders and their knit-hatted hangers-on. As the sun began to set, I was struck that I could still feel the day's intimacy. Between my confession about Cassia and the revelation about Alan, Catherine and I were coming to know each other, and I saw that I had found a comfort in her presence that was missing with other friends. But I also wondered if I could trust this. Was it really possible that a 70-year-old who used to be my mother's best friend could become a trusted confidante of my own?

6

When I awoke to a purple sky, Becca was gone.

I circled the tree under which I had slept, then the surrounding ones. Was I dreaming? Had a bear run off with her? How dare she leave? I began walking in the direction where the light seemed brighter, but I hadn't gone more than twenty feet when I decided to mark my path. This time there would be no one to stop me. I let pebbles slip through my fingers, turning a few times to make sure that the path was indeed marked. "Becca," I called out, but there was no response.

The sky turned a lighter purple, and the rim of the horizon, especially to my left, glowed orange as I arrived at a clearing. I kept walking toward the glow. Even as I reentered the tree line, the horizon brightened and expanded. There were fewer pine needles below, the trees thinned, and soon a field of grass was before me, damp on my toes. My nose ran. I ran. Up a gentle slope to where I could see, some distance ahead, a house. Was it the Morrows' place?

It stood three stories high, had a peaked roof, a chimney and windows with white paint flaking off the sills, a roof of dulled, worn wood. I kept running, joyously and fearfully, my fastest dash. The backdoor was locked and rounding the bend, I spotted three parked cars, one our dusty Datsun. Past an S-shaped cobbled path was the front door, which opened easily. Inside was a sight I knew only too well: the carnage after a dinner party (only later did I realize how unusual this was in a home run by Catherine Morrow). In the living room, a platter with cheese rinds and an edge of paté, and an ice bucket, now holding a puddle. In the dining room, a scatter of cloth napkins, two forgotten forks, a tin holding a third of a peach pie, and five empty bottles of wine, all but one the same deep purple I had awoken to. Above the swinging door to the kitchen, a clock read 6:11. Ahead, the creaky carpeted stairs, leading up.

On the second floor, I recalled JT having said, during the rushed tour upon our arrival, that "your room is second on the left." Sure enough, behind that door lay the four-shelved dresser, the wooden chair with ovular mirror above, the bed with floral quilting and brass posts. I expected to find Becca already tucked in it, but the blanket was still folded with hospital corners. I crawled on top, shoes on, laces tied, and curled into the sheets, pulling, twisting, until they wrapped me tight.

* * *

Yellow light flowed through the corner window. I felt snug and rested. My back was not sore. My throat was not dry. My nose was not running. A new day? But I was wearing damp pants and socks, and my sneakers were on. I fumbled through my backpack for my other jeans and fresh tubesocks (little good they did; the insides of my Nikes were soggy). Still no sign of Becca. The hallway, the bathroom, down the stairs. The clock now read 9:26. I followed voices into the kitchen, where Mom, Dad, and Catherine sat at the table, all in bathrobes. They were bleary eyed as they sipped steaming mugs of coffee.

"Good morning, Gabriel," Catherine said, and then turning to Mom, "See? I told you."

"We had a bet," Mom said. "Catherine said you'd be the first one down."

"The first kid?" I asked.

"We knew you'd be the first kid," Mom said. "She thought you'd be down before Alan, who apparently now sleeps as late as a teenager."

"Now we owe them tickets to the *Nutcracker*," Dad said.

"You can come too," said Catherine. "But the Staubs are on the hook for the tickets."

They sat in front of a window looking onto the field where we had seen stars last night, which I had run across at dawn. As in my room, the light was brilliant. The grass was a lush green, trees in the distance sparkled, even the blue sky with its wisps of white shimmered.

"You were out late," Mom said. "Did you have fun?"

"They must have," Dad cut in. "It's a late morning for you, Gabriel. Becca, too—but especially you. You and I are usually the early risers."

"Well, he probably caught the sleeping bug from my boys. They've become impossible to get up. One of the many blessings and curses of teenagers."

"Jonah thinks sleep habits are genetic, don't you, hon?" Mom said. "He thinks Becca and Gabriel get up early because he does. Maybe last night proves it's just circumstance. Look at you, Gabriel, it's nearly 9:45. And Becca hasn't even come down."

"She hasn't?"

At first no one reacted to my question, to the alarm I felt as I asked it. Each of them, Mom, Dad, Catherine, continued to sip from their mugs, their eyes still cloudy. But then Mom said, "She isn't upstairs?"

I shook my head.

"Well, teenage boys sleep late, and teenage girls get lost in the bathroom, don't they?" Catherine said.

"Wouldn't we hear her?"

"She could be in the basement," Catherine said.

"Would you check, Gabriel?" Mom asked.

I passed through the basement door and found a room so much more welcoming than the one I remembered. Light spilled through side windows, eliminating shadowy corners. Unlike the dining room, this space was tidy; not only were the butts and ashes gone, but the ashtray, too, as well as the beer and soda cans. The coffee table had been swept clean; its glass surface sparkled in the light. "Becca," I called out, but my voice was meek. I tried the windows, hoping I might see her strolling across the yard or lounging on a blanket. Even a patch of bent grass or trail of pebbles would have been better than nothing.

"Anything?" Catherine asked when I returned to the kitchen.

I shook my head.

"I'll go upstairs... ask the boys," she said. "You know, just in..." Her words disappeared into her mug, which landed, now empty, on the table. "They should be getting up, anyway."

Mom took a long look at Dad and followed Catherine to the stairs. But Dad smiled at me and asked what we had done the night before. As I stumbled in search of an answer, he asked if I was hungry and began poking around the counter, finding a bowl, spoon, milk, and box of Cheerios.

"We went out to see the stars," I finally said.

"How was it?"

Mom was back, wearing jeans and a cardigan. "Do you have any idea where she could be, Gabriel?"

"Not really. I..."

Catherine reappeared, too, announcing that Becca was not in the attic. "But the boys will be down soon."

"Do they know where she is?" Mom asked. "Do you, Gabriel?"

She began pacing, the only one to project concern. Dad merely encouraged me to eat but began to ask questions—sensible, practical questions—Had we checked ALL the bathrooms? The living room? The entire attic? All of the basement? The garage?

Alan appeared in the kitchen, holding a newspaper.

"Where's the best hiding spot in the house?" Dad asked.

"Is that a trick question?" Alan asked, reaching for the coffee. "Really, it's too early."

"Oh, Jonah, she'll turn up soon enough," Catherine said. "Don't worry."

"Who'll turn up?" Alan asked.

"We can't find Becca," Dad said.

"She's probably hiding in some corner with a book, or out on a walk," said Catherine.

"On a walk?" This was Mom, her words sharp and nervy. "She has no idea where we are."

"She's an intrepid girl, Donna. And there are roads and paths here. It's not like it's the middle of nowhere."

"For a city girl, it is."

No one reacted to the edge in Mom's voice, but I felt fear stirring inside me. And over the next several minutes, I watched as each adults grasped the reality of Becca's absence in his or her own way. Dad and Alan went to search through the house, leaving me to contend with Mom's growing agitation and Catherine's unflappable blasé. As the one paced and fumbled with stray spoons and mugs, the other calmly opened cabinets and drawers, gathering flour, eggs, oil, a bowl, and mixing spoon.

"Do you think people would prefer pancakes or crepes?" Catherine asked. "Gabriel, what do you think?"

"Pancakes," I said, though the second syllable was a whisper, chastened by Mom's hard glare at Catherine.

"Donna, it'll be fine. She'll turn up any moment."

I faced the wooden table and listened to the only sound, Catherine's spoon, mixing the batter, occasionally ringing the edge of the metal bowl. I felt such relief when Alan and Dad returned, but they announced that they had been to every room, the basement, the attic, too. "She's not here," Dad said. "We checked everywhere."

JT, Kyle, and Connor soon emerged, each dressed for the day, though Connor's hair was a greasy wedge sticking up from his head like a ski jump. Soon they were engulfed in the swirling conversation, and the facts of the previous night came out. Dad asked questions; Kyle answered, sheepishly, staring at the floor. Finally, Dad turned to me. I don't remember how he put things at first or how many times I had to repeat to myself; I just remember that he, and sometimes Mom, in more frantic tones, asked slight variations of the same questions, making me repeat the very thing I had just said, as if hoping that I would answer differently or correct a misunderstanding.

"Gabriel…" Dad gripped my shoulders and stared into my eyes. "I want to be sure I understand. When Kyle and Connor walked out of the woods, did you walk out, too?"

I shook my head.

"You spent the night?"

I couldn't meet his eyes any longer. I bent my neck and nodded.

"And Becca was with you?"

"She was when I went to sleep."

"And when you woke?"

"I didn't see her."

"Did you look for her?"

The room was silent, even Catherine had stopped her breakfast preparations. I didn't dare lift my eyes from the pale wood floor. "I walked around. I called her name. There was light and I walked toward it. I found my way out of the woods and—"

"See," said Kyle. "It was easy. That's what—"

"Shut up," said Alan. "Let Gabe finish."

"Alan, please," said Catherine.

"Was Becca in the room when you got back?" Dad asked.

I shook my head.

"We have to search for her," Mom shouted. "We have to go now."

I finally looked up, right at her. Her cheeks were ghost white but her lips bright crimson, as if she'd done up makeup for a masquerade. Her eyelids trembled.

"Everyone, get dressed," Alan said. "Everyone." He addressed us all, but he looked directly at Catherine, who dropped the spatula, rattling the countertop, and followed the others up the stairs.

Only Mom and I remained in the kitchen. We were the only ones dressed—well, maybe the boys, too, but they went upstairs with the others, likely for a moment of reprieve.

"Your cereal's getting soggy," she said. "Have a few bites."

She turned to the window, which looked onto the backyard, now a lush healthy green beneath the bright sun. Her eyelids had stopped twitching, but she still wore that pale, bloodshot mask.

Dad reappeared first, the others soon after. There was a pause as Alan questioned Catherine's woven sandals, which he said were for the beach, not the woods, but she gave him a disdainful look and opened the backdoor. One by one, we headed outside.

We walked in loose formation, each family clustered together, Connor tagging along in the rear. Mom and Dad were silent, but we could hear Kyle and Alan, the two furthest ahead, their voices raised.

"How could you?" Alan kept asking. "How could you leave, Kyle? I don't understand."

"We were barely in the woods. I thought they were fine," Kyle defended himself several times before eventually falling silent.

The conversation might have ended there had Catherine not stepped in. "This isn't helping, Alan. You heard Gabe. He found his way back easily." Then she would shift from the Morrow cluster to the Staubs and say, "She can't be far," or "We'll find her soon," or "Please don't worry." In response, Dad attempted a smile, while Mom was stone-faced. Now and then, Dad called out, "Becca... Becca," then uttered a loud "Shhhh," putting a finger to his lips. But there was never a reply, not even an echo. And we resumed our march.

In quieter moments, you could hear the clomp of Catherine's sandals, like a noisy horse hoof. I also noticed how small the grassy field seemed in the clear daylight. The sharp inclines and declines of the night had become faint dips and rises; the higher grass as we traveled from the house was barely perceptible. The journey to the edge of woods was achieved in a matter of minutes, hardly the vast distance of the night, nor my epic run at dawn.

"There." Kyle pointed to a spot in the trees. "That's where we entered."

"Are you sure?" Alan asked.

"I think so."

"You *think* so?"

"Alan, please," said Catherine.

We passed into the woods single file, Kyle and Alan ahead, then the three Staubs, with Catherine, JT, and Connor in the rear. Alan kept badgering Kyle about the direction and Kyle kept saying he thought he knew the way. Like the march up the field, the trail through the woods was underwhelming the day after. Most of the trees were thin enough that I could reach around and clasp my hands on the other side. And the gaps between them were wide. I looked back several times and could easily see where the trees ended, and the open sky began.

In little time, we came to a clearing, which was also smaller than expected. Kyle slowed and the group formed a loose circle.

"We came here last night. We crossed through about there"—he pointed ahead—"that's where we played hide and seek."

"You're sure?" Alan asked.

"I am."

We looked in all directions, taking in, I felt sure, the same set of facts: first, that Becca was nowhere in sight; second, that the woods were not thick and the field behind the Morrows' house remained visible.

"Where exactly did you begin playing?" Alan asked.

"About there," Kyle said.

"About?" Alan said, his voice again rising. "*About?*"

"Do you think it's possible…" Catherine said. "Do you think Becca might have—?"

"What, Catherine?" Mom said, glaring at her.

"Hear me out, Donna. Do you think it's possible she didn't want to be found?"

Mom's jaw clenched. The bone at her lower cheek stuck out like some Frankenstein bolt, twitching like a muscle under duress.

"I'm just asking if…"

"Say it, Catherine. I want to hear you say it."

"I'm just wondering if maybe she isn't lost, if this is deliberate."

"Like she ran away?"

"I'm just asking, Donna. Is it possible she's being difficult, or playing a game?"

"How could you say that?"

The thing is, I had wondered the same thing as Catherine. Not consciously—it had taken her words to make me realize it—but I had also imagined that Becca might not be lost so much as playing a more elaborate version of hide and seek. But Mom's reaction made clear I should utter no such thought out loud. Her barbed fury was a warning, doubly so if you knew her usual calm demeanor, knew how out of character it all was. And who knew better than Catherine, who often teased my parents for their reversal of gender stereotypes—Mom the stoic, the breadwinner (though also the primary cook), the driver, the handyman, while Dad was the chatty one, the gossip, an occasional "hysteric." Catherine knew how unusual Mom's displays of fear and anger were, but she didn't back off.

"Can we all take a deep breath," Catherine answered.

"A deep breath? This isn't yoga class. My daughter spent the night in the goddamn woods."

"I'm trying to get you to relax. I'm trying to get everyone to relax."

"Let's split up," Dad cut in.

"Good idea," said Alan. "I'll lead one group. JT, you take the other. Jonah, Kyle, come with me. The rest—"

"No," Mom practically screamed, her eyes fixed on Catherine. "I'm coming with you two." She neither pointed nor named "you two," but I knew instantly that she meant Alan and Kyle.

"Fine," said Alan, as Catherine retreated a few steps. "Me, Donna, Kyle. We'll start where Kyle says they began to play. The rest of you go the opposite way."

"Dad?"

"Yes, JT?" We all looked up, so unusual was the sound of the older Morrow boy's voice.

"Someone should go back. In case there's a phone call."

"Good idea," said Catherine. "I'll go. Connor, you, too. You don't need to be part of this."

Without another word, they walked off, an odd pair with nothing in common other than their heads bowed in palpable shame.

The rest of us split into our groups and headed off in separate directions, not unlike at the outset of hide and seek. It was JT, Dad, me. For a few seconds, we heard Kyle and Alan in the distance; then, they faded from consciousness. JT walked with a limp, which I hadn't noticed before. At first, I doubted myself, but if anything, the hitch in his left leg grew more pronounced with time. Still, he took the lead, determining our direction, even as he said little beyond, "Let's go this way," and occasionally called out, "Becca," in a poor echo of my father's persistent, though increasingly raspy, cries. But mostly we were quiet, and for minutes on end, I heard nothing but the pounding of our footsteps.

"Do you know the woods well?" Dad asked after some time.

"Not really. I've only been here a few weeks." JT reminded us that he'd had a summer job that kept him in Katonah through July. "But I have a good sense of direction."

Dad was silent. If JT's words alarmed him, he kept it to himself, but it seemed pretty clear that he was thinking the same as me: we were in Search Party B. In the movie, the other guys would get more screen time, and they would be the ones to find her, while we offered comic relief, perhaps going around in circles.

To make matters worse, JT periodically asked, "Does this look familiar? Is this the right way?" It would take me a moment to realize that he was asking me, and then I would feel like an idiot as I replied, "I don't know" or "I wasn't with her, remember?" or "It all looks the same to me."

We'd been walking awhile, at least half an hour, when I remembered my trail of pebbles. I blurted the news out, ashamed at having forgotten up until then, but neither JT nor Dad seemed upset. JT turned us around and, proving that his claim of a good sense of direction had merit, led us back to the field behind his house, where amazingly we found my trail of pebbles from that morning, right near the spot we had first entered, followed them to the opening where Mom and Catherine had yelled and we had divided into search parties, and then into the woods beyond. Dad screamed "Becca" with new vigor, which exhausted the little voice he had left. We searched for footprints, bent grass, a fallen flashlight, strands of hair, any clue at all. Nothing. The pebbles verified my story but gave no hint as to Becca's whereabouts.

Increasingly JT's phlegmy voice took over as Dad's shouts cracked and wilted. I added my high-pitched squeal, too. Still nothing.

We took a different route than earlier, JT claimed, but it all looked the same to me. No blazes. No clear paths. At times, openings between certain clumps of trees, or runs of bushes seemingly pressed to the side, suggested someone had been there, but then we would explore only to discover that no human had passed this way recently, perhaps ever. Despite the limp, JT was a reliable leader. He walked a stretch, stopped and looked, called out Becca's name, noted the position of the sun, and only then, went a distance further. At one point we came upon another trail of stones and followed it a while—was it my other Hansel trail? A sign from Becca? But it stopped before a clump of bushes, and we realized it was nothing at all.

What alerted me to the passage of time was hunger. Then, the heat. I tied my sweatshirt around my waist. Dad pulled off his sweater, too, but JT kept his heavier sweatshirt on. Even under that dark, baggy layer, his body looked slight. He kept sweeping hair from his forehead and eyes, tramping with his head down, doing all sorts of things that hardly inspired confidence, but he remained calm. Whenever I felt Dad's temperature rise, JT found a way to "talk him down" without, well, without really talking to him at all. He would call to Becca or point at a certain tree or stone or indicate our direction, and generally act as if we were on an ordinary walk in the woods.

We passed three more clearings, one wide enough for a game of touch football, the other two notable only for their temporary bursts of sunlight and grassy floors. We hunted the environs of each for scratches in the dirt, a misplaced flashlight, bubble gum, any sign that someone had passed through. But mostly there was little to do but call out Becca's name and press onward. Finally, we came upon the sort of persistent light that signaled an edge of the woods and emerged onto an open field, knee high grass at its edges, a cropped pale green beyond.

"Oh god, don't tell me we're back where we started?" Dad said, his entire well of suppressed disappointment spilling out of him. "Have we been going in circles this whole time?"

"Not at all," said JT. "This is somewhere new."

Sure enough, the structure that came into view over a hill was not the Morrows' rental but a red farmhouse with adjacent barn. The sun blazed above; it was likely past noon. I felt another pang of hunger as I clomped across the field, which was marshy in parts. Near the house, a fluffy brown dog bounded toward us, but some twenty feet away it halted, sniffed the air, eyed us suspiciously, and turned around. We came upon a dusty road, where a man with a ginger beard and dirty overalls stepped out of the barn, introducing himself as Len.

JT explained the situation, and the man said not to worry. "I haven't seen a girl, but the woods aren't thick. You can't get lost in there, at least not in daylight."

He brought us in the main house where a woman with thick glasses was scrubbing a soiled oven pan.

JT repeated the story, and she pointed to the phone.

As Dad dialed, she asked JT, "You the Morrows' boy?"

"How'd you know?"

"You've got your Mom's eyes."

I heard Catherine's clipped hello through the phone. Dad asked if there had been a call—there hadn't been.

"What about the others?" he asked. They were already back at the house, Catherine answered.

Ten minutes later, Alan pulled up in the red Chevy. On the ride back, he told us that he, Kyle, and Mom had walked awhile but found nothing, returning to the house nearly an hour earlier. "We were waiting for you," he said. "We were all hopeful, but now Catherine has called the police."

JT poked around in the seat pocket, pulling out a giant bag of nuts and offering them to me. "Hungry?"

The bag was empty by the time we pulled into the Morrows' driveway, right behind a white and navy police car that blocked our Datsun.

7

As a city kid, I'd always been a walker, and when I moved abroad, I was more than happy to keep at it. In my first months in Paris, I would go to the Gare de l'Est or Gare du Nord or Gare de Lyon and take a train to some random city: Ghent, Brest, Geneva. I'd immediately drop my stuff at a hotel and go out to explore. I discovered a pattern on these trips. After two, maybe three, days of heavy walking, there came a moment when I knew exactly where I was: I recognized the cafe with red countertops or the florid iron fencing of the leafy park across the street. I didn't yet know this new city—how could I?—but how its puzzle pieces snuggled into one another was no longer a riddle. I no longer *felt lost*. On day two or three, there came a moment when a smallish city surrendered some of its mystery, at which point, as in a game of tag, I became the wild one, suddenly restless, ready to leave. In larger cities, the three-day principle hardly applied, but it could for neighborhoods. So, I brought the game home to Paris as well.

And after Paris: Milan, then Bratislava, then Paris again. After each arrival, there was always this period of exhilaration—like the boyish anticipation on a birthday morning. Now in New York, being with Catherine brought me back to those earliest joys. Together we visited outer-borough destinations I had never known as a Manhattan kid. Arthur Avenue, Jackson Heights, Bensonhurst, vibrant neighborhoods that had only been names on a map beforehand. We passed days exploring, six-, eight-hour chunks, breaking only for food and the bathroom (or to walk Catherine, who was often tired well before me, to the subway or a cab). But unlike when I was abroad, the usual restlessness didn't follow, because now I had a companion. And what a cheerful companion she was. And maybe more. Gradually the thought crystalized in my mind. A friend. That's what she was, right? A genuine friend.

But of course, there was an issue. The more time Catherine and I spent together, the more I began to worry that our relationship was a betrayal. Of the memory of my parents. Of Becca, still very much alive.

One sweltering July day, our plans for a walk through Chinatown were canceled in favor of backgammon in the air-conditioned common room at the East River Home. Still, summer seeped inside. Residents shuffled and wheeled between tables at a languorous pace. Beads of sweat bubbled at the edges of the glass wall overlooking the garden. Amazingly, after two narrow losses, I was ahead in our third game.

"You're getting good," Catherine said, her emphasis on "good" suggesting this was more than some throwaway compliment.

I tossed the dice. A 4 and a 6, lucky and luckier, allowing me to create a 6-point prime, enough to establish a nearly insurmountable position.

"Well, well," she said. "Look at that."

My first victory. Finally. After dozens and dozens of attempts. The sudden flood of pride surprised me, though as I thought back on the game, I realized that several moves prior, Catherine had left a blot when safer moves were available. And I wondered if this was a rare slip in concentration or if there had been similar blunders in the past, which I'd failed to notice.

"Should we bother playing it out?" she asked.

"Would you deny me the satisfaction of crossing the finish line?"

"I always say, Act like you've been here before." She extended her hand. "Shake?"

I had learned to grip her fragile hand without worrying that I would crush it, but her cool palm surprised me on that sultry day, and a memory came to mind. It was maybe ten years prior, early in my stay in Paris, when I started to be overwhelmed by the press releases, notices, and even hand-stenciled invitations on expensive paper-stock, all related to Becca, that cluttered my tiny mailbox.

One day, I received an invitation to an exhibition in Lyon—*Becca Staub: Recent Paintings*. I had a brief chuckle about the word "recent"—Becca wasn't quite 30, what wouldn't be recent?—but I knew I would go, and some weeks later, the morning of, I trained early to Lyon Part Dieu and wandered awhile, arriving at the gallery after 6:00. It was a modest space—a small entryway with a reception desk, a larger exhibition gallery behind, and presumably hidden offices through the back wall—named for its owner, Maurice Leplanc, whose picture I had scouted online. He had a shaved head and a distinctive purplish mark above an eye (in proper light, his left eyebrow looked like a bird flying across a pink sky), but what made him easy to spot was something the pictures hadn't revealed: he was six and a half feet tall.

A small crowd stood in line to chat and rise to kiss his long pale cheeks. During a rare gap, I made my approach. My French was more than passable, so I was taken aback by his facial contortions when I introduced myself and praised his airy, light-filled gallery. At first, I took this for awkwardness, but it only got worse when I asked if Becca was coming. He blanched, then disappeared into the back, only to emerge a quarter hour later with a hard glare, as he planted himself before the gallery's lone pillar, white like everything else in the space, except for the shadow he cast on it. His odd reaction made sense only after I had learned of the several misunderstandings my question had provoked and the different levels of shame inherent in each—an early lesson in the esoteric codes of the art world. Maurice Leplanc was not a first-tier gallery; not really second-tier, either. He had organized this show without Becca's cooperation (despite a dozen fawning letters), and my question was at first received as evidence that she was in fact coming, a surprise for which he was entirely unprepared. Apparently, a few phone calls in the back office cleared up this misconception, at which point he reinterpreted my question as mockery—hence the unfriendly glare.

Finally, as I stood before a particular painting—titled *Karen H.*, from Becca's breakthrough series on her high-school class—which unbeknownst to me was the most valuable work in the show and also the one whose loan he had secured through less than savory means (calling in a "favor" from Chantal de Marin, a Parisian dealer who, unlike Leplanc, was someone Becca cared about), he decided I'd been sent as a spy, to block the sale he had in the works. That thought surely corresponded to the moment when a gallery employee—an emaciated man, likely my age though his wan face could have given him an extra decade—asked if *perhaps* I wanted a tour, if *perhaps* I didn't wish to see *all* the paintings, rather than *linger* before this one. "Sure," I answered innocently, consenting to a brisk tour that culminated unsubtly at the front door, where he offered his hand—a surprisingly dry touch, given the sweat on his brow and the nervy odor wafting from his jacket—and commented snidely about my outfit, which is when I noticed the streak of grease across my left pants leg, likely acquired during my afternoon stroll through the city.

I unraveled the mystery of this baffling behavior only after speaking with Becca the following day. After a good laugh, she said, "My God, that Leplanc. What a little man."

"Actually, he's enormous."

"Gabriel, you know I never use *small* like that. His suspicions were ridiculous. You weren't scheming; you were guilty of nothing but naivete"—the naivete, that is, of thinking that every notice about such and such opening mattered to an artist as in demand as Becca.

Becca explained that while she had put me on various mailing lists as a courtesy, unless she said otherwise, I could ignore the invitations to exhibitions in Osaka or Naples or the press releases about her having won some hyphenated, unpronounceable prize. She would alert me to the important ones. The rest, I could assume, were schlock.

It was an easy mistake, and the very one that Catherine made each time she announced some news gleaned from her Google alert. Perhaps this was why I had paid little attention at first when she spoke about Becca. Or maybe it was because Catherine dropped mention of my sister into conversations so seamlessly—and rarely broached the topic of the historical Becca, that is, the temperamental teenager, as opposed to Becca Art Star.

In fact, that very afternoon when my improved backgammon skills declared themselves on a tropical July day, Catherine mentioned an exhibition of Becca's in Lausanne.

"I don't think it's important," I said. "A lot of those shows aren't. Half of the time you have some art dealer who locates a few of Becca's paintings and organizes a show without her participation. Sometimes she doesn't even approve."

"I didn't know that."

"It's not like you can track her movements through the exhibition schedule. She tells me about the big ones, and she never mentioned Lausanne."

"What about New York? Surely, she must come through the city?"

Another lesson I had learned about the art world: Just as certain galleries mattered more than others, certain cities did, too, and New York was chief of all, with a second tier, depending on whom you spoke to, consisting of London, Berlin, LA, and increasingly Beijing or Hong Kong; maybe also Paris, Zurich, Milan, Tokyo. But New York was still the undisputed capital of the art world. Any significant artist had a New York gallery and debuted their best work there. In this regard, Becca was unusual. She gave her newest work to galleries in LA and Berlin, who managed her career, and worked with a less prominent New York dealer. Though obliged to be present in the city, she kept her footprint small.

Another discovery (this one dating back a few years): Becca had a studio in New York. A *studio* not in the sense of a large open space where an artist hangs canvases and has a dirty table topped with stained palettes and coffee tins sprouting a bouquet of brushes; no, a *studio* in the New York sense: a cramped, single-room apartment with a small bathroom and tiny corner kitchen, the sort of apartment that some of my college friends, even Derrick Banter, who was married and had a baby, might live in, Manhattan real estate being so damn expensive. I had learned of Becca's New York studio a few years prior when, at the end of one of our annual meetups in our old apartment (it was a requirement of the sublease that the tenants had to vacate for a week around the winter holidays), my flight to Paris had been canceled because of a snowstorm. With the tenants returning the next day, I would need a hotel room.

"Stay at my studio?" Becca asked.

"Your studio? Here?"

She shrugged. "You can't have an art career and avoid the city completely. And I can't stand the thought of staying in a hotel in my hometown. Neither should you—so come with."

The place was on the second floor of a nondescript five-story walkup, less than a mile from our childhood home. A couch abutted the bed. Had Becca been any taller, we could have dreamed with touching toes.

"Why do you ask?" I asked Catherine, after briefly explaining Becca's relationship to New York.

"I figured a big-time artist would have to come here."

There was something else I had discovered about Becca over the years. How often had I received a call or email saying, "Quick stop in Paris tomorrow. Free for dinner?" Or "Brussels on Friday. Can you train up? I have a few hours in the late afternoon." Such an invitation, always apologetically last minute, revealed that while exhibitions might be planned months in advance, personal appointments were always a secondary concern, which suggested the relative importance she put on public and private life or, more disturbingly, on our sibling relationship. Still, whenever I showed up, I always found the same Becca. In a hurry, yes; partially preoccupied, yes; sharing only the sort of facts that might appear on a public calendar, while I was expected to divulge intimate details, yes; but also, present enough. For however long she had set aside, she would be available. Sure, I saw a more relaxed and vulnerable version of her during our holiday week, but I never felt that she was shutdown or withholding, only that private life occupied little of her attention.

But I would also learn, through some sleuthing or news that accidentally slipped out in a conversation weeks later, that there were other times when she passed through Paris or Milan or wherever else without alerting me.

Why didn't you call? Why didn't you ask to stay with me?—for years, I asked such questions and always got the same response: "I was busy, I'm sorry, there wasn't time." And eventually, I learned that there was no point in holding a grudge. This was Becca. She was available, *sometimes*. You could take it or leave it.

But Catherine's question confounded me. Had Google provided her with intel that I lacked about some upcoming visit by Becca to the city, during which she might pass a day or two in her studio and leave—all without telling me?

"Why do you bring up New York?" I asked.

"Curiosity mostly. But I did see that she had a show around New Year's."

"Ah," I said, relieved. "That's when she usually comes for vacation."

"I know, you've told me, but it's unusual, isn't it? Her New York shows are often in spring or over the summer."

"You pay better attention than I do."

She smiled coyly, and I again found myself questioning her motives. Was she angling for an invitation to the show? A reunion with Becca?

I looked back to the backgammon board, because despite the handshake, I wanted to complete the game and savor my victory. But as I eyed my remaining checkers, my mind continued to churn: Was backgammon more like chess than I realized? Did players of Catherine's caliber plot out future moves several turns in advance? Was this entire friendship just some long play to get to Becca? These doubts mixed with an awareness of my own evasions and mis-directions. How in recent calls and emails with Becca, to whom I shared almost everything, I still avoided any mention of Catherine. And how with Catherine, I always described a white-washed, press-releasey caricature of Becca, not the actual person—complex, impetuous, erratic—who had once been, all but officially, her goddaughter. I normally didn't tiptoe around my sister's shortcomings, but with Catherine, who was otherwise my primary confidante, I was entirely disingenuous on this topic.

"Speaking of coming to New York," Catherine said. "You do realize that you've never told me what brought you back."

As I pondered how to answer this question, one seemingly so simple but which perplexed me to no end (so that the most banal of responses, "I just felt like it," was the only honest one I could offer), I saw that my conversations with Catherine, however open they seemed, were riddled with gaps and evasions. Yes, our friendship was full of warmth and ease. But was this only possible because we avoided the most crucial topic of all?

I turned from Catherine's smiling, expectant face again to the backgammon board, hoping to discover a quick and elegant finale to this game that I was finally on the verge of winning. Much of course depended on the dice. I gathered them in my hand, shook vigorously, blew…

"Hey, Ms. Morrow. Hey, Mr. Gabriel."

Harvey was at the table's edge.

"Oh, Harvey, we've already had our treat for the day," Catherine said. "And dinner is soon. Wouldn't want to spoil our appetite."

"I'm not here to take an order, Madame K. I wanted to show you something."

He lay a piece of paper on the space between us:

"Why it's lovely, Harvey," Catherine said. "I didn't know you were an artist."

"I'm not a good one. But I do like to draw. And you two make a pretty picture. I'll just leave it here. It's for you, darlings. Both of you. Now please share nicely, you hear?"

I told Catherine she should keep it, but she insisted I take it home, as "a victory prize," and that evening I set the picture on the living-room windowsill, where it sat unobtrusively for about a week. But one night, light glinted off the frame and I saw the picture anew—instead of two friends, two loners in need of companionship, but who couldn't quite be straight, not even with each other, which would be their undoing. It was a troubling premonition, and I buried the drawing in the depths of a desk drawer, in the hope that I would banish such foreboding and quickly return to my sunnier version of reality.

8

Two beefy men were talking with Catherine in the living room. The stouter of the two, spinning at my entry, asked, "That the kid?"

Catherine nodded, they indicated they wanted to talk to me in private, and she said, "Gabriel, why don't you take them to your room?"

I led them upstairs to the room I had slept in that morning, but whose brightly striped wallpaper still made me a do a-double take, so unfamiliar was the look of the space. The stouter of the two men had fleshy cheeks and a large, flat nose. He strutted ahead of his taller partner and was obviously in charge.

"Is it ok if I call you Gabe?" he said.

I nodded, though I hated Gabe. Normally the Morrows were the only ones I let get away with it.

"Tell us everything, even the tiniest detail, ok?"

It was the first time that I would tell the story that I would go on to recount dozens more times in years to come. I described the same sequence of events I have here. The game of hide and seek, waiting to be found, the slow realization that we wouldn't be, walking through the woods, the clearing, the flashlight, the decision to rest, falling asleep.

"What happened when you woke up?"

"What do you mean?"

"Did you see Becca?"

I shook my head.

"Did you look for her?"

"I looked around the tree. I called out to her."

"But you didn't find her?"

I shook my head.

"Any sign at all? Footprints? Broken twigs?"

"Dale, he's not a tracker." This was the second guy. Maybe half a head taller than his partner, he had dark hollow eyes and gazed at me sympathetically. Until then, he had mostly been staring at a spiral notebook, making marks each time I spoke.

"So, you didn't find her," the first guy said. "Then what?"

"I started walking. I saw light ahead and thought it might be a way out. I found a field. I started to run and saw the house."

"At this point, or really at any point as you ran back to the house, did you think about Becca?"

It's a question I would return to again and again. As I recalled each moment of that night and day after, I would ask myself: Did you think of Becca here or only of yourself? My answers were usually inconclusive or, worse, disappointing. I concocted various excuses for my oversight—Becca had left me, not the other way around; it was so easy to find my way out, I figured she could too, I figured she already had; with Becca you never knew, you never knew anything; I was so scared I wasn't thinking at all, not of her, not of myself—but I knew they were all rationalizations. The truth is I didn't think much about her, if at all.

I can't recall my exact words to the cops. I must have stumbled awhile or just shrugged.

"Can you tell us what thoughts ran through your head?"

I struggled here, too. Facts were easy, but how I felt, what I thought—this baffled me.

"It's ok, Gabe," the second cop interrupted my silence. "Tell us what happened when you returned to the house?"

"I went to my room."

"This room?"

"Yes."

"And when you came to the room and she wasn't here?" the first one asked.

I faced the corner window, which even later in the day still emitted a warm bath of light. "I don't remember."

"That's OK, Gabe. That's fine. What happened when you came in the room?"

"I got into bed."

"And what time was that?"

"6:11." The moment I blurted it out, I felt scared. Would they think it suspicious that I could recall the time so precisely while I hadn't the foggiest clue about my missing sister? "There was a clock," I added.

Their eyes didn't stir from me; they didn't blink.

"And you fell asleep? You were tired, right?"

I couldn't look at the guy asking questions. Only the other one— not-Dale; the friendly one, whose name I didn't know—who had smiled each time I turned to him. As he did now, lowering his notebook and asking his partner, "We done?"

"No, just a few more things," Dale said. "Gabe, you've been very patient and helpful. I want you to know that we're doing this for your sister. We're going to find her, but we need your help."

"Ok."

"I want to go back to something you said earlier. About the pebbles. Could you lead us to the spot at the edge of the woods, so we can follow them in?"

"I think so."

"Good. We may ask you to go back with us. That ok?"

"Ok."

"Good. Now I want to go back even further."

I went backward, at their request, to the previous night when we lay on the lawn beneath the stars, and then to the basement, the dining room, the drive up. They asked about the other families. Did I know

Connor? I said I'd never met him before. But I knew his family? Connor's family? Not at all.

What about the Morrows? I knew them well, they're our best friends. The hollow-eyed cop wrote this down and underlined it twice.

"Can I ask you something, Gabe?" the stout one asked. "Do you have any idea what could have happened to Becca? Any idea at all?"

"Not really."

"Do you think she might have decided to go away? Did that cross your mind? Any reason at all she might want to be alone?"

Yes, it had crossed my mind. But I also remembered my mother's blanched face and how she had balled out Catherine for making the same suggestion, and I felt a kind of choking guilt. "Not really," I said.

"Not really what? Not really, she might have no reason to run away? Or not really, it didn't occur to you that she might want to be alone?"

"Neither. I'm not sure. I—"

"Dale, cut the kid some slack."

"Let's return to what happened right when you entered the woods. I know we've been through this, but I want to talk about it again."

Again, I told them about hide and seek. About hiding behind the tree. About waiting. They asked how many flashlights there were, and I said three. No four, but JT had taken his and gone back to the house before we'd gone into the woods. Kyle had one, Connor another, Becca the third.

"Ok, so you were hiding, waiting, then what?"

We were going in circles, like the night before in the dark, like that morning while we searched. The same questions leading to the same unsatisfactory answers. After another run through the full script, the hollow-eyed guy asked, "Dale, shouldn't we talk to others? Maybe the father?"

"In a minute. I want to hear a bit more from Gabe."

They asked again about when we entered the woods. They asked about the first round of hide and seek—it was the second round when we got lost, right? I nodded. So, what happened during the first round?

It was right then that there was a shout from downstairs, then another. Dad burst through the door, announcing, between heavy breaths and with a cracking reed of a voice, that they had found Becca. She was fine. At a nearby farm.

He hugged me tight, so tight it almost hurt. "Let's go," he said.

9

In mid-July, Catherine and I played a terrible game of phone tag, and some ten days passed without a visit, the longest break since our reunion. When we finally connected, she asked, "Are you free *now*? Please come."

I had never heard such urgency in her voice and hurried over, but when I arrived half an hour later, she wasn't waiting at the bench by the entrance, or the garden, or in the sunny common room. Instead, the scowling receptionist pointed to the elevator and indicated that I should go to the dining room on the second floor.

The dining room was directly above the common room but lacked all its charm. It had rows and rows of cafeteria style tables with detachable chairs, and in place of the glass window that made the common room sunny and expansive, stood a white wall with a patchwork of papers: a weekly menu, first-aid instructions, ads for adult education courses, a concert schedule at a nearby church. The room could probably hold a hundred people, but only a handful was present: three solitaries at separate tables and a uniformed man clearing tin foil trays from a long table in the room's center. It was Harvey. He caught my eye and gestured to a back corner, where I saw Catherine sitting with a man.

"Gabriel, welcome," Catherine said, beaming, as I approached. "This is John."

Tall, lanky, with a gray ponytail and a scruffy black goatee, he was clearly too young to be a resident. As we shared a wordless handshake, Catherine said, "Don't tell me that you don't recognize each other?"

Had we met? I couldn't place him. He had stood to shake my hand, and as he adjusted himself to resume his seat, I noticed a slight limp.

"JT?" I asked. "What are you doing here?"

"I should be asking you. I'm visiting my mother, of course."

Catherine asked me to join them, but something held me back. At first, I sensed some unresolved tension between them, but now, I was simply processing the situation. If this man was JT, rather than some other "young friend" or East River Home staff member, I'd have to revise my first impression. He wasn't *young* at all, but older than expected. Perhaps time hadn't been kind to him. But the true surprise was Catherine. How could she have failed to mention JT beforehand? Were things so casual between us that she hadn't thought it necessary, or was this a deliberate withholding, as if she had feared I wouldn't have come had I known, or some response to my reticence about Becca?

"Are you sure I'm not interrupting?" I asked.

"Nonsense. Sit," said Catherine, even as JT looked to her impatiently.

She gestured to Harvey, who soon appeared at the tableside. "The usual, Ms. K?"

"Yes, but a double. Actually, we'll have three brownies." She pointed at JT, looking first to Harvey and then to me. "He loves them, too."

As Harvey's footsteps sounded across the linoleum, JT tapped the table with his long fingers, a clever percussion duet. "Where do we begin, Gabe? You first, all right? Give me the five-minute recap of the past twenty years."

I offered my canned response. "I'm a freelance writer and editor, and recently returned to New York after many years living abroad. I'm staying in my parents' old place as I figure out my next move."

"That's it?" JT asked. "Guess you didn't need the full five minutes."

"Gabriel's too modest," Catherine said. "He lived in Europe for years. France, Italy, even Slovakia. He's actually more adventurous than the two of us combined."

"That right?" JT asked.

"You might need to buy him a drink," Catherine said. "He has some stories to tell."

"Sure thing, but I'm about to take off. So, next visit," he said. "As for me, well…"

What followed was remarkably similar to the summary of JT's life that I'd heard from Catherine. He lived in Mission Hills, in San Diego. He worked "in music"—"a technician"—mostly in L.A., but he was sticking around San Diego to be near his daughter, Sophie, who was 15, and whose mother had remarried a chef at some fancy La Jolla resort.

"She's become a total food snob," he said. "Find her on the wrong day and she'll lecture you on how to caramelize an onion or roast a potato. It's even transferred to my daughter. And don't get me started on Stu. Apparently, he's a master at making stew. No joke."

Even when talking about Stu, JT had the same flat affect I always associated with him, and I could feel his flash of curiosity upon seeing me diminish like a leaky balloon. He had always been reserved and laconic, but surely some of this had to do with his relationship to us, the Staubs. Just as Kyle was usually at the center of things, in memories, JT was often the odd man out, someone who hung back and never quite belonged—as if he were the physical embodiment of the gaps in the friendship between the families, or some omen of the future separation. He seemed always in retreat, perennially in the background despite his great height, was improbably teased by his younger brother, and seemed part of some half-generation separating the other three kids from the parents. And yet when I recalled that night in the Catskills, JT seemed to be linked to several contingencies. More than once, I had wondered how things might have gone differently had he remained with us on the dark field behind the house—or had I left when he had.

As he finished his tale, he said, "Sorry, Gabe, if things seem tense. But before you got here, my mother and I were in the middle of a conversation. And I only have a few minutes before I head to the airport..."

"No problem," I said, happy for an excuse to leave.

"But you've barely caught up," Catherine said. "Swing your legs back onto the chair and make yourself comfortable. Don't forget your manners." That last sentence followed a pause, and I couldn't tell whether she was talking to me or JT.

Harvey arrived with the coffee and brownies. Catherine and JT slurped in unison. She put the brownies on napkins and pushed one to each of us.

"Are you coming back anytime soon?" I asked JT, feeling a need to pierce the silence.

"That's what we were discussing."

I soon learned that this very topic was the source of tension between them. Catherine wanted JT to return to New York for Christmas, but he wanted her to go out west. He and his daughter were both in San Diego. "Plus, if we do it out there, maybe Kyle would come; he's up the coast," JT added, though with less conviction.

"But Sophie wants to come to New York," Catherine said. "You know that."

"See that, Gabe. She always does that, uses my daughter against me."

Catherine began listing objections—from her tone, I could tell, not for the first time—"What about a white Christmas?" "I've just moved here." "What about your father?"

"Dad's the other excuse, when it suits her," said JT, again appealing to me. "But Mom left *him*. And I remember her exact words. 'He's too far gone to keep us tethered.'"

"No, John. I decided that I could no longer take care of him, myself. That's all. And I don't appreciate you criticizing me when I finally have a chance to take care of myself."

"Mom, I'm just asking you to come to me for Christmas."

"But we've done Christmas here for years."

"Not *here*. In Westchester. And Dad was always around."

"He's still around."

"So, bring him along."

"To sit in front of the tree and drool?"

"See, Gabe?" JT said. "When it suits her, she can't leave him. Other times, she can't bring him anywhere. Which is it, Mom?"

She reached for her cup, but behind the mug, I noticed a smile, which communicated that some of this had been a performance, which we would discuss once JT had gone.

"Let's stop, John. Please," she said, setting the cup in its saucer. "Why spend our last minutes bickering? And I'm sure Gabriel has no interest in this."

JT hit another drumbeat with his fingers and exhaled a dismissive chuckle. Soon he was explaining that "the other reason" he had come to New York was to see a fancy recording studio that had been fitted with some new equipment that his boss coveted for the studio in LA. "You wouldn't believe what this thing does. It transforms the studio, brings you in, so close. It's like what HD does to a TV screen, but with sound. You can hear *everything*."

JT's flash of enthusiasm was my opportunity to leave, and I took it, but Catherine called later that evening. "What did you think?" she asked.

I was in the living room, watching the sky darken over the East River, and I could feel her waiting, expecting me to say something meaningful. What came to mind was how JT's tone had changed when he briefly mentioned Kyle. The conversation had breezed right on past, but that moment laid a marker in my mind and keyed my guilt—both that I was betraying my family through this renewed contact with the Morrows, and for my role so many years ago in the Catskills: that I had abandoned Becca to the woods, that I had returned to the house and fallen asleep before reporting her absence, that I had forgotten about the trail of pebbles for hours, that I hadn't convinced JT to stay with us or hadn't left with him—any of the missed moments that might have altered the course of events.

"You do it, too," I said, "whenever we mention Kyle."

"Why do you keep bugging me about this, Gabriel?"

"I hardly think I'm bugging you."

"But you keep asking about him. Why? Sometimes people don't respond to a question because there's no good answer; there's nothing to say. I don't see Kyle much. That's all. He has this ability to forget, to move on without looking back. It served him well as an athlete, but… it extends to family, too, and that crushes me. He goes long stretches without any communication, and when he finally reaches out, he says so little. And Gabriel, I'm hurt by your reaction. You meet JT after decades and you only want to talk about Kyle."

A tugboat was passing below; the sky was just dark enough that I couldn't read its color. "I just asked a question. Don't be so touchy. Besides, how often do you ask about Becca?"

"That's absurd. Why would you compare…" She breathed deeply. "I've already fought with my son today. If we continue this conversation any longer, there's sure to be another."

The line clicked dead, and only then did I realize that Becca would also be coming to New York at Christmastime, and Catherine knew this. Was this part of the reason she wanted JT to visit over the holidays? So that he could see my sister, too?

10

Paved road led to dirt, and soon we saw a two-story wooden house with nearby barn, both colored a dark brown. A floppy iron plate on the façade told us this was number 39.

A woman emerged through a screen door. She had a chunky bronzed face topped with messy gray hair, a wide frame, and heavy legs. She wore a t-shirt that read Sybil Ludington 25K Run beneath an open plaid button-down.

"Becca's up there," she said, gesturing to a path between the house and barn. "About a quarter mile. You'll find her in the same spot I found her an hour ago, I reckon."

Dirt tire grooves marked the sides of the path, with a wooden fence further to the right. Beyond was a rolling field, where I made out the bobbing heads of a few horses. We all walked fast, but I rushed ahead of my parents and spotted Becca first. She wore the same outfit as the previous night—Cornell sweatshirt, jeans, Stan Smith tennis sneakers—and at the sight of her, I filled with rage as I recalled her doodling with the flashlight on the leaves, leading us on an aimless march through the woods, that she had gotten us lost and made us spend the night in the dark and cold.

But Mom and Dad began calling Becca, Becca, Becca, and I knew I couldn't express these thoughts.

Becca leaned against the fence, gazing through a gap between the rails. A gray blanket hung loosely from her shoulders, a mug of hot chocolate perched on a fence post. "Beautiful, aren't they?" she said, without turning to me.

She was pointing at two horses, one black, one mottled white and brown, standing on a ridge some thirty yards from the fence.

I mumbled something about liking horses too, and she said, "See how their muscles ripple beneath the skin, even when they're standing around doing nothing? There's no fur or wool or fat in the way. They're totally open books."

Mom and Dad were behind us now. Becca warded off their hugs and deflected Dad's questions: *how was she, what had happened, was she ok, was she hungry, was she cold, where had she gone, how was she.* As soon as he stopped, she returned to the horses. Now there were four on the ridge, and she pointed them out one by one: Miss Muffet, Chicory, Black Day, Polly-Ann.

A fifth horse ran up to them and whinnied. It was light brown except for the white cuffs above its hooves and black rings around its eyes and nose. "I named her Cedar," Becca said, "but Harriet says her real name is Star. She's the rambunctious one. Watch."

The other horses seemed more interested in the grass and dandelions than the people by the fence, but Star pranced back and forth, always facing our direction. After a few showy laps, she shook her neck and took off at a gallop, over a ridge and out of view.

"Watch," Becca said again.

In a few seconds, there came a pounding sound, and the horse reappeared, heading straight toward us. The fence separated us, but she whizzed by like a train past an abandoned station, causing Dad to jump backward and Mom to shriek.

"Don't be scared," Becca said with a chuckle. "It's just a horse."

That's when she finally faced us, and I saw the scrapes on her forehead and the deeper mark across her left cheek. A swollen patch just beneath the bone with a finer red line extending from lips to earlobe, like a crimson thread across a purple pillow. Dad reached toward it, and

Becca pulled back. There followed a new volley of questions—*what happened? was she ok? was she hurt?*—until Becca replied distantly. "It's nothing, I'm fine."

I recalled our scuffle over the flashlight, and how she'd cried out when she was alone with Connor. Had it been there all night without my noticing?

"Does it hurt?" Dad asked.

"I think a branch got me," she said, exasperated. "I told you, I'm fine."

Harriet appeared then, breathing heavily and carrying a tray with three pots, plus cups, saucers, sugar, and milk. "Coffee, tea, hot chocolate," she said. "Thought I'd offer a selection."

Behind her was a bald, white-bearded man in a tattered harlequin sweater. "I figured you might also want this," he said, dropping a dusty brown blanket in Mom's hands.

"What are *they* doing here?" Becca asked.

She was pointing at the two cops, who were standing some fifteen further down the path, Dale tapping his foot expectantly, as his hollowed-eyed partner looked at the horses.

"We just need to ask a few questions, is all, to wrap things up," said Dale. "We'll need to speak with you, Becca. And you, Mr. Staub."

"I'll go first," said Dad and walked over to them.

Harriet and the man also took their leave, and Mom spread the blanket on the grass and poured drinks. Becca refused a new hot chocolate, but I sat beside Mom and sipped mine. It was warm and delicious. Mom tried to coax Becca to join us on the blanket; then, when Becca refused, Mom started again with questions, like Dad's but in a softer, hesitant tone.

Becca deflected a while, before saying, "I walked, Mom. What the hell do you think I did? I walked and walked and walked... and then I walked some more. What idiotic questions."

Mom blinked slowly and, without another word or glance to either of us, stood and headed to Dad and the cops.

"So how was your day?" Becca asked me, her tone suddenly relaxed, friendly.

Joining me on the blanket, she sipped from my hot chocolate, handing it back to me with a smile. But the red splotch on her cheek glistened, and I felt a flash of guilt. "When I got up, Becca, the sun was coming out and—"

"So, you made it back?" Her voice offered no hint of accusation, though the weight of her eyes unnerved me.

"I called out to you, Becca. I really did. I tried to find you. I promise."

"I called for you, too. Probably a hundred times. Then I started to wonder, *Who is this crazy person calling out my brother's name?* So, I zipped it and walked. You know what I realized later? My big takeaway—I mean, what I imagine I'll be saying about this, years from now—being lost is boring. Going in circles, seeing the same scenery over and over. Trees, trees, trees, and then… you guessed it… more trees. Uhh."

"Were you scared?"

She shrugged. "I think the fear is mostly to fill your head and give you something to think about. An antidote to boredom. Know what I mean?"

"So, you're not mad? I really did…"

Becca's brows furrowed, and she shot to her feet. Turning, I saw Mom hovering at the blanket edge. She attempted the same questions as earlier, *What happened, Becca? We were so worried. Are you ok? Please tell me, honey. I want to know*, though her voice was practically a whisper.

Becca returned to the fence, where Star, having completed another lap, was again bearing down on us. This time, she thundered by without making us jump, though I did catch a gust of her barny odor. "That a girl, Star," Becca shouted. "Faster, faster."

Becca also called to the other horses, who continued to loaf on the ridge. "Hey, Miss Muffet. Hey, Chicory. Hey, Poly-Ann." If you were being generous, you might say that the horses acknowledged her, but in truth they merely followed the sound, oblivious of their new names, given by this girl who had been their friend for a few hours.

Dad was back and, unaware of the futility of Mom's recent questions, asked, "What happened, Becca? Where did you go?"

"Sorry, Dad, but I'm afraid I can't give you a satisfactory answer."

"Why not? Did something happen?"

"Well, kinda… It was like this… I went into the living room and sat on this big fluffy couch. I had a big bin of popcorn and slipped *Top Gun* into the VHS. And there was Tom Cruise. I just got lost, he's soooo dreamy."

"Becca, please. We want to know what happened."

"Right, right. The truth? Fine. I went to the underworld. I was in a dark woods. A spirit came, tapped my shoulder, and led me to a cave that just kept going down and down and…"

"Ahem." The nameless cop was blinking his shy, sympathetic eyes. "Becca, can we ask a few questions? It'll be quick and painless. I promise."

As Becca spoke to the cops, Mom folded the blankets, Dad carried the tray, and soon we were heading back to the car. No one said a word.

Harriet was waiting outside the house. "Something for the road," she said, handing Mom a paper bag. "Chocolate chip cookies and sodas. I hope that's ok."

"Thank you so much," Mom said. "For everything."

"Not at all. She's a great kid. Kind and very perceptive. Been watching those horses for hours…" She turned, then said more loudly, "Everything all right, sweetie?"

"Of course," said Becca, who was coming toward us several paces ahead of the cops.

"I'm so glad we met you, darling," Harriet said.

"Me too," said Becca, her warmest, fullest words of the day. "I'll never forget you, Harriet. I promise." She sunk into the woman's thick body, and the Cornell and Sybil Ludington 25K Run decals met at the center of their tight embrace.

Dale said to Dad, "Turns out it was nothing big. Just got lost in the woods. We've seen it before. A temporary fright but shouldn't last. But if anything comes up, please call."

Dale headed to his car, and we to ours. As Mom fastened her seatbelt, there was a knock on her window. It was the hollow-eyed cop. "Ma'am, do you know the way?"

Mom answered that she did, though hardly in a way that inspired confidence, yet to my surprise, some five minutes later we pulled into the Morrows' driveway. The front door opened and Catherine loped across the driveway, the clack of her sandals on the pavement reminding me of Star's hard strides. "Oh, Becca, I'm so glad—"

Dad exited the car and slammed the door behind him. Neither Mom nor Becca budged, and, though at first I reached for my door handle, I sensed I should follow their lead.

As Dad and Catherine headed inside, Becca's Walkman, which had remained in the backseat, clicked on, and I heard the familiar sounds of *True Blue*. Madonna. An obsession in an earlier phase of her life, the album had provided songs for every single girl who had participated in the lip synch contest at Becca's 10th birthday party. She had gone with "La Isla Bonita," and of course had won first prize.

Dad seemed to take forever, but the dashboard clock said only five minutes had passed when he reemerged onto the driveway. Becca's backpack was slung over one shoulder, mine over the other, he carried his briefcase in his left hand, and in the right, the suitcase that he and Mom shared, nicknamed The Discipline, because it had been purchased to force them to pack lightly, whether for a weekend at friends' or last summer's trip to France and Spain.

Alan followed Dad outside, but Dad waved him off before reaching the car, and Alan retreated to the house. Dad threw the bags in the trunk and climbed back into the passenger seat. "Becca, Gabriel, did you bring anything else? Ah forget it. If we left anything, we'll get it later."

I heard the click of the ignition, and Mom reversed out of the driveway. Catherine and Alan stood in the frame of the doorway, waving vigorously. Almost like our arrival the evening before, except that smiling Catherine had replaced silent JT.

* * *

After a few minutes of twisty, back-road driving, we reached a straightaway and Dad pushed Carly Simon into the tape deck. It was a car-ride staple, one of the few albums where the two generations found common ground. Like *True Blue*, it played on a loop all the way home.

Otherwise, it was a silent ride. No word games. No punch buggy. No red cars blue cars. No discussion of the week ahead. Nothing about German reunification or Dad's impossible boss or the novel Mom was reading or starry skies or summer camp or the start of 6th Grade. But perhaps an hour into the drive, Becca stopped her walkman, lowered her headphones, and said, "I don't ever want to see them again." Then she slipped the headphones back on and hit play. Neither parent reacted, the highway offered the same monotony of trees and concrete, and I began to wonder if I'd merely misheard some lyric of "You're So Vain."

In the days that followed, I dismissed Becca's pronouncement as another of her typical provocations. But maybe a month later, as we prepared for a trip to Katonah, she declared that she wouldn't be coming, and the parents offered no objection. Half an hour later, alone in the back seat, I felt bitter. This sort of visit had never been presented as a choice; here was yet another privilege of the eldest child that wasn't extended to me. Dad gave his usual response that "life isn't fair," followed by a novel argument that since JT was back in college, maybe it made sense—instead of 4 and 4, 3 and 3, the two eldest children absent. But he spoke with so little conviction that I doubted he believed his own words.

There was a BBQ lunch on the Morrows' porch. I ate a hot dog with ketchup and mustard, then went with Kyle to the basement and watched him play Nintendo. He'd been working on Super Mario Brothers 3 and already knew how to get to World 8, where you have to rescue

Princess Toadstool. His game lasted forever—he was only on World 6 when Mom called down that it was time to leave. "Check ya later, little man," Kyle said without turning from the screen.

"That was quick," I said in the car.

"We have to get home," Dad answered.

I soon drifted off, but around Yankee Stadium, as we inched along in bumper-to-bumper traffic, I awoke to the sound of my parents whispering.

"I don't know, Jonah. I can't look beyond it."

"But can't we move on?"

"I don't know. I'm not sure we can."

And that was it. My parents denied for a few months that anything was amiss with the Morrows ("We've gone elsewhere is all." *The Nutcracker* was sold out." Or, conceding a little, "We haven't called, but neither have they. It's been a busy time for all of us."). But in the spring, more than six months after the Catskills, Catherine left a rambling message on the answering machine. "Please call…," she repeated desperately, "Please… please…," like the refrain of a song.

Here, finally, was proof that something dramatic was happening, or had happened; that I wasn't imagining that the Morrows had been eliminated from our lives. But no one sat me down to explain why or even to admit to the simple fact of the change. Mom erased the message that evening, and I never heard it again. Nor did we ever so much as mention our former best friends in the weeks or months to follow.

11

One bright September morning, I met Catherine as requested in the lobby of the East River Home. She wore her usual walking attire—a comfortable summer dress, Keds, fanny pack—and indicated that we were going to the subway.

Heading south on the 6 train, I asked about our destination. "It's a surprise," she said. "By the way, I've been meaning to ask, when's the break-fast?"

"That's changing topics."

"It's that time of year, right? Rosh Hashanah?"

"Actually, Yom Kippur, and it was last Thursday."

"But I thought it was in late September. Why didn't you invite me?" she asked, wearing a sad puppy face that felt mostly for show.

The obvious answer was that I hadn't planned anything for the holiday, as had been my way for years; but with Jews aplenty in New York, I'd had multiple invites to break-fasts and had actually attended two, which were so similar—at each, a cramped apartment with some dozen people, standing around with paper plates loaded with bagels, lox, and cream cheese; or rye bread with tuna salad or whitefish salad or egg salad; or cucumber salad, pasta salad, or salad salad; with rugelach and butter cookies and dry chocolate cake for dessert—that they might have passed for a single occasion, had not the second, at my friend Peter's, had a much lighter feel, the explanation for which I discovered on my way out: They had broken the fast with shots of whisky at sunset, which, Peter said, "pack quite the punch on an empty stomach." He poured me a double for the road, and I felt the comforting warmth in my stomach as I stepped into the cool evening.

"I wouldn't have thought you'd want to come," I said to Catherine. "It's not something you ever did with us."

"But I did. Don't you remember?" And she recounted the time she had come to our place—alone, no husband or sons—and met an Uncle Gershom, an ancient man who had wheeled up and begun a monologue to which she'd nodded along, though she couldn't understand a word. Only later did she learn that he had been speaking elegant Yiddish, not senile gibberish.

"I never met Uncle Gershom," I said. "It must have been before I was born."

"But you were there. Maybe you were too young to remember."

I shrugged. "Now will you say where we're going?"

"King's Highway."

Brooklyn, then. Midwood. An area we'd visited on an earlier walk, but hardly one I knew well. "And what'll we do?"

"It's a surprise. Why are you so impatient today?"

We had switched to the B train, which emerged from its subterranean tunnel and began climbing onto the Manhattan bridge, rolling above tenement rooftops and then the East River, as morning sun streamed through windows, in one side, out the other.

"*Ahmet*," I said excitedly. "*His restaurant*?"

"No more clues. You'll find out soon enough."

The river, the buildings at the river edge, the steel escarpment of the bridge, were visible a few seconds more and then we were back in black tunnel, now in Brooklyn, heading southeast.

When we rose to the street at King's Highway, Catherine did her best to make it seem like one of our walking adventures, as if what steered us was the random pattern of green lights or mere whim, but she clearly knew where she was going. After half a mile, we came upon a storefront with a glass window and a checkered floor that might have passed for a barber shop had its sign not read "Coney Island Chess Club."

A man at a table asked for our names, checked them off a list, and gestured down a hallway toward a large, windowless space with rows of tables topped with backgammon boards, numbered 1-16. A paper banner along the side wall read "Summer Backgammon Tournament"—by the look of it, made by a dot-matrix printer with a sputtering ink cartridge. Some 50 people milled about, almost all men, many with the darker skin of the Middle East, thick black or gray mustaches, and the occasional beard. A smaller group had the pale-faced, circular-rimmed glasses appearance of your standard American nerd, though I overheard a few words that reminded me of Slovak and imagined it might be Russian or Polish. There were precisely four women, Catherine included, the other three my age or younger.

Between the din of unknown languages and the odd smells (a cocktail of cinnamon and mildew?), I felt instantly out of place; add the prospect of being walloped at backgammon, and, despite Catherine's enthusiasm, I could foresee only a day of boredom and humiliation.

Then one of the other three women lifted her chin. She had a perfect ovular face, olive skin, and dark, delicate eyebrows—bewitching. I couldn't pull my gaze away, but the instant I found her deep brown eyes, she turned her back, presenting a loose ponytail atop a purple sweatshirt.

Catherine approached a table at the far end, which held vats of tea and coffee, Styrofoam cups, quarts of milk, sugar packets, wooden stirrers, and a plastic tray stacked with a hard, flaky pastry. "Hello," "Good day," she said exuberantly to practically everyone she passed, though it seemed obvious that she didn't know them.

The man who had taken our names in the entrance stood at the front of the room. He held a clipboard between his stubby fingers and cleared his throat loudly, then began talking in a monotone, reciting the tournament rules and rattling off all sorts of terms (chess clocks, gammons, doubling cubes) I barely understood. "It will be a great event but a lengthy one," he concluded. "Please play with urgency, lest you be the cause of everyone else's delay."

"How did you find this place?" I whispered to Catherine.

"Yellow Pages. 2009. But I guess it's still here."

"Have you been before?"

"Shhh."

The man had begun to speak again, in a wholly mysterious language, presumably repeating the same directions. As he went on, I read the tournament draw pasted on the wall. It listed 53 names, 16 of which were the "seeds," each marked with an asterisk. They all had byes into the second round, as did a few non-asterisks. Neither Catherine nor I was so lucky.

I was at Board 4, against Walter Sergiviski, the epitome of the circular-rim-glasses nerd. Catherine was on the opposite side of the room, her opponent the stunning girl who had rejected my glance.

"Hello," Walter said, too softly for me to detect an accent.

He smiled, and I looked at the table before us. Now what? The board was already set. I was on the white side—with Catherine, white always went first—but Walter handed me a shaker and dice. "Roll," he said. At other tables, some players remained standing. Should I stand, too? And what was I rolling for?—to go first? to be white? Walter rolled a 2. I rolled a 5. A minor victory. At least, I got to remain in my seat.

But now what? I reached for the dice to roll again.

"No," said Walter. "That's your roll. A 5 and a 2."

In his annoyance, he had given himself away—a slight Eastern accent, Russian, maybe; probably moved to the U.S. as a teen. Did I dare a bit of Slovak? What was I thinking? I had never played backgammon for points before; I didn't know a gammon from a backgammon; I didn't know how to use the clock or doubling cube; I had no clue what the Crawford Rule was. Now was hardly the time to trot out a distant Slavic language I hadn't spoken in years.

Unfortunately, the luck of my first roll predicted little of what was to come. I followed with a series of middling combinations, while Walter got fortunate doubles twice and rushed to a sizable advantage. Good luck aside, he played with comfort that I lacked. He knew how to use the timer—which I learned only by watching him hit my peg with increasing vehemence, until I waved him away. He slid his pieces with ease, while I was caught off guard by the weight of the stone checkers, so much heavier than the cheap plastic chips at the East River Home. His advantage seemed to grow with each move, and I only removed a piece from the board on my final turn, thereby preventing what I now realized was a gammon.

Game 2 started without a pause, and on his second move Walter turned over the doubling cube. I needed a moment to process my choice—forfeit right away and be down 2-0, or play on but risk losing two points, hence 3-0 and the match. I accepted, but it took me a quarter hour more to realize that I should obviously redouble, at least this way, I could also win the match on this game. Walter accepted my redouble with a contemptuous wink, knowing as well as I, that it hardly mattered. Three turns later, he removed his final piece.

We were the first ones standing. I was the tournament's first kill. Walter walked straight past me and through another door, then returned to grunt that I had to go to the front room to sign a scorecard, a brief formality that we accomplished wordlessly. After that, he went outside to smoke, and I returned to the snacks table. I poured a coffee, which was grainy and weak, even worse than at the East River Home, and watched Catherine and the stunning girl, leaning intently over their board. The scoreboard indicated that they had split the first two games; the position of this third game was about even. I tried a tea; it was tepid and bitter, barely improved with a heaping spoon of sugar. Catherine and the girl were moving quickly, battling each other and also the clock. Back and forth they went. Rapid moves, hurried rolls. Catherine won game 3, the girl game 4. The other matches ended one at a time, then half a dozen in a flurry. A few men stood beside me watching Catherine and the girl—perhaps only watching the girl. Finally, Catherine lifted her last piece and stretched her hand across the table. I felt some envy as the girl's long olive fingers closed around Catherine's brittle knuckles.

She rushed to me with a glowing smile. "How'd you do?" she asked.
"I lost."

"Bad luck?"

"Yes, but—"

"Me too. I should have won sooner, but I got 2s when I need 3s, and 3s when I needed 2s. I thought I had her on Game 4, but at the end she had this incredible streak with the dice. And that damned timer. I put myself in a hole by going too slowly. Thankfully, it's more points per round from here on out, so skill matters more. You'll stay and watch, Gabriel, won't you?"

Stick around? I was hoping to get out of there as quickly as possible.

"Come on, it's almost lunch," Catherine said.

Over her shoulder, I read her vanquished opponent's name on the tournament draw: Jessica Haddad. She was reason enough to stay, wasn't she? Those dark eyes alone were enticement. "Sure," I said. "I'll stay for a bit."

"Yay," Catherine said, with a girlish clap, and the very next instant I spun to search for Jessica Haddad. But she was gone, and not only her. The space seemed emptier, and the man who had announced the rules was again before us, peering at his clipboard. "Please. Your attention. It's time to commence round two." Catherine was at Board 5, facing off against a man with a silver mustache, named, no joke, Apollo. Walter was two spots over, at Board 7. As board after board found its combatants, I realized that the first-round losers had left... all, but me. Catherine was seated at her table, her back rigidly upright, studying the board, oblivious of me. She tapped the timer, practiced hitting it, then reset her clock to 15 seconds, and practiced again. Would she really mind if I left?

Mr. Clipboard, the only person not at a board other than me, eyed me like some foreign curiosity, and for a moment it felt like another of my New York social misadventures, in which I was the most clueless person around, unsure how to talk the language, or play the game.

Grabbing a pastry, I sat in a long row of chairs under the tournament banner, telling myself the wait would be short, that my presence was only a minor humiliation. A week prior, after I'd recounted sheepishly to my friend Sebastian some of my recent awkward exchanges with women, he'd sent a kind note, which included a link to an essay about the "Theater of Love," whose central idea was that you had to be out there, on stage, practicing, rehearsing, to find the genuine thing. *Jessica Haddad*, I now asked myself, did our interaction even qualify as a scene in the Theater of Love?

At least, no one paid me any attention. Everyone focused on the table before them. It was all rolling dice, clinking checkers. Some players counted spaces in their heads; others tapped the point of each pip with the checker's edge. I had a decent view of Catherine, especially when it was Apollo's turn and she sat upright, studying the board with quiet intensity. Watching her lean over the table, I recalled a memory from years earlier, a scene that had played out countless times. There was Catherine, sitting this very same way, watching keenly as some constellation of Morrows and Staubs played a board game. But in the memory, it was Dad against Alan, or two of the kids, maybe Kyle and Becca, with Catherine in the background, hovering, and yet her tense shoulders, her vulture eyes, communicated a will to win no less intense than the player plotting his next move.

And now came other memories: fierce games of Risk against Kyle, family bouts of Trivial Pursuit and Scrabble, how the parents compared our grades and accomplishments so casually. Harmless, petty stuff, but tiny scenes of competition containing the seeds of our undoing. A subtle rivalry had always been the dark underbelly of the friendship between the families, and as I sat in that windowless room watching a crowd of strangers play backgammon, I began to wonder if Catherine might have brought me to this strange venue in distant King's Highway, fully anticipating the day's minor indignities, as if she were still engaged in some ancient clash with the Staubs—as if the very purpose of this trip was to make me watch her vanquish foe after foe, in some perverse reversal of how a generation prior, she had watched from afar, silently reveling, as Kyle destroyed my last army in Axis and Allies and brought an end to our long game of war.

As round two matches ended and the crowd thinned, I noticed a man sitting a few chairs down from me. He was older, with a wide, rubbery forehead and a red mole on his cheek. I didn't recognize him from earlier, but before I could ask if he was a recent elimination, he leaned into the space between us and whispered, "This isn't my game."

"I'm a beginner too," I said.

"Ponies," he continued. "You know, the track. Ever go?"

I shook my head.

"Neither does he." He pointed to Board 3. "That's Yilmi, my son." It wasn't hard to tell which of the young men he was referring to, since the one on the far side had a triangular cleft between his thick eyebrows, just like the man whose tea breath I was smelling. "He says, 'Baba, the track is boring, no skill.' 'No, Yilmi, the horses take skill,' I answer, 'and besides, what is wrong with luck?' So, he says, 'Baba, backgammon has dice. That's luck, but you hate the game.' So, I shake my head and explain to Yilmi about the two different types of luck. The first, I call random. 'Dice are random, a computer is random, a coin flip is random,' I say. 'This is the luck of machines, dull and lifeless.' The second luck, I call chance. 'Chance does not mean *anything* can happen. It means that things are beyond your control. At the track, we think about weather and dirt, about the stretch run and the mysteries of animals. They have moods and characters, just like people, unpredictable. You could study everything, show up prepared, and it is still beyond your control. That's chance. That's life, too, Yilmi. There's no greater lesson.'"

His words were obviously practiced, and when he finished, I followed his gaze toward Yilmi at Table 3. The few moves I saw felt rote, listless, as if dictated by a script neither player believed in, whereas across the room Catherine and Apollo confronted one another with passion and resolve. Despite the resentment that had flared with my memories, I couldn't help but admire my friend. *Catherine and Apollo*—how could one dislike the sound of that? An encounter with the god whose chariot rounded the sun; who commanded the muses;

who provided order and beauty; who had innumerable lovers. And she was clearly meeting his divine challenge, every bit his equal.

"Look—" The man pointed to Board 3, where only a handful of his son's pieces remained, while his opponent was far behind. "Yilmi will win."

The match at Board 3 soon ended, and the man ran to Yilmi, grabbed his wrist, and pulled down on the younger, taller man, so that he could kiss both checks. They walked toward the door, arm in arm, but the father turned to wink at me before passing through.

Catherine wrapped up her match soon after. The winning play passed without climax. No cry of victory, no triumphant expression or jolt in her gait. *Act like you've been here before.* But after going to the front room to sign the scorecard, she rushed back to me with a smile as wide as a child who's won the first trophy of his life. "Four points to one," she said. "And it wasn't as close as that."

She slipped into the sweater that had been tied around her waist and beckoned me to the door. "It's lunch break," she said, as she steered us to a restaurant two blocks away, where we ordered from a window in a brick wall and stood to eat at sidewalk tables.

"How is it?" she asked, pointing to my kibbe wrap (her suggestion). "You'll stay for the next round, won't you, Gabriel? You must. You're my good luck charm."

The last thing I wanted was to return to that stale club, but I knew that I wouldn't refuse Catherine. In all these months of exploration, I'd never once abandoned her on some random corner and gone my separate way; even at my most restless, I couldn't possibly tear myself away before first helping her into a cab or bringing her to the subway, or simply continuing on at her slow pace. If some of this was the good manners I'd been raised with, there was also that stern internal voice that wouldn't permit me to leave others without explicit permission. I had spoken to shrinks about my difficulty parting from others, and we had linked it to the Night in the Woods. But if therapy had revealed the source of the problem, it had done nothing to resolve it.

Still, as I watched Catherine battle her next opponent, a young man in a dark green hoodie, with an anxious, drilling leg, I couldn't help but pray that she would lose, and quickly; and when it became clear that she would win once more, and again finish late, I felt tremendous relief when I noticed a missed call from Sebastian and seized the opportunity to go outside. The sky was cloudless and the air fresh, and although I reached Sebastian's voicemail, I knew I would remain on the street awhile, soaking up the day's glory.

After a little, I saw Yilmi, head slumped, leave the club, followed by his father, who wrapped an arm round his son and offered what I imagined were warm, consoling words. They embraced tightly, but then, to my surprise, moved in opposite directions, with Yilmi crossing the street and his father walking up the block, right toward where I was standing.

"My friend," he said with a gleam in his eye. "I'm glad to see you. Come."

"Where to?"

"It is close. Come." And he threw an arm around my shoulder and gave a little tug.

I saw no harm in accompanying him and fell in stride beside him. The street rose at a faint incline, and we walked past a pleasant succession of low buildings with ground-floor businesses: a real-estate lawyer, a flower shop, a toy store, a barber. Rounding a corner, he pointed to a busy storefront, with a large crowd before it, mostly men, but older and more grizzled than those at the backgammon tournament. As we drew near, I peered through the window and saw a wall of TVs showing horses lining up for a run.

"OTB," he said, as he pushed open the door and led me inside, adding that friends called him Freddie and shaking my hand. "Pleased to meet you, Gabe."

A clerk called out, "Last bets," and Freddie advised that while the next race was "the big one," if I wanted to "get a taste for the action," he'd counsel Keep At It or Showboat.

Preferring the former name, I made a bet using the only horse term I knew. "To place. Five bucks," I told the clerk.

Having a rooting interest made the race surprisingly tense. Keep At It started poorly, but, true to his name, by the second post he was at the head of the pack chasing the three leaders, who had broken free right out of the gate. He came on strong during the stretch and nosed past the initial frontrunner to win third place. I pumped my fist triumphantly, but Freddie clicked his tongue softly and explained that a bet "to place" meant that you thought the horse would finish first or second. "But he came third, so you lost. I did, too. Don't worry, we're about to make up for it."

The "big one," he explained, featured two horses with Triple Crown lineages: Lightning Field and Blackbeard. "You couldn't go wrong with either one, but I've got a good feeling about a longshot, Castaway. He's at 14-1."

Freddie began talking me through a range of possible bets, dropping phrases like Exactas and Daily Doubles, a terminology no less arcane than that of the backgammon tournament. As he rambled on, I noticed the static buzz of the TV sets, the room's cheap plastic chairs and dull gray tabletops, the overflowing garbage cans in the corner, and an aura of sadness suffusing it all, so I was more than happy when my phone buzzed in my pocket.

"Where are you?" Catherine said without a greeting. "When you left, it broke my concentration. I nearly lost."

"Nearly?"

"Yes. I was the far superior player. But I need you for the next round. Come back, please?" I could picture the sad puppy face from earlier and again couldn't manage a No. I wished Freddie good luck and hurried back to the club.

The next round of the tournament was already underway when I found a seat. These matches were a big enough deal that a few other losers from earlier rounds had stayed to watch, making me feel a little less foolish. I sat beside two men named Huseyn and Tamar. Their thick black beards made me imagine that they belonged to an older generation, though my better sense told me that I was likely the eldest of the three.

"She's good," Huseyn whispered. "Quite prudent, but cunning."

Catherine was again on the room's far side, but the space had opened, and I could see her clearly. Tamar explained that her opponent, an older man named Faisel, was a past winner of the tournament, perhaps the strongest one there. Sure enough, he jumped to a big lead with a gammon, two points, in game 1, delighting Huseyn and Tamar, who patted one another's knees and whistled, then spoke excitedly in what they said was Azerbaijani. Catherine won game 2, narrowly, especially after a shaky move at a crucial moment, but as Huseyn said, with apparent admiration, "A win's a win. Against Faisel, nothing is easy. You should be proud. Your godmother, no?"

I asked why he thought Catherine was my godmother, but Tamar lifted a finger to his lips and pointed to the board, where a new game was beginning. "We'll talk after."

Game 3 was slower than the first two. The position was cramped and defensive; Catherine and Faisel gazed at the board absorbedly. After some time, the room's silence was broken by a sharp hiss at Board 4, where a player protested some perceived disparagement. Mr. Clipboard hurried over, and, after one more shrill, contemptuous wail, the whistling stopped.

Faisel finally pulled out a tight victory, and Huseyn resumed our earlier conversation. "She said that your parents passed away when you were young and that she looks after you, even as you are an adult."

"And that you have become her backgammon student," Tamar added. "You are fortunate to have such a teacher. This is the best way to learn."

Unsure how to respond, I smiled, thankful that the next game was beginning. After a few moves, Faisel had taken a narrow lead, and he managed to maintain it straight to the end, despite Catherine's numerous efforts. With only a few pieces left on the board, she faced the audience and lay her glasses on the tabletop. It was a surrender, and a ripple passed through the audience, aware that the match's drama was spent. Catherine sank deeper into her seat with each of her final three moves, and in less than a minute she and Faisel were politely shaking hands, then walking in lockstep, on opposite sides of the table. As Catherine rounded the table's far edge, I saw Faisel nearly slap her shoulder with brotherly warmth. Instead, he whispered in her ear.

"I lost," she said to me with a subdued smile. Huseyn and Tamar complimented her, but Mr. Clipboard, with a gesture toward Board 1, where play continued, shushed us. Catherine and Faisel validated their score in the front room, and then we were on the sidewalk, waving to Huseyn, Tamar, and Faisel, as they crossed to the shady, far side.

It was after 7:00, a brassy orange sunset blanketing the sky.

Catherine said she had chosen a special restaurant for dinner, but I told her that I was exhausted and wanted to go home. As a compromise, she insisted on getting takeout from a baklava spot, purported to be the city's best, on the way to the subway.

Once we were on the train, I asked, "Catherine, did you really tell them I was your student, and your godson?"

"I did," she said as she bit into her first piece of baklava.

"But why? It isn't true."

"And what would you have me do, Gabriel? Say that your mother and I used to be best friends but then we had a falling out and didn't speak for twenty years, and then you and I bumped into each other on the street and ever since have been playing backgammon and going on walks together?"

"You could have said I was a friend."

"No, Gabriel, they'd have thought that was weird. I didn't know them. I wanted to keep things simple." She took another bite of baklava, chewed slowly, and then started to relate, in a considerably softer tone, the details of her various matches, analyzing the character and style of each opponent, culminating in Faisel's caginess. As awareness of how he had entrapped her into a terrible risk during the crucial, second-to-last game slowly dawned on her, she said, "My gosh. Now, there's a lesson to learn from."

The train rose aboveground and climbed onto the Manhattan Bridge. The last rays of daylight colored the sky a lush umber. The water below rippled silver-orange.

"You have to try the baklava," Catherine said, for what felt like the millionth time.

"I'm not hungry."

"One bite won't kill you. Live a little."

We were descending again, passing between dark brick towers, then again in black tunnel, and I heard the crinkle of parchment paper and practically felt the baklava on my chin, so close did she hold it to me. I finally consented to a bite, and she smiled proudly. "You must admit it's extraordinary."

When I didn't reply, she went on, "By the way, Gabriel. Did I tell you what he said?"

"Who?"

"Faisel. When our match was over, he whispered,"—she leaned toward me, gripping my neck with her hand so that her lips were right at my ear, repeating his gesture along with his words—"'I needed my luck this time. Usually, I am fine without it. But against you, I needed it all.'"

She released me and patted her knees triumphantly. "I know it's silly, but I can't tell you how special it made me feel. I may have lost but I feel certain that I'm glowing. Can you see it? Just a little?"

Again, unsure how to respond, I smiled meekly and turned away.

We got out at Bleeker and I consented to share a cab—out of sheer apathy, a wish to be home as quickly as possible.

"You know, it's too bad about the break-fast," Catherine said as the car pulled up to her corner. "I've been thinking it would be nice to celebrate a holiday together. Maybe Thanksgiving? Think about it, that's all I ask. I'm planting a seed."

But my only thought was that a good long break from Catherine sounded nice.

12

While everyone else in my family acted as if the Catskills trip had never happened, I couldn't stop thinking about it. I revisited every detail in my mind, interrogating myself like those cops, hoping that the next re-telling would elicit an elusive clue to the mystery of why it all seemed so fateful. Sometimes, my internal conversation spilled outward, and I eventually developed a practiced version of the story—from the arrival at the house to the dinner table to the basement to the moonlit back-yard; out to the woods, getting lost, sleeping on tree roots; to the morning light, the return home, the search for Becca; to the horse farm, where we finally located her—that I would share with others. And with time, the story expanded to include later developments, which to others might have seemed barely linked to the Catskills, though to me the con-nection was crystal clear—for they were essential facts of my life, central to the story of the new me who had emerged from that night in the forest.

The first of these new developments concerned Becca. She had al-ways been "moody" or "difficult," but after the Catskills, I became aware of a new intensity to her discontent. At first her complaints seemed reasonable. Dinner was too late, or Dad kept interrupting her, or Mom had forgotten that her latest diet excluded dairy. I would find myself nodding along, but then Becca's voice changed, grew high pitched and harried, and soon she was screaming or banging the table or slamming a door.

Some evenings, alone in my room and seeking calm after a Becca blowout, I would picture her as she had been that night in the woods. I would focus on the period when we had been alone. *After the provocation but before the fallout*—is how I thought of it. When Becca, my know-it-all, good-at-everything, precocious, smart-as-heck sister, was rendered impotent, with no more sense than I about how to escape a dark forest with nothing but a weak flashlight, when she lacked all words of comfort, was instead silent, fiddling with the flashlight, picking at bark. Small, helpless, pathetic.

Hadn't her tempestuous adolescence begun right there? Becca had always had the wild in her, but that night when she had been small and frightened and at a total loss for solutions, was when this one of several possible futures became actualized. The Catskills woods were the kindling. They had to be. And when I told my story, as I did to people close to me, this was the part I emphasized.

During her final years of high school, Becca was a hurricane that frequently soaked and battered us, though never in a way that you could anticipate and prepare for. In response, the other three of us grew defensive. Some weekend mornings I caught Dad literally tiptoeing around the living room, so wary was he of waking her, and some evenings I watched Mom hold her eyes closed (lest she cry) as Becca once again mocked "the utter banality of the *How was your day?* dinner routine." I looked for excuses to go out. I joined clubs at school I didn't care about, began playing basketball in Carl Schurz Park just to be away, and when all else failed hung out with an awkward, friendless fourth grader in the building named Randy. Yes, I pocketed the money his mom secretly gave me, but I justified this by giving half to a homeless guy who sat outside the deli across the street. His name was Clyde, and he took to calling me Henry. I never thought to ask why.

More than anyone else, Becca determined the rhythm and tenor of our family life. Was she home or not? Calm or crazed? In some known place or "out"? And yet, more than once, I found myself wondering if

she was really as "out of control" as my parents suggested, or if the out-
bursts were a kind of performance. Her most extreme actions—entire
weekends spent unseen in her bedroom; the six weeks she inexplicably
moved in with Uncle Nick and Aunt Rita; regular screaming sessions
at both parents, especially Dad—all shared something in common: they
resulted in periods of solitude. So, was there some discipline even in her
most impassioned moments? Was it possible she was just trying to
carve out a space for herself?

After one particularly bad outburst, Dad found me in the living
room. I was at the window, looking out at boats floating down the East
River. "You have to look after her," he said. "Like she used to look after
you."

"Yeah, right. When was that?"

He ignored my question. "You'll take turns, I suppose, and now
she's the one who needs help."

Though I resented them, I never forgot his words and even began
to conceive a sort of "sibling code" that bound Becca and me together.
After that, if a Becca freakout hadn't left me too bruised, I might knock
on her door when things had calmed, and I soon learned that, even as
she still raged at our parents, she usually let me in. We'd sit on her bed,
listen to music, read. She might ask about my friends, but if the conversation turned to her, if I dared approach her personal life, a wall of
sarcasm and evasion shot up. In this way, I understood that the sibling
code might permit certain intimacy but still had its limits.

And Becca's erratic behavior wasn't limited to her "fits." There was
also the parade of obsessions—what Mom called "phases" and Dad
"crazes"—that gripped her for a few weeks before being discarded for
the next: veganism, ultramarathoning, Zionism, the 7-snacks-a-day
diet, Aikido, Zen meditation, Brazilian Jiu Jitsu, Kaballah, liquid fasts…
on and on. One quiet Sunday morning after a bellowing-to-the-point-
of-hoarseness Saturday night tirade, she barged into the living room
and started spouting words—"caprices eccentricities idiosyncrasies
kicks kinks quirks vagaries vogues whimsies whims passions infatua-
tions fads fancies fashions fevers frenzies furies madnesses manias

rages derangements"—like some wild-eyed spawn of Circe and Roget. She always needed to have the final word.

Becca's hair. She dyed it purple, cut it short, dyed it red, then black, as black as hair can be, so that it emphasized the pallor of her skin, which caused the reemergence of faint freckles on her nose that I associated with a more youthful, summery version of her. This pale-skinned, jet-black-haired look is how I recall her high-school self; she kept it awhile, letting the hair grow until it reached the small of her back, when, in the summer before college, she razored it down to the roots, bald.

Becca's clothes. She was never particularly fussy about what she wore, except that her clothes always seemed baggy. Sweats, wide floppy pants, loose dresses, oversize sweaters. Only later did it occur to me that she was hiding her body, which was not only small but skinny, too skinny.

Both parents, Mom especially, were always encouraging her to eat.

"I eat plenty," Becca'd say.

"For an anteater on a diet. Eat more."

It was an antic back-and-forth that never led to changed behavior but invariably left both Mom and Becca eager to flee the table. At times, Becca ran to her room and cranked up the Rollins Band, Nine Inch Nails, Sinead O'Connor, Ice Cube, Guns N Roses, Pearl Jam, Rage Against the Machine, Cranberries, or any others whose names I cannot recall, all of them loud and angry, full of screams. But she wasn't the sort to lock herself in her room and blast music for hours, nor did I see evidence of furtive trips to dance clubs. Again, the result of so much of this frenzied activity was a kind of negation: Becca, exiled to her room, silent.

Sometimes, I tried to ask about the Catskills. She mostly ignored or evaded my questions, but once I learned something new: that when Connor had first "found" Becca in the woods, he had tried to kiss her. This revelation added all kinds of nuance to the fact of our getting lost. I had heard the boys' laughter and dismissed it as wind, while Becca, knowing more than me, had heard it differently. But did this explain why she hadn't wanted to call out? I pressed for further details—had Connor succeeded in his attempt? had she welcomed it?—but got none.

She was also reticent on the mystery of how we had failed to connect the next morning. I'd imagined all sorts of explanations—she had wandered off to go to the bathroom, or gotten up to explore, she had continued to lean against that tree, fast asleep. I even wondered if she had heard my calls, but kept still and silent, and in this way willed our separation. I asked many times, but she offered only impenetrable sarcasm. "I ran to the store for milk for our cereal." "I took a dawn constitutional." "That old story? To be honest, I don't remember it well. Do you?" "Why do you keep asking? Why do you think there's some neat and tidy answer to be found?"

Or she did the classic big sister move of twisting the conversations around, and soon she was grilling me.

"The night before we couldn't see," she said. "The flashlight was useless, I thought it made sense to wait for morning."

"But what happened to you then? Where did you go?"

"What happened to *you*, Gabriel?"

"I went to sleep. I didn't go anywhere."

"And when you woke up?"

"I looked for you, Becca. You weren't there."

"So where was I then?"

"That's what I'm asking you."

"I was in the woods, Gabriel. I. Was. In. The. Fucking. Woods. Maybe *you* should have looked harder."

Politics were a frequent obsession. She wanted to free Tibet and end Apartheid. She read every report issued by the UN Working Group on Enforced or Involuntary Disappearances. She cried for hours on the day that the US bombed Iraq in the Gulf War. When I asked why, she said she was crying for me. "I hope it's over before you turn 18." After a summer in Israel, she returned with a wardrobe of knitted hats, sweaters, and ankle-length skirts, able to sing dozens of Hebrew folk songs; she kept Kosher, which in practice meant she was vegetarian again, but she also talked about the end times and the coming of the Messiah.

Then, a few months later, she became an atheist, and shortly after a Palestinian activist, who wore a keffiyeh and hung a poster of Hanan Ashrawi on her bedroom wall.

Amid it all, drawing was the one consistent activity in her life. When she was alone in her room, when she nestled in an armchair, when she was silent in the backseat of the car—it was a good bet that she had a sketchpad and pencils, or a pen, or crayons, pastels, charcoal, oil sticks. She didn't think of herself as an artist; she just drew stuff. But she could make whatever she wanted, and even if I didn't yet have the vocabulary to express it, I began to understand that she had a special talent.

Still, it took an outsider to reveal this truth more fully. One evening, we had a visit from Jen and Donovan, one of the seemingly interchangeable couples our parents frequented in those days. They had come for cocktails before the four adults headed to dinner at 8 1/2 and a concert at Carnegie Hall—was it Brahms? Schumann?—and Becca and I were called into the living room to make polite as the parents spiffed up in the bedroom. We were mostly just a delaying tactic, but we were also meant to perform as hosts; I hated how they trotted us out like this. And Jen had never shown interest in either of us, while Donovan had a single trick in his arsenal; he could talk to me about the Knicks.

On this evening Becca sat on the far side of the room, curled in a ball on the couch. She had a pen and pencil in her lap, both hidden in the hollow of her body; I doubted that Jen and Donovan even knew. Donovan asked if I'd seen the Bulls game, and Jen wandered over to the window to watch a passing yacht (on each visit, she managed some comment on "the view," which I had understood was a dig at her husband for not earning enough for an apartment "overlooking the river"). After a bit, Becca left without a word, and shortly after Jen said, "Don, would you take a look at this?"

As he rushed to join her at the window, she bent down to the couch and they nearly collided, which elicited a rare moment of shared hilarity—the three of us laughing together. Jen settled on the couch, holding

Becca's notebook, eyes transfixed. After a good half minute of silence, she passed the notebook to Donovan. Shortly after, he passed it to my parents, who had emerged from their bedroom. Eventually it made its way to me. The picture was of Jen, lifelike and detailed, though indicated with only a few marks, standing at the window, looking out at the dark sky. A kind of Hopper in reverse, black streaming in where he would have had light. I had seen this sort of drawing often enough, but Jen's reaction made this one stand apart. When Becca reappeared in the living room, Jen rushed over and asked, suddenly solicitous, what grade she was in, what colleges she was thinking of, whether she studied art, if she was thinking of it as a career. It was as if Jen had been struck by a sudden brainwave that this small sullen child might someday become an adult worth knowing.

13

I next heard from Catherine a week later. "I'm just calling to let you know that I'm going to San Diego," she said over the phone.

Still annoyed by our trip to King's Highway, I answered snidely, "So why are you telling me?"

"I didn't want you to think I'd disappeared."

After that, we didn't speak for some time. My part in this was half lingering resentment, half uptick in my social life. It began when Vic and Helene invited me to a murder mystery dinner party. I had just arrived and was still shaking hands when I was handed a cyanide-laced Manhattan, but unlike at the backgammon tournament, I was not treated as some forgettable first corpse, but was immediately brought a "safe" cocktail and "plate of munchies," and then attended to the entire night, well fed, boozed, companioned. More promising, Peter brought me to a few parties downtown, one of which spilled into an afterparty in Brooklyn, where I met Cathy and Calinda, a perky pair of advertising copywriters who were seemingly attached at the hip.

It was well past midnight, and several G+T's had loosened my tongue by the time they invited me to join their weekend getaway in Montauk. I agreed, and a few days later, was heading east on the Jitney with a change of clothes, two bathing suits, and a towel in my backpack. There were nine of us in the house, six girls, three guys. They mostly already knew one another; only a woman named Jill and I were first-timers. For three days, we alternated between the sort of absurd debauchery you might see on reality TV—plastic cups filled with beer and cigarette butts, empty vodka bottles stacked on the deck, a constant parade in and out of the rooftop hot tub—and a quiet, much duller experience, with people keeping to their bedrooms and grunting responses at one another as they prepared solitary breakfasts. But the final night Calinda and I hooked up, with Cathy passing the night in my closet-sized single. Calinda was all giggly the next morning as she kissed me goodbye, but she didn't return my call three days later, nor the one three days after that.

It was about then that I heard from Catherine. After describing a few uneventful days in San Diego, she said, "I have to tell you something, Gabriel. I fell."

I had a momentary fright that we were about to enter some new phase of our relationship, that I would become a caretaker, the first person she'd call after each tumble and new set of fractures, but I was still annoyed by our last encounter and made little effort to check my tone. "Sorry to hear that," I said. "But what do you want from me?"

She laughed. "I'm not asking you to push a wheelchair or anything. It was only a sprain, and I'm mostly recovered already. Harvey helped. Would you believe he used to be a physical therapist? I'm just telling you to explain why I haven't been in touch. What do I want from you? Well, I need to build up my strength, so I want you … to go on a walk with me. I need my old walking partner back. I miss you."

Feeling foolish and a bit guilty, I consented to a walk the following day along the East River. October was a spectacular time in New York. The brutal summer heat had passed, and the city was at the peak of its understated splendor. Within minutes, I was glad to be with Catherine again. She didn't carry a cane or limp; she seemed no slower. It was as if nothing had changed (so much so that I wondered if the fall had been real)—and though I didn't say it out loud, I realized that I had missed her, too.

We walked often those next few weeks. It was unseasonably warm. ("Ah, global warming October," Catherine joked. "There's nothing like it.") Battery Park and the banks of Lower Manhattan, across the Brooklyn Bridge and into the alleys of Brooklyn Heights, up and down the Coney Island boardwalk, through Flushing Meadows Park, Van Cortland Park, and Forest Park. Now, we were at Fort Tilden, on the southern end of the Rockaways. We tramped through the former army base, then settled on the sandy beach. In the distance, half a dozen surfers floated on stirring white tops, the only ones willing to brave the chilly water.

Catherine spread a blue bedsheet across the sand. She took off her Keds and sat on a far corner, clasping her knees.

She had recently begun to ask the very questions we had avoided at the outset of our friendship—what will you do now? what are your plans?—that, when asked by friends, had stumped me months earlier when I'd first returned to New York. The questions didn't nag at me as they had in the spring. Perhaps it was the passage of time, perhaps who was asking. Catherine's tone conveyed a mixture of curiosity and concern, without any hint of envy or judgment. But the thing was, she already knew the answers. In my half year back in New York, I'd had several short writing assignments. Nothing major, but enough to stay intermittently busy. When faced with the inevitable party icebreaker, "So, what do you do?", I could respond respectably, "I'm a freelance writer."

"And women? Are you dating?" she pressed.

I didn't mind this question either. It didn't feel like prying, and I liked that she cared enough to ask. "Now and then. No one who's stuck," I said.

"Maybe you shouldn't be spending all your time with an old lady like me."

I opened my backpack and took out the bag with sandwiches. "I'm hardly spending all my time with you."

"Someone needs to say these things." She brushed hair from her face and unwrapped her egg salad sandwich. "Someone needs to worry about you. Just a little. I want you to know that I am… worrying about you… just a little."

It was corny, but sweet. "You have my permission."

She bit into her sandwich, lifted the top piece of bread, and picked at the lettuce on top. "Have you thought about Thanksgiving?"

I'd told her that Thanksgiving was never a big holiday at our house; that when I was growing up, we had never settled into a fixed tradition, instead bouncing around, a few years at this aunt and uncle's, a few years at those ones'; and that after a decade in Europe, I had lost the habit of celebrating it entirely. Now it was just another Thursday in bleak November.

"Not really," I said. "It's only October."

"Well, I'm giving it thought for you, Gabriel."

A wetsuit-clad surfer emerged from the gray water, dragging a white and orange board. Somehow, I had missed his passage from the far-off waves to shallow water, so that he seemed to have grown a hundredfold, suddenly a giant, in a matter of seconds. Shaking his head and shooting spray in all directions, he walked straight toward us, but with the board a mere body length from my head he veered sharply to the left and walked along the line of dark sand marking the recent high tide. He reminded me of Star.

As he walked down the beach, shrinking again to the miniature size he had been when on the waves, I began to speak about something else Catherine had mentioned recently.

"You asked about Milan," I said. "About what happened after Cassia and I broke up."

She nodded, making eyes that said, "Go on."

"You have to remember, I'd moved to the city only a few months earlier. I barely knew the place and felt lost in just about every way you can imagine, heartbroken, life-broken, you name it. I remember calling Becca to run through my options—stay in Milan, return to Paris, back to New York? She said I had to stay awhile, if only to arrive in a better place to make the decision. Which sounded sensible until the phone clicked. Then a new wave of grief hit me and, though I'd promised not to, I found myself dialing Cassia's number. It rang and rang and rang until a strange voice, a man's, said, 'Pronto. Mi dica.'

"At least, writing kept me busy. I wasn't slavishly typing away ten hours a day, but freelance assignments arrived with regularity. They were mostly small lifestyle pieces about some hot chef or fashion trend, travel listings, also occasional news briefs. If I wasn't the essayist or short story writer I had once fantasized about becoming, I was making a career. Of course, I still had so much free time, so I turned to an old standby, exploration. Milan had three subways lines, which intersected in three stations, a little triangle of connections; otherwise, each line stretched out in both directions, away from the centro. I went to each station, visiting the surrounding neighborhood for hours and hours, like some spinoff of my three-day game that treated the subway map as a master plan. After several months with this my primary pastime, I faced a decision on renewing the lease.

"Once again, Becca helped me decide. 'You talk about leaving or going, but going where? Is there some other option I don't know about? Maybe stick around and see what happens?'

"So I did. Then, one day on a crowded subway car, I felt a tap on my shoulder. The woman behind me was attempting to suss out whether I would be getting off at the next stop, in which case I would not have to move out of the way so she could pass, she would simply follow behind me out the door. She was tall yet peered up to speak; her voice, though dry and deep, came out as a shy squeak. It was a momentary awkwardness that I would have easily forgotten had I not passed, later that day in the park near my house where I liked to read, a woman on a bench who asked if I had a cigarette.

"About what followed, there is some disagreement, but according to her version, I reached into a pants pocket, then the other, then a breast pocket, before saying, 'I'm sorry, I don't smoke.'

"'Then why did you check your pockets?'"

"'What do you mean?'" I asked, for in my version of this conversation I didn't check any pockets, just answered her question.

"Regardless, this is where our stories converged, and also when I recognized her from the subway. She recognized me too, we shared a *What a Small World* moment, and soon, after I told her where I was from, I noticed that she gave none of the usual responses (*You don't seem American* [a compliment], *That was my guess* [politely condescending], or *I love America, how I want to visit* [earnest]), but instead said, "New York. Che bella città. I visited 10 years ago with my parents. My uncle lived there, in a giant building on the 24th floor. I had never seen snow from above. I felt like I was in a fairytale.

"'To this day,'" she would probably say, if giving her version of our meeting, 'I don't know why he didn't ask *where I was from*. Was my accent flawless? Was he shy? Did he lack some basic social grace? Do you know what else, and this was even stranger, we gave each other a certain look, you know, *that look*—I couldn't have been more obvious—but still he didn't ask for my number. What a clod, and yet that's why I remembered him and spoke up the next time he walked by. So maybe it was skillful, after all.'"

The point is, as I discovered when I came upon her the next day in the same park, we were neighbors with similar schedules and paths of travel, and there seemed to be a certain serendipity, which you could read as fate, to our meetings. But, yes, I totally missed the fact that she too was a foreigner.

It was only the following day, during our next meeting in the park, that I heard the slight hitch of uncertainty as she approached the penultimate syllables of longer words.

"I'm from Bratislava," she said.

"Czech?"

"Slovak, thank you. It's an independent country, don't you know?"

Despite this hiccup, we spoke a good quarter of an hour and then I was on my way, only to regret within seconds that while I'd finally learned her name—Lina—I'd again forgotten to get a number. But amazingly, we bumped into each other at another park later that afternoon. As we walked, she told me about Bratislava, which she said I would enjoy, since it had large, beautiful parks, which I seemed to love as much as she. Over conversation led to dinner at a local trattoria. Then a walk to a bar for a digestivo.

"Do you know Fernet?" she asked. "My father used to sell it. I've never forgotten the smell."

I recoiled at the first sip, then talked myself into liking it.

"Now, you need to introduce a new taste to me," she said as we stepped into the warm night.

Which I did a few days later when I offered a bite of my favorite candy bar, a vanilla Charleston Chew. She gagged, then giggled. "Serves me right for asking an American to introduce me to a new taste."

I can't say when exactly we fell in love. It just kind of happened, and by the time I realized it, I saw that it was already old news. Everything was so natural between us. Even her moods, which were intense—she reminded me of Becca in a way—seemed familiar and manageable. Our days together flowed into one another, as if some magical spell had changed the nature of time's relentless march. I was surprised to find myself so often at a loss for words; happiness, I discovered, required so few of them.

Gazing at Lina across the room, I might slip outside myself, amazed at my new life. Who was I? How had I ... won *her*? She had dark blond hair with windswept brown streaks. She was tall and long with small breasts that would disappear beneath certain dresses but then surprise you in others. Her teeth were slightly misaligned, but a narrow smile covered this up, sometimes also a tiny web of saliva. She carried a ratty crocodile skin purse, a gift from a beloved, late grandmother; otherwise, everything was new, her dresses, her sandals, a new pair of sunglasses every week, it seemed. She drew in a coloring book when she felt nervy, she remained ticklish at the tip of her chin, she cooked a devilish goulash, she slept on the couch most Saturday afternoons even after sleeping until noon that very morning, she had the videos to prove that she had once been a star at team handball—a goalie, vicious and fearless. I couldn't tear my eyes away from her; I didn't even want to blink.

In her presence, something came over me. I was smooth and witty, always ready with a quick retort. I felt unencumbered; it was like I had become *someone else*—as if Gah-BREE-el were not the same as Gabriel, but a Milanese twin who had inherited the bulk of my virtues but only a fraction of my shortcomings, a suave person who moved through the world without a hitch between thought and action. You should have seen me. I could smile wide and hold that optimistic expression for hours, without feeling like a fool. I wasn't a brooder. Not at all. I was light and carefree.

My writing was never busier, the same sorts of pieces, but more of them and of greater ambition. Some even affording opportunity to travel. Day trips to Rome and Florence, overnights to Geneva and Zurich, longer trips, too: back to Paris; Copenhagen, Helsinki, Istanbul. Returning to Milan, there was always this awkward transition before I sunk back into Lina and rediscovered the Milan me. So, when she suggested, around October, that we go to Bratislava, not to meet her family, but for good, I didn't have to consult Becca. "Why not?" I said, without skipping a beat.

For a few weeks, the move felt fantastical, but when Lina said that she wanted to go for a weekend in Bratislava to search for apartments, I knew it was real. I had a writing deadline and couldn't accompany her, but I went on her second trip. We stayed with her parents, a middle-aged couple much younger in spirit and body than I remembered my parents ever having been. I could hardly communicate with them, and they kept their distance, but I felt their kindness in glances across the living room and the food and towels and the Slovak Koruny they left by my seat at the dining room table.

Lina found an apartment on a third trip, also taken on her own, as I crashed another article. Back in Milan, she showed me pictures—the breakfast nook, the courtyard view—and where it fell on the map: close, but not too close, to her parents. It was December. Our move-in date was in February. I bought Slovak language books and practiced each morning. Lina indulged me with conversations in the evening, which often devolved into riotous laughter, as my toddler vocabulary veered into unintended malapropism.

Shortly after New Year's, we were at a favorite bar, on a second glass of Fernet. We sat in our niche by the window, two tight, but private, seats, perfect for a date, looking out on a clear night sky in the midst of a mostly gray winter.

"I'm going to Munich," she said. "I'm moving there."

I wish I could have seen my expression—shock? incomprehension? terror?—but the window glass was clouded over. "I… I don't understand."

She had found a job in Munich. And not only a job. A new boyfriend, too—who was, actually a former fiancé whom she had dated on and off for eight years and lived with until two years prior. For months, she now explained, Karl had been calling, courting her. He had made clear that he wanted a new beginning. She had seen him during her first weekend trip to Bratislava; also, a few times when I'd traveled for work. There had been signs, I now realized. She'd changed perfumes, to something more rustic, earthier, which I noticed but hardly objected to, for it had spiced up our sex life. She left some mornings without kissing me awake. She kept rejecting my efforts to replace Fernet with Slivovice. "Shouldn't we practice?" I'd say; "in due course," she'd reply.

For a few heartbeats, I doubted her, not that she was going to Munich but the excuse she had given. Karl? Was he real or just some invented figure meant to explain away a Becca-like need to vanish? But I quickly saw that I was the one telling stories, and for no reason but self-protection—better to think that she was fleeing demons than just leaving me, right?

"I'm so sorry, Gabby"—her nickname, which now revolted me. "I'm so sorry. I'm not one to live a double life. I hate dishonesty. It has happened to me, too; it is the reason Karl and I broke up in the past… I can hardly believe I am on the other side."

"What about Bratislava? All our plans?"

"I'm so sorry."

I left the restaurant and walked for hours, a good long walk in a city that I now knew so well, walking past the point when my thumping heart had slowed to its normal beat and a familiar calm overcome me, at least for a few moments, whenever I could put aside the churning rage. As I reentered the apartment, I noticed what should have been another clue. Earlier that day, the place had been sparkling clean, my clothes folded perfectly on the shelves. Now I faced the same exaggerated orderliness, except for the pair of bags, lined up by the arm of the couch, where Lina sat. She asked where I had been, if I was OK, if I wanted to say anything.

When I responded with total silence, she said, "I can stay the night, or I can leave. It's up to you."

I faced the courtyard window, solid black on all four panes, as if our neighbors had cleared out for this dark scene. I looked down at the floor, the wooden planks dustless; even the tassels at the rug edge seemed aligned, combed. Lina peered up at me, she kissed my lips. A minute later, she was gone.

We had no second act, not even a brief one. I received a postcard a year later, then never heard from her again. One night, some years later, I had a nightmare. I was back in the woods, but instead of Becca, it was Lina, and instead of telling me to relax, to sleep, she turned to me with a sort of gleeful smile and begin scratching herself, her arms and elbows, gently at first, then tearing at hairs, digging into the flesh, pulling back skin, then her face, her nostrils, her lips, her eye sockets, clawing, excavating, paring away until she hit bone.

Until then, I'd resisted Googling her; now, I relented and found scenes of a life that appeared happy and conventional. As far as I could tell, she had stayed in Munich, married Karl, had two boys, in quick succession, and kept a handsome German Mastiff. She had also gained weight and cut her hair short. Her online presence consisted of sterile headshots on a professional profile and a handful of posed family portraits on social ones, photographic clichés from which it was impossible to infer emotion, but I also knew that whatever one saw on that face could not be trusted.

But back to Milan, 2008. In the days after Lina's departure, I learned that her plan had been in the works for months. It was not just the Munich train ticket or the suitcases packed. She had also prepaid the following month's rent and communicated to our Milanese landlord that she assumed we would move out afterward, though I would confirm one way or another.

So, what did I do? I went to Bratislava. I managed to piece together the plans that Lina had, at least partially, set in motion, and through many awkward phone calls featuring two people expressing in different languages their inability to communicate with one another (at least that was my half of the conversation), to secure an apartment for myself. Whether it was in fact the one that Lina and I were "planning" to inhabit or not, I cannot say. Nor do I know if I was taken for a ride on the price; I know only that the fee was reasonable by Milan standards and that it served my few needs, a bed, a place to sit, a corner kitchen, a bathroom, working appliances, all of it furnished and reasonably clean, proximity to the city center.

The question of "What the hell am I doing here?" presented itself often enough over the next several months. I took a beginning language class and learned to order a loaf of bread or bottle of wine but hardly became conversational. The Americans in the class seemed too young or too sad to hang out with; with the Europeans, I found myself on the opposite end of the same judgment. I quit the class after three weeks.

I never made friends in Bratislava nor found a way to blend in. Many people pegged me by sight as a foreigner, and whoever could, addressed me in English. My work had slowed (I wish I had collected the emails from editors asking some version of *Bratislava? Are you serious?*), and I was hardly assertive in seeking new assignments. So, what kept me there? At first, a mixture of apathy and sadness—leaving felt like defeat. I think there was also some reluctance to leave in winter, and I didn't have a plan. But soon it became something else.

In the hills above the city is Bratislava Forest Park, and I went there some days at dawn. I often came across a club of birdwatchers, who let me linger, indifferent to my presence, as if I were a squirrel on a treetop, innocently watching their watching parties.

In my neighborhood, I found a favorite café for morning coffee, a favorite lunch spot, and, as seemed to be the case in every city I spent time, a favorite park bench, where I went each afternoon to read. Here too I came to know a cast of characters: Wanda and Wencel (my names for them, not necessarily theirs), an older couple who circled my bench again and again each afternoon, deep in conversation that sounded tense, though their smiles suggested otherwise; Silent Pavel, who passed each morning leading a pack of dogs on leashes, all well behaved and never barking out of turn; and Book Guy, who set up a table each afternoon with a familiar hippy syllabus of fraying paperbacks. Only toward the end of my stay did I learn that the books weren't his; he was selling them as a favor to a dying friend.

Some nights I went to bars alone and a few times even noticed female eyes upon me. I had one minor fling consisting of two dates, one night together, and an awkward morning in which we quickly reached the limits of our ability to communicate. I began carrying cigarettes, offering them to whomever asked, like alms. Later, I carried a lighter too and loved watching the flame that I could instantly bring forth with a flick of my thumb. I walked often by the building where Lina's parents lived, greeting them whenever I saw them on the street; I have no idea if they recognized me.

I let my beard go and soon discovered on my left cheek my first gray hairs. I stopped trying to speak the language, made do with grunts and glares, and learned to carry myself with a sort of apish pride. I lost twenty-five pounds without really trying. I took to walking by dusklight, on and on to the point of being lost, no matter that my sneaker soles had withered, and my toes blistered. Many nights I walked straight through the darkness, arriving at the train station along with the first glimmers of morning. And I rested there, outside, regardless of the weather, lingering at the edge of the derelicts, who paid me no mind, as if I were one more member of the gang, as if I had become invisible.

Half a year later, back in Paris, I was able to identify the night Lina left me as the moment I knew I would return to New York, though I would not make the move for several more years. *Can you understand that, Catherine?*

I had been going on so long, lost in memory, barely aware that she was beside me, on a blanket spread on dry sand, with the sound of lapping waves before us, at an improbable beach before a dozen surfers in frigid water, in New York City, my home, that I had not known even existed a year earlier.

Catherine faced the water. Two more surfers had emerged, made the same hard pivot as the first, their boards momentarily as threatening as spears, then goofy-looking, oblong pancakes fading down the beach. Catherine pecked at bits of egg white that had fallen from the sides of her sandwich. She hugged her knees, then reached behind her head, removed the girlish headband holding her hair, and shook it loose, gray locks falling on her shoulders. Sometimes she didn't seem old—*older*, but not old. There was something about this combination—that she was neither ancient nor a peer—that created a space for sharing, even as I was fully aware that for all our openness, there was an overwhelming amount, or rather a single heavy topic, that we hardly discussed at all.

"The six months I spent in Bratislava were something I've tried often to describe without ever finding the right words," I went on. "Becca didn't get it. I heard her impatience on our calls. All my life I'd told her pretty much everything about me, and she was always sympathetic. But Bratislava, and my return to Paris, surpassed the limit of her understanding. "'Just go, Gabriel,'" she'd say. 'What are you waiting for? You're not a child anymore.'

"But it made perfect sense to me. I know it sounds crazy, but can you understand why I needed to stay, Catherine? Do you get it at all?"

It was midafternoon, and small shadows spread before us, occupying corners of the bedsheet like additional members of our party.

"Of course, I get it." Catherine smiled warmly. "Sometimes, you aren't ready to leave, even if you don't really want to stay, either. It was what you had to do. It's something only you could possibly know."

I'm not sure I believed her. I'm not sure I got it myself. But I liked that she said it. I liked that she had made a show of caring. And maybe that's all that *getting it* is. An act. As if.

The tide was coming in, darkening the sand only a body's length before us. Yet the waves seemed smaller. Maybe it was the light, the subdued tone of the latter part of the day, which did not shard the sea with harsh glimmers but instead gleamed above it, like some film on the roiling surface. Waves as rhythm, no longer pounding. Catherine leaned back on her elbows and kicked her feet forward. A breeze rustled her hair. With a sweep of the hand, she uncovered her forehead, liberating her eyes. She turned to me and smiled, then looked back to the ocean as a seagull flapped above us. She had no thoughts of leaving. She was going nowhere.

The words came to mind suddenly, and a moment later I said them out loud. "Thanksgiving? Sure, we could do Thanksgiving. Why not?"

14

It wasn't only Becca. Dad changed, too.

The pale, twiggy legs. The knotted knees. The twisted blue lines that ran along his inner thighs like a tangle of wires in an electrical panel. Had he always been this way? Or was this new? Certainly, his morning routine had changed. Once an early riser, dressed, shaved, buzzing through the kitchen with a coffee in one hand and a cereal box in the other, now he sat for hours in his favorite living room chair in his robe, gray bristles on his cheeks, staring out the window, even as I left for school.

A new order reigned in the house, and Mom reluctantly stepped forward. But temperament is unchangeable, and even in his subdued state, Dad issued resonant groans from the living room, let his hair grow wild, made grand pronouncements about his exhaustion. As Mom always reminded him, "Becca is YOUR daughter."

Dad's transformation was not without its silver linings. As he no longer set the morning tone with the odor of bitter coffee wafting through the apartment and his mess of newspaper across the kitchen table, I sometimes rose to an empty apartment, flooded with glorious light—nothing to disturb me, let alone his caffeinated morning inquisition. These calm mornings were welcome respite in an apartment that still echoed with Becca's fits.

But spring and summer passed, it was my freshman year of high school, the first fall with Becca away at college, a time when I expected the air in the house to lighten. Yet it hadn't. Why not?

One evening, Mom, Dad, and I lingered in the dining room after dinner, each waiting for someone else to declare that the meal was over.

"Can we talk, Gabriel?" Mom said. "In the living room."

We went to the big couch, which was plenty large for the three of us, but Mom practically sat on my knee, her thigh pressing against mine, until—whispering, "Jonah, why don't you sit here"—she scooted over, so Dad could squeeze between us.

He turned, bent, lowered his body. Such a simple thing—to sit—and yet...

He finally settled in the space between us and lay a cool hand on my knee, where moments earlier Mom's leg had pressed warmly. I saw her above his slumped shoulder. A white monster had settled on her face, covering everything but lips and pupils, though even these had been drained of color. I had seen this look only once before, that morning when we searched the woods for Becca, and instantly I understood, even before Dad cleared this throat and mumbled, "Cancer." Still, the word struck like a bullet, and I could feel the rush of blood through my chest, my neck, my face, my shoulders, my arms, my fingertips, every-where but that stone-cold knee.

"It'll be tough," Mom said softly. "But we'll make it through."

Blustery Becca had left us, and Dad the Doomed had filled the void. He lost weight, wore the same outfits days in a row, abandoned all pre-tense of caring about his breath. It felt like we had traded a terrifying roller coaster for a slow descent into a deep, inescapable cave. Down-ward, downward, downward, he descended, but always some new depth awaited. If that blanched terror never returned to Mom's face, she continued to cringe after each coughing fit and turned away when she came upon him in his living room chair, scrawny blueish legs slip-ping from a loose bathrobe. The smile she gave, when she noticed me beside her and said, "Come, shall we make dinner?" did not hide the twitch of her eyelids.

Yet life carried on. Sure, there were horrid throat clearings and sudden, unexplained clutches of his chest, but we could still play tennis (though only a single set, and later, noncompetitive rallying) and walk along the river. He developed a new interest in TV, perhaps because it allowed him to lie down. If you lined up photos, you could see the cheekbones pressing outward on an increasingly skeletal face, but day to day you could easily forget that a death sentence hung over him. Mom told me that his first, and only, round of chemotherapy affected him hard. He was nauseated, lost weight, and grew irritable. I had been away at camp, and my first thought when I came home was that he had buzzed his head for the summer.

Throughout it all, Mom worked long hours and took on new chores, shopping, cleaning, taxes, homework help. Ragged with exhaustion, she never complained. We had always been the quiet two, and with Dad sick and Becca at college, Mom and I faced odd silences at meals. We looked back and forth awhile, each expecting the other to speak first, before bursting into laughter.

I continued to think about the Catskills. I began to see that it wasn't just the friendship that we lost that night. It was something much greater, more profound, a sort of optimism, I suppose, or maybe just luck. It was as if that night in the woods opened a hole in the universe through which bad things started to emerge, bad things that affected Becca, and now Dad, eventually Mom and me, too. I obsessed about the Catskills, because I wanted to figure out how this one event had changed so much. But what I always wondered, what was never made clear to me, was this: Did that night set in motion those changes, or had a darker reality always been lurking? Was the night in the Catskills the cause of what followed or the event that allowed me to see clearly what was already foreordained?

For the rest of the family, the subject rarely arose, and when it did it was often with a light touch. If Becca was home from college and in a milder sort of mood, Dad might ask, "Donna, is your daughter lost in the woods again?" To which Mom might respond, "No, she's staring at the horses. I'll knock and see if she's ready to return to civilization."

Even Becca joined in from time to time: "Sorry, Gabriel, I was off in the forest. Just wasn't myself."

And so, when the topic did arise in a heavier context, it felt significant. It must have been the winter break of Becca's junior year in college, and bad weather had kept us cooped up inside for the better part of a week. Dad was going through a bad stretch, and Mom, Becca, and I were in the living room, restlessly flipping through magazines or gazing out the window at the gray sky and pale river below.

"What doubly sucks about this weather," Becca said, "is that as soon as it clears, it'll be Christmas. All those silly jingles, cheap tinsel, embarrassing light displays, everyone smiling, wishing you a Merry this and a Happy that, all governed by the cringy Hallmark police."

"Don't be a snob, Becca," Mom said. "Don't you remember how we used to pass our Christmases? When we had a special dinner invitation and could see what makes the holiday so special?"

It was true. Whatever Christmas magic we'd experienced was because of the Morrows. They celebrated Christmas Eve and Christmas morning alone, but dinner on December 25 was a public affair, and we were invited along with cousins, aunts and uncles, other friends. As soon as we got to Katonah, all the things that made Christmas seem corny or alienating to a Jew made perfect sense, from mistletoe to eggnog, to simply saying, "Merry...," without cracking up. Kyle and JT wore pressed slacks and blazers. Alan appeared in the wire-rimmed glasses you forgot he had and offered Dad a taste of some exotic brandy saved for special occasions. Their home's mixture of warmth and formality felt revelatory, as if a lesson in how domestic tranquility can tame the gray universe, even its coldest days. We reciprocated with an invitation to our Seder, which I knew they loved, Alan especially, though I never felt we matched their lofty example. And yet what pride I felt as I welcomed them at the apartment door, taking their coats and receiving the bottle of Kosher wine or flourless cake they had brought, and again at the meal when Catherine complimented me on my Hebrew after I read the Four Questions. "How well you read," she said without any of the usual adult condescension.

"Too bad you hadn't kept your wits about you that evening," Mom said to Becca. "We might be on our way to Katonah right now."

Everything about this barb was new, and while I had always felt entitled to complain that Becca had not taken better care of me that night, I could see no reason why Mom would hold a grudge. What had Becca done wrong? Not refused to play Hide and Seek? Not revealed our hiding spot sooner? Not recognized our location in those unknown woods? But I also saw that while Dad was usually the one who complained, Mom had lost something too. A best friend, which is no small thing.

Becca's reaction also surprised me. Yes, she stormed to her room, but by lunchtime she was at the kitchen table, explaining that she wanted to visit the Coke store on Fifth Avenue. "That Always Coca-Cola jingle is just too addictive. Can we go when we see the Christmas windows?"

What had I just witnessed? A skirmish that shed new light on a mystery or an entirely forgettable dustup? When I questioned Mom a few days later, she denied the whole thing before conceding, "I was in a mood, Becca was in a mood. I shouldn't have said it." Becca was even more nonchalant. "I think Mom just misses the pudding, you know, the savory kind. Where else can she eat that sort of thing?"

Still the memory of the Catskills burned in my mind, and I looked for signs of its imprint on others. It seemed significant that, while my parents never purged their photos of the Morrows, the albums from those years had been banished to closets, whereas another one, showing Becca and me as babies, had pride of place on a bookshelf in the living room, where guests were invited to discover it and flip through.

A few years later, when I was in college, Mom seemed willing to engage the topic a bit more. Perhaps I was older, perhaps more time had passed, who knows? Still, her answers disappointed. She insisted that there had been no major fight between the families; she had just been terribly disappointed with how the Morrows, Catherine especially, had made excuses for Kyle, had minimized the entire event, and in the aftermath had accused us, that is, Mom and Dad, of making a mountain of a molehill.

"That was the last straw. Had they apologized rather than grow defensive, we might have gotten past it. *Might have*. But it's not like we ever officially broke up, Gabriel. There was a period when we were very upset, and before you know it, the prolonged silence becomes a fact of its own, reason enough not to call, not to arrange the next visit. Soon, you begin to question your fonder memories. Were you really so close? Weren't the seeds of distrust always there? There was no breakup, because there was nothing to break. No contract. No obligation. What happened is as simple as they stopped calling us and we stopped calling them. Anyone could have picked up the phone at any time. But no one did."

Her words made sense, but did I believe them? Regardless, I would get nothing more from her on the topic. From Dad, even less. Or maybe it seemed wrong to even try with him. He was sick; regrets seemed like a topic to avoid. My obsession with the fate of the two families felt trite before the awesome force of his diminishment.

And yet I also remember walking beside him on the promenade along the East River on a clear autumn day. At some point, I inadvertently walked ahead and, recognizing he wasn't beside me, felt a fright that he had simply vanished. Turning back, I found him, only feet behind, as a blast of sun lit his chiseled face. Always handsome, he had rarely seemed so rugged—as if some hidden heartiness had emerged through his struggle. In this way, I came to understand that dying and death were such different things. That dying was a phase of life, rather than its opposite. A vision of infinity at the very limit of the finite.

That was the paradox of Dad's sickness. For years, I had watched him wither, thin, bald, pale, stop going to work, rarely leave the apartment, but always he remained Dad, witty and sentimental, ever ready to tease or to stoke the past, surprisingly resilient.

Then one day—this was my junior year of college—Mom called: "He hasn't eaten." Her tone made clear that this wasn't her typical worrying and I was back in New York that evening, arriving to the news that the doctor had visited and Dad had managed some toast with butter. Some, but not too much.

Two stories stand out from his last days. We were on another walk, one of our last, though I didn't know it at the time. We were on York Avenue, heading to Antonio's, a favorite pizza spot. Passing Key Food, Dad handed a dollar to a homeless man sitting on a packing crate. "Thanks, Henry," came the reply.

I didn't recognize the man, but I later realized that he was Clyde, who used to sit outside the deli across the street, and who had also called me Henry.

"He's been doing it for years," Dad said. "I have no idea why but I find it endearing."

When I related my Henry story, Dad and I had a long laugh, but what did it mean? Were we all Henry's to this man, or was there something about me and Dad, some bond that only this man, who sat all day peering into every face that passed, could detect? Unfortunately, I never saw him again, never had a chance to ask.

A few weeks later, I came into Dad's bedroom. Mom and Becca were already sitting at his bedside, as Dad talked about a baseball game he had attended with his father. A concession man came through the stands, peddling Cracker Jacks, and Dad asked Papa, who was an immigrant, if he could have some.

"Cracker Jocks?" said Papa.

Dad tried to explain, the proper name, what they were, why kids like them. Meanwhile, the Yankees had loaded the bases and he'd missed it all.

With Mantle up, a Grand Slam opportunity, Papa asked, "These Cracker Jocks... I don't understand... Why...."

Dad wanted to watch but felt obligated to explain. He went on and on to no effect and eventually gave up. "Just give me a quarter, Pop, would you?"

When Dad purchased a box, Papa was quite curious about this apparently desirable snack. "But he spat out the very first bite," Dad said.

"He coughed and took a long gulp of water. He never asked for any-more."

As he said this, Dad looked up and smiled. He wore a placid look that dissolved, as he shifted his gaze from Mom to Becca to me, into an inscrutable, almost alien expression. I waited for some punchline, but apparently that was the end of the story. Only later did Becca explain that shortly before I had entered the room, Dad had spit up the Jello that she'd tried to feed him. It was a final attempt to keep something down in a long succession of foods. He'd refused them all.

* * *

The August before Dad's passing, we rented a house in the Hamptons, but then Dad went through a bad patch and couldn't go. Still, Mom insisted that she and I go for a few days, and, with Dad urging me, I finally accepted. The weather was unseasonably brisk, and as neither Mom nor I particularly loved the beach, we mostly stuck to inland ac-tivities like tennis and hiking. But our final evening, we ate at a lobster shack on a pier jutting into the Atlantic, and it was there, between sips of salty margarita, that Mom told me about her own diagnosis.

"Stop it," I said. "Come on."

I must have repeated that, or some version of it, some half dozen times. For a good minute, we traveled in circles, until I came to under-stand that this was not some perverse joke. As I grasped the truth, her face was so flat, inexpressive. Now when she had more to fear than ever before, she was a vision of perfect calm.

Then she turned to the pulsing water, her hair ruffled in the dusk breeze, her newly tanned arms utterly still. A pair of sunglasses hung over her shirt collar, but she was ever resistant to them, even looking back to the setting sun.

I said the first thing that came to mind. Sebastian had called a week earlier, all impassioned because he said he had discovered a topic for his senior thesis. "The literature of war," he'd said. "I'm reading all these novels, World War 1 mostly, and also watching Vietnam movies, *All*

Quiet on the Western Front, *Platoon*, *Full Metal Jacket*, and so on, and I keep noticing something. What breaks the soldiers, what drives them mad, is not the fear of death or the discovery that one has become a killer—which is what I'd always figured. No, it's watching your friends die."

A smile cracked on Mom's face, a first expression since her revelation, but she had nothing to say, at least not out loud, about Sebastian's theory. She signaled for another round of drinks, then slurped away the watery dregs of her present glass. "One for each of us," she told the busboy, who looked even younger than me. "And more chips and guac, please."

She was on her third margarita. I had noticed that she had started to drink more freely. Perhaps she had always wanted this and only now felt free to do so. On this trip, she had asked each night, as we settled at a table for dinner, if I would be ok driving home. I was secretly pleased; she had always been a smiley, giggly drunk, and I was flattered by the responsibility.

"I feel fine," she said. The disease, she explained, lived as future possibility, not a present reality needing to be confronted. It was as if she'd been told she had a gene, not the thing itself. But she also made clear that she wished to speak of other things and soon was asking if I was sure that I wanted to major in history; if I planned to play intramural tennis again; if I was interested in a semester abroad. She said nothing about Sebastian's thesis, but I suppose it lingered in my mind, which is why—or maybe it was just Mom's openness—I asked about the fight with the Morrows, the friendship's collapse. "Mom, I remember once, a fight between you and Dad, over who ended it," I said. "Whether it was you or Dad."

"It was hard for both of us," she said, "but I think Dad had it worse. We both lost dear friends, but he also lost a fantasy. A friend and a dream. A piece of himself. I think that's why he couldn't see beyond the damage. But the truth is—and I've thought about this many times—I don't think reconciliation was possible. The trust was ruptured. Sometimes you have no choice but to walk away."

The slow sips of her drink. The serene face. The rejected sunglasses. The calm, reasonable words—Mom had always been philosophical. I could see it then. Could see a true self breaking through the fog of motherhood. Giggly but firm. Of the earth and the air. A spirit attuned to the essential frequencies and willing to discard all others. Mom was hard to emulate because it took so long to discover that she modeled anything at all; but when I did, I saw that her example was too subtle, too refined. I had no chance.

Despite her devastating revelation, those four days in the Hamptons were a blessed time. For what followed was cruel. The course of Mom's disease was entirely different than Dad's. His was like watching a sandcastle slowly eaten away by a rising tide. Hers was invisible erosion that you didn't notice until the structure had collapsed and the flood was already upon you.

That fall, as Dad lived his final days, Mom seemed unchanged. She hustled through the apartment, cooking, cleaning, bringing Dad his morning coffee, his TV dinner. She kept going to work. It was easy to forget that she was a patient too. She forbade me from staying home— we compromised: I returned home on weekends—and, after Dad passed away in October, she insisted I return to Ithaca when Shiva had ended. I was offered a brief internship at a San Francisco magazine for winter break. "Take it," she insisted. But only weeks later, back home for President's weekend, the sight of her shocked me. Her lush red hair had dulled brown and, though she would never admit it, thinned too. She looked like the victim of a scandalous facelift. A chemical smell emanated from her bathroom, the source of which I never discovered.

I didn't return to school that spring, and this time Mom didn't fight me. Some days she stubbornly cooked and ran errands as if nothing were going on. Other days, exhaustion made it hard for her to make it to the bathroom. Shortly before Passover, in a mood of peak obstinance, she insisted on going to the store for milk. Half an hour later, I got a call from a strange number. Mom had collapsed on the sidewalk. She had bruised her face and arm and was barely coherent. I reached her half a minute before an ambulance pulled up. She lay in a hospital bed for nearly a week, delirious the first day, then lucid and upbeat, begging to return home, the next five. Except for the bruises, she seemed fine, but the doctor said her cancer had advanced rapidly. We had to think about the end. Did I want her to return home or go to hospice? After a call with Becca, we decided on a full-time nurse at home, with daily visits from hospice beginning the following week.

Becca was at Cal Arts for an MFA. She came home as soon as her semester ended, skipping graduation, which she said was pointless. She didn't have a return ticket. "I'm staying as long as it takes," she said.

By then, Mom was mostly bedridden. When she was awake, Becca and I sat in her dark bedroom—Mom hated overhead lighting until the end—talking and reading to her. Becca was surprisingly adept at this. She seemed to know when to be solemn and when to lighten the mood with a joke. But as soon as Mom's eyes closed, Becca and I retreated to our separate bedrooms. We met in the kitchen for dinner, then separated a second time. We barely spoke when Mom wasn't with us.

Dad's decline had been drawn out but his end swift. Mom's trajectory had an entirely different shape, a steep descent, but right near the end, things slowed to a crawl. Later, I would remark that you could track each baby step of her passing. The last doctor visit. The last day she left the apartment. The last day she got out of bed. The last day she sat up. The last day she spoke. The last day she ate. The last day she opened her eyes.

When it became clear that she would live past Labor Day, I called the dean at Cornell to discuss taking off the first semester of my senior year. Mom begged me not to. "Won't it knock you off schedule?" she asked.

"What schedule?"

"Gabriel, you know what I mean. But I don't have the energy to fight."

The truth, which I didn't bother explaining, was that I had already sorted things out. Between packing a busy schedule in the spring and some AP credits from high school, I could graduate with my class, even if I missed the entire fall.

Mom died in early October, five days before the anniversary of Dad's death. The laying of his headstone had to wait until after her Shiva ended. Becca remained in New York afterward, helping with arrangements and keeping me company. After a few weeks, she returned to LA and I to Ithaca. I arrived on campus days before Halloween, then crammed a semester's worth of work into a month and a half. Friends kept coming around, asking me to go out to parties or bars, to campus theater and concerts, telling me I should get out, do anything, it would be a helpful distraction. But I preferred work. The library felt like the safer companion.

There was something else. It felt almost shameful to admit, but there were these odd feelings that I can only describe as bursts of joy that stole over me at the most unexpected moments. That I was alive. That I was young and healthy. That I had escaped the misfortune that had befallen Mom. I soon realized that I had experienced a similar sensation at Dad's passing and also, years earlier, as I became aware of Becca's turbulent adolescence and realized that it might have been cover for some inner anguish, some crippling despair. Which made sense, because the memory that came to mind, the moment I pictured during those earlier flashes of elation, was that morning in the Catskills, when I had seen the purple light and walked toward it. As a field appeared, and the light was rimmed with orange, I began to run, boundless, unrestrained, hurtling down the slopes, the morning sun warm on my cheeks. It was then that the familiar house had appeared, and running still, a full sprint, my feet unfazed by the squish of dew in my shoes, glorying in my panting breaths, I saw the Datsun. Our dusty, gassy Datsun, and I knew that soon we would be home.

15

The doorbell rang at 9:00 am. Catherine handed me her peacock over-coat and stepped into the foyer. She wore the same orange and blue dress as on the day we'd met on the street below my building, but her beatup Keds had been exchanged for elegant heels.

"Are you OK in those?" I asked.

"I have half a century of practice. I'll be fine." She handed me a shopping bag. "I hope you like pumpkin pie. I made it yesterday."

After a hug, fuller and more demonstrative than usual, I watched as she stepped into the living room, looking eagerly in all directions as her movements slowed, her steps, the twists of her neck and head, even the blinks of her eyes.

"Remind me," she said suddenly, as if yanking herself from a rev-erie. "Where's the kitchen?" Only then did it occur to me that during these many months of our re-acquaintance, I had yet to invite her over.

I pointed to the doorway on the left and followed her in.

"My, my." She brushed a hand along the marble countertop. "It's just as I remember. But there's something… maybe the wallpaper?"

The wallpaper had changed several decades prior, but whether this was before or after we had cut off the Morrows, I could hardly recall.

"There were stripes," she said. "All these bright lollipop colors… Or maybe I'm thinking of someplace else? It's been so long. Anyway, how amazing it must be to live in the same apartment all your life."

"But I haven't lived here all my life," I said.

"No, no, of course not. It's just…" She looked wistful as the words trailed off. "Maybe later, you'll show me the rest of the apartment. First things first, where's the turkey?"

I opened the fridge and lifted the heavy tin tray, a giant bird in a thick salt brine, just as she'd suggested.

And it had been her suggestion to invite others, to make Thanksgiving dinner into a party. I asked around tentatively, but to my surprise, my invitations brought forth tremendous expressions of relief—that a friend could avoid a long trip to California, or not have to wince through another family reunion, that a couple could escape the skeleton crew of malcontents who had become their holiday tribe. Even better, those who could come were the friends I felt most affinity with—not necessarily because we had once been close, but because they were now quasi-outsiders like me, slightly peripheral to the general flow of things. For instance, Laura and Carlos, two self-described "workaholic obsessive-compulsives" who actually convinced you when they claimed they'd be childless forever. Or Michael and Silvia—Michael, once a central cog in the college gang, but married to Silvia, who I sensed hadn't meshed with his closest pals (perhaps not coincidentally, she was the one significant other I'd hit it off with). Or Peter, still pining for an ex from three years prior, earning him the nickname "I'm not ready yet." "Yes," he practically shouted when I invited him. "Otherwise, it's back to Sebastian's, where I'll have to fight off another Sherrie setup attempt."

I carried the turkey to the counter, where Catherine joined me, standing so close I could see her chest rise with each breath. After months of friendship, I hardly expected to feel awkward in her presence, but there was something about her energy on this day, or perhaps it was the simple fact of standing beside her in my childhood kitchen, that felt new, like we stood on the threshold of … of what exactly? I suppose, some new intimacy. Or rather an older intimacy, a return to that time when she had been a surrogate mother-figure, except now with my mother gone forever, Catherine and I had been toeing this line for months. Had we finally crossed over?

"So, you're not a turkey fan either?" I said.

"One weekend a year is my limit. I permit leftovers through Sunday. Then I'm done."

"I hear brining changes everything."

"Let's make it through dinner before we start believing in fairy-tales."

I passed her a red-rimmed apron, which she slipped over her neck and tied tightly, before moving to inspect the stove and oven, the pans, the knives and cutting boards, the spice rack. She pre-heated the oven and grabbed the baster. "I returned to that club in Midwood last week," she said. "And guess what happened?"

"You won the tournament."

"Hardly. They were playing chess. Not a single backgammon player in the place. I don't know why I didn't anticipate that."

She grinned so wide that I could see the craggy tops of her molars. This felt like an apology of sorts, as if she were establishing parity between us, admitting that she too had received her comeuppance in that place.

The oven had reached 350, and, at Catherine's direction, I dumped the salt water and slid the turkey inside. She took a rainbow assortment of vegetables from the fridge, grabbed a knife and cutting board, and began chopping. She turned to the sweet potatoes. "How would you like them?"

"I'm not sure. Some friends are bringing a casserole."

"Then we won't mash. We can eat them with melted butter, baked-potato style, or cut them up and throw them in a salad."

"I like the salad idea."

"You got it, boss. Now what about the stuffing? Do you mind if I cook it separately, rather than putting it in the turkey?"

"You're in charge."

"But you'll help, won't you? I need a good sous-chef."

"Of course." But I was sous-chef in name only. Over the next hour, my primary responsibilities consisted of locating the occasional mixing bowl, measuring spoon, or serrated knife, and keeping her company— while she had the run of the kitchen. She sliced a head of broccoli, little green florets flying off in all directions. She got olive oil going on the stove and sautéed onion and celery for the stuffing. She chopped cauliflower and speared the sweet potatoes with a fork. She tore kale leaves from stalks, prepped baking sheets with layers of carrots and brussels for roasting, diced, spiced, and cooked an assortment of mushrooms. She was in a zone, zipping through the kitchen, in command and at ease. A joy to watch.

The timer sounded. Two hours had passed, though it felt like much less. "Would you pull the oven tray out?" she asked.

She held the baster, loaded it with turkey juice, and squirted the bird's every curve and crease. "Did you see how I did that?" she asked, as I slid the tray back in the oven. "Because that's your job. Every half hour, just like that. And the cranberry sauce."

Oh no. "The cranberry sauce? How do I do that?"

"Scoop it onto a platter and lay a spoon on its side. It's pre-made. Fool proof. The guests are coming at 4:00, right? I'll be back at 1:30 to finish the veggies and potatoes. The gravy and sides, too. Now, if you don't mind, this old lady needs to go home and nap."

Fool proof? Really? I felt certain that this was where I would screw everything up. "Do you want to nap here? Save you two trips."

"Are you sure?" She looked straight into my eyes, inquiring, and in that glance, I recognized an awareness that we again stood on the edge of our fraught history. *Which bedroom?* I couldn't have her go to mine—it was filthy, a week's worth of clothes strewn across the floor— and Becca's would have been a clear violation. So, I brought her to my parents' room but without naming it as such.

"The guest room," I said. "Will it do?"

"Of course."

Catherine faced the window looking onto the East River and the bright sky above. She turned to me wistfully and lowered herself onto the edge of the bed, where her body instantly seemed to fold into itself, as if a puppeteer had suddenly released her strings. The bed wasn't all that large, but I couldn't recall having ever seen her appear so thin and feeble. I stepped to the window to lower the blinds.

"Leave them," she said. "I like the view. You would think we had views like this in our bedrooms"—again, a reminder that despite our many visits, we hadn't once seen each other's homes—"But I don't, and this is special."

I waited a few seconds more, but she just gazed out the window. Pointing out the bathroom in the corner, I shut the door behind me.

Over the next two hours, I pulled the turkey from the oven every thirty minutes, basted it lavishly in its juice, pushed it back in. I neatened the corners of the counter where Catherine had placed various bowls and plates with afternoon ingredients and tightened the tin foil over the stuffing and salad. I prepared toast and cheese for lunch, then sliced an apple for dessert. I flipped through magazines and watched the start of the first football game. Mostly I leaned over the counter, nervously watching the oven timer.

A few minutes after 1:15, I heard the toilet flush, a door open, footsteps. They started and stopped, started and stopped again, circling me, without seeming to come any closer. Catherine was touring the apartment.

"I looked around," she said, appearing at the kitchen door, not quite ready to step through. "I hope you don't mind. The place has barely changed. So many memories…"

And yet, memory told me that this apartment had rarely been the friendship's true setting. I recalled Catherine once saying of New York, "A weekend a year is enough for me," as if our hometown were some second-tier poultry. And city references had never been part of the relationship—ballet at Lincoln Center, art house movies (even at 9, I knew that we only discussed whatever blockbuster was playing in the White Plains mall), the subway, the buses, this neighborhood or that. Likewise, I never understood the Morrows' suburban language of bikes and second cars, of lawn mowers, grungy garages, and daily commutes.

I didn't know how to compare their large house with musty corners to our smaller, more pristine apartment, or why the Morrow boys could wear sneakers and jeans to school, while we had a dress code, or why they played baseball and football but rarely basketball, or why they always complained that Katonah was "boring" but wanted to do nothing more, when they did visit us, than play boardgames, watch a VHS, and snack on Doritos. We might as well have been in the burbs.

But what we shared with the Morrows we shared with no one else— in a word, *home*. They saw us asleep on couches and chairs; they heard Dad's baritone snore and could tease Mom for her "stomach problems" without causing her to blush. With my parents' other friends, there was always some activity, some *occasion* (couples bridge on the first Friday of the month, a bagel brunch on Marathon Day, some regatta or July 4 fireworks to watch from our window onto the river), but the Morrows slipped into the seams of our lives. Some days we lay about the apartment with them, pursuing our separate, parallel quests, as we might with no guests at all.

Yet even as a child, I also saw that there were limits to this intimacy, spaces we did not share or gaps in our knowledge of one another. More than once, I thought about the fact that the Morrows saw us only on weekends, when Mom and Dad, after tense weeks, breathed more easily; when whispers of petty bosses, indecisive colleagues, and unappeasable clients suddenly ceased; when Mom splayed on the couch reading novels or disappeared into the kitchen to make beef stew or roast chicken or *real* bolognese sauce ("Don't mention the pork to Dad, OK?"); when Dad bestrode his armchair and listened to late Beatles (or the Mamas and Papas, the Byrds, Smokey Robinson, etc.) or muttered through gritted teeth as he "attacked" the *Times* crossword puzzle. Was that really us?

How odd, I always thought, that the Morrow boys considered Dad to be a cool guy who listened to hip music, when I knew him to be frequently short-tempered, a weekday stress case. How strange that Catherine expressed envy at Mom's "way in the kitchen," given that five

nights a week Mom complained about how little time she had to prepare anything and frequently gave up and ordered Chinese.

The same had to be true for them too, right? There had to be more
to their lives than leisurely meals and weekend putzing around the
house. Even as a kid, I picked up hints—"concerns" about the boys,
Catherine's loneliness, money struggles—but I saw no evidence of it
when we got together. If tempestuous Becca could somehow present
herself as a well-behaved though strong-willed girl, preserving her tantrums for only us three, I figured the Morrows still had to know the
truth, right?—because Mom said something; because they could simply
feel it—I mean, how could they not?

But what if I was wrong?

On the hourlong drive home from Katonah, we Staubs often slipped
into what Becca called "a stresserfall," a sudden outpouring of tension,
as if it had all been bottled up the preceding 48 hours, and I began to
question if we'd really been ourselves in front of the Morrows, as opposed to some gang of genial, weekend imposters. So, did they know
us? Did we know them? Did we have any idea what happened once they
gave their final wave and slunk down the hallway as we backed out of
their driveway? Once you started with these questions, you quickly
crashed down a rabbit hole, wondering what it meant to know another
person at all. If we didn't know the Morrows, did we know anyone?
Even ourselves?

"I see these scenes with Becca," Catherine was saying. "Disappearing into her bedroom for long stretches and thinking we wouldn't
notice. I would think of her after a visit ended. How unusual she was,
and what that must have meant for the rest of you. Your parents worried. How could they not?"

"Don't all parents worry about their kids?" I said cautiously, concerned about the direction the conversation was taking. "Didn't you
worry about Kyle and JT?"

"Of course, every child presents unique challenges," she said. "My
boys have given me plenty. But Becca was different. *Is different.*"

"What do you know about her?"

My words had an edge, and Catherine smiled enigmatically. "Gabriel, please. There are friends I've lost touch with, who I hear about secondhand, but I *read* about Becca. And every time, I think, 'I saw her on training wheels. I saw her with missing front teeth. I watched her bawl when we reached the bottom of the ice cream tub.' But the unusual part about your sister isn't the fame, it's that nothing about her surprises. She's always been beyond surprises, hasn't she?"

With that, Catherine finally stepped into the kitchen. She poured a coffee and took a long sip, before looking at me, her eyes lively, glimmering in the light. "Tell me, Gabriel, was it hard for you... to live with someone so... exceptional?"

"Catherine, I don't want to have that conversation. I'm—"

"Very well."

She placed her coffee mug in the sink, washed her hands, reached for the knife and cutting board, and again began chopping vegetables. She lined a baking tray with foil, placed the sweet potatoes on top, and slid it in the oven. But then she looked up suddenly and said, "Gabriel, there is one thing I must ask."

She held my gaze, and I felt a rush of anxiety.

"Can we skip football?" she said. "Promise me? Not a minute of those horrible games."

She wore a wide, self-aware smile, and I nodded at her joke.

"By the way, did I tell you about San Diego? It's warm, sunny, water everywhere—*holiday land*, I call it. But when Sunday rolls around, they go football mad like some tiny town in Texas or Nebraska. It's bewildering. Why would anyone want to ruin a Sunday, let alone Thanksgiving, with that brutal game?"

I told her there would be no football, and she pinched my cheek. "Thank you," she mouthed.

After that, she declared it was "time to focus," and soon she was buzzing through the kitchen, counter to oven, stove to sink, back to counter, working half a dozen dishes at once. It became clear that she envisioned a much grander meal than I had understood, even as I had shopped for the ingredients on her list. Not only turkey, stuffing, sweet potato, cranberry, and salad; somehow, there would also be carrots and toasted almonds, roasted brussels with herbs and parmesan, a spicy braised kale and scallion in coconut oil and soy sauce. Again, I sous-chefed, which meant performing the occasional mini-chore (*Where's the salt, Gabriel? Do you have a slotted spoon? Should we fill a pitcher with water?*). But mostly I watched as she glided through the kitchen—selecting which plates to use, comparing the wide wine goblets to the narrow ones with gold trim, recalling and then asking again and again until I finally found it in some dark closet corner, a particular crystal pitcher, which she filled with ice cubes, cucumber slices, and water, then placed it in the fridge to cool. As the clock hit 3:30, she began hunting through cabinets and the fridge herself. She located serving trays, cheese and dessert knives; filled a bowl with olives and a platter with raw vegetables; whipped up a dip from Greek yogurt and leftover herbs; trimmed four rinds of cheese and arranged them on a tray as if they had had been purchased for this occasion. (*We need hors d'oeuvres, right? Why not set these out in the living room for people to pick at before the meal?*) At the backgammon tournament, I had marveled at how she always seemed to know where to go, what to say, how to move, both herself and her pieces; but in this Thanksgiving kitchen, she achieved an entirely new level of bravura. Chopping, whisking, stirring, basting, tossing, plating, she exhibited Becca-level virtuosity. In command and at flow. A total absence of strain.

The buzzer sounded at 4:00 pm sharp. Derrick and Patricia, punctual as ever. I brought them into the kitchen to meet Catherine, but she told us to go to the living room and enjoy the hors d'oeuvres. Peter arrived minutes later. Then Vic and Helene. Then Michael and Silvia. The same script played out with each: a greeting at the door, the presentation of a bottle of wine (plus, from Derrick and Patricia, the promised sweet potato casserole, and from Michael and Silvia, an unexpected apple pie), an introduction to Catherine in the kitchen, hellos to the others in the living room. I carried wine and glasses to the living room, and time slipped by. Somehow two bottles of wine had emptied, and we were nearing the bottom of a third when Catherine finally appeared in the living room, ready to accept a goblet of her own.

"Cheers."

She made the rounds, clinking glasses one by one, always with eye contact, as if honoring whatever superstition the lack of it supposedly implied. Her hair seemed prepped anew, her clothes were smoothed, her sleeves buttoned at the wrist, yet her left hand still clutched a wooden spoon. "Are you ready to eat?" she asked.

"It smells so good."

"First, sit, Catherine. Give yourself a break."

"Can I make you a plate of munchies?" Helene asked.

"Did you make the vegetable dip?" Laura asked. "It's wonderful."

"Thank you," said Catherine. "I can't sit just yet. I need fifteen more minutes." Leaving her goblet atop a bureau, she and the wooden spoon returned to the kitchen.

Fifteen minutes, she had said, but somehow this became another half hour, which I only noticed when the grandfather clock in the corner of the living room chimed 6:00 PM. I led the group, all of us a bit tipsy, into the dining room, where Catherine was arriving with a salad bowl. Her apron was back on. A headband held back her hair, though a single gray lock had escaped and tumbled over an eyebrow.

"Excellent timing," she said. "I'll need help with the turkey. It's a monster."

"Gabriel and I can take care of it," said Peter. "It's time for you to relax and enjoy yourself."

But Catherine followed us into the kitchen and remained there as we carried the turkey to the dining room. After a few minutes, I returned to the kitchen and found her staring into the sink basin; the faucet off, the room silent.

"Catherine," I called to her.

She faced me with a smile, but her eyes immediately fled to the floor. "Go on," she said. "I just need a minute."

"But Catherine—"

"Go visit with your guests. I'm sure they would be happy to see you."

"I'm sure they would be happy to see you." A perfect echo of so many years earlier, that night in the Catskills, when she had used the identical phrase to urge me from the dinner table down to the basement, to claim my rightful place among the other kids—a seemingly meaningless action but one that might have set in motion the very set of circumstances that had torn us apart.

Back then, Catherine had been trying to ease my doubts, sharing her confidence with me, telling me that I, though only 11, belonged among those teenagers; whereas now, those same words oozed melancholy, as if some implacable wistfulness had overwhelmed her and she was preemptively declaring defeat.

When she appeared in the dining room a few minutes later, we had assumed our seats but not disturbed a single dish. This was less politeness than some communal awareness that the splendor of that table had to be savored before it was ravished. The pitchers, the napkins, the goblets—it was my parents wedding china, their cutlery and tablecloths, all of it spruced up by some aesthetic sense possessed by Catherine, such that it had somehow found its inner beauty while hiding its 1970s tackiness.

And the food—nine abundant dishes, each neat in its tray with a pretty serving utensil to the side, an array of color and textures. The sort of spread you might see in a food magazine, the work of an artist who had used her full palette. There was even a dish whose preparation I'd entirely missed, a pastry loaf, which when sliced into revealed a bed of mushrooms between the flaky crust—"a Fungington," Carlos called it, as odors of earth and butter spilled out.

Derrick began a rambling paean to the "beautiful table setting," which concluded with calls for a picture. He took out his phone and snapped away. First the table setting, then, gathering us at one end of the table, the entire group. He propped his phone against a tray, set it on timer, and told us to smile for a "Selvies."

I carved the turkey. The side dishes made the rounds. We ate.

The meat was moist and delicious. The sides fresh and crisp, or warm and savory. Everything was exactly how it should be, but also fresher, tastier, juicier.

"Derrick," Peter said after a few silent minutes. "How do we take a picture of *this*? How do we capture this… I don't know what to call it… divine sustenance?"

"Ambrosia," said Derrick, his mouth full. "It's Olympian. Amazing."

It was the standout Thanksgiving of my life. And surely of everyone else, too. The compliments continued over the duration of the meal. And these were hardly your typical, perfunctory dinner-party compliments, but genuine expressions of joyous surprise. When we circled the table offering thanks, Vic, a smoker, said, "I want to thank Catherine for helping me rediscover my taste buds." Derrick and Patricia's sweet potato casserole so clearly stood apart as the work of a lesser cook, though it was actually pretty good. And yet could they really care? It was like feeling bad about your sketch after seeing Becca's contemporaneous attempt.

As good as the food was, the spirit of the meal was at least its equal. The free-flowing wine, the steady conversation, the easygoing atmosphere—it was probably the most joyful time since my return to New York, an evening in which self-consciousness, as faithful a companion as my shadow, actually let me be for long stretches of time. At recent gatherings, often with these same people, there was always someone who undermined, or judged, or needled, who enjoyed sprinkling a few drops of disquiet into the air. This meal lacked any such complication. It was the sort my father used to extol when he rhapsodized about friendship—the very sort when he would have told his famous story of the Morrows and Staubs—and a sign, when I left the moment and entered a more reflective space, of what was possible, even for me.

Everyone shared in this spirit. Radiant eyes, pure laughter, relaxed talk, flowing like many streams into a single riverbed. Everyone but Catherine. She barely spoke. If right before the meal, she had repeated the very words that had sent me down to the basement in the Catskills so many years earlier, from that moment forward, she had assumed *my role* once I got to that basement—the odd man out, separated from the others by age and experience, forgotten in the corner.

Lost in the haze of food and wine, connected to the others in the flow of laughter and conversation, I mostly overlooked this. And Catherine skillfully interjected the odd word here or there as if having mastered that quintessential introvert lesson: that quiet draws less attention than silence. Seated on my side of the table, but with chubby Derrick between us, she often fell out of view, and for long stretches I barcly recalled her presence. Other times, I'd see her hunched in the corner, frail arms stiff at her side, barely uttering a word, and try to understand what had become of my chatty afternoon companion, my sometime confessor, the seemingly youthful spirit who had been reduced to a sad, sullen wallflower, and on this evening that she had requested and shaped. Was the conversation too quick? Were the references too obscure? No, I had been with her in the East River Home with words flying in all directions. Was it her hearing? No, we had been in crowded restaurants and coffee houses. Was it slowness of mind? Hardly. Something else was happening, a shyness I hadn't known before, a reticence, a retreat. Was it the aura of this house, the weight of the past?

When it was her turn to share words of thanks, she raised her glass and said, "To friends, new and old"—how I wanted to read into this, to feel her joining our joy, but it was mere cliché, giving just enough not to draw undue attention. More than once, I tried to coax her into participation, only to receive an inscrutable smile in response. Other tried, too. Silvia and Peter asked about her family, where she lived, her impressions of New York. Catherine's answers were polite, but terse, and they moved on. Amid the wine, food, and laughter, it was easy to forget Catherine's silence; it was easy to forget she was there at all.

The meal lasted hours. Michael had fourths. Most others had thirds. Only Catherine stopped after seconds. We finished six bottles of wine and were midway down a seventh. Catherine and Silvia helped me clear the plates. We stacked them by the kitchen counter after I insisted they not worry about the dishwasher. I brewed coffee and tea. We carried out dessert: apple pie brought by Michael and Silvia, pumpkin pie made by Catherine. One from the finest bakery in the neighborhood, the other made at the East River Home the day before. You couldn't tell them apart. Michael, who had claimed not to like pumpkin pie, declared a willingness to reconsider—and to reconsider again.

Again, we cleared the plates. Again, I had to warn off Catherine and Silvia from doing the dishes. We returned to the living room, everyone settling in the same spots as when they'd arrived, with Catherine at first refusing a spot on the couch, claiming it was already too crowded, and only consenting to sit when Carlos carried in a dining-room chair. We sat in quiet serenity. It was hard to say anything beyond how stuffed we were, how satisfied. It is odd how language fails when we are most content.

We finished wine bottle seven and uncorked lucky eight. Peter suggested we watch football, but Catherine shot me a look.

"You promised," she said.

"Promised what?" Laura asked.

"It's true," I said. "No pigskin. Sorry."

"Thank you, Catherine," said Helene. "For the second time this evening, you're my hero."

It was nice to see Catherine flash her gracious smile, but even then, she didn't really meet Helene's eye, and silence filled the room. Laura began to detail her Black Friday plans (apparently, she had half a dozen nieces and nephews to buy gifts for). There followed talk of some app that could tell you how crowded stores were in real time, but the room was seeping energy fast. Derrick and Patricia announced that they were "conquered by wine and turkey." Within minutes, the others had also stood to leave. A round robin of hugs, a chorus of thank yous, and out the door they went.

All except Catherine. She had hugged everyone goodbye, she had stood by the door and waved as they walked to the elevator. I expected her to announce her departure, but instead she asked to help with the dishes.

"You've done enough, Catherine. Please leave me something to do."

"But it's no trouble at all. Don't be silly."

She marched to the kitchen, leaned over the sink, began to scrub. I followed her in and reached for a sponge, but she swatted my hand, as if she were the host and *I* the solicitous guest. She wiped down the kitchen counters until they glistened, then took out a broom and dustpan. It was too much, a parody of her earlier excellence, and I was sad that we had reached this point, which recalled the dreary end of our trip to King's Highway.

Wanting her to stop, wanting to be alone, but also unable to kick her out, I suggested a nightcap.

"Do you have cognac?" she asked.

We returned to the living room, sat of facing couches, clinked glasses, and sipped.

"What's that?" she said after some time, pointing to a tattered picture album on the bookshelf. "May I see?"

They were ancient pictures: Becca as a baby in a green onesie atop a plaid blanket; or later, a little girl with pigtails, cuddling a swaddled baby, who was me. There were pages of pictures with an arty feel, the subjects uncentered, some backgrounds flatter than you'd expect, others hazy as if plucked from a dream sequence, all taken during the two-year stretch before my birth when Dad had fancied himself a photographer. Then, it was back to standard family shots, candids that were a little too posed and portraits not quite posed enough, plus the occasional picture marking a summer rental or the pine-needled path we were about to hike on, or a view from the hilltop where we had picnicked, or the Datsun, windshield dusty and stuffed with suitcases, or some country lake with a hard-to-pronounce Indian name.

"Are there others?" she asked after turning the final page.

"In closets. This was the one my parents always kept out."

"I was curious if I'd see myself," she said with a forced smile. "With black hair and high cheeks, can you imagine? But most of that album is from before we met your parents. Before *I* met your parents. It happened right before you were born. Do you know that?"

"Of course. Dad used to tell the story."

"Yes, your father was always telling that, wasn't he? But, Gabriel, do you know my version?"

"Is it different?"

"Not what happened. But how it felt. What the friendship meant… to me." She placed her glass, now empty, on the table between us. "Do you mind?"

"Not at all," I answered, thinking that she was asking about putting her glass on the wooden surface, without a coaster.

"You aren't too tired? You have time?" she asked, and I realized my error.

Her eyes shimmered as they had that morning when she'd arrived, and I wondered if all of the day's drama, from her star turn in the kitchen to her withdrawal at the table, was mere prelude to this.

"Go on," I said. "I'd love to hear."

16

"Fine," I said. "Then I'll do it like Dad. In his words."

Dr. Marks, the shrink I began seeing a few weeks after Dad announced his cancer, had complained for weeks that, though I'd already told the story of the Catskills several times, whenever it came to Dad's story, the one about the Morrows and Staubs, I skipped right over it. Finally, I was relenting.

"However you want," he said. "I'm all ears."

"Ok, here goes." I cleared my throat and tried to mimic Dad's scratchy voice:

"*So, I transferred to Cornell for sophomore year, and it wasn't an easy adjustment. But there was this pretty girl in my American History seminar, Diane Silverstein, who had a dimple in her left cheek and laughed at my wry retorts to the prof, and I somehow got it into my head that she was the key, well, to everything: to fitting in, to making this whole college thing work, to being happy. A few days later I worked up the nerve and invited her to a party. It was a warm fall evening. The house was packed and sweaty. Diane and I were in the backyard of this giant house, sipping beer from plastic cups. I heard her slurp the bottom of her cup. "Can I get you a refill?" I asked. The line at the keg moved quickly enough, but when I looked back Diane was gone. I'm tall and can generally see above crowds, plus Diane had curly blond hair tied in a purple bandana—you couldn't miss her. I looked everywhere, left, right, up, down. Finally, I spotted her on the porch, bandana off, hair down, talking with a guy, leaning in close. He was handsome and tan. He wore a rugby shirt and had a killer smile. I knew I had to move quick. 'Hi Diane,' I said seconds later, presenting the beer only to realize she already had a drink in hand. She barely acknowledged me, didn't even introduce me to her new friend. Confused and distraught, I retreated to a quiet corner of the yard to gather my thoughts. After a few minutes, I found my determination and went back, but again Diane was gone. This time, nowhere to be found. They were both gone. Vanished like a poof of smoke. Anyway, that's how I met Alan.'*

"Then Alan would jump in. That's the thing, Dr. Marks. Dad began telling the story, but the other adults had their parts, too. Alan said this:

"No, no, no. It was like this. I'm walking across the quad in the fall of my sophomore year. It's early October, one of those first chilly days, and this guy runs up to me, a gangly guy tall enough to play basketball but much too awkward, and says, 'You broke the code.'

"I give him a long look. He's a head taller than me, his body's a series of herky-jerk motions, he has elephant ears and rings of curly black hair way too long for his own good. Not the sort you'd meet and forget. 'You must have the wrong guy,' I say. 'I've never seen you before.'

'No, it's you. I'm sure it's you. You broke the code between men.'

"I keep walking, but he refuses to let me go. He follows me into the cafeteria, and when I take my tray to an empty table, sending what I thought was a clear signal, he sits next to me, not across from me but next to me, like in a theater. 'The code between men is simple,' he says. 'You don't steal another man's woman, you just don't, even if the situation is ambiguous.' He insists that everyone knows this, that the world can't function if people don't follow these sorts of rules. 'It's a first principle,' he says. 'You can build an entire ethical structure around it.' He doesn't stop, the code, ethics, some theoretical gibberish I've long since forgotten, interrupting himself only to tell me that mayo is disgusting, I should put mustard on my sandwich instead. Eventually he turns to his plate and digs into his roast beef sandwich—and with passion: he eats like he

speaks. At least I can finally get a word in. I explain that I went to a house party Saturday night and met plenty of girls, but they all seemed unaccompanied. He slams his sandwich on his plate, blurts out a girl's name— not one I recognized—and gives this long hard stare. At this point, I'm no longer scared, just weirded out. He's the farthest thing from mellow you could imagine, but I suppose he's charming in his way. I decide to stare right back. We both stick with it at least a minute; he turns away first. He shrugs, takes a giant bite from the second half of the sandwich, and starts back again about the code. He explains that he's developing some proposal to protect passions with the same sort of legal structure that existed for property. 'We need rights about passions,' he says, slamming his fist on the table. 'Affirmative ones. It's a key to solidarity, fraternity. Exactly what our society lacks. That's how Jonah and I met.'"

I had been seeing Dr. Marks for a few months. We were meant to talk about Dad's illness, but I found it so much easier to discuss the Catskills. I could tell the tale of my time in the woods on autopilot. But not Dad's story. Recounting it for the first time to Dr. Marks made me totally self-conscious, and though I knew his friendly eyes were only a few feet away, I looked everywhere else, touring the room's already familiar visual landmarks: the Egyptian scarab he used as a paperweight, the bulky answering machine, today with a blinking light, the many rows of dustjacket-less books on his shelf, a good half of them, it seemed, about "development" of some sort, the dirty window blinds that kept the room insulated and dim.

"They went on a while longer, Dad and Alan," I said, realizing I still had a ways to go to complete the story. "They would talk about how they became friends, super-close, roommates, inseparable. At college and after. Then the slow drift. 'It was circumstance, mostly,' Dad always said. Alan moved to Seattle for work, met Catherine, moved with her to Sacramento, they got married, had a kid, moved to Dallas, had a second kid, moved to Virginia. Meanwhile Dad remained in New York the whole time, single into his 30s, living an entirely different life. The old friends tried to write, tried to call, but it was tough. They drifted further and eventually lost track of each other entirely."

From the corner of my eye, I saw Dr. Marks lean back in his chair, clasping his hands on his lap.

"Still with me?" I asked. "Because now comes the other key moment."

"Of course."

"I'll try again with the voices. This is Catherine's part:

"*I didn't want to leave Virginia. My parents were half an hour away. We could go to the family farm on weekends. After moving so many times, we'd finally found a place we loved. But when the opportunity came to go to New York, I did a complete 180. Still, I insisted on the suburbs. I was nervous that the city itself would be too big a change. We had moved a lot, but this one was more of a challenge. I usually made friends through activities. Hobbies, clubs, stuff for the boys. But when we arrived in Westchester, the boys were older and didn't need me as much, or maybe New Yorkers are just too busy, too cold. Who knows? The upshot is that for a good year I was lonely and bored and started going to the city in my spare time. Museums, restaurants, movies. Sometimes I'd sit on a park bench or walk around for hours. I took a pottery class and an aerobics class. These weren't particular interests of mine; I just wanted an opportunity to meet people. I was twice the age of most students in the pottery class, but at the aerobics studio they were others just like me, middle-aged mothers, lonely though unwilling to admit it. I asked a few to join me for coffee or lunch. A couple said yes, but there was always something off. They were in a rush, we never connected.*

"*Then one day, this woman, who had mostly avoided my friendly smiles until then, points to a book poking out of my bag. 'How is it?' she asked. The truth is, I hadn't read past the back cover; all I knew was that it was a memoir about taking care of a dying stepmother. 'Good so far,' I lied. 'I'm happy to lend it when I'm done.' She nodded and looked to the door. I figured she was about to say how busy she was and run off; instead, she launched into this story about how that writer had 'changed the course of my life,' about how, before she became a lawyer, she had worked for a publisher and bid on that writer's first book but lost out, which basically caused her to go to law school. As she spoke, I realized I'd* gotten her all wrong. Those times she'd turned from my smiles, she was being shy, not arrogant. Unlike many New Yorkers, she didn't seem to enjoy talking about herself and shifted quickly back to the writer, who apparently received glowing reviews on that first book, but it didn't sell well and afterward had sort of disappeared. No second novel. The woman figured the writer had given up. I handed her the book and watched as she flipped through it, read the first few paragraphs, examined the spine. 'Good for her,' she said. 'I'm glad she stuck with it.'

"I thought our conversation was over, but she didn't leave. She looked at me and said, 'You know, there's something else about the writer. She played a very minor, very bizarre role in my husband's life.' And she began to talk about an incident that had happened to her husband in college. Which sounded shockingly familiar."

"Then Mom jumped in:

"That writer was Diane Silverstein. Catherine didn't know the name because it wasn't part of Alan's version of the meeting with Jonah, whereas Jonah and I had discovered the odd coincidence years earlier and already had a million laughs about it. But now, outside that aerobics class, Catherine and I began to put one and one together. I suggested a couple's dinner and felt such relief to see she was as excited as me. We decided to make it a surprise, and I've got to tell you, I don't think the men recognized each other at first. They'll deny it, but they shook hands politely, nodded, sat down. Even when they realized, they were quiet, both of them. But Jonah was so happy. Alan too. Beaming. Like little boys on their birthdays.

"Shortly after, we invited the Morrows to visit us, and that's when the kids met. And well, it's been what... ten years now? And here we are."

"It could easily have ended there, but of course Dad needed to have the final word. He'd say:

'There's one more detail, an amazing one. The title of the book by Diane Silverstein, the second one that reunited the two families? Providence. Because that's where her stepmother lived, where she went to care for her when she was ill.'"

I had finished, and the prospect of meeting Dr. Marks eyes was too much for me. I looked to the door and felt a sudden desire to jump to my feet and bolt.

"So, what does it mean to you?" he asked.

I had no idea how to answer, but the ensuing silence was intolerable, and I just started to talk. I said that Dad's story was all about good luck and how things just sort of worked out in the end, they just seemed fated to unfold in a fortunate way, and that was how I thought the world worked when I was a kid. But after that weekend in the Catskills, the lesson seemed entirely wrong; instead, life was random and chaotic, often cruel. That weekend in the Catskills seemed to mark a crossing from the time of good fortune to one of bad fortune, from the gift of friendship to the loss of friendship, and onto Becca's wild years, and Dad's illness. It was like a chain, each thing connected to the next, all pointing downward. So, I felt sure that more bad was soon to come. (This was all before I'd even heard that Mom was sick.)

Dr. Marks listened patiently, and only when I'd finished did he offer his thoughts. And he offered them gradually, cautiously, over several future conversations, rather than all at once, allowing me ample space to respond. He said that Dad had a story that he liked to tell over and over, and that I had one, too. But he said that Dad's story was positive and hopeful, whereas mine was cramped and bleak. He said that Dad performed his story for a public and got others to join in, whereas I whispered mine as if it were some shameful secret, safe to share only in backrooms with a few friends, a girlfriend, and now him. Perhaps most significantly, my story was a continuation of Dad's. It completed it. Even if my story was dark and sad, it was a tribute, nonetheless. Surely, that meant something, didn't it? And how had it felt, Dr. Marks wanted to know, to give voice to Dad's words, to conjure his presence, to bring him to life? "Like he's in this very room with us," he said.

In this way—skillfully, I recognized in retrospect—Dr. Marks succeeded in steering our conversation back to Dad and his sickness and how it made me feel. Which helped, I guess. We spent the next year or two working through some of my anger and fear. Which made those years of high school a bit less dismal. But Dr. Marks never led me to discover a positive and hopeful story of my own, nor did he cure my obsession with the Catskills saga. If anything, he just helped me add a new chapter, as I incorporated the telling of Dad's story into my own.

* * *

At Cornell, I saw a Dr. Fleckstein, and it was more of the same. After hearing about the Catskills a few times, he asked the obvious question (the same one my friends kept asking): why was I obsessed with an event that had affected others so much more than it had me? I wasn't the one who got lost. I wasn't the one who lost a best friend. I wasn't the one who was dying. So why was I the one who was obsessed?

He had me focus on the time in the Catskills itself, not the imagined afterstory, and together we reconstructed the events that led Becca and me into the woods and then what happened there, culminating with the still unexplained mystery of whether I had left her, or she'd left me, the lingering uncertainty over which of us had violated the sibling code. Dr. Fleckstein, whom I called Roy, had a smooth, boyish face and reddish nails bitten to the quick. He won my trust and helped me identify the feelings that the story evoked in me. *Guilt*—that I had left Becca, and in so doing, unleashed the events that had seemingly caused so much harm to my family. *Fear*—that if such a thing could happen to Becca (and to Dad and Mom), then it could happen to me, too. Then he helped me see the illogic of those very feelings. How could I possibly be responsible for whatever had happened to Becca in the woods, let alone to Dad and Mom years later? That strange night was no omen, just a freak event. Finally, he helped me recognize that the vulnerabilities I might have had at 11 no longer applied to the college-aged me, who would have easily found his way out. Also: *cell phones*.

That summer, days before we went to the Cape for what would turn out to be our final family vacation, an email arrived. Roy was moving to Berkeley. He offered phone sessions but suggested I find someone new in Ithaca and concluded his note with a few names and numbers.

I pretended not to care, but the very thought of him enraged me and I never wrote back. Still, when I returned to campus in the fall, I tried the numbers he'd given me and made an appointment with the first person to respond. Leigh was older than Roy but still young enough to be attractive, which made me nervous, as did the way she leaned forward in her chair, right into the no-man's-land between us. At first, we talked about my feelings of abandonment toward Roy, but then we shifted to normal college stuff and of course all the chaos back home. Before I knew it, the Catskills was again front of mind.

"That's very interesting," she said when I finished recounting the story. "But you spoke so much about everyone else. It's hard for me to tell what it means to you."

She suggested a thought experiment: what if I stripped the memory of the other characters so that I could see myself more clearly. I was mystified by her request, but soon she had helped me to reimagine the key moments without the presence of others, almost as if they were forest sprites rather than human beings. So, instead of sitting in the dark woods with my slippery sister, I was only beside a knobby root at the base of a tree, which did not move, talk, flicker the flashlight for amusement. Instead of JT and Dad trudging through the woods before me in single file, there was just a breeze that gusted intermittently, bending branches and leaves, opening a path. Or, at the farm, there was no one before me watching horses, just a lone fence post, disconnected from the others but oddly left standing, as if to mark a lookout point, from which I spied those beautiful beasts.

"Close your eyes and imagine," she said. "How do you feel?"

"Alone."

Obviously. I had voided a seminal memory of others; of course, I was alone. But that's not what I meant. I was *aware* of being alone—even as I was among others. It didn't matter if JT was with us on that starry field, if Kyle and Connor were still looking for us in the dark woods, if Becca leaned against the opposite side of the tree. It didn't matter—none of it mattered—because all the while I was alone. I always had been.

"And how does alone feel?"

Leigh asked me to stay in the moment, to concentrate on whatever came to mind. Eventually I described a sensation of insecurity, an unsettledness almost physical in nature. That was how alone made me feel. Which I recognized because it was how I felt so goddamn often. It was how I felt right then, facing Leigh as she leaned toward me, her eyes wide and emotive, her freckled face resting on the pedestal of her open palm. It was how I felt when Dad told me that he was sick and dying, and it was how I felt walking, my head bent, through school hallways, or as the crosstown bus passed from city grid into Central Park, or as I stumbled from the nightly news to some crappy 70s sitcom with the remote, or all too often as I lay in bed and closed my eyes.

What I found in the Catskills was a premonition of the sadness that would steal over me at the oddest moments, blanketing everything, as unseen dew wets a field in the cover of night. "It was," I declared grandiosely, "my first real memory." Not that I didn't remember my life beforehand, but all earlier memories featured some character who was not quite the me I had become. *My* first real memory. Paradoxically, the night I got lost in the Catskills was the night I found myself, the person I still was.

* * *

Winter break of my senior year, a few months after my mother's death, Becca was waiting for me at home, just as she'd promised when we'd parted after Mom's Shiva. Over the next three weeks, we ran around New York—restaurants, bars, clubs, a hill in Central Park where teenagers sledded at dusk, a movie theater where we binged four Christmas releases in a single day—the sorts of things that kids unencumbered by parents might do. We hung out at home with giant bowls of popcorn and heaping plates of Nachos and watched James Bond and Indiana Jones and Star Wars and The Godfather, or sprawled on the couch, covered in blankets, spreading out at a right angle from the same shared pillow, reading or listening to Discmen or gazing out the window. We fell asleep, side by side, on our parents' old bed. For the first time in years, my mind wasn't running to the Catskills. Between Leigh and Becca, the story was losing its grip on me.

Some of my college friends had moved to the city, and one night I took Becca to a party. She was surprisingly socially adept, and more than once, a classmate approached me to say something like, "I feel compelled to report how cool your sister is." *Smart, incisive, accomplished, amazing*—over the course of the night I heard the litany of compliments that had clung to Becca throughout my childhood, except without any suggestion of her dark side, which to me was as fundamental to the real her. (Even odder was when Casper, an occasional tennis partner, said that Becca was cute, he liked her "pizazz," and began fishing around for her relationship status.) At first, I didn't recognize the Becca my friends were describing, but then I had to concede that there was something to it.

So, was Becca the shrimp, Becca of slammed doors and silent treatments, Becca of that night in the Catskills, Becca the victim, left behind, wandering aimlessly, a thing of the past, just like the version of me that obsessed about that weekend in the Catskills? *If only*. Life offered no such absolutes, and it was only too plain when we were alone that Becca would never fully tame the black dog. But partial change? Sure. Our parents were gone, and her career was in a rush of early success. She had traded the shadows and wind tunnels of New York for LA's unrelenting sunshine. She'd become a lighter soul.

On Christmas Eve, we went to Chinatown, where an enormous second-floor banquet hall was filled with others just like us—Jews, atheists, Chinatown locals. The revelry spilled from table to table, and we fell in with a group of eight, probably closer to Becca's age than mine. I didn't catch every name, but "you" sufficed, and I was more than happy to forgo our plan of attending midnight mass (which we had done with our parents) to accompany the others to a karaoke bar, where we sang loudly and off key until dawn—well, everyone except Becca, who somehow managed to command the stage as she belted out "No Sleep 'Til Brooklyn." I woke the next morning to the garlicky aroma of something

Becca called "hangover soup," the ingredients of which she wouldn't reveal. "You liked it, didn't you? Isn't that enough?"

Over the next days, more of the same. Becca and me cruising the Fifth Avenue holiday windows, boozy afternoons at swanky hotel bars, long meals at hip restaurants, a second movie-theater binge, lounging at home with cold pizza and more hangover soup, watching more Bond and Indiana Jones, turning down the volume at key moments, so we could recite the script out loud. It was a joyous, nonstop run, and there were long stretches when I simply forgot about Mom and Dad. Just forgot entirely. For minutes, even hours at a time.

Back at school in the spring, I spoke often with Becca on the phone, and she gave me the gift that none of those shrinks could offer: a vision of the future. Between Mom's death and the cramming to graduate on time, I'd put so little thought into the question that haunted my friends—*what next?* There had been a time, before the shit really hit the fan, when I'd considered a junior year abroad, and this became the spark of inspiration for the idea that took hold. There were other reasons, too—to get away, to have an adventure, to mark a new phase of life with a new beginning, to experience some of the childhood that had been robbed of me. Like Becca, I had creative ambition, though unlike her I had no clear path, only vague sentimental notions. Would I write a cycle of short stories? personal essays? a screenplay? Make a movie? Take up photography? I had some ideas and few obligations. My parents' early passing had left an inheritance; I didn't *need* a job. I had time to figure things out.

"Paris?" I said dreamily when she asked about my plans. "Isn't that where restless young Americans like me go?"

"Where will you live?" she asked. "What'll you do?"

I was taken aback until I saw that she wasn't trying to dissuade me but rather to help refine the practical details necessary to give my dream a chance to flourish. Soon she was sending me rental listings, information about a French immersion class, recommending a favorite luggage store, reminding me to double check the date of my passport.

She joined me in New York after my graduation, just as she had the previous winter break. "The apartment can be yours," she said. "I'm lucky," she said. "I don't need it." She'd settled in LA and had already begun the globetrotting life of an art star; her portion of the inheritance would last some time. "Also, you have a place to stay in Culver City, whenever you want. There's a guest room, you know."

When I assured her that my heart was set on going abroad, she found a management company to vet and take care of potential subtenants. She also suggested the one unusual stipulation of the lease: We would reserve the apartment for ourselves one week a year—right around Christmas. The tenants would have to temporarily vacate, so that we could return home together, just like we had six months earlier. In this way, I saw, she was helping to clarify our future—*our shared future*. We would live in different cities but reunite for regular visits. So, we would never drift like Dad and Alan had.

We threw a party on July 4th. Our window onto the East River was a perfect spot to view the fireworks, and the next day's sunrise filtered through handprints and faceprints of dozens of people—a handful of Becca's friends, plus a good dozen of mine (who had already begun calling themselves paralegals, bank analysts, editorial assistants, screenwriters), plus friends of friends, and friends of friends of friends, more than fifty people in total. How many times that night did friends and strangers alike ask that awful question, "And what are you up to?"

I might have stammered until the wee hours had Becca not, time and again, thrown a steady arm around my shoulder and declared, "He's going to Paris."

"To do?"

"Just you wait and see," she shot back.

Two days later, sitting across from me in the backyard of a bar, she even indulged a conversation about the Catskills, a topic I hadn't dared broach with her in years.

"Becca," I asked, "that morning in the Catskills, when you woke up, what happened?"

"I walked in the woods. What do you mean?"

"But why didn't you leave? Couldn't you find your way out?"

"I was looking out for you, brother."

The impact of those words would seep into my consciousness over time, but right then I wasn't ready to meditate on them, or perhaps I was trying to ward off their meaning. "But you were the one who got lost," I said. "*You.*"

"Was I?"

She faced me with a knowing smile. Her freckles glistened in the afternoon sun, and her tongue dabbed the salt on her lips, transferred from her margarita. A long sip finished her drink, and an ice cube sloshed through her mouth.

The next day, the day of my departure, she accompanied me to the airport. After I passed through security, I turned back and saw her on the opposite side of the glass, waving. A small person stuck between all sorts of jostling bodies, who had managed to find a place where she couldn't be dislodged. She blew a kiss. I blew one back. Then she turned and walked away, disappearing into the crowd. "Wait," I thought, "isn't it supposed to happen the opposite way? Isn't she supposed to watch me walk away?" But that was Becca; she always left first.

And I saw that she'd prepared me for so much, even this.

17

"My home was so masculine," Catherine said. "JT all stoic and aloof, Kyle the athlete, Alan … well, he wasn't exactly the sort to confess his innermost feelings. The first time I saw your parents together, I sensed something different about them right away. Alan laughed and said, 'Maybe she's pregnant,' which turned out to be true—with you, Gabriel!—but I felt sure there was more to it.

"Your mother invited us to join them at a street fair, and the moment we arrived, Becca was waiting for us and took charge. She was so little, but what confidence. 'Hello, friends,' she said, 'Catch.' A beanbag flew through the air. Kyle reached up and grabbed it. She winked. 'Nice one.' I've never forgotten that vision of Becca. She was fearless.

"And that's when I realized that the different quality I had sensed in your family was the presence of a daughter. I suppose I'd always wanted one. Someone to cuddle with, and buy clothes with, and to teach to wear makeup. Who would tell me, honestly, how I looked in a new dress.

"As our families grew closer, I watched Becca grow into a bold and bright young woman. She was the closest I'd ever came to a daughter of my own. Do you know that we used to go shopping, just the two of us? One winter we visited you in the city, and your mother ran off to purchase tickets for a musical, leaving me and Becca alone for hours. We had a blast. We bought jeans, a handbag, eye shadow, sunhats. After that, whenever I visited, Becca would ask to go shopping—'just with Catherine, Mom,' she'd say, answering a question no one had asked. Becca loved to pick at your mother, and if I'm honest I kind of liked being in the middle of things, an object of jealousy.

"Your mother rarely reacted, but once she was feeling a bit testy. 'Why?' she asked. 'Why her?'

"Becca began to pace. She looked at some photos on the wall but didn't face either of us. She was milking the moment. 'Don't be offended, Mom, but Catherine and I share the same...' She walked further, settled before another photo. '...sensibility.'

"Almost anyone else—child or adult—would have said, 'taste.' Not Becca. She needed the more challenging and subtle word. She was a special girl, and I was caught up in it. It was a vulnerable time for me. The boys were growing up and would soon leave for college, there was money stress, I felt a kind of emptiness. And I got attached to your sister, which meant she could torture me a little, just like she tortured your mother.

"There was this time in the Catskills, earlier the same summer. July 4. You were at camp, I think. The night before, we had watched fireworks. The next day, a baseball game took the men away, which left Donna—I hope it's ok if I call her that—Becca, and me.

"'What should we do?' Donna asked.

"Becca shrugged, but some minutes later she whispered to me, 'Let's sneak off, just the two of us.'

"I saw the cruelty, but I was also flattered. I wanted to have my cake and eat it too. 'We can go into town,' I said, 'the three of us, and maybe you and I will peel off for some shopping.'

"'Not shopping. Just spend some time together, the two of us. I'll come up with a plan.'

"I doubted she'd manage, but soon enough Donna said to me, 'Becca says you know a place with a pond and hiking trails. It sounds lovely. We could bring our books and a picnic lunch and have the sort of quiet time that isn't possible with the boys around.'

"I had said no such thing, but I knew a few spots that met the description, so we gathered a blanket, bathing suits, towels, our books. Along the way, we stopped at a store to pick up sandwiches, a bottle of wine, and suntan lotion. Donna wanted a crossword puzzle book, and as she searched the magazine rack, Becca gave me these furtive, giggly glances. It felt like we were teenage girls planning to ditch the wet blanket in our group.

"At the pond, we settled on the grass just above the sandy beach. We went for a swim. Donna and Becca got out quickly; I went to a floating dock to sunbathe. When I came back, they were eating their sandwiches. Your mother had opened the wine and sipped from a plastic cup. Becca had an iced tea. They sat on opposite sides of the blanket, each with a book. Actually, Donna had two, her novel and the crosswords. She poured a second glass of wine and passed me the food without shifting her eyes. She turned onto her back, the novel above her head, blocking the sun.

"'Would you like to go for a walk, Catherine?' Becca asked.

"I looked to Donna, but she was lost in her book. 'Have fun,' she said.

"Becca slipped an arm through mine, and soon we were on the hill above the pond. It wasn't much, just an open field where they hosted outdoor events, like concerts or a county fair, with a path leading back to the parking lot and another past a stretch of higher grass and into the woods. I asked Becca what she wanted to do. 'Just walk,' she replied and headed toward the trees. We were on a trail marked with purple blazes. There were thick trees to either side, the path rose slightly, the ground was dappled with light that filtered past the leaf cover. All the while, Becca asked questions. All sorts of things, often personal, adult questions, slightly inappropriate for a girl her age, for the daughter of my best friend. 'What was Alan like when he was younger, when you first met? Were you attracted right away?' 'Do you know what JT wants to major in? Are you concerned he won't find a calling?' 'Does it bother you not to work? Don't you get bored?' It was an odd inquisition, invasive, even aggressive, but I also felt flattered by her attention and spoke openly. Now and then we came upon other people, and Becca always grew quiet and had us rush past; she wanted us to be alone. Unfortunately, I was wearing these damn sandals, horrible for long walks, and when we came to a large rock before an overlook, I suggested we sit. Becca climbed to the top of the jutting stone and went right on past. She settled on a grassy ridge of the opposite side and patted the ground beside her. We talked some more. But there were also silences, easy silences, and I had the thought that we had reached that special place where you didn't always need words. Where you could sit side by side in quiet communion.

"After several minutes, I became aware of Becca's eyes, how they often seemed focused on me rather than the view before us. Her gaze was almost comically intense, yet it felt thrilling to be looked at that way, to be desired that way—because that's how I felt: desired. Her eyes told me that we had a special bond, that whatever I represented to her—a confidante aunt, a big-sister figure—I was the very thing she was looking for. I tried to imagine what was going on in her head. I envisioned all sorts of confessions. About friends, boys. The sort of thing she might not tell her mom. It would be our secret.

"'I'm going to continue on my own,' she said suddenly.

"'But Becca—,' I started, at a total loss. 'I can walk, too. Forget the sandals.'

"'No, I'll continue alone,' she insisted, standing and marching down the path.

"I was startled and felt queasy. Part of me wanted to run after her, to cry out, 'Where? Can't I come with?' But reason told me that this would seem hysterical. She probably just needed a bathroom break, or to address a feminine hygiene issue. I waited a few minutes, then returned to the pond.

"Donna was lying down as earlier, book above her head, as if no time had passed. I sat on the blanket and picked at my sandwich. But I couldn't stay still. She giggled and I worried that she was mocking me— my unease, my sensitivity. Then I saw the wine. 'Want some?' She filled my plastic cup halfway before the bottle ran dry. 'Guess you were gone awhile,' she said, giggling more loudly. A few minutes later, she passed me her crossword puzzles. 'Try this, Ms. Restless.'

"Only a few people were swimming. Wind rippled the water. The sky clouded over. Maybe it was just my mood. Donna was lost to her book and wouldn't talk. And Becca was still gone, at least an hour, perhaps more. Now and then my heart would begin thumping, but Donna showed no concern at all, didn't even ask about her daughter.

"When Becca finally returned, glowing as earlier, and made no reference whatsoever to her time away, none at all, a new tumult stirred inside me. I even wondered if I had been the butt of some joke—if I had been the wet blanket, not Donna. Becca opened her book. I fiddled with whatever was around—the picnic basket, a towel, the bathing suit straps beneath my sundress. 'Another dip?' Becca said, and soon she and Donna were pulling off shirts and shoes, knotting their hair. Donna went in first, and I watched Becca—her body lean, hips narrow though adult, maturing—run down the grass, across the sand, and into the water, where she launched into a dive and swam to the floating dock. I waded to my knees and shivered.

"That trip left me confused, anxious, even hurt. I was sure there had to be some explanation for Becca's behavior, but she and I never found a moment alone, not that evening, not the next morning before your family left. That night, Alan, never hyper-sensitive, knew to ask what was on my mind. 'Just tired after a long weekend,' I deflected, much too embarrassed to admit that a teenage girl had gotten into my head.

"I soon put the incident aside, but maybe two weeks later, I got this."

Catherine pulled an envelope from her purse and passed it to me. On the front was Becca's handwriting and inside, a folded sheet of lined paper. It was a drawing, with hatches at the top indicating a hairline and slighter ones below hinting at neck and shoulders. Between stood crisp, confident lines defining a face that could only be Catherine's. The regal nose with its dainty tip, the high cheeks, the slender eyebrows, the dimpled chin. Though entirely gray pencil, the drawing somehow managed to convey the icy blue of her eyes.

The Catherine who faced me now—with pinched lips and a stiff, proper back—looked so similar to that generation-old rendering that you didn't have to be a family friend to recognize it as a past version of her. As I waited for her to go on, I folded the page along its crease marks and handed it back to her.

"Don't you want it, Gabriel? I thought you might…"

"I have lots of Becca's drawings. And this was given to you."

I held the envelope before her until her fingers closed around it and she returned it to her purse. She smiled but was silent, her face impassive. I found myself in the very situation she had described with Becca on that hill, waiting further words, anticipating what she would say next, imagining the point of this story, the message she wanted to convey:

It's how I see myself. When I imagine my face, it's not a photo or reflection but this drawing that I see. Or:

What talent she had. Only 14. Can you imagine? Or:

Even twenty years later, it makes me blush. I've often wondered if those closest to me had ever looked at me so intimately. Or, darker:

What do you see, Gabriel? A bored housewife? Some suburban cliché? Is that how she saw me? Is that how you all saw me?

Instead, she said, "When Becca asked me to walk with her, all her questions and the way she looked at me, it felt so intimate, but then she sent this picture, and I realized… I realized… it was only… Anyway, the point is that I hoped it might help you understand, Gabriel, that day months later when your sister went missing… why I thought… why I thought she wanted to be alone."

I didn't get it at first. We shifted to the window, looking onto the East River. I saw her in reflection, a faint smile, her eyes glassy, the wrinkles at the edge of her lips seeming to stiffen. At times, the water was depthless black; at others, sparks of color, the bright hues of reflected light, flickered on the surface. My thoughts were like that—unformed, fragmentary, but with flares of rising, incandescent anger. I felt enough of it to know I should keep quiet. We stood there awhile, silent. When Catherine finally spoke, I barely noted the words, only that they felt false and distant.

Only later did my simmering rage cohere into something like cogent thought: Was that *an apology?* Had Catherine just explained that she'd thought nothing about her son abandoning us in a dark, unknown woods, because a few months earlier she'd discovered that Becca liked to spend time alone, to draw? As if Becca were the one to will that betrayal. And what about me? I was there, too, and had asked for none of it. Was I just collateral damage? Had Catherine really waited two decades to share this infuriatingly lame excuse?

She called the next day to thank me for inviting her for Thanksgiving. I thanked her for coming, for the cooking and cleaning. I sensed her lingering, awaiting some invitation I wasn't about to make. Days later, a thank-you note arrived in the mail, courteous words in neat cursive, a formality from another age. The following week, I thought to call her before my rage flashed anew. Late November became mid-December. She didn't call, either.

BOOK 2

1

"Where are you?"

"What do you mean, I'm home."

"Meet me at this address. 74 Hester. Go up a flight of stairs. See you soon, Gabriel."

"Becca, wait—"

Click. The line went dead.

It was December 19. 9:13 PM, twenty minutes after Becca's arrival in JFK, which she'd announced with a text, "**Landed. FINALLY**" (her first words since the barrage of texts, written hours earlier from Berlin, announcing a flight delay and then providing quarter-hour updates). I called back, but the line went straight to voicemail. A bit resentful of the late-night rush, but eager to see her, I threw on my coat and hailed a cab.

74 Hester housed a typical Chinatown restaurant, with a corny name ("Bountiful Gates") and a lineup of blistery pink, skinless roast meats dangling from hooks near the window. Inside, six elderly men sat at a circular table before bowls of noodle soup and a metal teapot, the lone occupied table. But a staircase to the side led to a heavy door and then a second space, which appeared also to serve food but had the dimly lit ambiance of a tacky nightclub. A small group huddled by a bar; behind lay an open area, where I made out the corner of a stage; in

the background, I heard bad karaoke. Becca sat in a booth to the side. A suitcase nestled between her legs; a backpack lay on the booth beside her. She tapped furiously on her phone.

"Gabriel."

She leaned over for a perfunctory hug, without looking up from her screen, typed a bit more, emphatically hit send, lay the phone on the table, and reached for a dark bottle at its center. She topped off the glass before her and filled a second, which she passed to me. "Cheers."

After a long sip, she added, "Sorry, I just had this hankering for dumplings, it's one of those things you can't get in Berlin, good ones, I mean, and after the plane ride, which was one of those low oxygen clunkers and the guy next to me had sleep apnea, I think, I was starved. This place had good reviews, and Linda Fong told me it was legit. Ever been? By the way, this is rice wine, what do you think?"

I hadn't been before, I had no thoughts about the rice wine, nor did I have any idea who Linda Fong was. But what caught me off guard was Becca. How foreign she seemed. Every reappearance began like this. She lived life on a higher frequency than me, and my joy at seeing her always battled an initial sensation of dissonance. Luckily, the rice wine, which was plenty bitter despite Becca's claim that it was the best on the list, hit me immediately. After a few sips, I felt a lightness, more pleasant than not, flow to the top of my crown. As I finished my glass, the waiter arrived carrying two woven trays, each with 8 blond dumplings on a bed of lettuce, steamy hot.

"So," Becca said, soupy liquid squirting from her mouth, "what have you been up to?"

"Big question. Where to start—"

"Rebecca. Rebecca Stalb," crackled a voice over an old sound system.

Becca slid from the booth and pointed to a screen above the bar. "You can watch there." As she passed the bar, she said, "Would you please turn up the volume?" and seconds later, the goateed barman punched a button, releasing a static hiss.

Becca slipped around a corner but soon appeared on the screen, settling above a large X, indicated by strips of masking tape. Though perfectly framed, she looked tiny—either that or the speakers hovering behind her were ridiculously large. Music began. "Zombie," by the Cranberries, once an adolescent anthem. Becca jumped in half a note late and slightly off key, at which point the ambient sounds of the place, suppressed in expectation, let loose: whispered conversations, sloshing beer, shuffled legs. But as the first verse crescendoed, her voice gained confidence, and soon she was belting out the words. She sang a key or two lower than Dolores O'Riordan, which gave the song an earthy feel, and my, what force.

By the chorus, the rustling ceased; even the barman stopped his dishwashing to gaze at the screen. In the interlude before the second verse, Becca stood still as a statue, not even swaying, but everyone remained quiet. When she sang again, a tiny gasp from the audience revealed its secret: the place was in thrall to her. Back in New York for an hour, surrounded by suitcases, unwashed, perhaps without even pausing for a piss, Becca was already reminding me of the relentless energy that she could summon seemingly at will, but also of her ability to channel that energy into moments of true power. Every Christmas visit, she managed a trick like this, and though she was my sister, I couldn't help but fall a bit in love with her every time.

After the second verse, the music meandered. I kept waiting for Becca's next beginning, but instead the instruments faded. All was silent—then roaring applause. No previous singer had earned this reaction; in fact, none had registered as anything more than background noise. Becca winked toward the camera before hopping from the stage and soon had returned to the table, flashing an electric smile.

"I don't know what came over me. I was feeling it tonight."

She poured more rice wine for us both. As the warm liquid ran down my throat, I took note of a new song in the background—"Pour Some Sugar on Me" by Def Leopard. Becca leaned into the curve of the dark booth and sipped leisurely. I felt like we had entered a calmer place, the evening's second phase.

"So, tell me, bro," she said. "Any news? What about girls?"

I recounted a few escapades, including Calinda and Cathy. "But nothing major."

"Every time I see you, I wonder if you'll make an introduction."

"Sorry to disappoint again."

"And Lina?"

"That was a while ago," I shrugged. "What about you?"

Becca smiled but shook her head. She had been doing this sort of big sisterly inquisition more often of late but somehow always evaded the situation in reverse. "We're not talking about me."

"Now we are."

"Gabe. Gabe Reel. Gabriel. Stalk," cried out the loudspeaker.

"You didn't," I said.

Becca again flashed her wide smile. "Of, course I did. Go up and be a rock star, Gabriel."

Thank God for the rice wine. The inner voice that normally would have screamed No as my feet turned into deadweights and my knees into putty, put up only token resistance. "What song?" I asked.

"Go find out."

Passing the bar, I discovered an entire second wing to the place, with a crowd of several dozen people scattered among tables and a smaller bar along a side wall.

By the stairs to the stage, a tall woman with pointy glasses handed me the mike. On a screen to the side, I saw written, in white type on blue background, "Under My Thumb. Rolling Stones."

I spent a moment trying to decipher some special meaning to this choice, but then the woman said, "Ready?", the music started, and words scrolled down the screen. I did my best to follow along. I found the rhythm by the second verse and, from then on, did a passable job, or so I felt, though who can judge the sound of his own voice? I finished to a smattering of finger-snaps. The woman with pointy glasses held out her hand, wordlessly requesting the mike.

"Not bad, bro. Not bad at all," said Becca as I returned to the table, but she was staring at her phone, which pinged with new messages.

I hadn't seen her in nearly a year, but I was familiar with every subtle change in the rhythm between us. Our visits always began with a
flare of energy, which soon softened to a mellow glow. But what made
our Christmas vacations different was that they lasted long enough to
move beyond this two-step and break through to a quieter, more private space. Tonight was the ice-breaker, and Becca would soon crash;
only when she awoke would our real time together begin. Over the next
few days, we would enter a routine of family life, playing at domesticity,
until we reached the point where my sister, never much of a talker,
would share whatever closely held personal news she had carried with
her, as would I. Getting to that space took time, and when I caught
Becca for a stolen dinner as she installed a show in Brussels or Turin, it
simply wasn't possible.

Instead, I encountered some public version of her: the professional
self, the creative self, or the self-promoting self, three subtly distinct
modes that all came with a certain reserve. She wasn't so much withholding as someone who faced others from one degree of remove—in
a sort of neutral position that couldn't have been much different had I
been a high school pal rediscovered through Facebook or a professional
contact encountered for the third time. It was only during our Christmas break that we overcame such barriers and found the deeper
connection where we could share those feelings and announcements
that were too big or personal for the phone or email. So, things always
followed a clear pattern: first, frenzy; second, calm; third, intimacy,
which, as soon as you noticed it, was already in flight and you were in
the fourth and final stage, a few days of New York cavorting, which we
crammed with activities like two overeager tourists, before our rushed
goodbye.

"What's the weather been like?" Becca asked. "Have you checked
the forecast?"

Her tone was enthusiastic, but her eyes were squarely on her phone.
Over the next minutes, I would watch as she lay the phone face-down
on the table, an arm's length away, like some temptation she wanted to
escape, before a new ping interrupted whatever half-uttered sentence

she'd just begun. They called her name again on the loudspeaker; she didn't look up; eventually, another name was called. The waitress asked if we wanted another round; Becca was still lost to her phone, and it fell to me to politely say no. She did manage to fill our glasses a final time, emptying the bottle, and also raised eager eyes at the arrival of a third tray of dumplings—"a different flavor," she explained, "pork only, no crab"—which I hadn't heard her order. She must have done so while I was singing.

* * *

I saw Becca next at 2:00 pm the next afternoon. She emerged from her room fully dressed, went to the bathroom, and then suggested we go to Antonio's for our usual large onion, half mushroom, half sausage pie. We ate two slices each and carried the rest home in a delivery box. A minute later, she was in pajamas, yellow with green polka dots, a floppy string tie at the waist, a loose collar flapping open before her pale neck.

"What are you waiting for?" she said. "Get dressed," meaning, put on your pjs, too. Soon I joined her on our parents' bed, and she slid *From Russia With Love* into the DVD player.

We spent the next three days in the apartment, reading back-to-back on the couch, perched atop our parents' bed, watching DVDs, eating large bowls of Cheerios in the morning and larger bowls of spaghetti at night, in sweats and jammies the whole day, snacking on Antonio's leftovers, ordering a new pie the moment we had an urge for more, making no pretense to step outside, as if it were a rainy Saturday in October and all we wanted to do was cuddle under blankets and escape the larger world.

But as always happened, there came a morning when we both woke early, and I could sense restlessness, a desire to reconnect with the wider world. Becca was in the kitchen before sunrise, stirring her coffee intensely, turning an empty pizza carton into an origami menagerie. I recalled what she had told me, during the fall of her junior year of college, when I'd asked what she would do after graduation. "Make things," she said. "I think you've got four basic types of people. You've got lazy people, brooders"—saying this, she pointed a finger at me—"doers, and, probably the smallest group, makers. That's me."

"And what will you make?"

"That's what I need to figure out."

After three days inside, I wanted to go out and breathe in the crisp winter air, but the intensity in her simplest movements, and my memory of that conversation long ago, was already saddening me, for I knew that as soon as we reemerged into the world, we would already be on the backend of our visit. Yes, we would pass a whirlwind couple of days running around the city, but before you knew it, we would be facing off on opposite sides of a window or glass panel, then she would return to her life of making and I—I suppose—to my brooding. Sure, we would talk over the next 11 months and see each other on occasion, but we'd never approach this moment's closeness.

But I also knew that it was right now—in this gap between nesting and re-emergence—when our personal news came out.

"I'm moving back," she said.

"What do you mean?" I asked.

"I'm moving to New York."

"For good?"

"For now. And don't worry, Gabriel, I don't mean, *here*, the apartment. That's yours. I just mean, New York."

"Settling down?"

"I hate that expression, but I suppose."

For years, Becca had lived a nomadic life, never remaining in any single place, as far as I could tell from emails and postcards, longer than a few months at a time. She'd had several "homes" over the years. The longest standing were the Culver City loft and the narrow duplex in Mitte, in Berlin; others included the Maine sea house, the studio in the Old Quarter of Barcelona, the bungalow in Key Largo, the Pittsburgh warehouse, the whitewashed villa in Chios, and likely a few more I'd never known of. I once asked if those many homes had anything in common, and she scrunched her eyes, as if in deep rumination, before saying, "They aren't New York." But even this had turned out not to be true, for there was also that small studio in the city, where she bunked whenever she came to town outside of Christmastime.

"Why?" I asked.

"I promise I'll be out of your hair after the usual ten days. I'll go to the studio and eventually find my own place."

"It's not that, Becca. I'm just surprised. You haven't really *lived* anywhere—I mean, just one place—for years."

"I want that to change."

Becca setting up a home. Becca in New York. There was something momentous in this simple news, suggestive of some unstated explanation beyond her evasive answers so far. It certainly trumped my news, which I had agonized over in the days leading up to her arrival and even as we holed up in the apartment—*Catherine*. How to explain Catherine Morrow's appearance. How to break the news that we were friends, *good friends*, and that Catherine had mentioned that she wanted to see us, wanted to see Becca, during this visit. The anger I had felt toward Catherine after Thanksgiving had softened, and the idea of introducing them intrigued me. But I had no idea how Becca would react. Memories of her teenage tantrums came to mind. Anything from indifference to an encore outburst seemed possible. It had also occurred to me that I could use the brevity of Becca's visit as an excuse to avoid a meeting, but if Becca were moving to New York, it would be impossible to prevent it forever.

"I'm not getting a lobotomy, Gabriel. Just changing my address."

"But why?"

"Wow. Someone doesn't sound happy about this. Have I struck a nerve?"

Perhaps she had. Much as I cherished our Christmas holidays, I secretly loathed our lesser encounters, for being such meager copies of the former. Now they would be more plentiful, and my disappointment harder to mask. "I'm just surprised," I said. "I thought you hated the city."

"Well, I miss it. And I've been away long enough that I'm sure it won't feel too familiar, won't leave me overly comfortable. You know, complacent. Which is what I want to avoid. And what about you, brother? Why'd you move back?"

"We aren't talking about me."

"Now we are." She grinned the same snotty smile she used to tease me with when we were called upon to explain the origin of a fight to the parents and she had manipulated me into seeming like the instigator. "Look, last time I asked, you said something about needing to deal with our old tenants. But no one uproots themselves to solve a tenant problem. What's the real reason?"

"I wanted to come back. I was ready."

"Hmmm," she said. "We must be related." She walked to the window, where the sun was rising above the buildings in Queens, streams of light flooding the window and revealing the specks of dust floating before her. "More coffee?"

"No thanks."

Seconds later, she was back, steam rising from her mug. The sun was now fully visible. It looked like a cloudless day, which, given the season, likely meant frigid.

"Should we do MoMA today?" she asked.

And just like that, our conversation was over, and we were already shifting into the next phase of our Christmas break, when we would venture out into the city for a parade of museums and theaters, restaurants, pastry shops, bars, and boutiques. If this was anything like past years, she would have researched new places and already made reservations.

"Your first decision is our lunch spot," she said. "Korean or Greek?"

2

An hour later, we were walking through midtown, smoke steaming from our mouths with every breath. At MoMA, we rushed up escalators and through collection galleries to find the Die Brücke artists, Kirchner, Nolde, Pechstein, whom Becca had been studying, and lingered an hour. We lunched at Laxos: grilled branzino, lemon potatoes, Greek salad. We drank hot toddies at the St. Regis, walked south to Madison Square, and toured an outdoor installation of bamboo and cor-ten steel by Elena Evangelista, a Filipino artist Becca knew. As the sun faded, we headed south—Washington Square, Soho, giant bowls of steamy Pho on Mott, cannoli, limoncellos, and espresso on Mulberry. After midnight, we cabbed home.

As always when Becca reappeared in my life, it would take time to register certain things about her. To be struck, for instance, by how small she was. Barely reaching my chin, even in a pompom hat. Or the force of personality, the nonstop questioning (when she felt like it), the imperious way she ordered food or gave directions to a cabbie or asked for recommendations at the wine shop, her bristly intensity, which was raw and—to the unschooled—abrasive, as if the unceasing drive that fueled her ambition had temporarily lost its outlet and come bracingly to the surface.

"It's been nearly a year," she said of her absence from the city, indicating a desire to visit all her favorite neighborhoods. Battery Park and Lower Manhattan's few colonial remnants. Astoria to gorge on grilled octopus and blocks of feta. A full loop around Central Park. At the Whitney and Guggenheim, she arranged private tours with curators. She found us tables at hip restaurants usually requiring reservations a month in advance. A detour brought us to our high school—the students were on break, a friendly guard let us in—where we discovered a fancy new gym, picked up a basketball, and played horse.

We jogged, in hats and gloves, along the East River, then swam laps in an indoor pool on the seventh floor of a nearby building. Sitting across from her in the booth of a diner, I watched the maker in her stir alive. Within five minutes, she had constructed a metropolis of sugar packets, a dome from drinking straws, a paper-tablecloth collage.

We passed an epic day in Brooklyn. First, Williamsburg, a trendy Thai place and window shopping, walking through Hasidic neighborhoods and past the Navy Yard until we came to Clinton Hill, where she somehow knew the sommelier at a farm-to-table restaurant and got lost in a lengthy oeniphilic conversation, which turned into a tasting of the top bottles from their list, each paired with a course selected just for the occasion. When we were done, Becca wouldn't let me see the bill. It was late and we were tipsy, but she insisted we walk the Brooklyn Bridge, despite the cold. What a spectacular view; the harsh wind was no match for the Manhattan skyline, the gray towers silhouetted against a cloudy black sky, the intermittent sparkle of lit windows creating a radiant, if random grid.

At times, I returned to the topic of her move to New York, trying to tease out some hidden motivation I sensed she was withholding.

"There's nothing, Gabriel. No mystery. How many times do I have to tell you? I just want a change in scenery."

Could this be true? Was moving to New York nothing more for her than a change of attire or the repositioning of a couch from the south to north wall? I had returned when an entire phase of life felt exhausted, in a state of despair but eager for a new beginning. Was it possible that for Becca, such a move could be as trivial as painting the walls a new color so you can look at something different for a while? She still had her career, her "great passion." She had friends around the globe, none of whom clung too close, meeting another stated desire. She wanted neither husband nor kids—she had said this so often and so plainly that I no longer doubted it. Maybe place just didn't matter to her.

In the back of my mind, a second thought tugged at me: *Catherine.* But I didn't want to disturb our idyll and bit my tongue.

When we hit the Manhattan side of the bridge, a great levity came over me, equal parts energy and stillness, a heat without burn that tamed the frigid air.

"Let's walk," I said.

"Where to?" asked Becca.

"Let's just go, we'll let the green lights guide us."

I was thinking of the serendipity of some of my excursions with Catherine, and sure enough, some ten minutes later as we approached Houston, we heard festive shouts and fist banging, revelers marking midnight, a 30th birthday that had spilled onto the street. They offered shots of whisky in exchange for life advice ("Stop counting," said Becca), and we kept going. Proceeding in the general direction of home, we fell upon others—on 8th Street, 21st, 44th—groups of strangers wanting to dance a jig, or decorate themselves in tinsel, or, in the final case, a pack of Scandinavian tourists trying to locate the Rockefeller Center skating rink. We joined them for a few laps, skating until our butts were sore.

* * *

I woke the next morning to the sun already blazing in the sky and sat in the living room watching light ripple on the East River, the passage of tugboats, a flight of pigeons. Eager to begin our day, I brewed coffee and fried eggs, making just enough sound that I could plausibly deny trying to wake Becca.

Spying a clock that read 9:26, a time that still evoked anxiety, I felt a need to locate her, but across the foyer I saw that the front closet was open and her silver coat missing from its usual hook. Peeking into my parent's room, where Becca had crashed the previous night, minutes into *Empire Strikes Back*, I found an empty bed, the sheet folded downward. Her own room was equally still, clean and undisturbed.

In an instant, the morning glow was gone, curdled into its dark opposite. My mind raced in dismal directions. I imagined Becca curled in a window seat on a flight to Berlin. Or sprawled across some street, her body twisted and misshapen. Were we already at the end of our time together? Had she really left without a word?

I called her cellphone. It rang and rang.

I tried again minutes later: the same thing. The voice of reason within me was no match for my foreboding thoughts, and I trudged through the apartment, searching for distraction. I tried again to watch *Empire Strikes Back* but was too agitated to sit through it. I went to her studio and stood by the sidewalk intercom long enough to see the same person leave groggy-eyed and return carrying a tall Starbucks cup. I grabbed a slice at Antonio's and walked along the East River promenade. The cool clear sky brought momentary reprieve, but when I reached the awning of our building, desperation returned. I tried Becca again: straight to voicemail.

All afternoon, I prayed for her to call. Just to say where she was, where she'd disappeared to. And if not her, someone else. Sebastian. Peter. Catherine. Anyone. Amid this panic, I did have a moment of clarity. There had been days like this in Paris, hadn't there? At times, the loneliness had been terrifying—the awesome magnitude of it. Here was the answer to Becca's question, the why of my return to New York. It was the simplest, most truthful of reasons, though still impossible to utter out loud. I'd been running from loneliness, but it had caught me again.

The sky was already darkening when I finally heard keys jangling in the 15th Floor hallway. Becca pushed open the door. She was carrying several large plastic bags—from Key Food. "I thought I'd try something different," she said. "A home-cooked meal. Wanna help?"

"Where were you?" I asked.

"Oh, Gabriel. You look like you've seen a ghost."

"I kept calling, Becca. You never picked up."

"I was working. I always turn off the phone. It's the only way."

"I went to your studio. I buzzed."

"It doesn't work. Oh, Gabriel, I'm sorry."

She led me into the kitchen, unpacked the bags, grabbed a knife and cutting board, began chopping. Onion, celery, carrot. She heated oil and threw the vegetables in the pan. "Let me make it up to you. This is one of my specialties. Lamb two-ways. A lamb ragu, like Mom used to make, and a stack of chops." She unwrapped four lamb chops and searched the fridge and cupboards for balsamic, mustard, garlic, and rosemary to make a marinade. She boiled and skinned six tomatoes, and soon these went into the pot with the vegetables. Hardly inspired like Catherine, she at least seemed to know what she was doing.

We spoke little as she cooked, but she did manage to turn to me and say, "I didn't mean to worry you, Gabriel. I'm so sorry."

As the sauce boiled on the stovetop, we went to the living room. She had brought a bottle of wine, two glasses. "Cheers," she said, handing me one.

The wine was smooth and rich, unusually good. I should have known she'd pick a special bottle.

"Why did you do it, Becca?"

"Do what?"

"Leave like that—without even a note."

"I needed to go to the studio. I had the urge. It sometimes happens. Even on vacation."

"What did you make?"

"Some sketches. I'm trying to work out some ideas."

"Like what?"

"It's too early to say. When it's done, you'll see it first. I promise."

An empty promise, no doubt, but at least the tension lessened. She poured a second glass of wine. We drank in silence. Her return, the alcohol, the purr of the heater, cut the edge. But in its place, I felt a crest of sadness, the reality of the other 51 weeks a year crashing our innocent dream. Just as I fell in love with Becca on each Christmas visit, I also faced this, the sudden, wrenching breakup at a visit's end. It didn't matter that she wasn't gone yet, or that she would stay in New York—for it was still coming, and it would be no less jarring and severe.

After dinner, we sat on the couch, reading separate books back-to-back, as we had as kids. At times, I berated myself for the absurdity of my inner journey over the past 24 hours. Other times, I eased up on myself. This was just me. Who I was. Just as Becca was still the girl who always had one foot out the door. Even during this intimate time.

I looked out the window to the black river, unspoiled but for the dancing specks of reflected light.

"You won't believe who got in touch," I said.

"Who?"

"Catherine Morrow. Remember her?" As the words escaped my mouth, I questioned my motivation. Was I introducing my sister to a friend, or was I exacting some sort of revenge on her for the day's abandonment?

"Of course."

"Would you believe, she lives a few blocks away. In an old age home on 75th and the river. I've seen her. We've become friends."

"And?"

"We could see her." Again, I spoke without thinking, only afterward realizing that Catherine would not be alone, that she had family visiting, too. "She asked about you."

"And do what?"

"A walk? Do things around town? What I do with her is like what I do with you, only much much slower."

Only now did I look to Becca, curious to see the expression on her face, whatever clue it would reveal, but she was already walking away. "Sure," she said, passing through the doorway. "Why not? Nighty night, bro. See you in the morrow."

3

I saw them through the window as our cab pulled into the corner of 59th and Fifth. Catherine, draped in red and brown fur with dark winter boots in place of her Keds. JT, beside her in a puffy navy ski jacket that still revealed the rail-thin body beneath. And some ten feet away, on the edge of the curb, a teenage girl in a pink parka with torn white jeans and red high tops with a rim of glitter above the soles. This was Sophie, JT's daughter. She had a long ponytail like her father, though her hair and olive skin were several shades darker than his, and she had already reached her grandmother's height. Her purple lipstick shimmered beneath the Christmas lights dangling from streetlamps above.

We greeted one another with a crisscross of handshakes. Sophie took my hand limply, but her eyes were elsewhere. Following her gaze, I saw a large star, made of wire, metal, and glass, spanning Fifth Avenue.

"I can't believe it," she said dreamily. "Fifth Avenue. New York's famous Christmas windows. Wow."

"Sophie's never been to New York," Catherine said, before whispering to me, "I knew we'd convince him to come."

"Yeah," JT said. "But she's seen so many movies, she knows half the streets already."

"Well, come then," said Becca and offered an arm, which Sophie grabbed without hesitation. "You can show me around."

The two of them bounded off, with Catherine, JT, and I settling into a slower pace behind. I hadn't seen Catherine in nearly a month and was surprised at how labored her walking seemed. She proceeded slowly, occasionally winced, and more than once had to pause to allow some invisible pang to pass. And with JT, there was that strange hitch in his step, as if one leg were longer than the other.

"I had a feeling they'd hit it off," Catherine said, pointing to the much nimbler pair ahead of us. "Sophie is very creative. She was just telling me that she's won the lead in her high school musical."

But Catherine was mostly reserved, offering little beyond quips about the crowd and the cold, and it fell to JT to fill the silences. Before the windows at Barney's, he slipped into a summary of the major details of his life—his work as a music technician, his weekend radio show ("6:00 am on Saturdays, no joke, I have like 14 fans"), his marriage, the bitter divorce, the nasty custody battle—giving a speech that was nearly identical, right down to certain phrases, to what I'd heard months earlier at the East River Home.

Before a stunning vase at Tiffany (sterling, with intricate carvings of birds of prey—hawks, eagles, falcons, condors, vultures), he declared, earnestly yet awkwardly, for it came out of nowhere and was more than a decade late, "a genuine sadness" to have learned of my parents' passings. And as we began walking again, he attempted to engage me with the usual questions—*How was being back in New York? What would I do?*—but his eyes were glancing all around, over his shoulders, or down Fifth Avenue, along the length of the tourists plodding southward, following the same pilgrimage trail as us, or up the skyscrapers lining the path, to the patches of blue between the spires, and I knew that he was only doing as his mother wanted, while his true interest lay elsewhere.

"You've been awfully quiet," I said to Catherine.

"Just taking it all in," she said. "Besides, I wanted to allow the two of you to catch up."

But it was Sophie and Becca who looked like old pals reunited. Half a block ahead, they came into view as gaps opened in the crowd, or when Sophie rushed back to us, staying just long enough to utter some ecstatic cry—"Wow, Dad. Wow, Grams"—before skipping back to Becca. I watched as their heads leaned into the space between their marching bodies, and heard the hum of their cheerful conversation (if not the words themselves) as it traveled on the breeze. If at first, I couldn't quite silence the cynical voice inside me, claiming that the only thing these two had in common was a desire to escape the weighty drag of their families, all signs suggested a simpler explanation. They were having fun. The very oddness of their pairing—the tall, perky teen and my late thirtyish sister, a head shorter and with prominent crow's feet by both eyes—was the best evidence that their rapport was genuine.

At some point, I looked to Catherine, who nodded permission (or so I imagined), and I surged ahead, joining Sophie and Becca in the twisty, velvet-roped line before Henri Bendel. Their conversation marched along—11th grade boys, the California winter, what San Diego had over LA, not exactly topics I knew much about—even as they let me sneak in beside them.

When we arrived at the first window, Becca quieted, then asked Sophie, "What do you think of this one?"

The scene before us was a wintry village, with an elaborate model train riding along tracks that crisscrossed at a river, a bridge above, a tunnel below.

"It's like the others," said Sophie. "Cool, but ... missing something. I'm not moved."

"But why does it matter if it's not moving?"

"Because then it's not art. Not real art. Maybe, it's some kind of phony twin, but that's different. Know what I mean?"

Sophie's bright eyes flashed toward mine, as if seeking acknowledgment of her clever comment, then her neck swiveled back toward Becca. "Becca, how would you describe the difference... between whatever this is... and real art?"

"That's a big question."

"And who would know better than you? When my grandma said we were going to meet you, I couldn't believe it. I'd heard so much about you. I figured you'd be amazing, but you're also so normal. That's a compliment, you know. I'm not sure if my grandma said, but I do creative stuff, too, and so does my dad. He's in the music biz, an engineer. So, he's in the studio, *behind the glass*. But I want to be like you, Becca: up front, on the other side. This spring, the school musical is *Grease*, and I just found out that I'm Sandy. I beat out a senior who played Beauty last year, and I'm only 15."

Without missing a beat, she lowered her chin onto Becca's shoulder and sang, "*Summer loving had me a blast Summer loving happened so fast.*" Her voice was soft and sweet, but it stopped just as suddenly it started, and then she pulled Becca from the window and back into the southward flow of pedestrians, leaving me behind.

"Oh, Gabriel, you're back," Catherine said as I fell in stride beside her and JT. "Any news from the front?"

"They seem to be having a good time."

"I can see that from here."

It was true. Even at a distance, you couldn't miss Sophie's unbridled eagerness, her admiring gazes and exuberant laughter, and you could also sense Becca's girlish energy, her willingness to match each of Sophie's bouncy movements. Knowing Becca, I also suspected that some subtler indifference, even some condescension, lurked below the bubbly surface of her enthusiasm, but I wasn't about to share these thoughts.

The sidewalk opened up before Sak's, its long line, four snake-coils deep, sucking up half the crowd. Sophie and Becca were a row ahead of us, but as the line shifted, we occasionally overlapped and were able to hear them. Sophie was peppering Becca with a series of rapid questions about her career, like an interview. How do you get a show? Are you nervous before an opening? What inspires you? Do you think up a title before you start a new work or only when you finish? To my surprise, Becca was patient, answering each question earnestly, and I wondered if there was anything in this for her beyond the simple pleasure of feeling admired, or if she were merely succumbing to that old weakness of hers.

They had reached the first window, which showed an old man in a workroom, before a shoe on a bench. "That's 'The Shoemaker and the Elves,'" Becca said.

"How do you know?" Sophie asked.

"I've read my Brothers Grimm. And look at the next one." Becca pointed ahead, to a window barely visible from where I stood. "You know that one, right?"

"Hansel and Gretel," Sophie clapped. "Let's go …" She grabbed Becca's arm and jostled ahead of an obviously displeased family of Italian tourists. As Sophie and Becca gawked at the next window, I half expected that Becca might recount our real-life Hansel and Gretel saga. Instead, I heard a lengthy discussion of details, the hem of Gretel's dress, the tiny wax candle on a second-story windowsill, the toy chest and slumped wooden doll on the kitchen table, the sooty grate over the black oven, the gingerbread men with their icing features—Becca highlighting each element, explaining how it was made, the materials, the stitching, the order of construction, the logic of its placement, delineating every consideration that went into such an exquisite diorama. It was a master class in holiday windows, offered off the cuff, like the most natural thing in the world.

"How do you know all this stuff?" Sophie asked when Becca was done. "I thought you were a painter."

"I make other things, too. Sculptures, installations, a couple of movies."

Sophie's cheeks glowed. Not for the first time, I felt sure that some wild fan girl inside her was about to burst forth, but her reply showed surprising restraint, "I also do lots of art stuff, you know. I told you before about my singing and acting, but I also take art class. We do everything. Painting. Drawing. Sculpture. We're about to learn the pottery wheel. I like charcoal sticks best. Do you ever use them?"

"They're wonderful for sketches."

"Right? I love how smoky it looks. I like being able to smudge with my fingers after I draw a line."

The crowd shifted, and Catherine, JT, and I finally achieved the first row. We stood before a small diorama that preceded the Grimm cycle: a conventional Nordic scene, a crowd in long coats, bundled tight, before two sleds, with reindeer looking out from a bank of trees. The shoemaker lay some ten feet ahead and we were only some dozen people from Sophie and Becca, but as I tried to push forward, I felt a tug on my arm—it was Catherine, gripping my elbow. "They seem in a hurry," she said of the family behind us, allowing them to pass. "And I want to spend time at this window. It's wonderful, don't you think? The sled, the trees, the snowy ground. So elegant and lovely."

An obvious filibuster, which JT recognized as well, smiling wryly in my direction, and for the first time I connected the unwieldy yet easy natured, gray-ponytailed man before me with the sardonic, gloomy teen I had once known.

We caught up to the others a few blocks down. They were waiting on the corner of 46th, Sophie bouncing on her feet to keep warm. "It's 12:30," she said. "We're starved."

At a diner on Madison, we settled into a booth in the rear. JT and I ordered burgers, Sophie, following Becca, a Greek salad, Catherine a tuna fish sandwich. As coats and hats came off, I saw that Sophie had a double piercing on her left ear, and a tangle of bracelets on her right wrist. "JUICY," declared her T-shirt, beneath her modest bosom.

"Christmas windows, check," she said. "Statue of Liberty, check. Next up, Greenwich Village and MoMA. That's this afternoon, right, Grandma? And of course, our Christmas Eve dinner."

"We have a reservation at Tavern on the Green," Catherine said proudly.

"Fancy, fancy," said Becca.

"And what about you?"

"Well, Christmas isn't really a big deal for us. But we'll figure something out."

"And guess what?" Sophie said. "Tomorrow, we're going to Broadway. I want to see *Phantom of the Opera*, but if it's sold out, I'll take anything. Anything. As long as it's a musical, right, Dad?"

"Of course, Soph."

"And later Wall Street, Central Park, the Empire State Building. But I'm not going to White Plains," she said, again looking at her dad. "I'll stay in the hotel if I have to, but I'm not going."

"Let's not discuss this here," said Catherine softly, demurring with a forced smile.

The waiter arrived, somehow carrying all our plates at once, including two platters heaped with fries. We passed around salt, straws, and ketchup, and everyone began to eat. JT was the first to speak again, returning to what seemed to be his favorite topic, his job. "I work with all kinds of bands," he said. "Jazz, rock, pop, rap, Latin, a few you've even heard of. I'm the old guy in the studio. They call me Gray Locks."

"Tell them about your show, Dad," said Sophie.

"I already told Gabe."

"But not Becca. Go on, Dad."

JT lay his burger on his plate and wiped a dab of ketchup from his cheek. "I DJ this radio show. It's 6:00-7:00 Saturday morning, an AM station, so you can imagine the size of my audience. But I love it. Mostly 70s tunes, but not the popular stuff. There's some prog rock and some jazz. It wasn't popular when we were growing up, and it sure as hell isn't now. But it's what I used to dig, what I still dig, and it's also important—at least, I think so."

"How so?" Becca asked.

"The past always returns, right? The jazz is sampled in rap and pop; it's hiding in plain sight. Prog rock isn't ubiquitous like that, but Kanye just borrowed from King Crimson, to cite one example. And prog is more than just music. It's really an ethos—big, bold, futuristic—and if it was all kinds of lame when we were kids, I figure that just means it's going to be hip again real soon. At least, that's the self-important version. Truth is, the show's just me playing the stuff I love. Jazz like Wayne Shorter, Chick Correa, Phill Musra, Don Cherry, Huey

Simmons. The prog rock's well-known bands like Yes, King Crimson, and Supertramp and also wackier acts like Mahavishnu Orchestra. It's just a hobby, but it's also my thing, my real thing. At the end of the hour, I do call-in requests. I have this one friend who's always on standby. He makes a load of picks."

This little speech felt as close as I'd come to the real JT. The music nerd. Undaunted by his stringy gray hair. Proud of the radio show no one listened to. Loving that one bud who helped trick the world into thinking he had a real fanbase. During the hour of his radio show, he probably backburnered all the rest, the punk kids calling him Gray Locks, the ex who made him fight for every minute of partial custody, Stu slow-churning his stews, maybe even the teenage daughter longing for things he couldn't deliver. So, it was odd that Catherine wore something like pain on her face, a wincing expression that might have made me think that her tuna was bad or that a glint of light had caught her eyes, except it lasted too long for that. And how unusual. In the months I'd known her, she had typically worn a glassy, unflappable poker face in her more somber moments. But here she'd betrayed herself—a mixture of shame and disgust, or so I imagined.

Back on the street, Sophie and Becca again surged ahead, though Sophie ran back to us after a few minutes. "Dad, what day do we go back?"

"Wednesday, the 27th."

"Becca has an art opening at a gallery the next evening. Can't we stay?"

"You know we can't, Soph."

She rushed back to Becca and grabbed her elbow, saying in a fake whisper that we could hear at a distance, "Dad says we can't change the tickets. I don't understand why. It's so frustrating."

Again, the two of them disappeared into the crowd, as Catherine, JT, and I trudged along, but then Sophie was bounding back toward us. "Dad! Grandma!" she said. "Becca says we can see her art *now*. In the warehouse. A preview of her show."

"I'm sorry, Soph. We've got a busy afternoon ahead."

"Please, Dad. You can't see these things every day."

"And we need to rest before dinner. Your grandmoth—"

"It's fine, John. Let's take a cab. I'll rest while we drive. It'll be interesting for all of us."

So, we piled into two taxis, in the same groupings as how we'd walked, and fifteen minutes later arrived at a nondescript red brick structure at the far end of West 31st, not more than 50 feet from the West Side highway. Wintry gusts from the Hudson slapped my cheeks as I opened the door and helped Catherine to her feet. Becca and Sophie were already waiting in the building's vestibule. We rode a clunky freight elevator to the third floor, where we stepped into a waiting room with facing couches.

A window in the rear revealed an open space of tables, crates, and storage racks, presided over by two men in paint-splattered corduroys, one wearing a baseball cap that shouted, in large green letters, "Pig Destroyers." The other, with a scruffy ginger beard, invited Becca through a door, while Pig Destroyers joined us on the opposite side of the glass, carrying a tray of Poland Springs and Pellegrinos. He led us around a corner and down a hallway to a spare white room with stark light that mottled his papery skin and revealed a sinewy vein across his left cheek.

Two other men arrived, pushing a cart loaded with crates. They unloaded the boxes one by one, surrounding us with a small cardboard army, then extracted from each a single painting, which they placed on little shelves jutting from the wall. As they set up the display, Becca came in and grabbed a Pellegrino. After a long sip, she began talking about the upcoming show. She downplayed it, saying it was "mostly old stuff," but the knowledge I'd accrued about the art world allowed me to hear nuance in her words. The exhibition wasn't full of debuts, but it also wasn't a showing of the sorts of retreads you might save for less important galleries. It would be a "retrospective," a museum-quality career overview. In other words, a very big deal.

"Tell us, Becca," Sophie said with a clap. "Tell us everything we need to know."

I had never seen Becca's work in a warehouse showroom, but the idea that I might learn something new about her art lasted only a few moments. As she gestured to the paintings and began to speak, I heard a voice and script that were all too familiar, her affable meet-the-artist routine, a practiced act she'd performed countless times, though as ever delivered with a cheery tone that made it seem fresh.

"First up," she said, "are two pieces from *CLI*, my first big show, when I got totally lucky and won some recognition straight out of college."

These were life-size depictions (waist up) of every kid in her high-school class, herself excluded, ranging from young adults in their glory years to others in an awkward adolescence that was painful to behold.

"It's a roman numeral," she said. "151, the number of kids in my graduating class. One hundred fifty paintings in total. Minus 1, for me."

The first showed *Caleb H.*, a handsome boy of ambiguous race with long loose brown curls and skinny arms poking through a light blue tank top.

"Becca," I asked, figuring I should play my part to make this theater successful—for both sides. "Is he the one who became schizophrenic and later homeless?"

"No, that was Craig H. Caleb H. was captain of the lacrosse team. He did well for himself. Went to Princeton and into i-banking, I believe."

The second painting showed *Maddie P.*, a pretty girl with blond bangs who had raised a hand to partially block her face. You could only make out only one eye and the perky tip of a nose. "To be honest," Becca said. "I don't remember her at all. And she's nowhere on the internet. A total mystery girl."

The next two paintings were from the *Delft* series, still-life assemblages of candelabras, bowls of fruit, wine bottles and goblets, and flower vases, arranged and painted in a classical late Renaissance style, except for the slashing brushstrokes on the top layer of paint, as if some Flemish master had thrown a tantrum before the canvas dried, a momentary outburst undoing weeks of painstaking work.

Then, three pieces barely larger than postcards, depicting, in photorealistic detail, a short-order cook, a bartender, and a grocery clerk in their places of work. These were from the *Men behind the Counter* series, all posed on the left side of the canvas and viewed frontally yet each with a distinct personality, as if there were a million ways to ask, "What can I get you?"

We heard a knock on the door, and Pig Destroyers wheeled in a second cart, holding two of Becca's *Chairs*, an armless wicker and an Eames lounge chair, both nearly perfect facsimiles of the real thing, except made of discarded paper and rags.

Catherine pointed at the Eames. "Can we sit?"

"Of course," Becca said.

"Comfy," said Catherine, who settled in the seat, which was fashioned from a patchwork of black headscarves and towels. "Surprisingly so. What do critics say about that?"

Becca smiled. "You'll have to ask them. I just make it."

The man with the ginger beard carried in a rectangular pedestal and a small box. He placed the pedestal in the center of the room and pulled from the box one of Becca's tabletop magnet sculptures, in the form of a red dragon. "Enjoy," he said and headed to the door.

"Thanks, Austin," Becca said, then turned to the Morrows. "The chairs and the magnet piece are a few of my early sculptures. The show will have others, but that's what we could fit in here."

For the next several minutes, we all looked quietly. From the edge of the Eames chair, Catherine toured the room with her eyes. JT and Sophie both moved counterclockwise through the space, though to very different rhythms. JT showed more interest in Becca's art than the holiday windows but still remained some distance from the wall, one hand clasping the opposite elbow behind his back. Sophie got up close to each painting, her eyes and forehead inches from the surface, whispering audibly, "Amazing," "Wow," "I can't believe…," and the like, before every single one.

I tried to see Becca as the Morrows might, to feel the first-time seduction of this dog-and-pony show which she had given over the years to dozens of prospective collectors, school groups, and gaggles of old ladies who made the gallery rounds with private guides. No doubt, the Morrows thought this was a privileged tour. And yet where they saw intimacy, I saw a slipping away, as Becca's true self gave way to her professional persona, a welcoming façade that masked an increasingly inaccessible core. Ironically, the truly private view of my sister was hardly this smiling, engaging figure, but someone much dourer, much harder to approach and to love, which is surely part of the reason she kept it hidden.

"Incredible," Sophie said, as she completed her tour. "What else, Becca? I want to know more. I want to know it all."

"After I did those three paintings series"—Becca pointed to her classmates, the Delfts, and the Men Behind the Counter—"I wanted to try something new. So I made little sculptures that I called *Maquettes for a Young Artist*."

"Are they here? Can we see them?"

"They're too fragile. Also, the guys need to close the warehouse soon. But I'll describe one to give you an idea. I had this clear water bottle, and I wrapped film around most of it, covering all but a sliver at the top. That sliver remained transparent, while the rest was now translucent. I kept the bottle in the studio and whenever I worked and got hot and sweaty, I collected droplets of sweat in the bottle. I filled the bottle until the sweat rose to the top of the film, then put the cap back on. I called the piece *90 Percent Perspiration*."

"I love it," said Sophie. "Then what?"

"After that, I made the Chairs and Magnet Sculptures, which you can see. I was 30 then and wanted a new challenge. So I made a film called *Goliath*."

This was one of my personal favorites. It comprised snapshots and brief film clips of the many cities Becca had visited over the years— from Rio to Bangkok to Copenhagen to Chicago to Vancouver to Shanghai to Cleveland, and so many more—which she'd melded into a seamless vision of frenzied, kaleidoscopic urban life. As one image bled into the next, you never knew where you were, which city, which neighborhood, only that you remained in an inescapable labyrinth of concrete, cars, streetlights, sidewalks, storefronts, construction sites, vacant lots, graffitied walls, grated windows.

"A movie? Wow," Sophie said. "Is it in theaters?"

"Well, it's not at Loews or on Netflix. But some museums have it. MoMA, for one. Also, LACMA, if you want to see it closer to home."

"Dad, can we go, please?"

"Sure, Soph."

"And what else, Becca? Go on."

"After *Goliath*, I started to get commissions. A museum would invite me to make an installation. I made one of giant kids—seven to eight feet tall—half in a straight line against one wall, the other half running toward them. It's called *Red Rover*. Next, I made a giant bird's nest, each twig a twisted tree branch, with plaster eggs as big as you and me. It's called *Nest Eggs*. Then I painted on twenty giant cloth banners, which filled an enormous exhibition hall. Each banner shows a lion, some mid-roar, some prowling, others with claws bent forward, about to pounce. The work's called *Pride*."

"*Pride* sounds amazing. How can I see it?" Sophie practically shouted.

"The paintings are all dispersed now. Different people's homes. Museums. One will be in my show, but it's too large for this room."

"Dad. I've got to see it. Please. It's just a one-day delay."

"I'm sorry, honey."

"You could try the airline, John," said Catherine.

"Mom, you know we have to get back."

"I'll have other shows," said Becca. "Including in L.A. I can put you on my mailing list."

"What about the others *Pride* paintings, Becca? Are any in California?" Sophie asked. "I bet you need a ginormous house, right? What else, Becca? You said, 'mostly old stuff.'"

Becca smiled. "There'll be pieces from two recent series, *Glassworks* and *Mirrorworks*. I'm sorry, but those are already at the gallery. And there's one new piece, but it's not the sort of thing I can just wheel out and show you. Besides, I have a superstition about showing new work before an exhibition."

"Can't you make an exception?" Sophie asked. "Please. Just this once?"

"Soph, she just said…"

This superstition was one of Becca's idiosyncrasies. I couldn't pretend to understand it, but I also knew enough not to question her about it. A few years prior, I had visited Becca's studio in London along with two septuagenarian collectors from Houston, a couple named Marge and Franklin. It was all smiles and gushing praise until Becca, rather suddenly, said that they couldn't enter the studio's back room, "I don't share new work with strangers," at which point Franklin's face went ashen and he began saying, "Strangers? We're hardly…," before grabbing his wife's wrist, "Let's go, Marge," and storming out in a huff. Becca's dealer was upset, because this killed a potential sale, but for Becca, the incident was merely proof that Marge and Franklin didn't get her and therefore didn't deserve to purchase it.

"Then we have to stay," said Sophie. "We have to go to the show. We have to, Dad."

"Your mother will kill me, Soph. You know that."

"She won't. I promise. Please, Dad. Pretty pretty please."

They went on like this awhile, with Sophie's frustration growing in intensity with each new plea. I sensed that she was used to winning such skirmishes but today found her father's obstinacy maddeningly elusive, and for the first time all day she began to lose her poise.

Flustered, eyes twitching, seemingly on the verge of tears, she said, pounding a fist into her palm, "Dad, we've got to see the new work. We've just got to."

"Surely, Becca can find a way to show it to us now," Catherine interjected. "Can't you, Becca?"

"I already told you, I can't," said Becca.

"But why not? We're not strangers. We're friends."

"No."

Becca hadn't raised her voice, but her refusal was sharp and decisive, achieving, with a single word, what JT had not with many more—an assertion of dominance that brought the discussion to its conclusion. As her No rang in my ears, Catherine, who had been rising to her feet, stumbled, falling back into the lap of the Eames Chair. JT, off by the high-school portraits, ran to his mother's side, offering a helping hand, but she slapped it away.

"Thank you, Becca," Catherine said coolly, as she finally rose to her feet. "This was special. Now we need to get going. To prepare for our big dinner. Come, John. Come, Sophie."

"But what about our plans?" Sophie asked.

"Soph, we're all tired," said JT. "We have to go."

She blinked sadly but the outburst I feared never came, and she meekly followed her grandmother and father to the elevator. I went, too, accompanying them to the nearest corner to find a cab, as Becca helped shut down the warehouse.

After a terse goodbye, the Morrows drove off, and I stood alone on the chilly street, in one of the few spots still reached by the afternoon sun.

A few minutes later, Becca joined me. "Ready?" she asked, her eyes bright, as if nothing had just happened.

"For what?"

"Our Christmas Eve. Don't tell me you've forgotten?"

Chinatown on Christmas Eve was a tradition dating back to when our parents were alive. We rotated restaurants in the early years, but for nearly a decade, Becca and I had been going to Chef Wan's. Egg Drop Soup, Peking duck, lo mein, one or two other dishes per the waiter's suggestion. We sat at a table for two, but the spirit of the place was such that it felt like we were part of something bigger. The restaurant was packed with Chinatown locals and others like us, Jews mostly, who celebrated Christmas with duck sauce, chopsticks, bowls of white rice, orange slices, and fortune cookies granted the temporary authority of true soothsayers.

After the meal, when our parents were alive, we would walk through the neighborhood, stopping for tea or ice cream, before heading to St. Patrick's for midnight mass. Since their passing, we let the evening's coda evolve on its own, and in recent years we'd stumbled upon a campy cabaret, an a cappella of Christmas carols in a Lutheran church, a raucous bocce tournament in a Lower East Side bar, and a long walk up Broadway, all the way to Columbus Circle, with a youth basketball team visiting from Belgium.

This Christmas Eve was more subdued. Perhaps we lacked the spark for a serendipitous encounter, but the meal was pleasant, and the walk home, a good five miles, full of quiet joy. Even if we spoke little, even if the air was frigid, even if this holiday meant more to almost everyone we passed than to us, Becca and I were together, which—for me, at least—was all I wanted.

Perhaps that was why I shared little of what was on my mind. To say that I already felt her slipping away would be futile—so much better to just enjoy that portion of her that remained. Besides, she would deny it, just as she would deny she had been even the slightest bit rude to the Morrows at the visit's end. With Becca, such topics were fruitless, and I didn't want the evening to take a turn for the worse.

So, I was surprised when, as we neared our neighborhood, Becca faced me with a wicked smile. "I think I've got them totally pegged." she said. "It's a triangle, right?"

"I have no idea what you're talking about."

"The Morrows. See, in one direction, it's all anxious pining. Catherine longs for Sophie's affection, she longs for JT's, he longs for Catherine's. But face the opposite way, and you've got all kinds of problems, feelings of neglect and disappointment and resentment. I'm no oracle, but that sounds pretty combustible to me. And yet, I gotta admit, I like that girl. Sophie. She's got spirit. She may be naive, but she's got spirit. And not everyone does."

4

We passed a lazy Christmas. We got up late, then had our ritual exchange of gifts. For me, a notebook and pens, which Becca said were "the fancy kind," with refillable ink cartridges; for her, a Buddha board, on which I drew a vase of flowers, or at least attempted to, as she cooked a giant hangover omelet. After the meal, we sipped Scotch in the living room, read, and listened to Dad's old 45s. We napped, had leftover Antonio's for dinner, shared a nightcap, and, a few minutes past 9:00, went off to our rooms to crash.

The next morning Becca left for her gallery, Lightworks, to install her show, and shortly after the phone rang.

"Catherine," I said, recognizing the number.

"No, it's... Sophie. My Dad and Grandma are visiting White Plains, but I don't want to go. Are you and Becca free?"

"Becca's working."

"Oh... I was thinking about a museum, but..."

"I'm free—if you'd like. And we can still go to a museum, even without Becca."

"Are you sure?" The voice on the other end was soft and squeaky, and I was having trouble connecting it to the perky girl of two days prior.

"Of course. Any museum in particular?"

"Maybe… the Guggenheim? I read a book about Frank Lloyd Wright."

Half an hour later, Sophie stepped out of JT's rental car and promised, loudly enough for the whole block to hear, that she'd "be good." As the car pulled away, she rolled her eyes. "Worry warts," she declared, her confidence regained.

We left immediately for the Guggenheim. It was warmer than recent days, though the sky was gray and dim. Along the way, we passed Antonio's, and I insisted we stop for slices. Sophie wanted cheese, but I also got her an onion/sausage, "the Staub special," I said. "You must try."

"Wow," she said after a few bites. "Guess New York pizza really is different."

"Told you."

"Let me pay?"

"I already have. It was my treat."

The big show at the Guggenheim was of the Zero group, a European avant-garde of the 50s and 60s who produced an abstract art at once messy and spare. "What an awesome name," Sophie said, skipping up the winding ramp, but already in the first gallery, I saw disappointment on her face. Before us were large monochrome paintings, "fire" paintings that sounded wilder than they looked, and other simple abstractions. It was the sort of modern art mocked by skeptics as something a five-year-old could make, and in the case of certain all-white canvases, a five-year-old Bartleby. I did my best to repeat the text of the tour that Becca and I had received the previous week and even embarrassed myself as I approached a woman, tall and lean with boy's-length sandy hair, to ask if she was Caroline, the curator who had given the tour; but no, she was a Swiss tourist named Ulrike, who, not understanding my question, offered to take a photo of us. Too embarrassed to explain, I handed her my phone. The picture wasn't half bad, showing Sophie and me before a work that featured a trace of gray soot across otherwise empty paper, like a lonely cloud.

"Nice recovery," said Sophie. "Let's send it to Becca and Grams."

Sophie seemed different than on our previous meeting. Before the Fifth Avenue Christmas windows, she was all youthful exuberance; here, I saw a more mature persistence. We spent an hour completing the upward slope of the Zero show, proceeding methodically, reading each text, looking at each work, and all the while she showed unusual patience, giving no indication of restlessness or a desire to leave. At the snack stand atop the atrium, she said, "I want to keep going, is that OK? I know that for you, this is an everyday thing, but for me it's special. Let's see the permanent collection? But first a coffee?"

When I looked at her funny, she said, "I'm fully grown, you know. Some of my classmates have a cup every morning."

I was dubious, but I still bought us each a coffee and bottle of water. As we finished, she repeated her desire to see the permanent collection.

"I won't know how to give a tour there," I said.

"That's ok. Sometimes it's nice to look without knowing, to make up your own mind, don't you think?"

There were collection shows of minimalism and pop art, meant to complement the Zero exhibition, and then some galleries with impressionism and early modern art, Monet, Picasso, Matisse, etc. Sophie proceeded at a rapid pace, a glance at this wall, a glance at that, though now and then she found a painting that gripped her and would stand, still but for her steadily tapping toes, before it for a good minute or two—a still life of flowers, a Kandinsky abstraction, two portraits of middle-aged women, a picture of a man and his dog, woods in full autumn splendor. Her tour was without rhyme or reason, but I appreciated the whimsy of her choices.

We reached the lobby and sat on a bench. "You know, I'm glad I didn't go to White Plains," she said. "My granddad... well, it's just sad. He's barely there. But the real problem's Dad and Grams. I hate seeing how they hang on his every word. They watch, waiting, as if this will be the word that finally makes sense, as if this one word will make Grandpa return. But he's not improving. He's not remembering. He's not coming back. The whole thing's pathetic, if you ask me."

"It's not an easy situation."

"Of course not, but it's also this game they play. Dad's always trying to get Grams to move to California, but I don't think she wants to. Grandpa's just her excuse."

"Why don't you think she wants to?"

"I think she's spent her whole life taking care of people. Her husband, her kids, her husband again. I think she wants some time for herself."

"Sounds reasonable."

"More than reasonable, if you ask me." Sophie popped to her feet and shifted her weight from one leg to the other. "Can I ask something?"

"Shoot."

"Do you have a girlfriend?"

"I don't."

"Why not?"

"I guess I just haven't found the right person."

"And Becca?"

"I don't think she has anyone either."

"You don't *think*?"

I shrugged. "Does your Dad know everything about you?"

"That's my Dad, not my sister."

"Speaking of which. What about your Uncle Kyle? No one ever talks about him. Do you see him often?"

"Dad says he's an asshole." She shrugged. "You ready to go?"

I stood and we took a few steps toward the door before Sophie stopped and pivoted toward me. "Championship baseball coach fired after barroom brawl," she said gravely.

"I'm sorry?"

"I found it by Googling. I had to hunt. It was on the third or fourth page. It said Coach Morrow went out drinking with some kids after a game and there was a giant fight. Someone got stitches, the pitcher and third baseman were suspended, Uncle Kyle spent a night in jail. Dad never said a word about it, but whenever he says something like, 'You need to be careful with boys, especially wild ones,' I always figure he has Uncle Kyle in mind. So, it's probably…."

Sophie paused mid-sentence, pointed to the museum's glass front, and ran ahead. Snow was falling hard and thick, probably an inch already on the sidewalk. She flung herself through the revolving door, and by the time I joined her on the street, she was hopping around, her nose raised, her tongue out, trying to catch the big airy flakes.

"It's amazing," she said, thrusting her arms skyward and twirling around. "I love it."

"First time?"

"I've seen snow. But not like this."

She stretched a hand to catch a floating flake as if it were a butterfly willing to rest a moment on her palm before fluttering away. As we rounded the corner from Fifth, she rushed ahead, arms spread wide as if about to take off. She was wearing those same shiny red sneakers as on our walk down Fifth Avenue and stumbled more than once, though she always managed to steady herself and remain on her feet.

I said we should go straight home, but now she was walking lazily at my side, looking up to the sky. "Why? Can't we stay out and play?"

"We'll play along the way. Let's go."

The snowfall was growing more intense, and we pressed ahead, weaving through other pedestrians, much as she and Becca had before the Christmas windows. At times, her pace increased, as if she were about to dash off. Other times, she slowed and swept her feet along the sidewalk as if skating. Or brushed her hand across car roofs and windshields, wiping them clean. Or kicked the higher banks forming along the sidewalk's edge.

"I wouldn't do that. You'll slip," I said.

"I already did. It was no biggie."

"What about wet sock?"

"What's that?"

"Just what it sounds like."

"Oh," she said with a giggle. "I already have that."

When we were blocks from the apartment, my phone rang. A number I didn't recognize. "Is that you, Gabriel?" Catherine asked, notably concerned. "Are you ok?"

"Sure, why?"

"I kept calling your landline."

"We went to the Guggenheim. We're almost back at my place."

"Why didn't you write back?"

"Write back?" Looking at my phone, I saw a series of texts I had missed in the museum.

"It doesn't matter," she said. "I sorted everything with Becca. We're stuck in White Plains. Between our late start, and some things with Alan, and JT being uncomfortable driving in the heavy snow, Becca said Sophie could stay over."

I wondered for a second how Catherine had been able to contact Becca, but then I remembered Ulrike's portrait, which I had texted them on the same thread. To my side, I noticed Sophie, who had evidently overheard the conversation, sweeping her foot along the snowy sidewalk with extra glee.

"Is it an imposition, Gabriel? We *could* take the train back. We're close to the stat—"

"Catherine, it's no problem. We'll see you tomorrow. How's Alan?"

"He's fine. Thanks for asking. Yes, fine. Are you sure, Gabriel? Are you? Thanks to you and Becca both. If you have problems, please call. Please. This is JT's number."

I handed Sophie the phone and she walked away, so I couldn't hear. But I could tell that she spoke to both father and grandmother, while doing her best to keep both conversations brief. Within a minute, she was back at my side.

As we entered our dead-end street, she walked right past the building's awning, toward the park. "I don't want to go home yet. Can't we do a snowball fight, Gabe? Or go sledding?"

I obliged with a few snowball tosses, then said I had to go up to use the bathroom. "No fair," she said, fake pouting. "I'm the guest. You're not allowed to be no fun." In the end, I could only get her inside with a vague promise that we would come back out when the snowfall had ended, that this was the better time to play in the snow, anyway.

* * *

Sophie was soaked. I told her to take a shower and that I would find her a change of clothes. I heard her singing *Grease*, as I hunted through Becca's old closets, selecting the baggiest items I could find, hoping they would fit the larger girl. They all did except for the ratty old winter boots. "I'm fine with these," Sophie said, pointing to her sparkly red shoes. "They got me here, didn't they?"

Becca arrived some fifteen minutes later. She didn't notice Sophie's outfit or at least made no mention of it. She carried a bag of groceries, which she'd purchased for dinner.

"Can't we go out to eat?" Sophie asked.

"It's not going-out weather," Becca said. "I'm making soup."

"But my Dad's mad I didn't take Gabe out for lunch. He says I have to take you out for dinner, to thank you for everything you're doing for me."

"That's very generous, Sophie. But you don't need to worry, it's our decision."

"If not dinner, what about a bar?"

Becca put down the knife she had been chopping vegetables with and gave the same look of skepticism I imagined I had when Sophie asked about coffee.

"I've been before," Sophie said. "I mean, with adults. I get a Shirley Temple."

"What about the snow?"

"Your brother said we could go out and play. Besides, this will allow me to do something for you. Please. My Dad insists."

Becca and I looked at one another and silently agreed not to refuse. "Why don't you guys relax in the living room? I'll call when it's ready," Becca said, picking up the knife and starting to chop again.

Our apartment was in a quiet, residential area, but a few blocks over was a handful of sleepy neighborhood bars. Warmed by giant bowls of Becca's hearty Minestrone, we bundled up and went out. The snowfall had died down. There was only a light dusting in the air, which might have been new snow or perhaps just windborne flakes dislodged from trees and car roofs.

"See, it's nothing," said Sophie, pointing to the blackening sky. "My Dad's a wimp. He could have driven back no problem."

She rejected the first pub we entered when three red-eyed men faced us the moment the door creaked open. But she was equally decisive in accepting the second, marching us past the tables in front, where people ate burgers and wings and drank beer from pitchers, toward the bar behind, with booths along one wall and a countertop with some eight stools before it. A youngish crowd milled about in the empty space in between, mostly twenty- and early-thirtysomethings.

Sophie settled into the one free booth. Almost instantly, a waitress appeared and pointed right at her. "How old is she?"

"I'm having a Shirley Temple," Sophie answered defiantly.

"All right then. And the two of you?"

"I'll have a gin and tonic; for him, a whisky water," Becca said.

As the waitress left, Sophie turned to Becca, "Up for a challenge?"

"Maybe. What do you have in mind?"

"A wingman contest. I'm good at it. Sometimes I help out my Dad."

"But no stepmom yet?"

"His follow-through can be pretty rotten."

"Ordinarily, I would say the same of Gabriel, but for some reason I have the feeling he's on the verge of a breakthrough."

The waitress returned with our drinks. Sophie popped a maraschino cherry in her mouth, took a long sip, and licked her lips. "Maybe all Gabe needs is the right wingman."

"And that would be you?"

"I'll find someone. I promise."

"That's some confidence. So, how does the challenge work?"

"We each try to set him up. Winner names her prize. You up for it?"

Becca turned to me. "Are you?"

I wasn't about to kill their fun. "Go for it."

"It's not what I expected when we agreed that you could sleep over," Becca said.

"We can still watch a movie when it's over," Sophie said. "With or without him."

Becca made a face at Sophie, then flicked her eyebrows provocatively at me. I expected some clever retort, but she just sipped her drink through the stirrer, occasionally spinning her glass, silent except for the occasional burst of giggles. As this went on awhile, I remembered all the time Becca and Sophie had spent together two days prior, and I began to wonder if this was some pre-planned joke, some high-concept gag that flew over my head. Or was this a real contest, a kind of farcical revival of the competition between the two families? I didn't get what was going on at all.

Figuring nothing would happen, I studied the room. There was a sameness to the crowd, an informal dress code of dark boots, dark jeans, and thick wool sweaters, in muted greens and grays. Newer arrivals boasted staticky hat head and frozen fingers; what gave them away was their frantic hand rubbing, trying to hurry both conditions away. The bar had grown more crowded since our arrival, and its accidental symphony of jovial shouts and laughter, of jostling ice cubes and clanking glasses, reached a higher pitch, at times drowning out the soundtrack of standard late-90's fare, which likely marked the bartenders as just about my age.

"You like redheads, right?" Becca said suddenly.

No, not especially. I guess Calinda fell into that category, but Becca had never seen her; besides, had I chosen her or had she chosen me? And Lina was blond, while Cassia's hair was raven black. If there was any common characteristic in the women I wound up with, it certainly wasn't hair color. I suppose Becca herself had once been a redhead, though her hair had since darkened into generic brown. A preference for redheads? How had she come by such an idea?

But she was already on her feet, approaching a group at the bar, two women and a man, plus a distant fourth whose hair was thick, shoulder length, and, yes, red. She leaned against the wall, gazing across the bar, looking bored.

The other three broke into laughter shortly after Becca's approach. But not the redhead. She spoke little, even as Becca whispered in her ear, just nodded twice and offered a few monotone responses. I watched Becca turn on the charm, but the girl barely moved; I saw only her profile, the contours of her body remained hidden beneath a loose gray sweater. As Becca stepped away, the woman smiled for the first time, revealing a few gappy teeth, but she was as still as earlier, not even glancing our way.

"I struck out," Becca said.

"See?" said Sophie.

"No crowing until you prove you can do better."

Sophie slurped up the melted ice water at the bottom of her glass and looked around. Becca ordered another round of drinks, and Sophie again plucked her maraschino cherry and chewed loudly. She downed half her glass and cracked her knuckles. "Here goes," she said.

She approached the bar and stood at the edge of a loose circle of some half-dozen people, without introducing herself or finding an entry into the conversation. A minute later, she shifted to a second group with the same result. It was hard to tell if she was sussing things out or terribly shy.

"Like I said, spirited but naive," Becca said. "Too bad, I'd actually begun believing in her."

Sophie shifted to a third group, and then a fourth, all with the same result.

"Did you finish the installation?" I asked.

"I think so, though there may be some last touchups tomorrow before the opening."

I followed Becca's gaze back to the bar. Sophie was off to the side, by the group that Becca had approached minutes earlier. She was speaking to them, including the quiet redhead. Soon Sophie broke free from the group with the redhead a few steps behind.

"This is Allison," Sophie said, marching proudly up to us. "Allison, I want to introduce you to Gabriel."

Allison was short and thick-hipped, with a pretty, round face and thin glossy lips. She blinked shyly, but her smile was wide and friendly.

"Hi." I reached out and shook her hand.

"Your hand is freezing," she said.

"I was holding my drink."

Sophie, who had been sitting next to me, slid into the booth beside Becca.

"Would you like to join us?" I asked, shifting over.

Allison remained at the table edge. "You know, I've never met a guy like this before."

"It's new for me, too. How did she get you to come over?"

"She said you were a dynamo with the older ladies, so you might be able to teach me something."

Becca looked at Sophie and the two of them burst out laughing.

"I was horrified too," Allison said. "But then she told me that the older lady was her grandmother, and she described your friendship, which sounded sweet. She made a hard sell."

"We only met a few days ago," I said. "She might not be trustworthy."

"My friends and I are about to head out. And this is kinda weird. I mean, very weird. But it's freezing and it's December 26th, and yes, I'm single…"

I felt a kick below the table. Both Sophie and Becca grinned widely; I couldn't tell which of them was responsible. "Yup, totally weird," I said. "If my face is red… Is it red?"

"Pinkish? Maybe a shade or two softer than her shoes."

"Well, you've seen me blush, so I guess it can't hurt to ask for your number."

I handed her my phone and she typed in her name and number: Allison Blum — 646 771 9814. "I'll be away through New Year's," she said, with a coyer smile than earlier, lips pinched, teeth hidden. "After that, I'm around."

Becca and Sophie held their laughter for a few seconds. But the sounds that followed—shouts, cheers, whoops—were as loud as after Becca's triumph at the karaoke bar. "I'll have whatever *they're* drinking," someone called out from the bar.

"Shirley Temples all around," Sophie screamed.

Allison's friends, who were on their way out behind her, passed our table. The women gave us a wide berth, but the man stopped before us. "Allison's great," he said.

"So's Gabe," called Sophie.

He lifted his thumb and winked back at us as he headed for the door.

"You're not the smoothest," said Sophie moments later. "But you're better than my Dad."

"Closing's closing," said Becca.

"That wasn't closing. That's just opening the door a tiny crack," Sophie said. "Can I claim my prize now?"

"And what's that?"

"Convince my Dad to let me stay longer in New York. I want to see your show."

Becca looked at me, communicating that I had to be the one to say No. "Sophie, we can't do that," I said.

"Pretty please."

I shook my head. "Not possible. What else?"

As at the warehouse, I worried about tears or some other scene, but again she kept calm. "You know."

"I do?"

"I told you. I want to play in the snow, duh."

"That we can do," Becca said. "Come on."

We were back outside minutes later. One of the advantages—or disadvantages—of living in a dead-end is that yours is never one of the first streets to be plowed after a snowstorm, even if you live only blocks from the mayor's mansion. The moment we returned to our block, Becca grabbed Sophie's hand and the two of them ran halfway down the street, then jumped into a giant bank of snow on the curb. As I drew near, they bombarded me with poorly packed snowballs, powder spraying in all directions. Becca grabbed the plastic top of a garbage bin, ran to a pile of snow on the lip of the dead-end, and sledded down into the street. Soon more snowballs flew at me, these packed tighter and holding firm until they splattered on my jacket or the street beyond.

I ran to the opposite side of the street, hid behind parked cars to avoid their bombardments, popped up to launch snowballs back at them. I held them at bay until they figured out how to approach me from opposite sides. Once I ducked and a snowball Sophie had intended for me sailed right past and smacked Becca squarely on the nose. Her face was pancaked white; she wiped off a clump, then, pausing with a laugh, one eye still coated, asked for a picture to mark the moment. Sophie gladly obliged. Then Becca grabbed the garbage saucer and said that we should go to the hill in the park where we used to sled as kids. It was after midnight, and we were all alone. We took a few sled runs each, then flopped down, exhausted. When I sat up, I saw Becca sweeping her arms back and forth, making a snow angel. There were two more to her left, and another three behind, beside a grinning Sophie.

For the next quarter hour, they kept going, lining the hill and field below with an army of angels, as I lay back and looked up. It was a clear city night, but between the lit windows and streetlights, even in that shaded park, the stars stood no chance. Nothing but endless black sky, plus a single wisp of dark gray cloud—like a misplaced work of the Zero group, missing only a frame.

5

"It's so perfect out. Does it last?"

Sophie leaned against the living room window, looking onto the promenade below, where more snow had fallen during the night, creating a near virgin surface now marred only by a single pair of human and dog tracks.

"They'll plow the street and salt the sidewalks," I said. "Before you know it, it'll be gone."

"Who are *they*? I want to talk with them." Sophie twisted around. She wore Becca's old Eurythmics nightgown, and for the second time that morning, I momentarily mistook her for my sister.

"Good morning." This was the real Becca, behind me, rubbing her eyes and yawning. She invited us to the kitchen, where two cups of coffee wiped away her dazed look. "What now?" she said. "How about popcorn and another Bond?"

The previous night, she and Sophie had crashed on my parents' bed toward the end of *The Spy Who Loved Me*, Becca on Dad's side, Sophie on Mom's. Now, Becca began *Moonraker*, and soon she and Sophie were riffing on a joke from the previous night. Sophie pretended to have a crush on Jaws, the oafish, metal-mouthed villain. She swooned each time he appeared on screen, cracking Becca up every time.

The landline rang at 9:00. It was Catherine. "Can you believe it snowed again? We dug out the car last night; now, we have to do it again. And Sophie and JT's plane. What a mess. We should already be on the road... Hold on... It's another call, the airline. I have to go."

Becca used the break to heat up leftover minestrone. She carried in three bowls and restarted the movie. Soon, the joke was on me. Every few minutes one of them would put down a spoon and ask when I was going to call Allison. *Slurp, Allison, slurp*—it became a running gag, each trying to outwit the other in the elaborateness of their teasing.

Catherine and JT arrived just before noon. JT recounted the highway crawl back to the city, the nearly hourlong holdup at the Alamo garage, Delta's deadly dull hold music. "JFK's totally backed up, our plane is delayed," he said to Sophie. "But if we pack and head straight to the airport, we still might get out tonight."

"I don't have school until next week. Can't we wait?" Sophie looked to Becca for support, but Becca wasn't offering any.

"What a great visit, Sophie," she said coolly. "Thanks for coming."

Sophie's face soured, and I felt sure she was about to begin her *please pretty please* routine, but instead she went wordlessly to my parents' bedroom and soon reemerged in her own clothes, which had dried on the heater overnight. "I had the most amazing time," she said at the door. "Thank you both so so much."

We rode down to the lobby and said goodbye with a round of hugs and promises to see one another soon. We were all sad—at least, Catherine, Sophie, and I were—and when the Morrows crossed the threshold onto the salty sidewalk and offered another wave, it had the finality of a true parting.

Yet I was hardly surprised when Catherine called the next morning for details about Becca's opening. "It'll be all three of us," she said. "The snow has the airport all backed up. Sophie and JT couldn't get a flight till tomorrow morning."

* * *

Lightworks was in the heart of Chelsea, on one of the glam-gritty stretches of the West 20s, between 10th and 11th Avenues, where white box contemporary art galleries vied with greasy auto shops for sidewalk rights. There were hundreds of these places, but Lightworks was the only one brave enough (or dumb enough, I suppose) to schedule an opening on Thursday, December 28, when the vast majority of its audience would be at some ski lodge in the Rockies or the pool at St. Barts or a hipster bar in Bushwick, or before the Christmas tree at home. On the other hand, if you were in Manhattan and wanted to go to an art event, well, this was your lone option. "Small supply, small demand, is also a market," my friend Peter, a banker, liked to say. With snowbanks piled high on either side of West 27th and only a single lane to drive down, it seemed like Lightworks had placed a losing bet, though the afterparty couldn't have been easier to find, at Marty Shinn's duplex, directly upstairs in the same building. Yes, you had to trek through the lobby to an elevator bank in the rear, but you could get there without another risky venture onto the sidewalk, with its chalky salt pellets and sinister black ice.

I arrived at 6:45 and, entering through the double glass doors, recognized the place immediately. A reception area, with small book display, to the left. A circuit of galleries, starting to the right. The second of these had a staircase to the tiny mezzanine (roped off; a smaller show was set to open in January), with offices through the rear of the third gallery. Completing the circuit was an open area featuring a bar that led back to the reception.

There was a decent crowd, but the gallery was spacious and hardly felt packed. The Morrows were already there, dressed up for the occasion though still standing out. The color of the day was black, even the snow boots, but Catherine's long dress, which slipped from under her fox coat, was red, and Sophie's had a white front with pink sleeves that billowed around the wrists; and of course, she still wore her shiny red shoes. In a gray jacket, jeans, and cowboy boots, JT might have passed for an eccentric regular, if not for the thick gel darkening his gray hair.

I waved to them but walked in the other direction, into the first gallery. The setup was similar to what we had seen in the warehouse days earlier, with the paintings of classmates, still lifes, and men behind counters, as well as a few *Maquettes for a Young Artist*, a group of small works made from household materials and bearing clever titles (*Don't Let Perfect Be the Enemy of Good, Escape Goat, Don't Dwelling, Second Winds, Be Born Rich*). These dated from the 1990s.

In the second gallery were works from the 2000s: the two *Chairs*, a plinth topped with four tabletop magnet sculptures, a large *Pride* banner (which spanned an entire 18 foot wall) plus a photo montage of the original installation of all 21 pieces in an enormous empty warehouse, and two of the *Red Rover* kids.

Many guests had clustered in the third gallery, which featured Becca's *Metalworks* and *Glassworks*. They were large sculptures whose shiny metallic and dulled mirrored surfaces were twisted, bent, rolled, and sometimes partly painted over—then hung on the walls as reliefs or placed on the floor as freestanding sculptures. These had debuted in 2010 and 2012, respectively.

The opposite end of this gallery opened to the booze and snacks, but the exhibition checklist indicated a fourth gallery, which I had to double back to find. In a back corner of Gallery 2 lay a narrow opening covered by a white curtain that, when not fluttering, barely stood out from the wall. Surely, I was not the first visitor to have missed it entirely.

Beyond the curtain was a dark hallway, perhaps 10 feet long, along which you gradually lost your ability to see in the pitch dark. At its end, on the side wall, I felt another curtain, which I pushed through and entered a second corridor, perpendicular to the first. It was no less dark except for the words projected in dim white against a third curtain on the far end:

Once ashore, when you reach the city of Cumae
and Avernus' haunted lakes and murmuring forests,

there you will see the prophetess in her frenzy,
chanting deep in her rocky cavern, charting the Fates,
committing her vision to words, to signs on leaves.
Whatever verses the seer writes down on leaves
she puts in order, sealed in her cave, left behind.
There they stay, motionless, never slip from sequence.
But the leaves are light—if the door turns on its hinge,
the slightest breath of air will scatter them all about
and she never cares to retrieve them, flitting through her cave,
or restore them to order, join them as verses with a vision.
So visitors may depart, deprived of her advice,
and hate the Sibyl's haunts.

Pushing through the final curtain, I entered a wide rectangular space, also dark, the sort I knew well from video installations, though without the usual benches to orient you in any specific direction.

After a few seconds, flickers of light dotted all four walls. The dots and splotches soon congealed into a cluster of trees, a thick, leafy canopy, a forest floor dappled with fallen leaves as others fluttered through the air. It was a vision of early fall, in animation but close to realism. In an instant, the peaceful scene was overwhelmed. A burst of wind beat the trees, rattling branches, hurling leaves in the air. The wind stopped just as suddenly, the leaves scattered to the ground, and the walls went dark but for a sliver of moon high in one corner. Another beat, and this too vanished; the room was completely black.

Then, I heard a voice, male and husky:

Oh, she was so shy, and so gentle. There is something of a child about her. Her eyes opened wide in exquisite wonder when I told her what I thought of her performance, and she seemed quite unconscious of her power.

Just after the words began, an image appeared on the wall to my right. A photograph of a woman in a blue sleeveless dress, a gray jeans jacket slung loosely over a shoulder. Her opposite hand thrust forward, fingers spread like a fan, showing off long nails painted neon pink.

The image faded moments before the voice went quiet. There followed a few seconds of darkness and silence, then a new voice, female and high-pitched:

> *A time will come when many days reduce*
> *my body to near nothing, and old age*
> *whittles my limbs to where they scarce can bear*
> *their meager burden; nor will I then seem*
> *to have inspired love in a god's breast;*
> *Phoebus himself perhaps will not remember,*
> *or may deny that he desired me:*
> *these are the changes I will come to bear,*
> *but when I am no longer visible,*
> *I will be recognized by my voice still,*
> *according to the promise of the Fates.*

A few beats into this reading, a new image appeared—on the back wall—a Polaroid of a teenage girl holding a red Dixie cup and standing on a wooden porch amid a mass of faceless bodies. It faded just before the voice ended, and the room was again dark.

Then a male voice with a posh English accent:

> *People she had never seen before would insist that they knew her. She would go to a picnic and have a vague sense of having been there before. A dress that she had not bought would be hanging in her closet. She would begin a painting and return to the studio to find that it had been completed by someone else—in a style not hers. Sleep was a nightmare. She just couldn't be sure about sleep. Often it seemed as if she were sleeping by day as well as by night. Often, too, there was no dividing line between the time of going to bed at night and waking up in the morning. Many were the occasions of waking*

up without going to sleep, of going to sleep to wake up not the next morning, but at some unrecognizable time.

The accompanying image appeared on the front wall: a woman, likely in her thirties, sitting on a bus, leaning against the cloudy windowpane with empty highway behind her.

The fourth voice was a young boy, who began with a singsong rhyme:

Listen, my children, and you shall hear
Of a lovely feminine Paul Revere

Who rode an equally famous ride
Through a different part of the countryside,

Where Sybil Ludington's name recalls
A ride as daring as that of Paul's.

The boy cleared his throat and, shifting into prose, attempted a sober tone that highlighted his struggle to pronounce the larger words:

Sybil Ludington's Ride *(1952), the first of many twentieth century books to be written about the girl rider, was published as Cold War tensions were escalating. Pitched to ten- to fourteen-year-old readers, it was composed and illustrated by the well-known children's book author Erick Berry. While driving through Putnam County around 1950, Berry had noticed the historical roadside markers about Sybil. Her interest piqued, as the* New York Times *noted, she set out "to unearth scanty facts about this teen-age heroine of the Revolution." Praising the book's historical angle, the* Times *declared that "fact-founded adventures like this one always seem a little more satisfying than purely fictional ones." Berry listed as her sources "a short poem about [Sybil] written some years back, a short write-up and map made at the time the historical roadside markers were put up," and a "brief and colorlessly written book" about the Ludington family. Despite Berry's claim that* Sybil Ludington's Ride *took only "a slight liberty with the Ludington household, but all other details are historically accurate," her book was essentially a work of fiction.*

Berry jettisoned six of the Ludingtons' children and their mother, leaving Sybil and her younger sister, Rebecca, to carry the narrative. In Berry's imaginative rendition, Sybil threw on her father's clothes, carried a lantern, and rode a sorrel colt, Star—details that would emerge in later "histories." Perhaps the most widespread invention Berry promulgated was the name of Sybil's horse, which neither Lamb nor Johnson had specified. Berry would likely have been pleased with that development because, as she reported on her book's dust jacket, "really it's the little horse who interested me as much as Sybil's ride."

Accompanying this reading was an iPhone snapshot of a young woman in a bikini, lying awkwardly atop a towel at the beach, shading her wide hazel eyes with a copy of *The Bell Jar*.

Someone entered the room. I could barely make out the shape of the body, certainly not a face, but the appearance of another person broke the spell. When the young boy stopped his recitation, the room darkened, and the animation of trees, leaves, and wind played again, followed by a new voice, male and professorial:

I saw with my own eyes the Sibyl at Cumae hanging in a cage, and when the boys said to her: "Sibyl, what do you want?" she answered: "I want to die."

The image that flashed by showed a teenage girl in breeches, boots, and a riding helmet, with a section of rope snaked between her fingers.

A third person entered, and again we saw the trees, leaves, the wind. I can't recall exactly how long I stayed, how many voices I heard, how many pictures I saw, only that no single voice, nor any picture, repeated during my visit, and that each time someone new entered the room, the tree animation played, after which came new voices (some male, some female) and new images (all female, most quite young), projected on all four walls of the dark, rectangular enclosure, in no discernable order.

I exited the same way I had entered and returned to the gallery, whose bright walls and gleaming ceiling lights now overwhelmed me. As my eyes readjusted, I saw that I was standing among some dozen people, mostly singles and pairs turned to the walls. Becca was a few feet away, talking with an older woman in a stylish dress and loud purple plastic glasses.

"Tell me, Becca," the woman was saying. "Your new piece, what was the name?—yes, *Sybil*. Tell me about it, I want to know—"

"Tina, you know I'm no good at talking about my work," Becca said.

"But this one *needs* to be discussed. It's begging for it." Tina paused for a response, even turning to me, a total stranger, for support, while Becca stared at her feet, feigning bashfulness. "Well, it's something else," Tina continued. "I want you to know that, Becca. I thought it was marvelous… and haunting. Marvelously haunting."

"That means so much coming from you, Tina. Thank you. By the way, do you know my brother, Gabriel Staub?"

Of course, we didn't know each other, but Becca had learned to play this game. As Tina extended a hand, Becca slipped through an opening to the next room.

"Why, Gabriel," Tina said, watching Becca vanish over my shoulder. "You must be so proud."

"Of course," I answered, though in fact I felt less pride than confusion. Like Tina, I was perplexed by Becca's newest work. So much of my sister's art was about heady concepts and exquisite execution—it projected order and control—but this one was looser, pushing toward an uncertain sublime. I'd left that dark room feeling more unsettled than when I'd entered.

Tina blabbed on about her "little house on the beach. It's in Baja. I fly out tomorrow, my New Year's escape. What are your plans?"

As soon as I could, I broke free and headed to the bar, and from there to the bookstand, which held a small library of Becca's old catalogues, the earliest of which were flimsy pamphlets, though one was housed in a glass vitrine, having improbably become an item of some value.

I felt a tap on my shoulder. It was Catherine, with Sophie and JT only a few feet behind.

"We had the most amazing day. We had lunch at Saigon Kitchen," said Sophie excitedly, as if it were no less famous than Tavern on the Green. "Do you know it?"

I didn't bother saying that there were probably half a dozen places of the same name scattered across the city. "I'm afraid not."

"An unassuming place on 74th, but we had the most wonderful lunch," said Catherine. "I'll take you one day, a special treat."

JT explained that they had a 4:00 pm plane the next day, but he wanted to go to the airport in the morning in case they could sneak onto an earlier flight. Then he whispered to me, "Sophie's mom was surprisingly calm on the phone. But I'm telling you, if I don't get Sophie on a plane tomorrow, there'll be hell to pay."

"What did you think of the *Pride* painting?" Sophie asked.

"Was that your favorite work, honey?" Catherine said.

"That or the reflective pieces. I can't decide."

"I'm still partial to the classmates," said JT.

"The *Pride* banner just moved me," Sophie said. "There was something about it I can't really explain. What about you, Grams? What was your favorite? And what about you, Gabe?"

I wanted to discuss Becca's newest piece, but something held me back, including my awareness that they might have missed it entirely, so I let them speak and listened as their discussion followed the usual pattern at these events: broad, open-ended questions leading to vague, banal responses, as if everyone was fearful of voicing a critical opinion or one that might be considered silly or unsophisticated. Only Sophie spoke with any courage, any freshness. If she relied on the most basic, positive adjectives (*good, excellent, astonishing, etc.*), this was mere innocence in her case, not fear of social faux pas. And she was right. The show was *wonderful*. My sister was a virtuoso who still knew how to surprise. When Sophie asked if anyone had detected a "through-line" to the work, "an overall theme," no one responded. What came to mind for me, though I didn't say it out loud, was this: Quality. Excellence. Mastery.

Which is why *Sybil* stood out. It landed a blow somewhere between the heart and gut, whereas most of Becca's art was more like a tap to the head. I knew that I would think about it at home that night. And even after Becca left the apartment in a few days, the feeling of *Sybil* would linger, like some residue she'd left behind. Tina had been right to call it haunting.

I drifted back to the bar and, finding no one familiar, returned to the catalogues. Somehow, it was only 7:30. I knew from experience that time can crawl at an art opening. People generally breezed through the show and then stood around chatting. If you had an aversion to small talk, it could be a torturous two hours.

Another tap on the shoulder. Rachel Shatner, Becca's Boston gallerist and one of the few dealers I'd met who was every bit the opposite of the horrible man in Lyon. Rachel was always friendly, playing her part to make art galleries feel like welcoming spaces. Of course, I knew this was no less a persona than any other and likely successful for her business. Still, she greeted me with a full hug. How was I? What had I been up to? I offered the usual replies, and she showed off photos of her granddaughter, a blond-tufted, toothless smiler, who had yet to emerge from her generic baby look. Rachel asked for my thoughts on the show. When she mentioned *Sibyl*, I heard myself utter the usual banalities. "I thought it was really interesting. Quite strange, but wonderful."

"Wasn't it?" Rachel replied, a gleam in her eye. "So strange, but also so wonderful."

Her echo highlighted my false witness, and I felt relieved as she tactfully excused herself and moved onto the next gab session.

At the reception desk, I read the show's press release, hoping it might offer some information about the new work. It was a long text, much of it familiar. This was Becca's fifth show at Lightworks. The exhibition was a career overview. Becca was one of "the most important artists of her generation." Yadda yadda. Several paragraphs described the many works on display, but on the second page, I came upon this:

The final work in the show, and the only one that debuts here, is Sybil *(2013), a multi-channel video and audio installation dealing with issues of female identity and representation.*

The work takes its point of departure from the soothsaying of the legendary Sybils, priestesses of Apollo who prophesied with leaves at the god's oracles. The work uses literary quotations about the Sybils, as well as other famous and legendary woman named Sybil from history and literature: Sybil Dorsett (or Shirley Ardell Mason), an art teacher and famous psychiatric patient alleged to have multiple personality disorder; Sybil Ludington, a teenage girl whose ride during the American Revolution earned her minor fame as "the female Paul Revere"; Sybil Vane, a character in Oscar Wilde's Portrait of Dorian Gray; *Sibylle Boden-Gerstner, the East German fashion writer; and many more.*

Juxtaposed with the texts discussing these women's real and imagined lives is a slideshow of anonymous women, mostly adolescent and young adult, as seen in photographs that Staub has collected during travels over several decades, at tag sales, flea markets, estate sales, junk yards, and thrift stores.

The full loop runs every 12 hours, but as the pairings of text and image are randomly generated, no two 12-hour viewings are the same. And every time someone new enters the priestess's cave, the leaves that the Sibyl uses for prophesy are re-scattered, and the work begins anew.

I had read this sort of description of a high-concept artwork at plenty of exhibitions in the past. Just as there was a code to gallery opening chit-chat, so there was a particular way to write these things. Yet for some reason these words had sent my mind racing, leaving me anxious and confused, not unlike the work itself. Sybil Ludington, the female Paul Revere? Didn't I...? I had no idea who she was, yet the name sat heavy in the brain.

I searched the gallery for Becca, finding her in the ever crowded third exhibition space, amid the *Glassworks* and *Metalworks*, with the Morrows beside her. "Hey, Gabe," said Sophie, as her grandmother and father—the one leaning into Becca's ear, the other roving the larger scene with his eyes—offered only distracted waves.

Sybil Ludington. It was the T-shirt worn by that woman. What was her name...? Harriet? The woman on the Catskills horse farm. *Sybil Ludington 25K Run*, her T-shirt had incongruously read.

As this memory flooded my mind, I turned back to the group and saw them all reshuffled: JT looking at Catherine, who looked at Sophie, who looked at JT: gazes of longing, none returned, the exact triangle Becca had described days earlier. A few heartbeats later, they shifted anew. Sophie gawking at Becca with awe-struck eyes. JT spying the two of them in the silvery reflection of an artwork, slowly uttering, "Wow." And Catherine, turning to me, whispering, "Isn't it grand?" her breath warm on my earlobe, practically a kiss.

"What do you mean?" I asked.

"Why, the five of us. The Morrows and Staubs. After so many years. Who would have thought, Gabriel? Who would have thought that you and I, such an improbable pair, would be the ones to bring everyone back together again?"

6

"Been in a house like this before?"

Catherine held a cracker topped with tuna tartare in her right hand and a clear, fizzy drink in her left.

We were in Marty Shinn's penthouse—the usual mix of lawyers, bankers, and other finance types, plus many guests with enigmatic work lives, which was hard to pull off in this city of "What do you do?" Some were the usual art-world hangers-on, and a few others belonged to that rarified slice of New York society for whom extraordinary wealth was no less a given than the color of light or the taste of water. And yet it took a practiced eye to differentiate this latter group from a third, and largest, group, those who constantly obsessed about wealth, caught as they were between the perilous nature of their own status and the permanence of everyone else's. What eventually gave them away were their exaggerated smiles and fidgety, roving eyes.

Had I been in a house like this before? Well, yes. Growing up, I had accompanied my parents to the homes of some of Mom's wealthier clients and law partners. Among my generally well-off classmates in school, there had been a few scions of massive fortunes with discreet mansions perched atop the most august Fifth Avenue tower. While my parents would surely have mocked the pretensions of this event at Marty Shinn's, they would secretly have loved being present for it. One difference between the Staubs and Morrows, I suppose, was that we had always stood adjacent to this elite and occasionally been invited inside its gates.

We had already been at "Marty's" for an hour, perhaps two, long enough for our little group to spread throughout the giant space, find favorite vantage points, and assume our evening roles. Becca was in full professional mode, distant and imperious, barely straying from Marty's side. They nestled in an alcove along the room's long back wall, the axis around whom the rest of us revolved. Between the depths of people before them and Becca's impervious armor, not to mention the cool touch of her hand as she parted from me upon entering the penthouse, I had recognized that tonight would offer no hope of real time together, at least not before the party's wee hours.

Catherine was in top form. She bounced from circle to circle with an alluring smile and a bon mot in her back pocket, sometimes with Sophie at her side. I overheard snippets of their conversations, with phrases like "only 15 years old" or "a bit of a painter herself, but her real thing is musical theater," or "why yes, a California girl." Sophie knew the precise beats when she was supposed to chime in, and her words always won a wide smile from Catherine, even if others raised haughty eyebrows in response.

But Sophie had less success on her own. She lacked Catherine's light touch, and when her teen perkiness didn't instantly charm, she had only blunt persistence to fall back on. From what I saw, she handled these rejections (including one from Marty, when Sophie had mistakenly asked if an Oehlen was a Basquiat, winning her a long stare at the back of his creaseless blue shirt) with aplomb, shifting quickly to another conversation, always leading with an outstretched hand, though I once noticed Catherine, watching nearby, grimace sourly, as if betraying a momentary flag in her faith in the night's promise—or perhaps in that of her precocious granddaughter.

JT stood at the party's edge. Whatever centripetal force pulled his mother and daughter toward its core, an opposite, centrifugal one drove him to the walls and windows. Looking out as often as in, he forayed into the center of Marty's expansive living room only to refill his champagne glass at the bar. Not unlike on that long-ago evening in the basement in the Catskills, his presence was vanishing, and for stretches of time I forgot he was there.

Fortified by two drinks at the opening and a third here, I circled through the party like so many others. Catherine and I crossed paths with regularity, and each time, like some cuckoo clock, she had stretched her neck, leaned toward my ear, and whispered, "What a wonderful evening," or "I can't believe it," or "Isn't it grand?"

But this time, she stood directly in my path.

"What's your guess?" I asked.

"My guess about what?" She was already looking over my shoulder, plotting a next move.

"You asked, *Have I ever been in an apartment like this*? What do you think?"

"With you New Yorkers, one never knows."

Clever, and not without edge, her comment spoke to the subtle envy that had always existed between our families, but also, to my mind, suggested a categorical error. Whatever Catherine may have thought of my parents, there lay a world of difference between our upper-middle-classness and Marty Shinn–level wealth. This was a veritable mansion in the sky—an apartment with separate wings for entertainment and domestic life (we guests were permitted to see, at most, one half of the place); with panoramic views across the city: to the west, the churning Hudson; to the south, the lonely Freedom Tower; to the East, the bridges to Brooklyn. Even if I had been here before (or anywhere like it), it was no less astonishing and absurd to me than it surely was to her.

Yet, it only took a glance at Becca to wonder if there might be something to Catherine's charge. After all, each time I circled past my sister—and it was always I who came to her—I was reminded that she had attained more fluency in this milieu than my parents or me. She spoke with ease about tech startups (where Marty was "parking" a good deal of money these days) and somehow managed to contrast the draft of a catamaran to that of a monohull credibly enough that the white mustachioed yachtsman beside her, named (I kid you not) Skip, said, "I know exactly what you mean."

And so, if you glanced from Becca at the party's core to JT at its farthest extremity, you could see how once subtle distinctions of class between the Morrows and Staubs had heightened over a generation. The two eldest children, both naturally shy and introverted, had such radically different social temperaments and levels of comfort in this setting.

"Well, I think it's marvelous," said Catherine, dabbing the corner of her eye with a napkin. "I just never imagined that our two families…"

So began a new rhapsody on time and fate, but even as Catherine spoke, her eyes sought out Becca and Marty, who stood at the center of a crowd, twin poles of desire and attainment. On the one hand, a skinny man in black suit pants and a light blue shirt, two buttons open to reveal a tanned, hairless chest, whom you might easily overlook until you noticed he stood in the frame of two faux columns, as if posing for a picture or possessed by some narcissistic grandeur. *A collector*, they called him, which meant that what set him apart from other dark-suited, plastic-rim-bespectacled, silver-haired eminences with a shit ton of money, was that he possessed that rare and most exotic of strengths: WALL POWER. Just about every square foot of wall that wasn't window or bookshelf was given over to canvases, plinths, and even two video projections, as were sections of ceiling and pediments above doorways. Two of these, *A Man Behind the Counter* and a *Glasswork*, were Becca's. On the other hand, the enigmatic, young genius Rebecca Staub, possessor of the one talent that money couldn't buy: *inspiration*. Theirs was a perfect symbiosis. Without her, he would have been just another rich New Yorker with windows wrapping around three walls of a living room that reached toward the clouds. Without him, her sibylline creations would have been totally unknown, never escaping their dark cave.

Soliloquizing on the reunion of the families, but shuttling her eyes between Marty and Becca at the party's core, and her son on its outskirts, Catherine betrayed her inner tension, the clash of her competing agendas: the family reunion, about which she kept talking to me, and a social ambition, to ingratiate herself into this scene. I felt as if I was witnessing her dawning awareness that the two wishes were incompatible—that no amount of skill and cunning could grant her both and still make the story neat and whole.

"Why do I feel like you aren't hearing a word I'm saying?" she said, though she was the one looking past me. "Oh, go on then, Gabriel. Mingle. Maybe you'll meet someone."

Mingle? Me? It was more her desire than mine, but what else did I have to do? I took a deep breath and, having nothing to lose, steeled myself to enter the party.

I wandered a bit and soon found myself before a woman named Isabelle, who addressed a small circle. "It was different back then," she said in a faint but intriguing accent. "Artists just made things. If you paid their way, they made their thing and left it with you before moving on. It was the unofficial contract. Later, these art spaces, not all, but many, took those things and sold them, some becoming very rich. I know all this, because my first job, right out of uni, was at The Warehouse, the art space run by Elizabeth Caughlin before she founded Right Edge Gallery. Some directors of art spaces even made a copy of the thing the artist had left behind, and now there was also a second version to keep or to sell later. The artists didn't object. They were making a career, traveling the world; what more could they want? And back then, nothing was worth that much, so who cared if your host made some money on the side? Now, it's all buttoned up. Becca's too savvy to stand for any of that. She understands the business, she keeps records. You can't pull a fast one on this generation. Then again, the money is so much greater now, so the dealers have an easier time making theirs, too."

I continued on, smiling at those I nudged past, until I could stretch my elbows and eavesdrop on another conversation.

"Beth," said a graying, silky skinned older woman to her platinum-domed contemporary. "Do you remember Heather, my friend who always has the best book recommendations? Well, she told me about the latest by Diane Silverstein."

"Speak of the devil, Joan. That's her, right over there." Beth pointed to a tall, plump woman with a puff of snow-white hair, her back to us.

"Heather's here?"

"Not Heather. Diane Silverstein. That's her. Go on up. I hear she's very approachable."

"But I can't just do that. At least not without another drink... Come to the bar, Beth. Help me."

Feeling little of Joan's inhibition, I presented myself before the fingered woman, who was standing alone, fiddling with the latch of her purse. "Did I overhear that you were Diane Silverstein, the writer?" I asked.

A chin lifted, and I saw a sallow face and a pair of warm, though rheumy eyes. "I am Diane Silverstein, and I am a writer."

"Did you go to Cornell?"

"Go Big Red," she said, pumping a flabby arm in the air. "Why do you ask?"

"You won't believe this, but my dad used to tell this story..."

As I launched into the tale of the Morrows and Staubs, Diane Silverstein smiled, the heavy lines of her face shifting and resettling. I had never seen my parents reach this phase of life and I was momentarily touched by the thought that only a few decades earlier my father and his best friend had competed for her attention.

But she quickly cut me off. "You must be Becca's brother. Yes, I can see the resemblance. I'm sorry to disappoint, but I don't remember your father at all."

"And how do you know Becca?"

"Artists, writers, we really aren't that many."

"It's still quite the coincidence."

"Yes, perhaps, I'm..." She waved to someone on the far side of the room and was off, leaving me as wordlessly as she once had left Dad.

As he had so many years ago, I stepped away to gather my thoughts and soon found myself in a clearing near JT, who stood at a window gazing at the Hudson and dark sky beyond.

"Doing ok?" I asked him.

"Absolutely. I'm admiring the view. Actually, *admiring* is too weak a word. I'm mesmerized. Look at those snowy roofs. The dark sky with those cloudy streaks of light. It's pure magic."

JT looked around eagerly, delight in his eyes, and I followed his gaze to the tide-rippled Hudson, the windows of the Wall Street towers, the glowing torch of the Statue of Liberty, the slate gray of the sky. As on the street a few days earlier, he seemed happiest when taking in the extremes of the city architecture, its inhuman scale.

"Out west," he went on, "you've got the ocean, the mountains, the desert. Where Kyle lives, up north, you have forests and things. But the city at night, with all these shimmering lights… It steals your breath. Is this what brought you back to New York? I bet…"

I heard a churning sound, and all at once saw a helicopter buzzing close enough that I could make out a passenger's gold-rimmed cowboy hat. "Would you look at that. I get it, Gabe. I get why he's up there."

"You wouldn't be scared?"

"I said I *get* it. But there's a reason I'm here and not up there." He smiled soberly and turned back to the window to watch the helicopter, which continued south, past the Freedom Tower, past Battery Park, until it faded into the sky, seeming to take some portion of his boyish enthusiasm with it.

I went to the bar for another whisky. A few sips brought on a new wave of fortitude, and soon I was back in the scrum of the party, pleasantly anonymous, sliding easily from conversation to conversation. In little time, I had passed from gawker to participant, which it turned out was more trick of the mind than a shift in space. Banish the thought that you're an outsider and—*poof*—you pass for an insider. It really was that simple. If you had made it up to Marty's, you were surely a friend, or a friend of a friend, or a friend of a friend of a friend. Everyone belonged. The only imposters were the ones who refused to play the game. Act as if.

But of course, not all conversations were created equal. Many bogged down in superficial chitchat, others rutted in the gawky "So how do you know Marty?" phase. Only a few avoided these dead ends and continued on at a leisurely pace. I had the most luck with older women. Perhaps they were more practiced at this art, perhaps less desired; perhaps Sophie was right, and I really did have a knack with them. A half-generation my senior, on the cusp of 50, the gray dyed away, the faces and arms barely wrinkled (though no amount of work could mask their thin, bony hands, the prominent veins coursing over knuckles and joints), in a word, *mature*, and aware that whatever sexiness remained to them they had for this very reason. Connie. Claudia. Sheila. Elaine. Shifting through the mass of bodies, I found that conversations stretched longer, smiles widened, groups of four and five gave way to private audiences. I was questioned longer, sometimes teased, my forearm, elbow, wrist, lightly touched. Astrid. Eleanor. Janine. Light flirtation with each, often so subtle I couldn't determine the line between playfulness and genuine suggestion. What is certain is that I was growing tipsier and less inhibited with each.

Catherine found me again, on a clockwise tour to my counterclockwise. "I've been watching you, Gabriel," she said. "You seem like quite the lady's man."

"Catherine, I've got to tell you, the most amazing thing happened. Diane Silverstein is here. Do you remember, the woman from Dad's—"

"Yes, I met her too," she said excitedly, then leaned forward and whispered, "But she's snooty, no? Way too proud to say that she doesn't remember Alan or Jonah. We'll have to show her, won't we?"

And she reached a hand into a passing tray of hors d'oeuvres, sipped from her fizzy drink, and laughed, a little too loudly, before slipping past me and back into the crowd.

Looking around, I could see that the party had entered a new phase, smaller, boozier, more intimate. The crowd of 100 had whittled down to half that size, with most gathered in two clusters: around the bar and around Becca and Marty.

Every time I looked to Catherine, she was among those inching toward Becca. When Catherine had taken off her fox coat earlier in the night, she had revealed a new layer of luxury beneath: a pearl bracelet and thin gold filigree necklace with a black leopard pendant—all new to me. Too much flash for this crowd, but not without purpose. No one would have suspected she lived in "a home." No, she could pass for the sort who went to society parties, mingled with the uber-rich, perhaps had a small art collection of her own. Among this crowd, being gauche might seem like a crime, until you realized it was so much milder than all the others. Sure enough, there was Sigrid Körner, Becca's Zurich dealer, sidling up to her. Sigrid, whom Becca had said was "always selling, it's the only thing she knows how to do." I knew Catherine would enjoy furthering the illusion, and I approached to listen.

Where did she live? "A small place on the East Side."

Had she lived there long? "No, I moved recently."

And why was that? "My poor husband got sick, and I finally escaped dreary Westchester."

As Sigrid stepped away, I was about to compliment Catherine's act, but Sophie brushed right past me and stood at her grandmother's side. "Dad says we should go," she said.

"I'm not ready," Catherine replied. "Are you?"

Sophie shook her head, and Catherine bent and whispered something, after which Sophie hurried back to her father with renewed purpose.

Just as Catherine kept pushing further into the center of things, JT remained on the party's edge, largely hidden from view. I next came upon him some twenty minutes later. Sophie and he were standing by the window at the room's southwest corner, the lights of Staten Island visible above the horizon.

"People do long distance all the time," she was saying. "You're acting like a loser, Dad."

"We live on different coasts."

I cleared my throat, alerting them to my presence.

"Gabe," JT said with a friendly smile. "I don't understand why everyone is over there." He pointed to the swarm in the center of Marty's living room. "How can you resist this view? Or is it commonplace for you? Is every day like this?"

"Hardly," I said. "This is far—"

"For Becca, it is," said Sophie, looking at each of us with a defiant stare. "It could be yours, too."

Then she ran back to her grandmother, who draped an arm around her and introduced her to Sigrid and some other new friend.

"Teenagers," JT said with a sigh. "She wants me to be more social, is all. Would you believe she's always trying to set me up? We go to a restaurant, she excuses herself to go to the bathroom, and the next thing I know she's talking up some strange woman at another table. I admire her nerve, but God can it be awkward."

Behind us, I saw that the party had thinned further, with a new trail of departees heading toward the elevator, including a cotton-ball head that I recognized as Diane Silverstein's. I mentioned her to JT, and he answered, "Who?" I tried the name Sybil Ludington, and his answer was no different.

"So, you didn't see the piece?" I asked. "The new one?"

He shook his head, I explained, and he stared at me, dumbfounded. "Are you telling me there was a large room with a video installation? Shit, we completely missed it. We thought the mirror works were the new ones. Gabe, please don't tell Sophie. It'll drive her bonkers."

"Don't worry," I said. "Not a word."

And I didn't say a word, nor even run into Sophie for the next half hour or so, though I couldn't help but notice her. While JT was able to remain hidden to those outside his family and Catherine to blend in at the party's core, Sophie couldn't help but draw new attention to herself. Several times, I witnessed her on the losing end of a snub—a turned back, a snide comment, a haughty dismissal. If earlier, she had handled such setbacks well enough, bounding about with the same irrepressible energy I'd seen at the Christmas windows and in the snow, now she rushed away turbulently, biting her lip and glowering, her leather purse bouncing from her sides like stirrups on a galloping horse. Again and again, she'd run to her father's side and implore him to join her among the crowd, as if his isolation were the cause of her humiliation, then hurry back to Catherine to greet whichever new friend was presented to her. With each passing minute, Sophie's movements grew more frenetic. Her once confident eyes turned red and heavy—just like the sloshy, syrupy liquid in the glass she perpetually carried. I'd assumed she was drinking Shirley Temples; now, I wondered if she was stealing sips of something stronger.

Once I caught sight of her running through the doorway into the library, and I followed her in. It was a spacious room with three walls lined with books (one interrupted by a fireplace), plus a couch, two chairs, and, in the center, a grand piano. To my relief, JT was also there, standing before a bookcase, a paperback in hand. He called us both over, and soon we found ourselves before the fireplace, eyeing a lineup of glass ornaments along the mantlepiece: an egg, a 6-sided die, a pipe, a nutcracker, and a snow globe.

"What's your favorite?" Sophie asked, but even before we could respond she reached for the snow globe and shook it. Crystal snowflakes floated in the liquid air—before settling on the ground to reveal a background of leafless trees with two ravens, carved deep to emphasize their blackness. She shook it again, and light hit the glass at an angle that revealed a prism, which cast a small rainbow onto the wall.

"Amazing," she said.

"I'd go with the die," said JT.

"For me, the nutcracker," I said.

"Well, you know which one I want," she said, again agitating the snow.

Which felt like an omen, for within minutes, the sky outside turned a softer gray, and then a dusting of white started to fall.

"Oh, shit, not again," said JT. "I'm getting this vision of Sophie's mom bawling me out. Excuse me, I better call Delta."

As I returned to the living room, Catherine beckoned me with an ostentatious wave. "Do you know Patrick?" she said, evidently referring to a young man with curly, brown hair and baby cheeks standing beside her. "He has one of your sister's high school paintings."

"*Patrick M.*," the man said, turning into the light and revealing a deep bronze that looked out of place in the dead of winter. "But it's a total coincidence. I'm a collector, not a subject. Meaning, I'm not *that* Patrick M. But oddly it looks like me, or so I tell myself—if you tilt your head and squint. You're her brother, yes? Has she ever made something of you?"

"Not that I've seen."

"Why you think that is? Too close to home?"

A poignant question, but he didn't pause for a response, just kept talking, now about his upcoming ski trip to Zermatt. As he droned on, I felt a slap against my back. It was Sophie, or rather her flapping purse, as she brushed past me and Catherine, headed straight to Becca and Marty.

"Becca?" Sophie said, loud enough that we could hear her several people away. "I have a question. Are you single?"

"I'm busy, Sophie," Becca said with an anxious cough. "Can we talk later?" She twisted her body toward Marty, leaving Sophie to face the knot of hair on the back of her head.

Some minutes later, I heard music, the evening's first, and followed the sound back to the library. JT was seated at the piano, playing a few notes as his iPhone issued the reassuring hum of "hold" music. He tapped the keys softly, creating the barest outline of a song I would never have recognized had not Sophie, standing a few feet away, begun to croon:

Met a boy cute as can be
Summer days drifting away to oh oh the summer nights

Spotting me, she ran up and grabbed my hands. "Sing with me, Gabe. Sing with me." She sounded loopy.

"I don't know the song."

"Of course, you do. Don't be shy.

"*Summer loving had me a blast*
Summer loving happened so fast"

As she sang, JT sped up his playing to match the pace of her words. "Do you really not know it? I don't believe it," she said, playfully swinging my hands. "I'll teach you.

"*Summer loving had me a blast*—that's your line—
Summer loving happened so fast—that's mine.
I met a girl crazy for me—that's yours.
Met a boy cute as can be—that's mine.
Summer days drifting away to—that's mine. *oh oh the summer nights*—that's both of us.

"And then the chorus:
Tell me more, tell me more
Did you get very far
Tell me more, tell me more
Like does he have a car

"Dad, you join then, ok?"

JT whispered, "It was the only way I could get her to quit bugging me. Are we too loud?"

I told him that I could barely hear them from the other room but that I had stopped by on the way to the bathroom, where I was still headed.

Back in the living room a minute later, I found myself beside Elaine, an IP lawyer who had chatted me up earlier. My glass was low, hers too, and I went to the bar for refills. I had barely handed Elaine her martini when Catherine was again upon me, slinging an arm around my shoulder and leaning so close that I could smell her stale, vodka-scented breath. "Gabriel," she said. "Aren't we having fun tonight? Come, I want to introduce you to someone."

She brought me to a woman with a sandy bob, whom I'd met upon arriving but hadn't seen since. "It's the funniest thing, Leslie," Catherine said. "Earlier this evening, Gabriel met, well, we both did, a writer named Diane Silverstein. Do you know her? Her latest novel was just reviewed in the *Times*, it's some sci-fi thing in which daughters become the mothers of their fathers. A bizarre concept, flew right over my head. Anyway, Gabriel comes up to me and says, 'Why, Catherine, Diane Silverstein is here. Don't you remember her? She's the one from our story.'"

"What story?" said Patrick, who had joined our circle.

"Tell him, Gabriel," said Catherine. "I bet you remember it better than I do."

Telling the story of the Morrows and Staubs seemed like an even worse idea than singing *Grease* with Sophie, and I looked for an escape. Thankfully, there was finally a clear path to Becca, who for the first time all evening was all alone before the alcove. She stared alternately at her feet and the window behind her, looking bored. When she noticed me, she scowled; had I not known her so well, I would have read the look as a not unsubtle request that I stay away.

"Here you go," said a voice to the side. It was Marty, returning through a swinging door and handing her a large glass of red wine.

"Marty had this bottle of Châteauneuf he wanted me to try," Becca said.

"I've been saving it for a special occasion," said Marty, "and what could be more special than tonight. Would you like some, Gabe?"

"He can have a sip of mine," Becca said.

Marty lifted his glass and made silent eye contact with me—*cheers.* It was good, of course, the smoothness hitting my tongue a beat or two after the first sip.

"Not bad, right?" said Marty.

"Not bad at all."

"A certain type would take this moment to extol its richness, to praise the subtle notes of magnolia and lingonberry. Not me. I just say, 'Not half bad.'" He sipped again and tipped his glass at me. "Sure, you don't want your own?"

For some reason, I turned to Becca for permission. Her lips were taut and her eyes stony and unyielding—I knew her answer without asking. And to think that I had approached her hoping that we might have an actual conversation, about Diane Silverstein, perhaps, or *Sybil*, about the heavy grip the past still had on her. But her sneer didn't shift, and I lost my nerve. I handed her the glass and turned to Marty, "Does it really have notes of magnolia and lingonberry?"

"Who the hell knows? I don't even know what lingonberry is. Do you?"

I felt something press on my opposite side. It was Catherine, standing so close that her arms and hips brushed against mine, clearly wishing to join our circle, though ostensibly she was still talking to Patrick. "Do you have New Year's plans?" she asked him.

"Skiing in Switzerland, didn't I tell you? I'd already be there if not for this opening."

"Do you know all the artists you collect?" she asked.

"A few. Becca's more accessible than most," Patrick said.

"Did I mention that she's a family friend?" said Catherine, her words growing louder, faster. "One of my oldest. I saw her on training wheels. I saw her with missing front teeth. I—"

Behind me, there was a hard, thumping sound, like a crash or something falling, but all I could see was Sophie stomping across the room with JT chasing behind.

She was upon us in a few long strides, cutting in front of Catherine and me. "Hello," she said to Becca.

"What's up, Sophie?" Becca answered dryly.

"Remember, I told you about *Grease*, how I'm Sandy? My dad and I have been practicing, and I wanted to perform for you. For everyone, really. But it's a duet, and I need a partner. Marty?" She pushed her grandmother aside and stood before him, her left elbow jutting out from her hip, her right arm dangling, inner elbow exposed, a pose meant to evoke sophistication or sexiness but which instead emphasized only the pallor and spindliness of her arms and neck. "What do you say?"

"I don't understand," he said.

"Sing with me, Marty. *Summer loving had me a blast Summer loving happened so fast?*"

"Now?"

"My dad can play the piano."

Marty blinked rapidly and wore a look of sheer befuddlement before erupting into a riot of laughter. Bent over roaring, smacking his knee, he showed more personality in a few seconds than he had over the past several hours. Between cackles, Sophie stammered, attempting to rescue the situation, but in the end she could only turn beseechingly to Becca, who smirked callously, which sent Sophie, eyes aflutter, down the very path she had taken to arrive before us, her steps long and ferocious, as JT tiptoed meekly behind.

Meanwhile, Marty, harrumphing a few times, stood upright, straightened his shirt, and, chuckling still, excused himself and headed to the bar, where he gulped down a tall glass of water.

The room, which had temporarily stilled, returned to its chatter, and Catherine slipped into the void abandoned by Marty and Sophie. "So," she said, leaning toward Becca with the same solicitous smile she had worn much of the evening. "Patrick and I were just talking about New Year's plans. What are you doing, Becca? Anything special?"

Catherine waited a few heartbeats for an answer. When none came, she pivoted to me, her face flushed. "And you, Gabriel? You'll do something with me, won't you? What about Times Square? I'm sure you locals think it's gauche, but I have to do it once, don't I? And I'm not getting any younger. What do you think—"

"It's late, Catherine," Becca said.

"I'm sorry, what was that?" said Catherine, spinning back to face her squarely.

"Maybe you should leave."

"Oh, never mind Sophie. She's just being silly. She'll pull herself to-gether."

"She doesn't belong here. None of you do. You should go."

"Becca, please be gentle—"

"Now."

Catherine blinked and blushed and sought out Becca's eyes, but my sister just marched across the room, where she gathered Marty under an arm and walked with him to the west wall, not far from where JT had camped much of the party. It was the first time all evening that Becca had abandoned the alcove along the south wall, and absent the shield of her body, I felt a chill in the air and noticed that a corner window was opened a crack.

"Well, that was…," Catherine began before her smile collapsed. She froze, trembling, and said softly, staring right at me, "How dare she? After everything I've done." Then, she brushed past me and the rest of the crowd and headed in the general direction her son and granddaugh-ter had gone moments earlier, calling out, "Sophie, get your father, let's go," though her head bowed low, as on that day long ago when she had left us at the edge of the woods before the start of our search.

I looked toward Becca. She faced the far window, her back to me, her back to all of us.

How dare she, indeed, I wanted to shout. *How dare she decide who stays and who goes. How dare she remain silent all these years about Di-ane Silverstein and Sybil Ludington. How dare she share none of it with me, the one person who has always stood by her side.*

The words sat heavy on the tip of my tongue. I thought to cross the room and shout them in my sister's face; instead, I swallowed them, as always. For I came from a family of hiders. Just as Becca was forever running, fleeing, obscuring, evading, even in the supposed freedom of her art, I too was a retreater, never willing to utter out loud my most urgent thought.

Still, the accusations roared through my mind as I followed the Morrows to the coat check. And moments later, with my jacket slung across my arm, I strode back across Marty's vast living room, fully intending to confront Becca with some portion of my rage and confusion, however muddled and incomplete.

But when I was some ten feet away, a new group having formed in her orbit, I heard some faceless male voice say, "Whatever. These things happen at the end of a party. I found it funny, actually. They could have stayed. It wasn't a problem."

To which Becca replied, "But how that woman galls me. She acts as if we're supposed to be friends because we knew each other twenty years ago. But she was supposed to be Gabriel's friend, not mine."

That was what I heard—words that I barely understood but which nonetheless arrested my progress toward Becca and had me instead hurry to the elevator bank, where JT and Catherine stood stiffly before the panel of brass buttons, as Sophie, slumped against the adjacent wall, looked back to the party like some cabaret singer at the end of an interminable night, at once mournful and defiant.

7

Pinching collars, pulling hats tight, slipping on gloves, we walked down 27th Street in silence. A dusting of snow coated the ground, but already the skies had cleared and darkened. Rounding the corner onto 10th Avenue, I saw middling traffic, a smattering of pedestrians, and no lighted storefronts, a reminder that this newly hip area of the city remained barren at night. A hopeful cab idled a few feet from a nearby corner, but none of the Morrows gestured to it, and it sped off the moment we passed.

Sophie rushed ahead, with JT following behind. Twice he tried to catch her, but each time she increased her pace like a jogger who refuses to be passed. I couldn't tell if she was truly too fast or if he somehow lacked the will to close the gap between them. As he drifted back after the second attempt, I noticed the return of his occasional limp.

"My son is hopeless," said Catherine, who walked beside me with her own labored stride. "And his girl has such promise, but she runs wild. Such horrid manners…"

Catherine continued in this vein, bitter and unfiltered. Becca's cold parting had surely burst an illusion. The tease of reconciliation, of renewed friendship, the closure of a painful past and promise of a new beginning, undone in an instant. If an hour earlier, Catherine had imagined that she and Becca were restoring an old bond, now the more prosaic reality had been laid bare. Catherine, her son, and granddaughter had merely tagged along to a party for someone they barely knew, someone they might never see again. Even still, her venting seemed excessive, and as she circled back to those words I had heard after Becca's rebuke—"After all I've done for that girl, how could she?"—I wondered if she might be speaking of Sophie, not Becca. They had both let her down, hadn't they?

"...And JT, how he just stands there. His career, his marriage, it doesn't matter what, he just stands and watches as things fall apart."

With a snort, Catherine signaled that her speech was over. I thought to ask about the words from Becca that had jolted me—when my sister had said that Catherine was supposed to be my friend, not hers—but another, stronger instinct held my tongue. The timing was wrong, the topic more appropriately addressed with Becca.

The street was empty but loud with the sound of zipping cars, their engines grinding and churning. Voices traveled poorly through the night air, but I gradually became aware that Sophie and JT, nearly half a block ahead of us, were yelling. Or rather, Sophie, peering over her shoulder at the father who kept pace some ten feet behind, was screaming at him: "You're a loser, dad. A loser"—similar words to earlier, but without a hint of motivational tough love, just pure bile. Like an old joke that had soured into resentful mockery.

This went on awhile until JT asked, "Sophie, what's that?"

"Nothing," she said.

"Is that... My god, Sophie..." It was then that I noticed something shiny in her hand, glistening beneath the light. "You have to give that back," he said.

He rushed toward her, and again she upped her pace, moving several feet ahead. How different from hours earlier, when he had sped up his piano playing to catch her runaway voice, and she had allowed herself to be found. "At least, I'm not going home emptyhanded, Dad," she taunted.

JT attempted once more to catch her and, failing anew, soon fell into step at my side. "Mind if I walk with you, Gabe? You're the only calm one."

"Not at all," I said, suddenly aware that Catherine was no longer beside me but some distance back. "What was that in Sophie's hand?"

"She took that snow globe. Can you believe it? She has this wild streak. It's no good, and she's going to get in real trouble someday... But don't worry about the globe, I'll find a way to give it back. Let's talk about something else. Anything really."

Yet he didn't say a thing, just looked around. To the opposite side of 10th Avenue, where a woman walked a large dog in a red and white sweater. Into the glow of a streetlamp, where tiny snowflakes seemed to hover, as if gravity had momentarily been suspended.

"Remember our talk at the party?" he finally said. "We were up so high. Here on the street, everything is right before you. It's still magical, but... I can't quite put my finger on it... It's almost like, when I was up above looking down, I felt like I was in it, but now that I'm down in it, I feel like I'm looking at it from a remove. Like the closer you are, the most distant it becomes. Do you understand, Gabe? Oh, I don't know. Maybe I sound crazy. Or maybe it was just a long night."

"At the end of a long week."

"Tell me about it."

Sophie was now more than half a block ahead, crossing 24th. The light was red, and the only car I could see was facing north on 10th, stalled at the same light that failed to deter her.

"Say, you never answered my question earlier," JT said.

"What question?"

"Why you came home. I mean, from Paris. What brought you back?"

Sophie was on the opposite side of 24th. The light turned green, and the car blasted through the intersection and was already beyond us. But JT wasn't looking at cars or Sophie. His chin was tilted up to the dark, empty sky. He was the only one of us in his element, and somehow this put me at ease.

There was something I had never said before, not fully. Not to friends, not to Catherine, not to Becca. It was about Lina. It was true that when I Googled her after we split, I saw that she was married to Karl, and that she had a child, and then a second. It was true that the few pictures I found online were cliché professional and family photos with an anodyne smile that revealed nothing more than a photographer with good timing. That's what Google spit up whenever I searched for her (not maniacally, mind you; just every few months). Until one day, I found something new: a death notice.

Using Google Translate, then picking away word by word with a German-English dictionary, I read it. I found a few more and read them too. They mostly lacked images, though one had a smiling photo from her professional site, unaltered. How? Why? What had happened? One after the next, the obits were vague on the cause of death, either skipping over it entirely or saying, opaquely, "the cause of death is unknown." But I knew, I just knew she had killed herself. I knew because on certain nights, even at the height of our relationship (when its end was inconceivable to me), well before we'd begun to talk of Bratislava, she would slink into a dark corner of the living room and stare blankly out the window, or because morning showers sometimes lasted an hour, and I would find her huddled on the chipped tiles in a corner, shivering, her lips and fingers blue, or how certain nights, beautiful and brilliant starry nights, the sort JT would have loved, when Lina and I were out walking, she would fall silent, even in the midst of conversation. Though I asked, and cajoled, and insisted that she tell me what was going on, I could get no explanation other than, "Nothing. It was nothing, ok?"

And I knew something further: The unnamed cause of death included me. There was too much sadness in me, too much silence. Too much brooding. Lina had not been that way when we had met, on the subway, in the park, as she introduced me to the taste of Fernet. She had *become* that way. Surely, the dark contagion had come from me. Where else had she learned such unshakeable gloom?

One night, one single night in my dark Paris apartment, I discovered all of this: her death, her suicide, my complicity—a succession of devastating revelations. They came at me fast and relentless, wave upon unexpected wave, and soon immense sadness gave way to nausea. I retched suddenly and some fifteen minutes later was searching for flights to New York. That was what brought me home. A girl I had loved was dead, poisoned by my sadness. I had infected her. Something in me. Perhaps not born with me, perhaps only learned, perhaps nurture not nature, but so ingrained by the time of our meeting that the distinction no longer mattered.

How can you disclose such things to others? They wouldn't understand. They would say that I was imagining things, I had no proof, I was crazy, I was torturing myself. They would say that only a misguided narcissism could place myself, five years after our final goodbye, at the scene of death. But I knew. I knew.

That's why I came home. I needed to flee everything that linked me to that grisly scene, to get away and start over. I had no choice. I had to begin anew.

Here I was a year later, walking along 10th Avenue on a bitterly cold night, not only reliving it all again but on the brink of confessing it for the first time. And to JT Morrow of all people. How bizarre. But first I looked back. I suppose to check on Catherine—indeed, she was still with us, walking steadily, though some distance behind; also, to see if she was within earshot.

And I looked forward. At Sophie, who was tossing the snow globe from hand to hand like a ball, though rarely catching it cleanly, so that each time you worried it might escape her grip and fall to the ground.

And then came one of those moments you sometimes read about, when your perceptions heighten, and your eyes see with greater clarity—so that you see not only the situation before you, but also what will soon follow.

Sophie tossing that glass object, though with little comfort.

The blinking Don't Walk sign at the corner ahead of her.

The dancing glimmer on the sloping sidewalk between her and that corner—a reflection of her glittery shoes on a sheet of black ice.

When you see not only what is before you, but also how it will fit together in the next instant—the glass object escaping her hand on an errant toss, landing on the sidewalk but without a crash, and beginning to roll, she chasing it, as the crossing light goes red, and the light at the perpendicular street goes green, with two cars some distance down that street gathering speed and racing forward without hesitation, and Sophie continuing to chase, bending lower to the ground, moving faster, slipping on the invisible ice—

I took off at a sprint, quickly closing the space between us, somehow managing to stay upright even as my shoes hit the slick hard ice, and launching myself upon her, after she had stumbled and was already sliding down the sidewalk toward the corner, as the ball of glass rolled ahead of her, into the heart of the street, where first one, and then a second car, roared by, oblivious of the fact that anyone, or anything, was in its way on that quiet December night.

"What the hell?" she said, twisting and pushing me away. "Get off me. Get off."

An elbow smacked my gut, and she slithered free.

"What the hell was that?" she cried, now above me, looking down contemptuously. "What's wrong with you? Did my Dad put you up to it? Geez, I was going to give it back. Now it's gone. See what you did? See what you did?"

Catherine had arrived at Sophie's side. JT stepped onto the street and waved at a lonely cab on the opposite side of 10th.

Rising, I took half a step toward Sophie. I lurched slightly—the ice was real—and she jumped backward behind her grandmother, as if I were some monster. The cab shot across four lanes, JT opened the back door, and Sophie slid to the seat's far side, muttering, "Creep."

Catherine turned to me. Her eyes were glassy, her bottom lip trembled, but she said nothing. Gripping JT's elbow, she bent to enter the cab.

"A long night, Gabe," he said, his hand still holding the open door. "It was great to catch up. Pity things had to end this way. Please apologize to Becca."

I stood on that corner a minute or two, unsure what to do. My pants were damp from the sidewalk, but I wasn't particularly cold. Should I walk awhile? Hail my own cab? Take the subway? Return to the party? A candle in a second-story window across the street flickered, and for some reason I pictured Becca—in her shapeless black skirt and gray blazer, as she encamped by the alcove in Marty Shinn's living room, lordly and remote, never once deigning to play the welcoming host or flattered guest-of-honor who made the rounds. No, I wouldn't return to that party. I couldn't stand to be around others. Not tonight.

A blast of wind slapped me hard, so hard that my eyes closed, and when they opened, I saw something... a rainbow. I blinked twice, but the rainbow was still there.

My god—the snow globe.

Pristine, undamaged, there it lay between slats of the gutter on the opposite side of the street, having somehow survived the perilous crossing. I waited for the light, but across the street, a man appeared, from where I have no idea. He bent for the globe and thrust it in his pocket. Back on his feet, he surveyed the street in all directions, and when his pale blue eyes found mine, they flashed with terror and he began to run—up the sloping sidewalk, growing smaller as he rose in the sky, until he disappeared into the blackness.

8

"Hello," I answered excitedly.

It was the next afternoon, the sun already setting, and I had spent most of the day desperately making phone calls and silently praying for one of them to be returned.

In the morning, Becca had appeared in the kitchen as I huddled over a bowl of Cheerios. She wore the same baggy Harvard sweatshirt she sometimes used as pajamas but also jeans and boots. Brewing a pot of coffee, she spoke about the weather, which would apparently warm considerably, and about how late she was out the night before. She returned to her bedroom, then was back some ten minutes later, dragging a suitcase. She filled a second mug with coffee and sat down at the table. In the ensuring silence, I felt desperation well up inside of me.

"I need space," she finally said. "To return to myself. You understand, right?"

Minutes later, we shared a loose hug at the door. "No need for a big goodbye," she said and walked toward the elevator. "I'm just going to my studio."

I busied myself with laundry, ordered a small pie from Antonio's, tried to make it seem like a normal day. But eventually the void of Becca's absence overwhelmed me, and though I beseeched myself not to, I tried her cellphone.

It rang and rang.

I tried her again. This time it went straight to voicemail.

That was what set me off.

Next, Catherine. I knew that at that very moment she might be saying goodbye to JT and Sophie, perhaps in Manhattan, perhaps at the airport—so what? she could take a moment to say, Hi, couldn't she? Also, she might be as alone as I, maybe on the long trek back from JFK.

The phone rang and rang until I heard a click, after which the usual voicemail message failed to play. I hung up.

Allison—though she had told me she was away until New Year's, though I knew I was hardly in the ideal mental state for that all-important first conversation. Again, voicemail.

Janine? Of the various women I'd met the previous night, I selected her. I had little to go on, but a bit of Google sleuthing led to two decent possibilities: one, a VP at a company called Manders PR, two, the wife of the managing partner at a private equity firm. Rather than make a total fool of myself by calling, I sent a Facebook invite to Marty Shinn, hoping he'd point me in the right direction. After an hour of busywork, in which I avoided all screens, I saw that we still weren't Friends and called the number at Manders PR. I left a message with a secretary, trying my best to sound casual but secretly cringing at the sound of my every word.

Finally, there was nothing to do but go out. It was indeed warmer than on previous days, and I stood awhile watching kids toss a football in the park. I followed the promenade north to the footbridge to Wards Island and turned back. I sat on a bench watching the still, empty river until the afternoon chill became too fierce. I tried the general line at the East River Home but lost my will at the sound of the receptionist's aloof greeting. "Sorry, wrong number," I said.

I read, putzed around the apartment, watched TV, lay on the couch, putzed around some more—the phone never far me. When it finally rang, I had begun to drift off.

"Hello," I repeated, after no one answered my first greeting.

"You've been chosen for a special…," said a robotic voice. The offer was a heavily discounted New Year's trip to the Outer Banks. I would have to leave the next morning, at 7:27 am, from Newark. No thanks.

I fixed myself a cocktail and stood at the living room window watching light flicker on the river below. The problem with winter, I decided, was less the cold than the long nights. Upriver, I saw through the dusk the outline of a tugboat, pulling a long barge on its southward journey. At its rear, a spotlight rotated in a half circle, casting thin beams into the sky, one of which, as the boat drew parallel, momentarily streaked across the glass before me.

The tugboat and its light drifted past, disappearing around a bend and leaving behind a sky even darker than the one of minutes earlier. I couldn't help but think of Becca's morning departure, which seemed more heartless than usual, almost inhumanly callous. As the boat's wake vanished into the lapping tide, a new idea took shape. Maybe it wasn't indifference that moved Becca in such moments but some confused form of caring. Maybe she imagined that she carried some contagion that would spread if she stayed anywhere, or with anyone, for too long. Maybe I was wrong to think that she had ever made progress in taming the black dog—maybe she was the one who had unleashed it on me. Maybe that was why she was always moving, always leaving people, even her brother, her only family. Maybe she could imagine no option but flight. Maybe, in her twisted, genius mind, this was what the sibling code required.

9

On New Year's Eve, I found myself in a large Tribeca apartment with sleek steel appliances, flat screens hovering subtly before walls, and blind-less windows with adjustable tinting. The central room was expansive and open, if not quite as magisterial as Marty Shinn's. The swarm of people spilled into hallways, the kitchen, and a frosty deck, dominated by smokers. Amid jostling shoulders and flocks of unfamiliar faces, the final minutes of 2013 flew by; aided by countless swigs of champagne, so did the first of 2014.

I had gotten there by way of a dinner party at Sebastian and Sherrie's cramped two-bedroom in the West Village. At first, it looked like I would be the ninth wheel among four longstanding couples, but half an hour in, a girl named Larissa showed up. Sebastian seated us next to each other at the long table, she smiled at me shyly, and I understood it was a setup, which explained why Sebastian had asked me three or four times to confirm I'd be coming. Larissa wore a stylish track suit made of a spongy purple material; it seemed so odd for a New Year's party, let alone a setup, that I took an instant liking to her, but we struggled to get beyond clumsy small talk, and the prodding questions and conversation starts from our 8-person inquisition panel hardly helped us to relax.

I tried to engage her anew at the Tribeca party, but even with alcohol and time, we weren't connecting. So, when I spotted her deep in conversation with a guy with long blond sideburns and a bland though handsome face, I felt happy for her, happy that at least one of us had made a match. But maybe an hour later, I saw the same guy with an arm around another girl, and though I searched, Larissa appeared to have left. Suddenly aware of the hour (after 2:00) and that the party had sifted down to a core group, to which I clearly did not belong, I shouted a few thank yous and stumbled down the entry hall to search for my shoes.

The front door opened, and in came a woman in a puffy green jacket. "So, I just had my second epic subway voyage of 2014," she said, attempting to de-static a crock of frizzy hair with one hand and to de-fog her glasses with the other. She spoke hurriedly and with an odd lilt; it was hard to tell if she was tipsy or flustered. "My girlfriend Hannah said, 'No more than two parties on New Year's, and definitely, definitely, do not switch spots post-midnight.' But I'm new in town and rotten at following directions. Please, please, don't tell me this one's already over? By the way, I'm Amanda."

I shook her hand. "Gabriel. The party's still going. I'm just heading out."

"Suit yourself," she said, but then added, after a few awkward attempts to move past one another in the narrow hallway. "You sure your subconscious is committed to going?"

"How could I possibly know?"

"Here, give me your hand again." She pulled a pen from a pocket, faced my palm upward, and inked "Amanda" and a phone number across the surface. "Like I said, I'm new in town. Also, one of my New Year's resolutions is to be bold and not worry about making a fool of myself. So, humor me, ok?"

When we met the next weekend at a bar in Turtle Bay, I wasn't sure if it was a date, and her casual outfit and lack of makeup likewise gave nothing away.

"What you called Turtle Bay, I called the East 40s," I confessed as we took the first tentative sips of our drinks. My knowledge of the city was a generation old, I explained, the city of my childhood, not the one of today.

"I live in Queens. Know where that is?"

"Ha ha."

Soon, I was telling Amanda about my explorations of the city, the long walks I had taken over the past year through so many city neighborhoods, including many in Queens. I gave just enough detail about Catherine to make clear that she wasn't a girlfriend or romantic interest of any sort.

When I had finished, Amanda asked, "Why do I feel like you're talking about this woman in the past. Did something happen?"

The only thing that had happened was that Catherine hadn't returned my calls, any of them. I had tried her several times in late December and also that first week in January. Sometimes I left a message, sometimes not. It didn't matter; no response. The situation was little different with Becca, though at least she had responded with voicemails in the middle of the night when she knew my phone would be off, plus a few texts: "Got your message. Sorry I've been busy. Thinking of you, bro," and the like. Nor had I heard from Janine of Manders PR or from Allison, whom I had tried half a dozen times, which was surely sufficient to show my interest or desperation.

"She's actually an old family friend," I said. "A friend of my mother."

"You mentioned that."

"Anyway, you've introduced me to a neighborhood. How about if I return the favor?"

"Tell me when, I'll be there," she said.

A few days later, Sebastian invited himself over for dinner. We ordered Chinese, and he spent half the meal standing, bouncing on the balls of his feet, speaking rapidly, seeming to choke on his every other thought. After dinner, he refused every suggestion of what to do until I offered, "A movie?"

"Sold," he shouted. "Let's do *Shawshank*? Please."

Even after so many years, Sebastian could still recite it straight through, though he limited himself to the Morgan Freeman parts. We cracked up every time he proclaimed lines like, "I have to remind my-self that some birds aren't meant to be caged. Their feathers are just too bright," but toward the end of the movie, he started crying. I asked if anything was going on, and he shook his head. "Just feeling emotional," he explained unconvincingly. "But it's the happy kind, don't worry."

Larissa's spongy track suit, the spark with Amanda, Sebastian weep-ing on my couch—it was barely a week, but already January 2014 offered surprises and had a lighter spirit than the dreary month preced-ing. Even more unexpected, in mid-January an editor I hadn't written for in years replied to my email from a year prior announcing my move to New York. "Still in the city?" she wrote. "I know it's last minute, but I'm about to go on maternity leave, and we're looking for a temporary replacement. Any interest? I seem to remember you've done editorial work in the past."

Days later, I found myself in a large, drab midtown office, entirely open plan except for the closet-sized, glass-fronted offices along one wall. I thought I had come for an interview with her boss, but it turns out to have been a fait accompli. Stacey, the very pregnant departing editor, trained me that very afternoon and the remaining three days of the week; Monday, I was on my own. A week later, my cubicle neighbor poked her head around the partition and said, "Don't take this the wrong way, Gabe, but I think Stacey suggested you because you were safe."

"Safe?"

"Not a threat to replace her, you know, if a few months from now she asks to extend her leave."

"Why would I—"

"Exactly. That's what she was counting on."

That weekend I met Amanda again. The neighborhood I selected was my own. I knew it was corny, but I also suspected she'd be charmed as long as I made clear that I hadn't chosen it due to proximity to my bedroom. Besides, who'd ever heard of Carl Schurz Park? My tiny cor-ner of New York was not one you'd have any reason to discover on your own.

We walked on the boardwalk by the river, watched the ball courts and dog runs, sat on the very bench that Catherine and I had shared on our first meeting. I again spoke about Catherine, giving a few more details and mentioning that I hadn't seen her in weeks.

"Isn't it terrible," Amanda said, "how in this city, you can go a month without seeing your closest friend and still feel like you're pressed for time during that one visit?"

I shared the odd case of Sebastian, who had been calling almost daily. One night, he had an extra ticket to the Rangers game, the next he wanted to catch the new *Mission Impossible* or show me this new Swedish bar. Then it was restaurant week. "Practically every fancy place in the city is offering discounted lunches," he said. "I already have resys on Monday and Wednesday." A Friday invite came soon after, but my new boss had taken note of my lengthy lunch breaks, and I had to refuse. No matter, Sebastian called Friday afternoon to rave about the beet salad and brick chicken. "Best meal of the week. But I hated being alone. I wanted to talk about Sherrie and also ask a favor"—a first hint of whatever was weighing on him.

"Well, there you go," Amanda said. "He was reaching out because he wanted something from you. It's never innocent, is it? What invitation comes without a string attached?"

That was one lesson, of course, but I was thinking of another. That the cycle of fortune and misfortune, of comfort and anxiety, of companionship and solitude, turns for us all. "What about this one?" I asked. "What's the string?"

"I'm not going to answer that, but I will invite you somewhere. Actually, right now."

She had booked tickets that evening for a play at a small theater on the Lower East Side. The play had been written by a friend of a friend of hers, and when it ended, Amanda was surprisingly critical, questioning its pacing and believability, before conceding that she had once considered scriptwriting. "If I'm being completely honest, I guess the string attached to this invite, was that you were supposed to agree that the play was juvenile and amateurish, OK?"

"Juvenile, amateurish, certainly a sign that your friend made all the wrong decisions in her life."

"Thanks," said Amanda as she squeezed my hand.

A few days later, visiting her overstuffed studio, I learned that she was older than I had assumed, 35, a year my senior. As she said this, I noticed that odd lilt in her voice for the first time since New Year's. "My nervous tell," she later conceded.

We were on the couch cuddling, and she asked why I never spoke of my family.

As I attempted to describe my parents and their passings, I was thrown off by her alternating expressions of shock and sadness as well as the way she kept repeating, "Sorry," like some Tourette's tic.

"Please stop," I said. "There's nothing to be sorry about."

"You're right, I'm sor—"

She caught herself, we laughed, and she told me to go on. If I felt little relief in sharing further details of my life, neither did it feel unnatural to explain so much about where I'd come from. And when Amanda said, "Hold on, I want to do something," and lay two fingers on the inside of my elbow and traced the course of my vein down to my wrist, I shuddered. Amid my joy, I was already imagining the day she'd disappear.

* * *

In early February, the doorman appeared at my apartment door, pulling a cart with a large cardboard box. "What'd you order, boss?" he asked. "Building a stone wall?"

He wheeled the cart through the foyer and into the living room. The box weighed a ton, and it took a considerable effort to lift and lower it gently to the ground, where it landed with a thud. I wasn't expecting a delivery and the postmarks gave nothing away, so I tore it open right away. Inside were piles of books, packed tight, mostly old hard covers missing dust jackets, the lettering on the bindings too faded to read the titles. But the mystery quickly resolved itself. On every other page, there were diagrams with facing rows of long, narrow isosceles triangles alternating in red and black, topped with patterns of red or white circles: backgammon books, 31 in total, in English, French, German, Arabic, Turkish, and two languages I didn't recognize.

There was also an envelope with a letter inside:

Dear Gabriel,

It's the morning of February 2nd, and this afternoon I'm off to the airport. By the time you read this letter, I'll be in California. Since Christmas, just about every moment of my life has been spent packing and planning for this move, which is why I haven't been in touch. I'm so sorry. I do wish we could have said goodbye in person.

Sorting through my things, I came upon these backgammon books. Naturally, I thought of you. They were a gift to me, from my teacher. Now I pass them to you. Someday, I hope you'll continue the chain and give them to a student of your own.

San Diego—wow! It will be a giant change, but I have some idea of what's awaiting. I spent a week there in early January. Each morning, I woke to the sun shining in a clear sky and forgot for a few moments that it was the dead of winter. I stayed with JT, in Sophie's bedroom (there are posters of the Jonas Brothers on the wall. Ever heard of them?). I will be there tonight, too, but we are looking for a place of my own and I hope to move SOON. We're also looking at homes for Alan and will bring him out when we can. Sophie lives with her mother half an hour away. Her mother is all logistics, no time to chat, but she's agreed that I can visit Sophie on Wednesday and Friday afternoons, and soon I plan to ask for more (don't tell her!). It will be a different life, and I'm nervous, but also excited. Besides, it's the good nervous, I think.

Oh, Gabriel, I miss you already. Please please visit.

Warmest,

Your friend, Catherine

P.S. Please send my best to Becca.

P.P.S. I made my radio debut. Please listen.

http://www.wfex.amamshow.com/87569

The next day, Becca finally called at a reasonable hour. "Guess what?" she said. "I'm in Brooklyn."

"Aren't you the ambitious traveler?"

"Ha ha. I mean, I found a place. A house and studio, both. Can you believe it? After all these years, the Manhattan girl, living in Brooklyn. Come over. I want to show you around."

Brooklyn. Of course. The gritty borough of our youth had become the chic spot creative types wanted to be. It was so obvious in retrospect that I couldn't believe I had just passed a month wondering about my sister's whereabouts.

Two days later, I took the subway to Bushwick. Becca had the top floor of a converted factory building. I rode a mechanical elevator with a grated door up to 6, and stepped into a vast space with 15-foot ceilings and thick, ponderous walls—a gargantuan room, monstrously large, or perhaps I was reacting to the sparse furniture. Large metal hooks and pulleys randomly placed along the red brick walls recalled a prior, industrial life, as did the enormous sink basins along the back wall. It was easy to imagine hoses where now there were faucets.

Becca gave a quick tour—after this entry/living room: a bedroom, second bedroom, den, kitchen, bathroom. From a kitchen window, she gestured to another structure with a ruddy stone facade. "My studio," she said, pointing to a hazy window on the second floor. "It has two large rooms, one for painting, one for everything else, and a small office in between. By the way, I'm looking for a studio manager. Know anyone?"

We settled in the kitchen. It had the usual appliances, cabinets, and countertops, but the proportions were off, everything too spaced out, so that even the jumbo-sized fridge looked miniature. And this was only one half of the room. On the opposite side was a sort of secondary living room with two couches and an armchair atop a sisal rug. I felt my feet itch just looking at it. Between the furniture and the appliances stood a long table that Becca might have made herself. A long wooden plank supported by stacks of cinder blocks at the midpoints and four corners, with eight wooden chairs surrounding it. The floor was a sheet of gray concrete. It looked too slippery for socks and too cold for bare feet; indeed, Becca wore black workboots.

"Hungry?" she asked, handing me the menu for a sandwich/salad place around the corner. "I bet you'll like the roast beef and Swiss."

As she ordered, I wandered by the couches, where I noticed a shelving unit stacked randomly with items that I assumed had been left by a previous occupant: old phone books, yellowing drug store novels, a deflated football and kicking tee, three billiard balls, and a stack of board games, including a checkers/chess/backgammon set.

"Wanna play?" I asked.

"Checkers?"

"Backgammon."

"I'm not sure I remember how. You'll have to remind me."

I set up the board at the cinder block table and gave a refresher on the rules. We played twice, and I beat her soundly both times. The delivery man arrived as we were setting up a third game.

"Phew," she said. "I was beginning to feel bad about myself."

As we ate, I told her about the role backgammon had played in my friendship with Catherine, how it had broken the ice between us, and about the books I had just been sent, which had once belonged to Ahmet. I was hoping that this would lead into the many questions I had for Becca, not only those I had wished to ask at Marty Shinn's party, but also two more: about why she hadn't returned my calls for over a month and about what I had learned from Catherine's "radio debut."

Becca nodded attentively as I spoke about backgammon, then shifted the conversation to more favorable ground—namely, all the work still to be done in her studio: the purchase of storage racks, canvas, stretchers, paint, brushes, cardboard, tape, Styrofoam, packing blankets, cleaning supplies.

After lunch, she suggested a walk. It was a mild day for mid-February, the sky still and sunny. Across the street from Becca's building lay two more converted factories, then a stretch of derelict structures, some boarded up with crisscrossing planks of blond wood. Two blocks past was an empty lot with high, unshorn grass, beside a small playground and a basketball court with iron backboards. The next street had a mix of small corner markets and hip restaurants, catering, I supposed, to the neighborhood's older and newer residents, respectively.

Becca moved at a brisk clip. We wandered without any clear direction, not unlike how Catherine and I had once explored the city. But Becca was quiet, her mind elsewhere, as if she were saving the better side of herself for later, or for someone else. It seemed clear that my questions would meet evasion or hostility.

Still, the walk was pleasant. I know few joys greater than discovering a new city within a city you already know; as your legs settle into the pace, your mind is free to wander. If I had little memory of childhood walks with Becca and my parents, it hardly surprised me that my sister would be drawn to this pastime, too. I was about to remark on this shared affinity when we rounded a corner, and I saw an entrance to the subway half a block ahead.

Wait? Was this it? "But, Becca, I'm not ready…" I started, taken aback.

She looked at me quizzically. "Is something wrong, Gabriel?"

"Are you taking me to the subway? We've hardly visited. Can't we talk?"

The sun was directly behind me, and Becca was drenched in light. She shaded her eyes with a hand but still squinted. "If you'd like," she answered. "Let's go back."

She pivoted and we began retracing our steps. She spoke little other than to point out the 24-hour market where she could get milk when running low and the pretty residential block with a row of Linden trees and porched houses. In the past month, I had read about her online. There were several reviews of the show at Lightworks, all positive, though none glowing, as well as a gossipy item about a second, larger opening, which took place the first week of January. Patrick, Marty, and others from the party had been there; I hadn't even been told. There were also notices of upcoming shows in Dusseldorf, Athens, and London. I had looked up Catherine, too, discovering little beyond an abandoned Facebook page. But I did find her radio show.

It was the evening I had received her package. I sat on the fluffy chair in the living room, the one perpendicular to my father's stiffer, preferred perch. The sky was already dark, though it couldn't have been much after 5:00. I clicked on the link and heard a momentary buzz, then a trumpet, playing soft and slow, then louder and faster.

The volume lowered and a voice said, "Good morning. It's the ungodly hour of 6:00 am, on Saturday morning in San Diego." The voice was nasally, but also calm and assured, almost soothing. "This is the AM AM show. I'm John Terrence Morrow. If you're listening, you're either a fan or lost, and I welcome you either way. Today we have a special show, which I'll introduce shortly. First, let's listen to 'Quiet Dawn' by Archie Shepp."

The music, which had been playing at a low volume as he spoke, became louder. It combined a haunting child's voice and mellow jazz rhythm, and the effect was trippy. It played for a few minutes before fading to silence.

"Welcome back. This is the AM AM show with John Terrence Morrow, on WFEX San Diego 710 AM, where I play the boundary pushing music from the 70s, experimental jazz and progressive rock, two musical styles that deserve more attention than they get nowadays. I try to give the music some much deserved love but also show how it never really went away. In fact, it's part of everything we listen to today. You just have to know how to find it.

"Longtime listeners know that every now and then I am joined by a guest, and boy do I have a special one today, someone who is on the brink of moving to San Diego after decades on the East Coast, and whom I affectionately call, 'Mom.' But before I get to Catherine Morrow—and yes, she is my mother—let's hear some music…"

On came a jazz duo, two guitars trading riffs or, as JT said, with the song fading in the background, "shooting the shit, squabbling, and making up, like the best of friends."

"So, Catherine Morrow, Mom, welcome to Southern California."

"Thank you."

"First impressions?"

"I've been here only a few days and—"

"But you're moving soon. Share your observations. Anything."

"I've seen the usual things. The ones you read about. The beautiful weather, the horrible traffic, the giant burritos, the salty air, the sandy beach."

"So, all the clichés are true? I guess it takes an outsider to let us know we aren't crazy. Thanks for that, Mom. Now let's listen to a song, which, as our guest, you can choose, though I'm going to steer you to a band you've heard a lot of. King Crimson. What do you say?"

"I'm thinking of a Roger Fripp song with Brian Eno. The one you always played when you were in a 'chill' mood."

"'The Heavenly Music Corporation?'"

"Exactly."

"That's not King Crimson and it's a long one, Mom, but I'll play a few minutes of it. This is from the duo's debut, *No pussyfooting*."

He played an excerpt of an instrumental song that seemed like it could go on forever, then read an ad for Chevy and another for a restaurant promising "the best poké bowl in Orange County."

There followed some polite back and forth between mother and son. It was jarring to hear them, Catherine sounding elderly, proud of her son but circumspect, clearly uneasy, while JT couldn't have been more comfortable, restoring a sense of order each time he spoke. A complete reversal from the party at Marty Shinn's.

"Is it ok, John," Catherine asked, interrupting herself in the midst of a ramble, "if I tell a story?"

"Of course. That's why you're here."

"This winter, I finally had my New York Christmas, which is something I've always wanted. But this story begins long before then when you were a boy. We were close with another family, let's call them the Sterns, though that's not their real name. My husband and Mr. Stern had been college buddies. Mrs. Stern and I were close, too. 'Like sisters,' we'd say, and on our best days we confessed all our secrets and finished each other's sentences. My husband and I had two boys. The Sterns had a girl and a boy, both younger, the boy just a baby at the time the families grew close. I loved their children, I watched them grow. Their daughter was the closest I had to one of my own, and I tried to arrange little trips with her, to the nail salon, shopping, the girlie stuff I could never do with my boys. The families vacationed together. We did holidays together. The children called each other cousins. Of course, there was occasional tension, envy, resentment—we were human, in other words. But we always managed to overcome it and remained so very close.

"But one day, there was an incident, a violation. It was something your brother did at the expense of the Stern girl. A joke that got well out of hand. In retrospect, I can see how my son's behavior was so upsetting, though I downplayed it at the time, and also how the tension that the two families had always managed to bury now rose to the surface. My son's action did not emerge from the void, the Sterns implied. The malice had surely been planted in his mind, and by whom if not his parents?

"So, when they blamed him, they were blaming me. And when they blamed me... well, the issue was no longer something that my son had done to them, but something they were doing *to me*. Such wild, exaggerated, thoughtless accusations. Especially from the mother, who I considered my best friend. "How dare she?" I thought. *How dare she?* I could go on and on, and at the time I did, spinning the entire situation around in my mind so hurriedly I made myself dizzy.

"But the point is there was a break. And if at first, I thought it was the sort of tiff that would pass quickly, I came to realize that the wound was deep. Even still, I wouldn't have imagined that the situation was irreparable. But what followed was a complete rupture. Silence. The friendship erased. Kaput. I mourned it a long time, until I had no choice but to resign myself to what had happened. And when I looked back, I saw that my son's joke really was vicious, and the trauma it had caused real and lasting. And toward the victim of that action, the Stern girl, who was as close to a daughter as I'd ever come, I felt tremendous guilt.

"A few years later, both Stern parents died, tragically young. We heard of their passings from mutual acquaintances. I felt a new stab of loneliness, as if they were leaving us a second time, and I was so devastated for those kids, but what could I do? What could I say? *I'm sorry*? I rationalized that they wouldn't want to hear from me, so I didn't reach out, which I suppose was cowardly. But I also vowed that if I ever saw them again—I wouldn't, but if I ever did—I would make it up to them, her especially. I had to. I just had to. And she was owed so much more than an apology.

"Fast forward several years, and one day I pick up the newspaper and there's an article about the Stern girl. She's a rising star in a creative field. She travels the world, doing her art, wildly successful. I start reading about that field in all sorts of newspapers and magazines and she appears again and again. She's pretty, smart, polite in interviews, ambitious, talented. After a few years following her in the papers, I decided to reach out. Her success made this easier. Seeing the things she had done with her life, that she was doing *so well*, reduced the risk that my approach would go wrong.

"I wrote to her and confessed that even after twenty years I couldn't think of her without feeling tremendous guilt. I apologized and said that I would never be able to right the wrong of what had happened. And then I told her about my life, not that she had asked, just because it seemed the polite thing to do. I summarized as best I could all that I had been up to these many years.

"What relief. What catharsis. Just sealing that letter in an envelope. I didn't expect a response. No, that's not quite true. For the next few weeks, I rushed to the mailbox every day. But there was nothing. I had to remind myself that she had never been likely to respond and that there was still comfort in sharing my words and having made the attempt.

"Then, some months later, a letter arrived. A long, wonderful letter. Ms. Stern referred little to the past and didn't even acknowledge my apology. She just wrote about her life, much as I had about mine. It was a spirited letter, and quite open, containing details that you would never find in those articles I read. She related one story—which I can't share; I don't want to break a confidence—that had me in stitches. I wrote back that very afternoon.

"Again, I waited. Rushed to the mailbox every day. Waited. She had been polite, I told myself. She had answered the first letter out of a sense of duty, but no second response was coming.

"But a few months later, there came another colorful, thoughtful letter, the sort you imagined had vanished forever with the invention of email. What relief, what joy...—that was when I allowed myself to fantasize that this new correspondence would bridge the gap of decades, that we'd again become close, maybe as close as in the past.

"I had to catch myself. Parenthood had taught me to take what you can get. You can wish for daily phone calls with your child, but sometimes all you get is a monthly text, and you should be thankful for it. Ms. Stern was setting the terms of our relationship. She was offering something more than a single conversation but something less than full-blown friendship. She was offering that we would be pen pals, neither more nor less, and by following her lead, I accepted.

"We didn't write every week or even every month. Which wasn't easy for me; I wanted so much more. And it was a difficult time. Your father wasn't well; I had to move him to a special home. I knew that Ms. Stern came to New York occasionally, and I was just an hour outside the city. I wanted to see her in person, and more than once had to remind myself that she was only a pen pal. But what a delightful pen pal. A generous and lively letter writer with whom I could discuss my life.

"Living in New York had been a lifelong dream. My husband's condition grew worse and worse; some days he hardly recognized me. Everyone was telling me to do something for myself. Finally, I did. Big Apple, here I come! I shared the news with Ms. Stern and her response surprised me. She asked a favor. Her brother was moving to New York, too, after years living abroad; she worried about him, she wrote. He had finished school and moved straightaway to Europe. He was a writer, a journalist, but whereas her career had taken off, he had bounced around. In his personal life, too, he had never established roots. She would visit him where he lived, mostly Paris, but also Milan, even Bratislava for a time. Every year they would return to their childhood home, their parents' old apartment in New York, at Christmas time, though they were Jewish and didn't celebrate the holiday. But with the passing of time and her career pulling her across the globe, she said she had a harder and harder time keeping track of him. He was distant, a brooder, possessing a sadness she couldn't penetrate. The favor was simple. She asked if I would contact him and tell her how he was doing. 'Not like a spy,' she wrote. 'Actually, yes, a spy. But a benevolent one. Just your impressions. I worry about him but have so little to go on. All the things that happened to us, even that night at the house for which you felt you owed me an apology, may have affected him even more.' It was her first and only acknowledgment of my apology, and it made her request impossible to refuse.

"I hadn't known this boy all that well. When the families had their falling out, he was still a child. I had never known him as an adolescent or young adult. Unlike with her, this boy and I had never been close. And spying? But how could I say No to this girl, to whom I owed an obligation of guilt? I was willing to overlook her manipulation because I was elated that she would entrust such a responsibility *to me*.

"I discovered that the boy lived in his parents' old apartment, which was just a few blocks from the home where I had moved. One day, I waited outside his building and pretended to bump into him. *Oh, hello there...?* He was standoffish yet open; if not overly friendly, certainly available. We walked and visited awhile. I soon understood his sister's concern. He was melancholy and quiet and let me lead the conversation. As I related things that had happened in recent years, my move to New York, my husband growing sicker, he nodded along, barely asking questions, sharing little of himself. But we ended our time together with a plan to meet again.

"And we did meet again. And again after that. And we became friends. It was the most unexpected thing. He was as lonely and unoccupied as I, an elderly person in a new city. I taught him backgammon, a game I knew well, and he was a quick study. We met at coffee houses and restaurants. We explored the city, often taking long walks. He was a good sport, moving at my slow place; I was a good sport, too, traveling the distances he wanted. I took two Extra Strength Tylenol before each trip, and often iced my legs or napped afterward—which is not something I ever told him—but I was happy to put up with the pain and exhaustion. At times I laughed at fate. Who could have imagined that that little boy, who had become a quiet, almost morose, adult, would be open to friendship? And that's what it was—not mere companionship, but friendship. It was like one of those spy novels in which the characters meant to trail one another instead fall in love, except here, it was platonic. We talked about everything. We confided in each other. We supported each other. I felt closer to him than anyone else in New York. At times, I felt I knew him better than I did my own sons.

"Now I faced a dilemma. I felt compelled to write to his sister, but I didn't want to break his confidence, so I wrote that we had seen each other many times and grown quite friendly, and that he seemed well to me. There was nothing to worry about. I assumed he would have communicated something similar to her, so I was surprised when she responded, more promptly than usual, saying that she was glad to hear that I had been in touch with him, because he hadn't mentioned it at all in their emails and calls. How strange, I thought. But then I recalled the incident from all those years ago. Perhaps my friend worried that he was betraying his sister by forming a friendship with me. And so, I saw that my bonds with each of them involved keeping secrets from the other. I saw that I had created a tangled situation and I felt guilty anew. But it also wasn't my place to break either confidence.

"Are you following me, John?" Catherine said, her voice suddenly raised, as if leaning toward the microphone.

"Of course."

"You know it all."

"Some of it, Mom, but I can't tell it like you."

"Well, all of that was buildup. We're only coming to the story now. The real story."

"Should I create some dramatic tension with a song or commercial break?"

"If you must."

JT played "Textures" by Herbie Hancock and then read ads for a landscape firm and a job board geared toward mid-career changes. Then the show resumed: "Welcome back to WFEX San Diego 710 AM on a beautiful Saturday morning. This is the AM AM Show, where we play the best music from the 70s. The special stuff. The hidden pearls. If you're looking for Classic Rock, this isn't the place for you. Today we also have a special guest, my Mom, and she's been telling us a Christmas story."

"Thank you, John," Catherine said. "As you know, you visited me in New York last month. I had been begging you to come for the holidays, and finally you agreed to it, also bringing your daughter, my beautiful granddaughter, whose name I won't mention. I was so excited, John; finally, I would have a New York Christmas. What a gift. I needed nothing more, but in the back of my mind, I nursed a secret hope. Ms. Stern, my pen pal, my new friend's big sister, would also be coming to New York. Finally, I would see her.

"I felt amazed at the way fortune worked. I hadn't considered any potential awkwardness, but my friend, her brother, had. He suggested we meet, the five of us, and visit the famous Christmas windows along Fifth Avenue. It's a classic New York thing but also safe for a reunion, because it's outside, crowded, and easy to split off at any moment. But things couldn't have gone better. My granddaughter fell for Ms. Stern's charm and success. As the two of them ran off like old girlfriends, you and my friend stayed by my side. My granddaughter was so excited to discover New York. She had never been before and she wanted to see every street, every store, every cafe. To visit with a famous artist was a dream. At the walk's end, Ms. Stern invited us to view her art. She was having a public show in a few days, but you were already going to be back in San Diego. No matter, we could visit a storage warehouse, where work from around the world had been shipped for the show. It was a rare and privileged visit, and for my granddaughter, a fairy tale. Ms. Stern deserves all her accolades. I felt overwhelmed by what I saw and such happiness for her success. It was a near perfect day. I only wished Ms. Stern would have been warmer. She was friendly to my granddaughter but distant from me, a surprise given the openness of her letters. You consoled me that evening, John. Deep wounds do not heal instantly, you said, as ever the wise and reasonable one; in your opinion, the afternoon couldn't have gone much better. I could see that beyond these words lay skepticism that anything more would come of the family reunion, also about the New York trip in the first place. But you were there to please me and your daughter, and to convince me to move to California.

"We had a fancy night out Christmas Eve and a special Christmas Day at home. A splendid meal, gifts under the tree, stuffed stockings. We ate pie and chocolate and drank eggnog. It wasn't the whole family, but it was a wonderful time. And the next day, we visited your father at his home outside the city. Those visits are always hard. My granddaughter has no real memory of when he was well, and I hardly blamed her for not wanting to come. But I was not expecting how resourceful she'd be. On her own, she called the Sterns and arranged a visit. I had to double check with them, but they assured me it was fine.

"You rented a car. It began to snow as we drove, and it kept coming down throughout the visit. We stayed no more than two hours, but by then, the roads weren't travelable. The Sterns generously offered that my granddaughter could stay with them, and we could delay our return to the next morning. When we arrived at their apartment to pick up my granddaughter, all seemed well. But the moment we left, she started asking to delay the return to California, so that she could attend Ms. Stern's show. She begged you, she pleaded with her mother on the phone. Her mother refused, but the snow had wreaked havoc at the airport; the return flight was delayed. The fates were on my granddaughter's side.

"The next morning, we shopped for outfits to wear to the opening and in the evening, we piled into a cab. My granddaughter frowned as we drew close. It was the dead of winter, and this area of the city seemed dark, cold, and deserted. But as the cab approached the venue, light spilled onto the street, and you could see through the glass door a crowd of people, fancy as we never could be, even in our new outfits. And the view from outside hardly did justice to what we found inside. Room after giant room, dozens of fancy people—all ages, a few as young as my granddaughter, others as ancient as me. And in each room, art by my pen pal—*my pen pal*—each piece more spectacular than the last, filling this giant, light-filled space.

"My granddaughter had wanted to see what a young successful woman got for her accomplishments. And what did she see? An evening in which Ms. Stern was feted and wooed by the beautiful and rich, even a few faces you might recognize from the papers. They said her work was "extraordinary," "spectacular." I overheard the word "genius" more than once. After the opening came a party in a home so extraordinary that you'd never expect to set foot in it. A grand apartment atop a skyscraper, spanning an entire floor with gorgeous views across the city. The living room could hold 100 people without feeling crowded. And from the windows, you could see the snow-covered city below.

"The moment we entered that apartment I saw that my pen pal lived in a different world than I. Here was wealth, beauty, and grandeur as I'd only seen on TV. Another fairytale. In my 70s, I was seduced. So, can you imagine how a girl of only 15 would feel? It's such a vulnerable and impressionable age. My granddaughter's eyes grew big with the fantasy of a new life. But such enchantment is fragile, and you, John, were a constant reminder of her reality. She kept urging you to join her make-believe dream, and at each refusal, anger boiled inside her.

"I realize that this has been a terribly long story. I know I'm rambling, but I promise I'm coming to the end. You and she began to fight. Oh, the usual stuff, plus the exhaustion of a long week, plus all this envy. You wanted only to return to your quiet life in San Diego, but your daughter wanted to stay in that apartment until she became a part of it, until the fantasy became her reality. I also got lost in the moment. Wanting to belong and secretly ashamed that I didn't, I flitted about all night, hoping to find that elusive entry point. But each time I saw Ms. Stern, this girl whom I had wronged, whom my family had wronged, I felt the goal slipping further away. She was my ticket in, but also, in her standoffishness, a reminder that the door was not fully open. Over the course of the evening, I watched her pass from friendly to tolerant to indifferent. Eventually, a simple truth was unavoidable. She did not care that we were there; she was merely humoring us.

"My granddaughter's frustration spilled over, and she made a scene. We were asked to leave. Ms. Stern delivered the message coldly, and I felt hot with shame and anger. What a shock it was when we stepped onto the winter street. All three of us, but also my friend, Ms. Stern's brother. Have I really not given him a name yet? Let's call him, oh I don't know, Gregory. But that's the thing about him and his sister, and how I viewed them. All night I had overlooked him. *He* was my friend, but at the party I had tried to win over his sister and barely paid him attention. And yet I had something important to say. Earlier that day, as we had dressed for the party, I had told you that I would move to California, that city life was too tough for me, the northeast winter too brutal. I wanted to share the news with my friend, but each time we crossed paths at the party, it never felt like the right moment, or I spotted someone alluring and rushed over to talk. I suppose I felt guilty that I would be leaving him. I knew that he had been hurt by other departures and I didn't want to add to his pain.

"On the street, you and my granddaughter continued fighting, and now there was no crowd to temper it. My friend walked patiently beside me. I knew I had to tell him that I was leaving New York. But I was scared and couldn't find the right moment. Of course, I worried that my news would send him into a spell of sadness but also, I must admit, that he might not react at all, that he'd be as aloof as his sister… Rather than expose myself to the risk, I complained bitterly about *her*, how snobbishly, how *cruelly*, she'd expelled us from the party. I was thinking only of myself.

"Half a block ahead, my granddaughter was screaming her disappointment at you, John. She was cruel, too—at 15, she already knew that words can scar. She yelled until her voice cracked and then yelled some more; she started to run. You followed at first, but she wouldn't let you catch her. We were tired; we felt insulted and sad, all of us, but my granddaughter turned her anger on us, as if we were the source of her shame. She took from her pocket a glass object that she had stolen from the house. She held it high, another taunt, and began playing with it like a ball. You had let her go by then, but Gregory was watching closely. My granddaughter dropped the glass object; it didn't break, but rolled on the icy street. She ran after it. Gregory ran to her. I thought he was doing the same as my granddaughter, or perhaps playing a game I didn't know, but no, he had seen the danger ahead. The street corner, the ice, the rushing cars. Now I saw it too. My granddaughter neared the intersection, reached for the rolling glass, with a car approaching. Such terror. Here was the possibility of a rupture so jarring, so destabilizing that my life—yours, too—would be forever changed.

"As terror spread from my mind to my body, an immense pressure weighed on my arms and legs and movement became difficult. But Gregory did not hesitate. He ran and hurled himself at my granddaughter and held her against the sidewalk until the car rushed by, the car that might have crushed her. My granddaughter stood, still angry, now cold and wet from the slushy pavement. I was still in the grip of the horror, barely processing what had happened. My granddaughter had no idea at all; she saw only further humiliation in her damp dress and the loss of her glass souvenir. And it was surely a relief to transfer her anger and shame from her father to this stranger.

"My first instinct was protective. I needed to hold her and carry her from danger. We rushed into a cab and left. Too quickly, I now see, leaving my friend alone on the street corner. But it was only in that car, as my heart slowed and my body released tension, that I began to process the events I've just described. In truth it took many days to recognize the full sequence and what it meant. *My friend had saved my granddaughter's life.* My friend, to whom I had been reintroduced by his sister, whom I had contacted because of decades-old guilt and a wound that still festered; my friend with whom I had shared a most unexpected friendship, who had cured my loneliness and whom I had hopefully helped with his own. Until then, our friendship had seemed so random, such an improbable turn of events, but now…

"John, it was a Christmas miracle, a set of circumstances so unlikely, but had any of them played out differently, my granddaughter, your daughter, would not be alive. You and I have discussed this. You think I'm a loon, but to me it all makes sense. The story that began with a letter of forgiveness and led to an unexpected friendship and the reunion of the families culminated in this miracle, of which my granddaughter is not even aware, which you barely believe in, but her life was spared, her life was spared, John, and for that reason, yours and mine, too. You see something like that—the corner, the ice, the approaching car—and you imagine the moment after, had things gone the other way. In that vision, I didn't see anyone else, just you, me, and my granddaughter; but in real life, my friend was there, too. The corner, the ice, the car—*and my friend*. Don't you see, John, if it had been just the three of us, that car hits her, and you and I are not sitting in a radio studio talking about a Christmas miracle; no, we're crying in separate rooms, on opposite sides of the continent, casting blame at each other, nursing our separate griefs. The entire course of our lives cast on a path of devastation, but for the fact that my friend was there, too.

"It turns out that I did not write that letter only to apologize, but to save my granddaughter's life. A prayer that I did not even know I had was answered. It's a miracle, John. I don't think there's any other word for it."

After a pause, there was a crackly sound—some shuffling beside the microphone.

"Thank you, Mom. Now we're going to play another song."

"Hold on. I want to thank you, John. I know you think I'm mad, but you still let me tell this story on the air."

"Sure thing, Mom."

"It means so much to me. I want you to know that, John, how grateful I am."

There was a click, a static hum, and then a trumpet blast, a single note, pure and strong, that lingered, trembling slightly until it suddenly ended. Drums began to play, then a sax, a trombone, a bass, joining too. The trumpet went on, playing mournfully, with the other instruments gaining momentum, growing louder and faster, mostly cheery and upbeat, like a family, or group of friends, trying to coax one sullen member out of a dark mood. The other instruments reached an almost fevered pitch, bordering on euphoria, and began to wind down, the bass disappearing first, then the trombone, the sax, the drums, until the trumpet was alone again, repeating its wistful prelude.

JT read an ad for a seafood restaurant, and the audio cut off.

10

I listened to the radio program three times that night and several more times in the days after. At first, I got hung up on Catherine's claim that she had been asked by Becca to look after me, my thoughts began racing, and I couldn't concentrate any further. But I managed to focus all the way through on subsequent listens, and soon I was replaying Catherine's story in my head with the same obsessiveness I once reserved for my tale of the night in the Catskills.

I kept returning to a few observations. First, Catherine had portrayed my actions as heroic, even angelic, but I knew the more prosaic truth: I had reacted instinctively, and probably overreacted; it's likely that the only tragedy averted was a more thorough dousing of Sophie's jacket in the curbside slush. Second, Catherine's logic contained a gaping hole. Had she never contacted Becca, Sophie would never have been running blindly on an icy sidewalk, in the first place. For a tale of fate and serendipity, Catherine's story was selective and illogical; anyone could see that.

Third—and this is the thought that weighed most heavily—was how I could practically hear Catherine transforming over the course of JT's program: from the tentative, meek voice at its outset to the poised, assured, and sometimes wry person who had become my closest friend. But what tormented me was a feeling that she had not stopped there but kept going, changing anew. It was hard to describe this third state, except to note that it was full of contradictions—philosophical but nonsensical, status-conscious but spiritual, tormented yet serene—and, most of all, foreign to me. Perhaps she had traveled back to some earlier version of herself or already leaped forward into a So Cal vintage, but whoever she had become, she was no longer the friend I knew. And when I combined this strangeness with the fact that she had not replied to my calls for a month and then only with a crate of books and a flippant letter, it felt clear that something profound was happening. The weeks of silence had made me question the basis of our relationship, but Catherine's story made me doubt that I had ever known her at all. At Becca's opening, at Marty Shinn's party, there had been signs that she had used me as a bridge to my sister. And the more I considered her story, the more it seemed to diminish our friendship further, turning the whole relationship into a mere plot device, necessary to move the action from point A to B. In her telling, our time together was only a footnote in a grander tale of decades-long guilt and the miracle of her granddaughter's salvation. Was it even friendship at all?

These thoughts buzzed in my mind as Becca and I walked back to her apartment that afternoon. Yet we mostly proceeded in silence, for I had no idea where to begin. If any of Catherine's story was true, I would have to rewrite the tale of my return to New York, but what role was I to assign Becca? Was she the wizard behind the curtain, controlling it all, or as peripheral to the unfolding drama as the person who fires the gun at the start of a race?

And what about *her* weeks of silence? A coincidence—or had they been tied to Catherine's? Had Becca waited for Catherine's confession before inviting me to her new home in Brooklyn? And where did we, sister and brother Staub, go now? How would we adjust to living in the same city, something we had not done since I was 14?

If I struggled to find the words with which to begin this talk, I did note that I felt more generous to Becca than to Catherine. The simple fact of being in her presence meant something, the proximity of her body worth more than a million gifted books and countless hours of radio confessions. Yet, how long that walk to her apartment felt, though it was surely more direct than the one on the way out. And what relief it was to finally pass through her building's rusty door and enter the rickety elevator. In that large metal box, I was even able to convince myself that Becca's thoughts mirrored my own, that she would start the necessary conversation if it turned out that I lacked the nerve. Then the door opened, and we stepped into the large white space, and I doubted it all, and felt such sadness, remembering anew that to feel close to someone is not necessarily to know them at all.

Becca excused herself to go to the bathroom, and I browsed a bookcase surely inherited from a previous tenant. It was filled with adventure novels, cold war espionage and more recent stories set in Africa and the Middle East. Did Becca skim these books from time to time? As with so much about her, I didn't have a clue.

"Gabriel, how about some coffee?" she asked, and soon we were approaching the cinder block table from opposite sides. She poured the coffee and spoke about the logistical challenges of life in Bushwick—the poorly stocked supermarkets, the hike to the subway, the difficulty of finding a dry cleaner or nail salon—but also the buzzing nightlife, the bars and restaurants and general air of youth, how some days, just walking around, she felt ancient.

"One night last week," she said. "I go to this bar and order a beer. I'm standing around and suddenly I feel this hot gaze, and turning, I see this guy with a bushy white mustache sizing me up. 'A lush,' I think, 'and a lech, yuck.' But looking more closely, I see that his gaze isn't predatory at all. No, he's just seeking innocent company. I was his only peer in a crowd of lusty twentysomethings."

And what then, Becca? I thought, waiting for the story's punchline. *Did you go up to him? Did you make a friend? Find a lover?*

"My gosh, I almost forgot," she said, crossing the room and returning with a long, yellow bar—a vanilla Charleston Chew. "I saw this in the store and thought of you."

I broke off two pieces, but she shook her head when I offered her one. "Sorry, I never liked it," she said, still standing at the table's edge, bouncing anxiously on her toes. "Gabriel, can I make an observation? You look different."

"I do?"

"It's a good thing, don't worry. You look... dare I say... like you're glowing. Kinda tender but also alert. I have an idea. Stay there, ok?"

She left the room, then returned carrying a metal box and an easel board holding a piece of paper with a metal clasp. "All these years, and I've never drawn you," she said, settling down at the table across from me. "How come?

"Is that a rhetorical question?"

"Hah." Her cry was playful but enigmatic—I had no idea what it meant.

The box held a wealth of pens, pencils, and other drawing instruments. She fished around until she found a stick of charcoal. I felt her eyes bore into mine, cold and intense. So I looked toward the charcoal, poised in the air between us, like a match before it scrapes the flint. After a long second or two, she swept it across the page in a long stroke that curved back on itself, an oval.

"Becca, can we—"

"You can't talk. I need quiet."

"But I need to know."

"I'll tell you this. She never told me anything."

Her gaze was insistent, intimidating; it was hard to look back. My eyes fled to the room's far reaches, the white of the appliances that barely stood out against the white of the walls, the black grilles of the windowpanes. When I returned to the page between us, I saw a new mark—a single line, simple and strong, cutting across the oval, nearly edge to edge. A hairline? My eyes?

"So, it's true?" I said. "You asked her to write?"

"Shh. Please look at me, Gabriel. Straight ahead. Not at the paper."

Her back was upright. One arm lay flat on the table, the other held the charcoal. The icy stare of the previous minute was gone; now her eyes seemed evasive (or meditative?), blank and unreadable. I sensed that at any moment she might stand and disappear into another room, to get a pencil or ruler or some other tool, to go to the bathroom, to take a nap, who knew? But right then, at the very moment when I felt sure she'd vanish, she leaned forward and made a new line.

The edge of a nose, its rounded tip.

"Becca, please."

"She wrote once and said you were fine and that I shouldn't worry. She also said you were a friend, and she couldn't say anything more because it would be a violation."

"Nothing whatsoever?"

"Gabriel, please. Look at me. Not around. Not down. I need to see you directly."

"I can't talk. I can't look. No fair."

"Who said anything about fair?"

The tiny flicker of a smile, followed by another weighty look that gradually lightened. And so it went. Long gazes that burned intensely before softening, like the balloon that fills and rises until it reaches the very edge of floating away—only then did she lean above the paper and make a next mark. Adapting to this rhythm, I soon found ways to peek downward without tilting my neck or chin. And I discovered that just as there was a rhythm to her gaze, so there was to her composition. A line, perhaps a series, that made no sense at first, followed by another that gave the whole group order and purpose. A nose, a mouth, two eyes, two ears, the cleft between my eyebrows. With this cleft, for the first time, I saw me—me as opposed to anyone else—though a much younger me, as I had been at 12 or 13. It was there in the roundness of the cheeks and the large dot to the left of my mouth, the exact location of a zit I had obsessed about throughout my adolescence. Did Becca still see me this way? In her mind, was I forever trapped in that end phase of childhood?

I kept trying to speak—the month of silence, Catherine, Sybil Ludington, the sibling code—but she would ask me to be quiet, say that she wasn't keen on talking, or a finger would cover her mouth and she'd whisper, "Tomorrow" or "We'll get to that later." And her hand would return to the page.

Her first lines were long and definitional. Next came a flurry of hatches, her pace increasing though the results were no less precise. The round cheek was cut by a line sloping inward, which marked the cheekbone and thinned the face. The zit vanished, too, into an array of dots smudged with flattened thumb into a passage of shadow. This gave the first hint of light, some invisible source streaming onto the page from the right. Next came a bevy of nicks and blemishes: pores, a blister, stubble, nascent wrinkles.

And in this way, a new version of myself, not quite me, certainly not how I saw myself, but recognizable nonetheless, soon emerged. As always, Becca was the first to see it.

A Note on Sources

The quotations in Becca Staub's artwork *Sybil* come from *The Aeneid* by Virgil (Translated by Robert Fagles), *The Picture of Dorian Gray* by Oscar Wilde, *The Metamorphoses* by Ovid (Translated by Charles Martin), *Sybil* by Flora Rheta Schreiber, "Sybil Ludington's Ride" by Berton Braley, "Sybil Ludington, the Female Paul Revere: The Making of a Revolutionary War Heroine" by Paula D. Hunt, and *The Satyricon* by Petronius (Translation in *The Waste Land: A Facsimile and Transcript of the Original Drafts Including the Annotations of Ezra Pound*, by T. S. Eliot, edited by Valerie Eliot).

ACKNOWLEDGMENTS

A reader of an earlier manuscript of mine offered this cryptic advice: "There's a difference between finished and complete." Julie helped me to make sense of this riddle, and she has aided me at each stage of this new book.

Close friends, foremost among them, my brother, have supported and sustained me for many years, shaping the person, and writer, I've become.

Jeremy was my companion at the outset of the journey that has brought me to the completion of this book. Without his constancy and trust, I would not have kept going.

My parents have been unwavering presences in my life. There is nothing more humbling than trying to account for all that I owe to them.

Sarah and Simone are my bedrock and teach me daily about love, patience, and belief.

ABOUT THE AUTHOR

David Grosz lives in New York with his wife and daughter.
Providence is his first novel.

NOTE FROM DAVID GROSZ

Word-of-mouth is crucial for any author to succeed. If you enjoyed *Providence*, please leave a review online—anywhere you are able. Even if it's just a sentence or two. It would make all the difference and would be very much appreciated.

Thanks!
David Grosz

We hope you enjoyed reading this title from:

BLACK ROSE
writing™

www.blackrosewriting.com

Subscribe to our mailing list – *The Rosevine* – and receive **FREE** books, daily
deals, and stay current with news about upcoming
releases and our hottest authors.
Scan the QR code below to sign up.

Already a subscriber? Please accept a sincere thank you for being a fan of
Black Rose Writing authors.

View other Black Rose Writing titles at
www.blackrosewriting.com/books and use promo code
PRINT to receive a **20% discount** when purchasing.

www.ingramcontent.com/pod-product-compliance
Lightning Source LLC
Chambersburg PA
CBHW030807210726
48290CB00002B/463